"HORRIFYING...UNIQUE...
SUPREMELY SATISFYING...
A near-perfect example of the
chiller thriller."
—*Cosmopolitan*

*

"THE *MARATHON MAN* THRILLS CONTINUE . . . *BROTHERS* IS SURELY A CAUSE TO REJOICE."

—***Philadelphia Daily News***

"REALLY AN INCREDIBLE STORY . . . and yet it's believable because Goldman is so good. If he's not hooking you with the plot he's charming you with his prose. From page to page to page you'll be dying to know what happens next—My God, what's going on?—right up to the very last page."

—**Elmore Leonard**

"SUSPENSE MOUNTS . . . *Brothers* moves well and twists and turns . . . It begs for a sequel!"

—***Boston Globe***

"WILD AND WOOLLY . . . a highly satisfactory novel."

—***San Diego Union***

"GOLDMAN IS BEST AT DEPICTING NONSTOP ACTION, AND THERE IS PLENTY TO SPARE HERE, MUCH OF IT WILDLY IMAGINATIVE."

—***Publishers Weekly***

Please turn the page for more rave reviews of *Brothers*.

✲

"A FINE THRILLER . . . a sleek, polished story. . . . This book has movie written all over it. But don't wait—the book is too good."

—*Cincinnati Post*

* * *

"A TRUE GEM OF SUSPENSEFUL WRITING. Ever so slowly the web is woven until you are snared in the story . . . a chilling way to spend your reading time."

—*Houston Home Journal*

* * *

"WILLIAM GOLDMAN HAS DONE IT AGAIN . . . BROTHERS hurtles along at breakneck speed, daring you to stop reading. From the first page to the last, Goldman grips the reader with the sure and steady hand of a master . . . a joy to read. . . . It's vintage Goldman. Anyone who enjoys a good thriller shouldn't miss it."

—*Milwaukee Sentinel*

* * *

"A ROLLER COASTER OF SERPENTINE TWISTS, DIABOLICAL SURPRISES, TEETH-GRINDING TENSION."

—*Boston Herald*

"A MARVELOUS BOOK! A near-perfect example of the chiller thriller. . . . The menace is horrifying and unique, the pace is breakneck, the denouement supremely satisfying, the writing on a level far higher than the genre normally attracts . . . will make a spectacular movie!"

—*Cosmopolitan*

* * *

"GOLDMAN'S BEST WORK IN YEARS—A SHOWCASE FOR HIS IMMENSE POWERS AS A STORYTELLER. As writers of contemporary thrillers go, Goldman is the absolute tops, the best of the breed. *Brothers* is classic Goldman, and that means it's better than anybody is likely to do for a long, long time."

—*Albany Times-Union*

* * *

"EXCELLENT . . . GOLDMAN HAS NEVER BEEN BETTER . . . *Brothers* has some surprising emotional depth to it . . . Goldman is at the top of his form, and that is very, very good."

—*Roanoke Times and World News*

## Also by William Goldman

### FICTION

*The Temple of Gold* (1957)
*Your Turn to Curtsy, My Turn to Bow* (1958)
*Soldier in the Rain* (1960)
*Boys and Girls Together* (1964)
*No Way to Treat a Lady* (1964)
*The Thing of It Is...* (1967)
*Father's Day* (1971)
*The Princess Bride* (1973)
*Marathon Man* (1974)
*Magic* (1976)
*Tinsel* (1979)
*Control* (1982)
*The Silent Gondoliers* (1983)
*The Color of Light* (1984)
*Heat* (1985)

### NONFICTION

*The Season: A Candid Look at Broadway* (1969)
*The Making of "A Bridge Too Far"* (1977)
*Adventures in the Screen Trade: A Personal View of Hollywood and Screenwriting* (1983)

### SCREENPLAYS

*Masquerade* (1965)
(with Michael Relph)
*Harper* (1966)
*Butch Cassidy and the Sundance Kid* (1969)
*The Hot Rock* (1972)
*The Great Waldo Pepper* (1975)
*The Stepford Wives* (1975)
*All the President's Men* (1976)
*Marathon Man* (1976)
*A Bridge Too Far* (1977)
*Magic* (1978)
*Mr. Horn* (1979)

### PLAYS

*Blood, Sweat, and Stanley Poole* (1961)
(with James Goldman)
*A Family Affair* (1962)
(with James Goldman and John Kander)

### FOR CHILDREN

*Wigger* (1974)

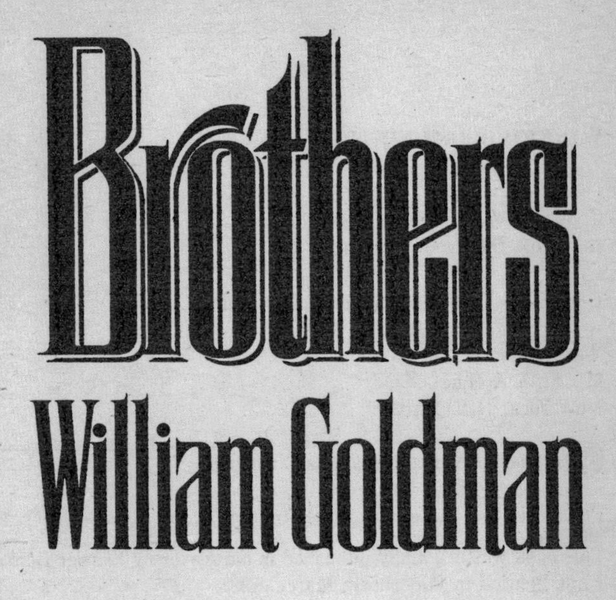

A Warner Communications Company

WARNER BOOKS EDITION



Cover illustration by Joe and Kathy Heiner

Warner Books, Inc.
666 Fifth Avenue
New York, N.Y. 10103

A Warner Communications Company

Printed in the United States of America

This book was originally published in hardcover by Warner Books.
First Printed in Paperback: March, 1988

10 9 8 7 6 5 4 3 2 1

*For the sisters*

# . . . before the beginning . . .

. . . dusk settling over the Caribbean . . . the giant emerged from the smooth waters, stood, walked to the beach . . . "giant" was the wrong word, he lacked the prerequisite size . . . but it came to mind because his naked body, tanned so deeply by the sun, gave off such power . . . and he was big . . . big in the shoulders especially . . . from somewhere on the small deserted island, the birds were doing their night vocalizing . . . they had been his chief companions for so many years . . . how many years . . . ?

. . . perhaps the birds knew . . .

. . . certainly he did not, nor did he care . . . any more than he wondered what the month might be . . . or the day of the week . . .

. . . he knew this much . . . today had been his swimming day . . . not entirely true, since he went into the water for some part of each morning . . . but today was when he set off in the morning, swam till the sun was high, turned then, swam back to the island . . . and if he got confused, missed his island, what then . . . ?

. . . perhaps the birds knew . . .

. . . he knew only that after his swimming day came the day for toughening his hands . . . once he could kill with either, but that was a dissimilar skill from riding a bicycle, you could lose it all, and quickly, so he worked on them, in case that talent was ever needed again . . . and after the hand day came the day for strengthening the rest of his body . . . and after the strengthening day he had his book day . . . then it was time for another endless swim . . . he had compressed the week into four days . . . no wonder the months eluded him . . .

. . . the birds were quieting . . .

. . . he walked to the only civilized part of the island, to the lean-to and the water purifier . . . he drank from the metal cup . . . drank again . . . then he ate the fruits and nuts he had gathered before he'd set off that morning . . . ate . . . drank again . . . the sun was going . . . he stretched . . . yawned . . . the swim always made him ready for sleep . . . again he stretched, the muscles under the tanned skin so well defined . . . he was an extraordinarily handsome man . . . or would have been had his dark eyes been more alive . . . it was hard to tell what was going on behind those eyes . . .

. . . perhaps the birds knew . . .

. . . truly a remarkable piece of work to look upon . . . but not perfect . . . the scar was too noticeable . . . even after these years, it made a red road up his flat stomach . . . a narrow road, but long, and the wound had been deep . . . not surprising, that . . . after all, it had killed him . . .

. . . dawn had already surrendered . . . and he had already breakfasted, nuts, berries, pure water . . . and stretched . . . and taken his dip, a fast crawl circling the island . . .

. . . now, dry, he walked the white beach, looking for a perfect place . . . no, not perfect, they were all the same, the beach was wide, the sand pale . . . an appealing place for what he was looking for . . . he selected one, knelt, made a tight fist of his right hand, drove it down hard . . . it made a very quiet sound . . .

. . . but the birds heard it . . . screeched, began to flutter from various places to the nearest trees . . . why they found it fascinating, he never knew, he certainly didn't, it was a job, his job . . .

. . . so he set to it . . .

. . . the right hand struck again, with precisely the same force, and after that again, and then a hundred "agains," a thousand . . . now there was a hole in the sand . . . he slammed his hand harder, faster, making the hole deeper and when it was the length of his arm he spread his fingers into the bottom of the hole and with his left hand, filled the hole in tight . . .

. . . and now he began to twist his hand, his arm, with the sand providing resistance . . .

. . . for how long in minutes, of course he had no way of knowing, but he judged from the angle of the rising sun when the proper length of time was gone . . . then he pulled the right hand free, began to hit down with the left . . . it was important, no, more, it was *everything* that both hands have identical power . . . identical killing power . . . it weakened you if you favored one hand in combat . . . it gave the enemy an edge and that was bad, every edge had to be yours, if you wanted to win . . . of course nobody won in combat, but every edge had to be yours if you wanted to survive . . .

. . . did he . . . ?

. . . insufficient evidence, Your Honor . . .

. . . he put a damper on his mind then, went back to pillaging the sand . . . he kept at it till the sun was at its peak, swam again because his body was so wet with perspiration it was difficult to get leverage for his blows . . . then back, kneel, hit, till the sun was dropping . . . the usual dinner, the usual water, and when it was dark he lay in the lean-to and closed his eyes . . .

. . . Babe was there . . .

"SHIT."

. . . he sat, cursed again . . . that was the bad thing about the hand days . . . sometimes, not often but occasionally, he was not sufficiently exhausted to sleep immediately . . . he could never predict when those "occasionallies" would come, but when they did, they brought Babe, his beloved kid brother, with them . . . and it was then that he wanted to chuck it all and run across the dark sand and flail the water, and whatever it took to reach mainland, however far it was, he would get there and a plane would be waiting and it would land wherever Babe was living now and Babe would be there at the airport and they would weep and embrace and . . .

. . . and such embarrassing sentimental shit the daydream was . . . even if they ever did meet again, and they would not, there would be no instant embraces, no quick tears . . . because Babe knew one certainty and it was this: his older brother was dead . . . and more than that, he looked so different now, he looked like someone few men had ever seen . . . "He's dead, my brother's dead, who are *you?*" was what Babe would say . . . and rightly so . . .

. . . he lay back down, tried with all the power of his mind to blank it, and he had a mind with enormous power, and he had worked as hard to make it work precisely for him as he had worked on his body, and he had brought it under control . . . most of the time under control . . . but there were nights, rare and surprising, when his mind broke loose, rushed to Babe, their childhood, the bad but mostly the good . . . and those nights, they were hard, very . . .

. . . high sky . . . he was in the treetops, chasing the birds, when he heard it . . . *rrrrr* . . . very distant but he recognized it . . . *rrrrr* . . . the birds were several branches below him and part of him knew he ought to get to ground quickly, be ready, but another part thought they enjoyed the horseplay . . . *hoped* they enjoyed the horseplay . . . so he dropped down after them . . . he was a superb climber now . . . originally he went into the trees to increase his agility . . . strength too, of course . . . he chinned hundreds of times from the thicker branches down below . . . but agility was the most crucial need, the need to be quick, so he took to climbing high and it was soon that he realized that the birds actually didn't mind . . . the first times they screeched and scattered but then they got braver and sometimes, he suspected, even lingered close to taunt him as he did his best to chase them down . . . of course he never caught up to any, and if he had, would have done nothing . . .

*. . . rrrrr . . . rrrrr . . . !*

. . . the helicopter motor was louder now . . . he slipped

gracefully down the branches then to the sand, peered . . . the machine wasn't visible but it would be, and soon, which meant his island time was over . . .

. . . they *needed* him . . .

. . . and how did he feel about that . . . ?

. . . insufficient evidence, Your Honor . . .

. . . but there was no denying a certain sense of excitement and he sat, listened to the motor, closed his eyes, heard the voice of Perkins, his best friend at Division, talking from years ago.

"—this has to go fast—you were essentially dead, we brought you this far back, far enough so you ought to be able to flutter your eyelids or squeeze my finger, can you do one or the other?—"

. . . flutter . . .

"—all right, the doctors don't think we can bring you any further than where you are—unless radical techniques are attempted—if they succeed, you still may be nothing more than a vegetable, that wound has torn your stomach apart and I promise you this, I won't let you be a vegetable, I owe you too much, I'll kill you myself before I let that happen—but I have an idea—you must listen—to my idea—you're of no use to us now and you may never be but if we can bring you back, you have one tremendous advantage—*everyone else knows you're dead*—all right, if we can keep you alive through the night and if we can pump strength into your body, I want to change you—your prints, your face, voice, state-of-the-art surgery—it will take years and I'll have false identification and shift you from one hospital to another while the alterations take place—will you risk this, it will be agonizingly slow and a lot of pain, a *lot* of pain, flutter or squeeze—"

. . . fuh-luh-terrr . . .

"—all right—there's an island—an isolated part of the Caribbean, no planes fly over, no boats float past—I'll take you there with a copter pilot and land you and the copter pilot will be remaindered on return so I'll be the only one who knows—if I die, no one will ever send for you—I may never send for you anyway—because if I do, it will only be for something of very great import—you will be the loneliest man alive—you may die on the island—no one will know—you may go crazy on the island, no one will know—you will be there at the least years, and you must get yourself ready for recall—I'm not sure you'll ever be strong enough again—what it comes down to is this: do you want to get away from the world, perhaps forever?—"

. . . flutter *and* squeeze . . .

"Done," Perkins said and so it was.

Now the helicopter was visible, low in the high sky. He moved across the sand, went to the lean-to, rooted around quickly, found the clothes he had come in, put them on, shirt and slacks, loafers. Awful constricting things, but they fit. Or at least covered him adequately.

The copter was circling to land now.

For a moment, watching it, he felt suddenly chill. He had worked so hard to get it back, all his power, but what had the opposition been, sand, trees, Caribbean water. What if they called for him now and he failed?

Lots of experiments fail.

And surely they would test him severely before they sent him into the field. If he did well, fine; if not, he would be quickly remaindered.

He walked to a tree. There was a fairly thick branch at shoulder level. Nothing trunklike, but not a twig. He struck it with his left hand, struck it with his right. It snapped and fell. He looked at his hands. No pain at all, surely not a bad sign.

Perhaps he was still Scylla the rock, not just the remains thereof. Part of him hoped so. The curious part. Because the roaring helicopter meant he was not being summoned for a child's task, these were not adolescent chores they would want from him, lawn mowing, tidying up children's toys.

No; horrible things must be happening out there . . .

# I

# THE CONTESTANTS

# 1

# The Tring Experiment

Strangely, no one wept for the brothers.

And they must have been brothers, though except for size they looked like twins, same haircut, same school uniform, same scrubbed complexion, Disney kids really, one perhaps an adorable eight, the other probably a cuddly six—the brothers, excited, walked in perfect unison through the mild English afternoon. An early summer Saturday, two weeks to Wimbledon, high skies, pale British blue, with cloud puffs spotted along for company.

They were walking along Spruce Mews in the village of Tring, careful to stay close to the side of the road, and their brisk pace increased, as up ahead they could see the intersection of the village High Street. The younger one paused, then sputtered the following: "I'm simply positive I heard a dirty word at breakfast—do you know what a 'phallic' is?"

"Oh, spare me," the eight-year-old replied.

"Well, do you do you?" His voice became conspiratorial now. "Mummy used the word as I walked in—but when she saw me her voice got all whispery, the way it does when we're not supposed to hear, and Daddy shushed her—which only served to conform my suspicion."

"Con*firm* your suspicion, Ollie. The word 'confirm,' I believe, would more closely 'conform' to your intended meaning."

"Thank you, Stan. I do so prefer it when you prompt me

in a gentle way. I don't like it when you're hypocritical of me."

"*Hyper*critical. You must think before you speak, and not just occasionally; mind your mind."

"I'm so stupid sometimes. It's the excitement."

Stan nodded, stopped at the corner of the High Street. "I know. Give me your hand now, Ollie, while we cross."

Ollie held out his hand, Stan took it, and in unison they skipped to the other side where the sweet shop was.

"Are we weirdly bright, Stan?"

The larger boy considered his reply for a moment. "Perhaps. I suppose so. It's not our fault. And yes I do."

Ollie blinked. "Once again, please."

"Before you enquired as to whether we were weirdly bright you asked did I know the meaning of 'phallic'? I just answered."

Ollie scurried in front of the larger boy, stopped him dead. "Tell me, tell me."

"I will do better than tell you, I will spell you. The first letter is: 'p.' "

"I've got that, yes, on, on."

" 'P' is followed by 'r.' "

"P-r-what?"

"P-r-i—"

"—I think I know, I think I know—go on."

"The final letter is 'g.' A phallic is a prig." With that they started walking again, again hand in hand.

"*Prig?*" Ollie said, obviously disappointed. "Is that dirty? It doesn't sound like a dirty word to me. When you say 'piss' you know you shouldn't. *'Piss!'* I don't think 'prig' is quite in the same class, Stan."

"I'm sure I got it right. Call a man a prig in the old days and 'slap-slap' would go his gloves and the next dawn you'd be dueling for your life."

Ollie scuffed his shoes on the sidewalk. "Well, if you say it's so, then it's so, but—" And then he stopped, took a quick step so he was half hidden behind Stan, as a middle-aged woman confronted them suddenly. She was heavy but dressed nicely enough and her smile was certainly pleasant. But Ollie found it very hard not to stare at her right eye—it drooped, almost to closing. "Aren't you the nervy ones," she began. "Out all alone."

"Since there are two of us," Stan said, "we are hardly all alone."

"Quite so; I meant without grown-ups."

"Ahhh. I personally, have done it before, but it is a special treat for Ollie here—he's to be seven tomorrow and we're off to buy him sweets."

"Fancy, all of seven." She reached quickly around Stan, squeezed Ollie's cheek, shook it, in fact.

"Ollie does not like being tweaked," Stan said. "He does not see how it benefits the world around us. And do not think of tweaking me, as we share the same sentiments."

"I'm terribly sorry," the droopy-eyed woman said, pulling her hand back quickly. "I was simply watching you both as I approached, and you seemed so bright and happy."

"Thank you, that's very kind," Stan said.

"You must stay that way," the droopy-eyed woman said then. "Promise me at the very least you'll try. It gets a bit harder as you age."

"Vowed," Stan said, raising his right hand, while behind him, Ollie kind of made a nod.

The droopy-eyed woman smiled, moved past them.

Ollie moved up next to Stan and they watched as she walked away. "I thought she was going to snatch us, Stan."

"Oh, spare me," Stan said. "You and the telly. She had a kind smile and usually that means there's nothing to fear behind it. She was just being lonely."

Ollie began whispering then. "Well then why does she go around scaring people, making her eye droop that way?"

"She doesn't do it on purpose."

"She doesn't?"

"No, it's a defirmity." Stan shook his head. "Informity." He shook his head again. "Piss."

"Prig," Ollie seconded, and then they both started to giggle as they continued their parade to the sweet shop.

* * *

Fern felt relieved when she heard their laughter. She knew that the smaller had been bothered by her eye, had slipped behind his brother for protection.

The drooping lid had been part of her so long, she usually forgot about it. It wasn't *that* much of a problem, nothing like a scar. Adults dealt with it easily, perhaps because she smiled a good deal with others, and her smile, no question, was a strength.

Occasionally, though, a child would become nettled, and that had just happened and it upset her until the sound of their high-pitched laughter made her know she was not anything but a brief shadow and not a lingering fear.

A relief, that was—the two were so adorable. Her directions had been to engage them in brief conversation and report her reaction. She wondered if she would tell of the clearly irresistible urge to squeeze the smaller boy's cheek? Part of her gesture was to assuage his fear, but more than that, it was to tell them that they were precisely what she had said: bright, happy. And well mannered. And well dressed.

Most of the youngsters today, Fern thought, were a disgrace; to their homes, schools, and if they attended, their churches. They were rude, without respect, and the Good Lord spare the world when this generation of brats took over, a third of a century on.

But these last two: perfection. No. Probably a bit too smart, and perhaps a trifle haughty. There was still no point denying that if she could have taken them home she would have. And made them decent meals. And walked with them on weekends, shown them off for all.

Look what I have created, she wanted to shout.

Look at what I . . .

Her mind had no place to travel. She stood still on High Street, staring at the window of the small tobacconist, and her mind slowed. The fact was this: Fern had no, well, little imagination.

Which, as much as anything, was the secret of her

success. She was superb at taking orders. "Fernie girl? Head of the class—tell her anything once and she's got it and you can forget whatever it was, she'll remember. Yet to make a mistake. Wish we had more like old Fern."

Today she had had two orders. The first, accomplished, was to intercept some children and chat with them briefly and, the next time she was contacted, give her impressions.

The second order, she knew from experience, was the more important. At the end of the High Street, where it intersected with Tring Mews, there was to be an old and scratched blue Ford. It would be unlocked, the key by the gas pedal. At 1:30 P.M. she was to enter the car, start it, take a left turn into Tring Mews, past the house numbered sixteen. She was to drive two houses down, come to an idle in front of number eighteen.

From there The Blonde would tell her what to do.

That was the extent of her knowledge. Some women, naturally, would have objected to taking commands from another woman, probably a pretty one as a person called merely The Blonde would likely be.

All ho-hum to Fern. Along with her limited imagination her other great virtue ran parallel: she was almost entirely without curiosity. She didn't care why she had to chat with the little boys. She had no interest whatsoever as to what would happen when she stopped the car in front of number eighteen. And if The Blonde was beautiful with eyes that didn't droop? Of no moment whatsoever.

Fern liked having limited knowledge. She realized the reason they used her the way they did was that if anything should go wrong, she could talk all she wanted, she wouldn't have much to tell.

1:28.

Fern moved slowly up toward Tring Mews. At the intersection she crossed toward the scratched blue Ford, stood alongside it at 1:29.

1:30 and she felt light-headed. 1:30 and her poor heart quit its pumping. 1:30 and the incredible had encroached on her reality—for at 1:30 she had reached for the car door, had actually spread her fingers to open it—had done all that *while forgetting to put on her gloves.*

She remembered in time, but that meant little in the way of bucking her up—she had erred! (What did that mean? A onetime wonder or the start of her downfall?) Fingertips meant fingerprints. On the door handle. On the key inside. On the wheel. And if there was to be blood spilled shortly—and her experience told her that was very much the case—then those prints of hers might have proved deadly. True, she couldn't tell much because she didn't know much. But the telephone voices that gave her instructions were not the end-all of the apparatus. There were other employees. And they would invalidate her. "Fernie girl? Back of the room. In the corner with her, dunce cap on tight. Used to not make mistakes, now they're her speciality. Such a shame about old Fern."

1:31. Gloves on, key in proper place, lift key, insert key, start motor, a bit of gas, left at Tring Mews, past number sixteen. Stop at eighteen. Wait for The Blonde.

Fern sat still, her eye drooping worse than usual. Why did she make such a howler? There had to be a reason. She gripped the wheel. 1:34, and she had it.

The jet lag.

She was never much on traveling and now they had her doing so much of it. Too much of it, too much for her, anyway. Greeting children outside London on a Saturday, tracking teachers in New York on Friday afternoon. The back and forthing was the reason.

Relieved, Fern took a breath, relaxed her grip, waited for the time to pass. And The Blonde to arrive. With new instructions. Fern went over what she had been told to do. Get the car, yes. Left on Tring Mews, yes. Past number sixteen, yes. Idle two houses down in front of eighteen. She was there now.

Clearly, number sixteen was the place. She would not have been told to pass sixteen unless that was true. They would have just said, "When you reach number eighteen, stop." No. Sixteen was crucial. She glanced back at the small house, totally detached from its neighbors, close to the street. Pretty place. But if she had to give a guess, it would be that whoever lived inside would have been happier with a different address.

Any other address in the world.

Ollie held his breath as he followed Stan into the sweet shop. And once they were inside, he still made no sound, but simply looked around, his eyes widening. "Fancy the treasures," he whispered.

It was not a large store, but extremely well stocked. Shelf after neat shelf of nougats and lollipops, taffies and toffees, kisses and creams.

The man behind the counter was old and, except for the fact that he was very fat, did not seem the type to run a store such as this. He looked sourly out at the two boys, ignored the excitement of the smaller, and rapped with his knuckles on a cardboard sign that said the store closed promptly at two on Saturdays. He hadn't had a customer in half an hour, and was contemplating locking up early when they had jarred the silence.

Ollie clung to Stan. "It's too beautiful."

The fat proprietor rapped at the closing sign again.

"Sir," Stan told him, "we are major customers, fear not."

"That's right," Ollie said. "For my birthday—I get to spend half a pound on whatever I want."

"A falsehood," Stan cried. He turned to the owner. "Do not believe that."

"But, Stan . . ." Ollie started, confused now.

"Hear that whine? Love it, love it."

"But, Stan, Mummy said—"

"I know, I heard her—half a pound. Tell me something—does *this* look like half a pound?" And he pulled a one-pound note from his pocket and waved it about. "It looks like an *entire* pound to me. And *that's* what you get to spend."

Ollie stared at the one-pound note as Stan waved it

around and around high in the air. More confused than ever, he began to whisper, "But where does the extra money come from?"

"Who cares?"

"Well, I don't want to do anything wrong is the thing, Stan; what if it's money that's not meant for me?"

Stan took a long time before replying. "My allowance is mine and I get to do whatever I want with it. And what I want is for you to spend it." He shoved the note across the counter to the fat man. "Keep it. We accept no change, under threat of torture."

The proprietor took the one-pound note, wondering how he had been so wrong about these two. The second they came in his shop he thought they were going to be trouble. The rich ones—and these were rich, no doubt, the clothes, the accent straight from Mayfair—were a pain. The way they looked at you, like you were a bug; the way they treated you, treated everybody really, like some servant. And what had they done?

They had been pulled from the proper womb.

That didn't give them the right to be superior. He had worked hard in his shop, he owned it, stocked it with the best he could afford, never minded the hours to keep it neat. He wanted his kids to take it over, but kids nowadays, they didn't want to spend their lives selling candy. Anyway, his kids couldn't stand each other.

Now, in the center of the shop, Ollie tried to grab Stan, but Stan dodged, skipped out of his reach. "I want to hug you," Ollie said. "You're so sweet."

"*I?* Sweet? Wrong, Ollie," and now he swept his arm toward the counter. "*These* are sweet." He waited, then looked briefly disappointed. "Silly, why didn't you laugh, that was a very good word joke, an excellent pum."

"A wonderful pum, Stan, and I will laugh, later, I promise, when I'm not so excited."

The owner beckoned for Stan to come close. "You're sure about this allowance business? My boys didn't spend their money on each other, I'm here to tell you. They hated each other."

"Oh, I hate Ollie too, a good bit of the time, but not today."

"Tell me, Ollie," the owner said then, spreading his arms to take in the store. "What do you like?"

Ollie started to answer, stopped, shook his head, making up his mind.

"Ollie likes chocolate, chocolate, chocolate, chocolate and chocolate," Stan said.

Ollie couldn't help giggling as he nodded.

The fat man leaned over the counter, then made his voice soft. ". . . I got a special kind of chocolate, the best, it's so good I don't even sell it, I just order it for myself . . ."

"What's so special?" Ollie wondered.

The fat man bent still further, his voice softer still. ". . . it's . . . it's *white* . . ."

Ollie quick turned to Stan. "Is he teasing?"

"Not in the face, he isn't."

"You both wait," and with that the fat man hurried behind a curtain to the back of the shop. "Close your eyes," he said after a pause.

"What do you think, Stan, close them or peek?"

"I'm going to close mine, you do what you will."

"Closed?"

"Yes sir."

"Okay, open your mouths," the fat man said, his voice nearer. "Now I'm going to put a little something inside and you take a bite and chew it good and tell me what you think it is."

They bit, chewed, opened their eyes. "Oh, Stan," Ollie said.

Stan nodded in agreement.

"Special?" the fat man asked. His hands were behind his back. "I take it we are in agreement as to quality."

"Ollie may never be the same," Stan said.

*"And what color is it?"* the proprietor asked in triumph, bringing two bars of white chocolate into view.

Ollie just stared at them, then gestured for Stan to bend down a bit, then whispered in the bigger boy's ear.

"What did he say? I, Abromson, demand to know."

"He wondered if somebody painted it that color," Stan said.

"*Paint?* Where?" and he broke the bars in different places, showing Ollie how white they were all the way through.

Ollie whispered to Stan again.

"Could he have some please, one pound's worth? That's what he wants for his birthday, Mister Abromson."

Mr. Abromson shook his head. "Not for sale, I told you that already."

"But—" Stan began.

"With this special white, there are no 'buts' allowed. I just get enough for myself. Besides, this is too expensive. It comes from the middle of Switzerland. It would make too skimpy a present. One of these bars here?" He held them up. "Many many pounds each."

Ollie bit his lip.

"For one pound, I could make a nice chocolate assortment. I stand by the quality. That what you want?"

"Thank you," Ollie said, and he stood watching as Mr. Abromson took out a thin brown bag and put some mints in and Cadbury's milk chocolate and some silver-wrapped kisses from America, he explained, and soon he was done. "Who carries?"

Ollie reached out his small hands, took the bag.

"Stop in again," Mr. Abromson said. "A few minutes ago, you were new customers, now I consider you standbys."

They started for the door. "We will come back," Stan said. "Someday."

When their backs were turned, Mr. Abromson said, "Could I ask a favor?"

They looked at him.

He held up the two bars of white chocolate. "Look. See? A bite's been taken out of each. I only eat whole bars, I'm fastidious about germs. These aren't any use to me now, do you happen to know anyone who might want them?"

"I would I would!" Ollie said.

"*Manners,*" Stan reprimanded.

Ollie said, "Please I would I would."

Stan shook his head. "Hopeless."

Mr. Abromson held out the white chocolate, put it in the thin brown bag. Ollie said, "Thank you," then "Thank you" again, and then he skipped to the door that Stan held open, and they both waved when they were on the sidewalk, and they kept on skipping, Stan doing it far better until they reached the intersection where the High Street met Tring Mews, and Ollie took Stan's hand and they crossed and when they were safe they both started running, with an occasional jump of happiness thrown in, and they passed number one Tring Mews and after that they skipped by number two.

It was 1:37 when they began to pass number sixteen, running now with no intention evident of ever coming to a halt. But at 1:37 Ollie stumbled and the thin brown bag slipped from his hand and spilt as it hit the area at the edge of the street and Ollie couldn't do anything but yell Stan's name out loud as he stared at his treasures, lying there, half covered with mud.

It was 1:36 when Fern realized she had got the sex wrong, for surely The Blonde was no woman. The man moving toward her as she sat in the blue car, the motor idling, directly across from number eighteen Tring Mews, two houses up from what she was sure would prove to be the center of whatever was about to happen, unlucky sixteen, that man would certainly stop when he reached her. And he would look at her and say, "Top of the afternoon, Fernie girl," and she would nod and then, well, the rest was his doing.

Fern had never done well with men, but even if she had, even if she understood their ways and how to please them, this fair-haired creature coming toward her now would have been beyond her. He wore tight gray slacks and a tapered white shirt and a blue club tie. His suit jacket was slung over an arm. He carried a small case.

If her beloved Gable had been blond instead of dark, that was an approximation. The body was powerful but it moved with quickness. The eyes were so pale, so large they dominated even the long blond hair, even the smile. "Top of the afternoon, Fernie girl."

She nodded, wondering what it would be like to have a creature like that pursuing her, caressing her sad form, kissing her disfigured eye, saying words that gave her confidence to caress back, words like . . . like . . .

Her imagination deserted her again. She said nothing, kept her hands on the wheel.

He moved quickly, opened the back door of the car, tossed his jacket on the seat. Then he opened his case, took out something that looked rubbery, elastic, a slingshot kind of apparatus, then another thing that looked almost pear shaped, except it was metal, grenadelike in color. "As soon as I start to enter, start to drive. Clear?"

Odd accent. Not English. The "clear" was almost "klar" but not quite, so he wasn't German either. Where was he from? She pondered that briefly, as if it mattered.

It was 1:38 when he brought the metallic object to his mouth, yanked something loose with his teeth, and then the metal thing was in the elastic thing and he was spinning with great power and as he let it fly, as he dove into the backseat, Fern glanced into the mirror and saw the beautiful little boys stopped in front of number sixteen, Tring Mews, and as she drove quickly away with her perfect companion she wondered how could he have done it.

Had she had more imagination, she might have also wondered why.

"Oh, Ollie, you'd best get up," Stan said as Ollie, on his knees, tried to clean the mud from the white bars of chocolate, stuff them back into the bag.

Ollie stayed on the ground.

"There's more candy in the world, you know."

Muffled: "Not special candy."

"Please. Get up now. For me. For Stan."

Ollie got up.

"And don't cry."

"Can't help it."

"If you cry it's the end of me."

"Sorry."

"But there's so much that's wonderful around us, Ollie, you're not concentrating. The sunshine. The sky. Look—" and he pointed across the street. "See that man swinging the slingshot? I think he wants to play a game, fancy that, doesn't that dry your tears?"

Ollie shook his head.

Stan stared at the object that came from across the street. It went very high, almost to the treetops before it began its slow arc down toward them.

Ollie was staring at the ruined chocolate, weeping full.

"Give us a hug?" Stan asked.

How could Ollie disobey?

The destruction of sixteen Tring Mews was of little interest to the newspapers—a boiler had exploded, and true, two had died, but a rock star was arrested at Heathrow, cocaine was involved, and that was of more lasting interest.

The man who owned the house, Frederick Webster, was an American businessman, according to the tabloids. The man part, of course, was correct. But his name was not Webster any more than he was in business and the only thing American about him was his employer.

Still, he had a loving wife and a fifteen-year-old daughter. They had been shopping at Harrods when the explosion happened. When they arrived at Tring Mews along about four, the area was barricaded. The wife, when she heard what had happened, tried not to become hysterical. She succeeded, at least for a while, even if her daughter did not.

The charlady who was finishing her chores at number sixteen—Evelyn Jones—also died. She had no husband, but her three children, when the police reluctantly informed them of the afternoon's events, dealt with the facts badly. They were young, their mother their only source of funds, and none of the three could imagine not having her to pull them along. She was not educated, but she was remarkably kind and even-tempered, and her loss decimated the offspring.

There was, to sum up, a good bit of legitimate mourning. But there wasn't much sadness centering on Stan and Ollie. None, in point of fact. Not a single tear honored their passing. For the brothers, no one wept.

# 2

# The Standish Atomizer

Even while she was still naked, still drying herself after the shower, Connie knew it was a night for the blue silk blouse. Buttoned all the way to the throat. Demure, kind of. But tucked tight inside her jeans, so her breasts wouldn't be invisible. To Stevie Wonder, maybe, but not to the world at large.

She tossed the towel toward the laundry basket, missed, shrugged, turned to study herself in the mirror that was still covered with steam so she couldn't make herself out all that clearly yet. Connie shrugged again, turned sideways, sucked in her gut, held the pose.

The steam was beginning to lessen, and her form began to become visible. God, what a shape she had. Not that the face made you want to turn tail and run. Nice long brown hair, nice enough brown eyes. But she wasn't tall, five one, and she'd never weighed more than one-oh-five. Most of it, she sometimes thought, chest. Since she was thirteen.

Male companionship had never been much of a problem.

She was clearer in the glass now, so she gave up the profile, went for straight on, bent forward. Someday when she did that her breasts would sag. But not yet. Not when she was less than twenty-five even, and worked out with the hand weights every day, sometimes twice. Just pectoral stuff. Making sure the pillows stayed firm, firm as well as soft.

Arnie was the first one to call them pillows. It was

probably the first thing she liked about him. Not the last, not near the last, but all the other guys, she hated the way they talked about her; tits, knockers, shitty words, and she hated dirty talk.

But pillows—that showed he had a tender streak. Gentle, kind of. Not that he was always tender with her, not near always tender.

The steam was gone from the mirror now as Connie pushed herself up on tiptoe, did a slow circle, watching herself very close. Summer was coming to the city soon, and already she'd grabbed a couple spare hours, gone to the roof with her Walkman, laid flat in her bikini, grabbed the sun. By August she'd be black damn near, and she wasn't close yet, but already there was a change in color to her skin. A good change. Her eyes seemed bigger, her hair more fair. Her skin . . . she really gave herself a solid once-over. A glow, kind of.

Sometimes she knew she was watching herself too much; it could get to be a rotten habit, people might think you were conceited about the way you stopped traffic when you swung your bottom and sucked in your stomach and when you could stop traffic in the Apple, well, maybe she had reason to feel conceited.

But she also knew she was lucky. Pillows were in in America, had been since Harlow. She'd read that once in a kind of intellectual rag she'd picked up at the hairdresser's. It was a long article about how beauty was in the eye of whoever was doing the looking and it said—truly it did—that when the Greek fags ruled the world, thousands of years ago, they were penis happy, no surprise there—the kicker was, what drove them wild was *little* ones. The smaller the cock, the more beautiful the guy.

Arnie would have been the ugliest Greek alive if he'd been around back then.

And she would have been a dog if she'd been around in the twenties, flapper time, when women bound their breasts to make the boys come coming. That was why Connie thanked whoever was Up There that she was born in the sixties, flowered in the seventies and now, twenty-four in '85, was never short for company, not male company.

She left the bathroom, found her favorite tightest jeans, lay down on the bed, and after the usual struggle, got them over her hips. Then she put on her sandals, went to the closet for the blue silk, held it carefully while she headed for the underwear drawer, grabbed a bra.

And hesitated.

What if she went without? Just the silk on the skin. She hesitated again, then thought what the hell, no harm in just seeing, so she dropped the bra on the bed, put the blouse on, buttoned it, gave herself a look in the bathroom mirror. The pressure of the material was enough to distend her nipples.

But was it tasteful?

She began to walk back and forth in the bathroom, studying the way her breasts bounced. Not floppy or nothing, she was years away from floppy, but you couldn't help but be aware that they were moving by.

Damn, Connie thought, continuing her private parade; she really wanted to go out just like she was, the nipples pointed, the pillows doing their dance—

—and someday she would—

—but it would have to be a future someday. For now she was just too shy, she decided, to risk it. So she unbuttoned the blouse, pulled it off, put on the bra, cursed herself for her modesty—Madonna would have pranced 42nd Street all night long with just the blue silk on—rebuttoned herself to the throat, ran a comb through her hair, grabbed her purse, took off.

It was 10:10 when she got to the Taj Mahal, a joke name for a joke bar, a dump smack in the worst part of Avenue C, maybe the only part of New York where if you *weren't* a pusher, people figured you for weird.

At least until two months ago.

Which was when one block down, Blythe Spirit had opened, a disco with mucho bread behind it, enough for publicity in all the columns, Liza and Bianca and Andy had all been limoed to the opening, and it had taken off from there. Crowds every night. Kids who made Boy George look like Nancy Reagan begging to get in past the roped entrance. Sometimes part of the overflow came slumming to the Taj. Yuppies. Briefcase guys. Some with dates, some without. Mixing with the ordinary Taj clientele, most of whom were either dealing or snoozing at the corner tables.

At 10:11, Connie ordered a Miller Lite on draft, gave Mulcahy, the Taj owner, five bucks for quarters, took the beer and the change, went off by herself to the two pinball machines. Blue Skies, her favorite, was closest, so she stuck in a quarter, took a sip, started to play. The Yuppies couldn't believe it, sometimes, when they saw the pinball machines. It was like they had stepped into a time warp, no video games. Once a salesman had tried convincing Mulcahy to give the games a shot so he tried one, but an angry snow salesman kicked it till it busted the first night. The Taj was not an upscale establishment.

10:15.

Connie concentrated on Blue Skies, when, from alongside her she heard, "My God, I haven't seen one of these since senior year." She looked at the guy. Big. Ivy League. A blazer tossed over one white-shirted arm.

Connie said nothing, played another ball.

"I stopped by the disco," the guy went on. "Dead. Will be for another couple hours. You be heading over then?"

Connie stopped playing, looked at the big guy a moment before she said it: "Look, mister; I got a boyfriend. My name is Connie, but I'm taken." Then she reached across his body toward the other pinball machine and the ashtray tucked in a corner. She took it in one hand, lost her balance a little. Was it her fault that her nipples grazed his shirt? Was it her fault the look came into his eyes?

Where had she gone? Out.

What had she done? Nothing. . . .

* * *

From day one, life had handed Arnie a shit deal. Maybe some would have held his cards and turned into Mother Teresa.

Not Arnie.

He hit out. At everything. In whatever home he was in, at whatever school. He came out swinging. The trouble was, he was always the smallest so people kept kicking the crap out of him. Some kids grew up with big ears. Arnie grew up with a bloody nose.

When he was thirteen one of the Fathers got him interested in weights, so he worked out with them, and he got strong. But he was still small. When he was sixteen, he sprouted to five ten, filled out to an even one sixty.

And found boxing.

He was quick on his feet and he had stopping power with his left, and his left was his weak hand. He began to train for the ring seriously then, and at night, in whatever flophouse he was spending the evening, he knew who he was: the next LaMotta. Only greater. LaMotta could take any punch and the only time he was ever stopped it was a fix. Arnie's chin was like that too. He waded in, straight at the enemy, and he took everything; nothing, *nothing* made him step back. LaMotta could stop you, but only with an accumulation, usually when you were fighting exhaustion as well as him.

Arnie could drop anybody when they were daisy fresh.

Except from day one, life had handed him a shit deal: his hands were brittle. Sure he could punch. Yes he could take you out. But his bones broke. Damn near every time he unloaded, there went a finger, a knuckle.

At eighteen, he gave up on the ring, decided to be a hero—so he tried joining the Marines.

Except, as always, life was there to give him the good old you-know-what. The Marines insisted on a high school diploma—

—a *diploma*—

—who the hell cared how smart you were when what you wanted was someone tough alongside you, someone who wouldn't step back, no matter how hard the punches coming at you.

Also, they didn't like it when they found out he'd had a couple little pranks when he was a kid. The asshole recruiter called them felonies but pranks was all they were. Scaring old people. Maybe helping them across the street for money.

At twenty he was driving a cab. Living alone near Avenue C. Boozing with whoever happened to be in whatever bar he happened to be in.

At twenty-five, two years ago, a girl got in his cab, a kid in jeans and sandals with pillows you could die for. He bought her a beer and told her so.

The shit deal died.

Up ahead now, was the Taj. Arnie looked at his watch. 10:30 straight up. In the darkness alongside the bar was the alley where he parked his cab. He pulled into it till he was just past the side exit. Then he turned out the headlights, killed the motor, got out, moved into the darkness, lit a butt.

And put the leather gloves over his brittle hands . . .

Standish sat alone at the bar, elegant in his three-piece suit. He had himself positioned so that without seeming to intrude, he could watch the movements of the couple that had begun their sex dance at the pinball machine, was seated at a secluded table now.

He could have risked moving in before the Ivy Leaguer, and perhaps he should have, but he had not attained his present position of eminence by making mistakes. And the atomizer would benefit from another week of testing before final fieldwork, because fieldwork, this kind anyway, could be dangerous. Or, in this case, lethal.

Standish knew the odds were against his living forever, but he intended giving it a very good try.

"You only want what I've got," Connie said, sipping her Miller Lite, seated at the corner table at the Taj, looking in the Ivy Leaguer's eyes. The clock on the wall said 10:20.

"I'm not that kind, I told you already," the Ivy Leaguer said.

Connie shook her head.

"Why don't you trust men?"

"'Cause they lie. They all lie, not counting my boyfriend."

"Some attentive fella if you ask me—leaving you alone at night in a dangerous place like this."

"He got a job." She reached across, looked him in the eyes then. "How many years you got? College?"

"Enough to get a law degree, no big deal."

"I got one semester secretarial school, think we're a match made in heaven?"

"I like you, Connie. You've got honesty. That's a rare commodity these days. When we first started talking what did you say right off? That you had a boyfriend. Most of the girls I meet only want one thing." He held up his third finger, left hand.

"They want your finger?"

"No." He tried not to laugh. "Marriage."

"Don't you fuckin' laugh at me."

"I'm sorry, and I wasn't—it's just I remembered something that happened once, a funny memory is why I was laughing, not anything remotely to do with you."

Connie weighed that.

"You want a double vodka, I'd like a double vodka."

"I'll drink you under the table, lawyer."

"Boy, you really don't trust men." He stood up quickly.

She watched as he went to the bar, ordered, got the drinks, paid, came back and started to sit across from her. She patted the chair alongside. "Sit next to me if you'd like; I don't mean to imply nothing, but it's easier to talk if someone's close, don't you think?"

"Oh, a lot."

"And it's getting noisier."

"My thoughts exactly." He sat by her.

Connie picked up her glass, indicated for him to do the same. "What do they say? Foreigners I mean? When they clink? Friendly foreigners."

"Will *'skol'* do?"

*"Skol."* She drained the double.

He looked at her a moment. "I'm impressed." He did the same with his, or tried to. Halfway through he coughed, took a long pause before he finished. "Another?"

"Just so you promise you don't get ideas."

"I promise, I promise," and then he was hurrying back to the bar, getting the refills, returning. He sat down, pulled his chair closer.

Connie said nothing, stretched her arms above her head, inhaled deeply.

He watched her, turning the glass in his large hands.

"You move well for a big guy, you know that? I watched you when you got the drinks. You a jock?"

He shrugged. "I was on the tennis team."

"You got a good face too. Handsome, at least to my way of thinking."

He held up his glass. "Here's to your way of thinking."

Connie picked up hers. *"Skol,"* she said. "I get it right?"

"I never heard it done any better." He smiled at her.

"You like me?"

"No complaints so far."

"Then why are you ashamed to be with me?"

He put his glass down. "Time out—where's that come from?"

"At the pinball, when you started talking, before I agreed to sit and chat and all, I let drop what my name was, Connie. You never said. You never said yet. And we been together what, ten minutes easy. I don't believe everyone's after you to get married, I think you are already."

He flipped her his wallet. "Name's on all my credit cards."

She shook her head. "I don't need to know—if you'd let me see, I don't have to. Anyway, I like calling you 'lawyer.' "

"I like the way it sounds when you say it." He put his wallet back into his pocket.

"Where'd you buy the jacket?" Connie said then.

"No place you'd have heard of."

" 'Cause I'm so stupid?"

"Why do you take everything wrong? No, not because you're stupid, because I've got a tailor makes things for me and I didn't think you'd have heard of him."

Connie looked at him a long time, then she put her hand under the table, touched his trousers. "He make these too?"

"It's not as expensive as you might think—and appearances have a lot to do with client confidence."

"How much?"

He shrugged. "This stuff's a couple years old, I'm not sure."

"About?"

"Maybe a thousand, that ball park."

"Jesus," Connie said. She kept her hands on his trousers, the fingers moving from the knee to the thigh, then back down.

"Let's get out of here. Let's go someplace."

"Not yet."

"Why not? I'm crazy about you, I swear to Christ."

Connie sipped her vodka. "I just don't know—see, men—the reason I take everything wrong is, I been lied to by so many men—in the night they're all crazy about me, but I'm not so much in demand once the sun starts shining."

"I'm not like the others," the lawyer said.

"How can I know that for sure?"

"You can't—you've got to give me a chance to prove it—we'll go to the disco awhile—"

"—what if they won't let us in?—Blythe Spirit's awful particular—"

"—bullshit, I'll pay whatever it takes, doormen are doormen, and we'll dance a little and talk a lot, really get to know each other, we'll drink and tell each other stories about what it was like before we met each other and what it's going to be like now that we have and . . ."

During this, her fingers were back under the table, moving up from his knee to his thing, then back down.

"Go all the way up."

Connie hesitated.

"Just do it."

Connie did.

"That's what just talking to you does to me. Imagine what it'll be like when we really know each other."

Connie stood.

He did too, started for the main door of the Taj.

Connie headed for the side entrance. "Shortcut," she said.

He followed her.

"Careful, it's dark," she said, as they left the bar, moved into the dark alley.

When the door had closed behind them, he put his hands on her breasts, pulled her into his arms, kissed her mouth.

"Don't do that."

"You want me to. You been sending out signals all night."

"Stop."

"I will if you really want me to." He kissed her again.

"Stop."

"You don't want me to—you know goddam well you don't want me to."

In the darkness now, a male voice said, barely in a whisper, ". . . I think maybe she does . . ."

Arnie's first punch landed while the guy was trying to get accustomed to the darkness; he pushed Connie off, half turned, and the blow tore into his stomach, taking away his air. Before he could bend double, the second punch was already on its way, a backhanded clenched fist into the cheek and nose.

Blood pouring, the big guy went down.

Arnie was lifting him back up almost before he'd fully hit, dragging him back into the rear of the alley, propping him in a corner between an alley wall and a fence, so that the body stayed upright and Arnold could use both hands. He went to the stomach again and again, all he had—his hands were at full strength as long as the target was soft.

When he hit the other guy's face, Arnie was more careful, the blows more gentle.

Now the other guy doubled over, pitched down.

Arnie brought him right back up, shoved him harder into a propped position, went back to work with his leather-gloved hands, and now his body was fully in balance, he had total power with his punches now, ribs were cracking, God knows what else, he didn't care as he went at it and at it, occasionally going for the face, not minding if the blood got his clothes, and then he was back at the body again and then Connie was going "Arnold—Arnold stop—"

"—why?—"

"—Christ, you'll hurt him—"

"—I already hurt him." He continued the slaughter.

*"Stop."*

*"Why?"*

"You'll kill him."

"I want to. What do I love most in all the world?"

"—touching me—"

"—and what do I hate most?—"

"—when anybody else does—"

"—and what do you hate most?—"

"—when anybody else does—"

"—well I saw him touching you and you hate that so why do you want me to stop—"

"—because of what I love most—"

"—an' what's that?—"

"—you touching me—"

"—so?—" He went for the face again, both hands.

*"—stop please Jesus—"*

*"—goddamit tell me why—"*

*"—on account of, I'm wet—I'm so wet, Arnold, and I need it, I need it and I need it now—"*

And then they were both of them heading for the backseat of the cab, and he threw the door open as she ripped at her jeans and his hands worked the fly of his pants and when she lay on the backseat she spread and he lunged and then they were rocking, in love and rocking, eyes shut in the darkness, listening as their bodies worked.

The sound, the loudest sound was the constant building moan from the figure in the corner of the alley. Sometimes, along with the moan, there were sobs.

Icing on the cake.

They were not the only ones to hear the moans. Minutes before, as his quarry had started for the side entrance, Standish had left the bar by the front, circled around, entered the darkness of the alley, moved as close as he dared.

He was there for the end of the slaughter, the discussion of wetness, was still there as they found passion in the backseat of the cab.

What a pair. Murderous, psychotic, moronic, and vile. And, as far as Standish was concerned, just perfect.

The second he saw Connie coming into the Taj, Mulcahy knew nothing good was going to happen. She was always a hunk, sure, a head-turner that ranked with the best, only tonight there was a difference. For the better. He studied her as she moved toward the bar, wondering what the hell it was, then cursed himself for not knowing immediately.

Tonight the nipples were damn near popping through the blouse.

And the blouse was different too. It wasn't just that she didn't have no bra, it's that her top was all scooped out down to the tops of her tits. Usually, she was a buttoned-up type. Now, as she moved and they jiggled ever so slightly, Mulcahy found himself half praying they'd fall out, give him a peep.

What he wouldn't give.

Except, of course, Arnie would kill him. They were so weird, the two of them. Good customers most of the time, no problem most of the time, come in, buy their drinks, sit, laugh together, spend their bread. But every so often she'd come first, hit the pinball, leave with some guy.

Bad for some guy.

Christ, a week ago the one they found in the alley had everything broken; almost everything. The ribs, the nose, the cheekbone, the stomach brutalized.

Anybody could have done it, there were no witnesses, except Arnie did it. Mulcahy knew few things for sure but one of them was that. "Lemme guess, a pink lady," Mulcahy said.

He got a laugh.

"A frozen Rob Roy?"

Just a look this time.

He took a glass, pulled her a Miller Lite. "Change your hair, Connie? You look different."

She almost blushed with her smile. "Nothing different 'xcept maybe the outfit. I seen that Madonna flick, y'know? —*Desperately Seeking Susan*. And after seeing her, I figured what the hell, go with what God gave you." She plunked down a couple singles, waited while he gave her change plus quarters for Blue Skies.

"I wish God had given me Ruth Roman," Mulcahy said sadly; he was fifty-five and a grandfather but he still had never gotten over the sight of her in *Champion*.

Connie shrugged, headed for the pinball.

"Clearly you're a man of taste," Mulcahy heard then. "For she was indeed a morsel. Standish is my name, a fellow lover of beauty."

Mulcahy turned toward the speaker, a little gray-haired fruit most likely, all decked out in a three-piece suit, fancy tie. He'd been sitting alone for a few minutes at the bar, fingering his Scotch in one hand, a pocket breath atomizer in the other.

"But would you rate her above or below Rhonda Fleming?"

Mulcahy shrugged. There was something about the pipsqueak that spooked him. He seemed like he was slumming, that there was a smell to the Taj which made him look down his nose at it. Of course, there *was* a smell to the Taj, Mulcahy knew he didn't own Sardi's, but most of his customers were good enough to hide their feelings.

"Personally, I would have cast them both aside in favor of Miss Ekberg."

"I guess you're a tit man," Mulcahy said then.

"Tit *person*, if you please; I'm also a feminist."

Mulcahy mopped the bar, making practiced circles until he stopped, suddenly and for just a moment he felt afraid—because the little guy with the vest could not take his eyes off Connie. "Don't do it," Mulcahy wanted to warn. "Don't do nothing, just nurse your booze."

Because if there was one thing Arnie hated worse than people looking sideways at his girl, it was fags. Fags and the blacks, Arnie hated them both. Mulcahy had heard the man going on about them often enough. Late at night whenever some straggler from the disco came in, some weirdly dressed guy.

Now the pipsqueak was standing.

"Lemme buy you a round," Mulcahy said then.

The guy didn't even answer, just started toward the machines.

I tried, Mulcahy thought. I honest to God did. And he went back to cleaning the bar, wondering, truly wondering if Arnie were capable of murder.

Connie was concentrating on the third ball when she heard, "Milo Standish is the name, *not*, please, Miles; Milo."

She looked at the shrimp as he smiled at her, toasted her with his glass, then squirted the general vicinity with the breath atomizer. "What's with that, for chrissakes?" Connie said.

"Apologies, apologies, a fetish of mine, my parents, may they rest in the reverse of whatever peace is, used to constantly be after me because of my cleanliness habits; halitosis, they said, body odor, they said—none of it true, understand, but it found its mark. I have a terrible fear of offending."

Connie went back to her machine. Some were strange and some weird, but this one, no question, was whacko. She didn't even much want to think about what Arnie would do. What was it they used to say about cattle slaughterhouses? —they only left the squeal? That's all Arnie would leave of this one.

"I didn't catch your name, my dear, I suspect the reason more than likely being because you're withholding it."

"Connie."

"Ah, Constance, from the Latin *constantia,* meaning 'constant.' Faithful. Are you constant, Constance?"

Connie looked at him. He was a wise guy, no question; asking for it. "Look, Milo, I got a boyfriend."

He laughed. "What a delicious coincidence, so have I."

He said it so fast and his eyes were so twinkly that in a moment, quite to her surprise, she was laughing too.

Outside in the alley, Arnie lit a fresh butt off the one that was down to a nub. He looked at his watch. 10:30.

Soon.

He slammed a leather-covered fist into a leather-covered palm. God, he felt—not angry, worse than angry, *foul,* there was a foul taste in his mouth, to the air, to the world.

Ten million dollars.

That was what the evening *Post* said. It was all a rumor but Spinks was going to fight the middleweight champ, Hagler, and Hagler was going to get ten—million—dollars. Here he was fighting traffic for buttons and Hagler was going to make that—

—and he could have killed Hagler.

Taken him out easy. Three rounds on a bad night. If only his hands hadn't betrayed him. He could have been retired now with a house bigger than the nigger Sugar Ray Leonard's. He and Connie could have had nigger servants to bring them whatever they wanted—(white cooks though, you couldn't let niggers near your food)—and they could have traveled to Vegas whenever there was a big fight and after they'd introduced all the cheese champs, Frazier and Ali and Robinson, the announcer would go, "Ladies and gentlemen, last and far from least, we are honored to have with us tonight . . ." and he'd go on and on only no one would hear the rest because by now Arnie would be in the ring, hands clasped high, and turning around for all the folks to get a good look, and most of them would have tears in their eyes, he'd brought them that many thrills, that much joy.

He inhaled deeply, slammed his hands together again. Again. *Again*. Goddam brittle betrayers.

Tonight the world was gonna *pay*.

"You gotta explain me something," Connie said, sipping on her second Scotch.

"If it is within the realm of human knowledge, Constance, the answer shall instantly be flying from my silver tongue."

"The way you look at me—like right now—you're staring at my nipples and I don't get it—you said you were gay, why do you keep watching me."

"That was just my little joke, Constance—let me put it this way: if it is ambulatory, it arouses my passion."

Connie didn't know quite what the long word meant, but the gist she understood. "You just want what I've got, you mean."

"Do you mean am I interested in your superstructure? Of course. What fool would be interested in your mind? You have yet—at least in my presence—to use a three-syllable word. Why in the world would anybody want to *talk* to you?"

Connie figured probably that wasn't flattering, but you couldn't get mad at Milo, not with his way with words.

"And don't bother with *my* boyfriend, if such there be, tell me about yours, start with his name."

"Arnie."

"And is he good?"

"Sweet you mean?"

"Expert I mean."

"Are you trying to pry into my sex life?"

" 'Pry' was surprisingly well used, Constance. Perhaps you have the makings of a quiz kid after all. The answer is yes."

"I like it in the rack with him, yeah."

Milo raised his glass and toasted. "Praise be—if he weren't, it would have been a tragedy greater than Lear's. A creature like yourself unsatisfied—it would have made the devil weep."

"I really turn you on, don't I?"

He nodded. "It's just a joy being able to watch you. Are you blushing, Constance?"

She was.

"It only adds to your blossoming appeal." He stood. "Where is this legendary boyfriend of yours that I may meet him?"

"Maybe that's not such a great idea, Milo."

"Let *me* be the judge of ideas, my dear; that way your brow will never need be furrowed." He gestured for her to stand.

She did. "He might be waiting by the side entrance."

"Come along."

"I don't think maybe you know what you're doing."

"Milo always knows what he's doing," Milo said.

As soon as he saw that Connie had brought him a fag, Arnie wanted to give her a hug. And he would. Soon. Plus a lot more. He could feel the bulge in his jeans and nothing had even started yet. He stood still in the darkness by his cab and was about to say, softly, "I think maybe you're in trouble, mister," when suddenly the little guy was going, "Arnold . . . oh, Arnold . . ." very loud, and looking around for him.

"Arnie?" Connie echoed.

"You want him, you got him," Arnold said, moving toward them.

"The great Arnold," the faggot began, "I must shake your hand," and then as he walked close he squirted the general area with a breath atomizer.

"What the hell you doing?"

"He's got this cleanliness thing," Connie explained.

"His parents were rotten to him, weren't they, Milo? He's afraid of offending, I get that right?"

"Oh, beloved Constance, could you do anything wrong?"

The leather gloves formed fists now. "I wouldn't call her words like that, faggot."

"Please—I have strange mannerisms, but I also have a way of endearing myself."

"He does," Constance echoed.

"I can tell," Arnie said. He held out his hand. "You want to shake, let's shake."

Milo held out his right. "To the luckiest man in the world."

Arnie took the small hand, held it tight, began to turn on the power.

The faggot cried out, went to his knees.

Connie moved in, said to cut it.

Arnie put both his gloved hands around the asshole's right, sent his strength into overdrive.

Now the guy was flailing like a hooked fish.

Connie slapped him in the face.

Stunned, Arnie looked at her.

Then he let the little guy go. In a moment, Milo was back on his feet, massaging his right with his left. "Nothing broken," he said. "Let's hope anyway."

Arnie blinked. "Did I squeeze that hard?"

"No," Milo said. "I'm just not, shall we say, physically strong."

"Hell, you sure nothing's broke? I can drive you to Bellevue."

"Please. Enough about my hand." Arnie could sense him studying his face. "Inside, when glorious Constance was going on about you, I tried picturing you in my mind's eye. But you surpassed my imagination."

"Oh, cut the shit," Arnie said, "I'm not handsome."

"That's right, you're not, but you're a good deal more, you're *fearless*, Alexander the Great would have made you his king warrior."

Arnie looked at the little guy. Maybe he wasn't a fag.

One of those both-way people you were always reading about. "Why am I the luckiest man in the world?" he asked.

Milo said nothing, merely pointed at Connie.

"I don't get it."

"She loves you. And you satisfy her. She could have any sheik, but she chooses you, don't you, wise Constance?"

"He's my man, all right."

"Would you both do me a favor?" Milo said then.

"Depends."

"I don't want our acquaintanceship to end yet—I want to know you both better—I want to tell you about myself and I want you to talk to me—but not here."

"Where then?" Arnie asked.

"Your place, perhaps, or mine."

"I didn't do such a red-hot job of cleaning today," Connie said.

Milo laughed. "Look at her, blushing again." He put an arm around Arnie. "My apartment then? It's just by the university. Ten minutes away in your chariot. I had it done by a world-class decorator." He gestured for Connie to come close, and when she did, he had an arm around them both. "And my maids did a very red-hottish job of cleaning this selfsame afternoon." He looked down at her, then up at Arnie. "Well?"

"Why the fuck not?" Arnie said.

"A Latin scholar after my own heart," Milo Standish said.

"Oh, I want it, I want it," Connie shouted, running ahead of the men into the enormous living room.

Milo smiled.

"Some place you got, Milo—we could stick our whole apartment into this one room."

"Life is more than square footage, Arnold. Believe me."

"Feel this *rug*," Connie said, touching it with her fingers, then kicking off her sandals, moving through the expensive carpet barefooted. "It's a foot thick I swear,

Milo, and look''—she pointed to the corners—''it just exactly fits this room.''

Milo smiled.

Connie went to the windows then, stared out. ''This is the whole Village, right? I never seen a view like this.''

Milo patted Arnie on the back. ''You truly are the most fortunate of men.''

''You don't seem to be hurting a whole lot yourself.''

Milo dropped his voice to a whisper. ''May I ask you a question? I don't mean to invade your privacy, and if you don't want to answer, please don't.''

''Shoot.''

''Who was her surgeon?''

''Huh?''

''The implants. Was it done here, Los Angeles?''

''I don't get you.''

''Surely you must.''

''You mean her breasts?''

''Obviously.''

''Those are real, Milo. The McCoy. Nobody's touched them but me and believe me, I know.''

Milo shook his head. ''Not possible.''

Arnie raised his right hand. ''Swear to God.''

Milo hesitated then for a moment. ''If you don't want to do this, don't do this, Arnold—but it would mean a great deal to me if I could ascertain the truth for myself.''

Arnie shrugged. ''Go for it.''

Milo crossed to the window. ''Constance?''

She turned.

''Bend down a moment for me, would you?''

''Why?''

''Just bend down,'' Arnie said.

Connie shrugged, did as she was told.

''There's a dear girl,'' Milo said, and he carefully put both his small hands into her scooped-out blouse, raised her breasts so they were free. ''Now would you stand very straight please?''

Connie stood very straight. "Want I should inhale?" she giggled.

"That won't be necessary." Milo took her right breast, examined underneath where the skin met the chest. Then he did the same with the left breast. "Incredible," he said.

"What did I tell you?" Arnie said, smiling.

Milo shook his head. "Ornaments of God," he murmured. He looked at Arnie then, then at the girl. "Please feel free to say no but it would mean a great deal to me if I could suckle them."

"My pillows you mean?" Connie said.

"I most certainly do."

"If it's okay with Arnie, it's okay with me."

"Hey, I'm no spoilsport," Arnie said.

"Lift your arms above your head like a dear," Milo said.

Connie lifted her arms up.

Milo untucked her blouse, pulled it off her body. Then he sucked her nipples for several moments. When he was done, he looked at Arnie. "You get to do this every day, how blessed a thing."

"They are nice."

"I do little exercises to keep them perky; free weights and stuff."

Milo nodded. "Never stop." Then he hesitated.

"Are *you* blushing?" Connie asked next.

"I feel so embarrassed asking you both this, and please *please* say no if you don't want to, but . . . it would mean a great deal to me if . . . if I could hit them."

Arnie took a step forward. "Hit Connie's breasts?"

Milo managed a nod.

"Isn't that kind of sick, Milo?"

"Why do you think I'm embarrassed, Arnold?"

Arnie lit a cigarette. "I'll tell you the truth, they're not mine, if it's okay with Connie, I got no gripe."

Milo smiled at her. "Connie?"

"They're awful tender, Milo."

"Of course they are, forget it, just forget the whole thing, I said it would mean a great deal to me but the last thing I want is to cause anything untoward to come between us so—"

"—you mean with your fists?"

"Oh, dear girl, no. Just a solid finger flick—the nipples enlarge when they're struck—they redden and swell and I find that . . ." He looked pleadingly at Connie. "It excites me."

"A finger flick is nothing," Connie said. "I don't mind that."

Milo struck her nipples.

Connie inhaled sharply.

"Oh God, look at them, come here, Arnold, see?"

Arnie approached, nodded.

"Doesn't that excite you?"

"Naw."

"What does?"

"Well, beating up on people with her watching."

"You see, we're all normal," Milo said. "Normal but with special appetites. Did that hurt badly, Constance? You gasped."

She shrugged. "Just sort of stung. Worse than that, but you know what I mean."

"Bless you for your bravery," Milo said, and he kissed her lightly on one cheek. Then he said, "For heaven's sake, where have my manners gone, I haven't offered you a drink." He pushed a button on the nearest wall and a cabinet opened, revealing a bar. "Arnold, would you be bartender while I slip into something more comfortable?"

"No sweat."

Arnie approached the bar when Milo had gone. "Jesus, Connie, look at this—Stoly and Chivas and J.D. and imported gin. State your preference."

"I guess Stoly. He got any lemon peel?"

Arnie nodded. "And olives and onions, the works."

"On the rocks then."

Arnie nodded, made her drink while she wandered to the entrance. "Arnie? Look—there's another whole floor. Stairs going up. Some palace." She came back to him then, kissed him, stuck her tongue in his mouth fast. "We'll have ours someday. I got faith in you, Arnie. I love you an' I got faith."

Arnie handed her a drink. "Do you hear a whirring?"

She listened. "Yeah. Oh." She pointed below the bar. "I bet it's that icemaker."

Arnie glanced down. "Right." He made himself a Stoly too, and they clinked glasses before chugging them down. "Another?"

"Oh yeah."

Arnie had just finished squeezing the lemon twists and pouring when Milo came back in, hugged them both.

Arnie stepped back, surprised. "Shit, Milo, you should have said you were going to get naked. You should have asked did we mind?"

"I thought I did."

"You said you were going to get *comfortable*, that's not the same."

"Now I'm embarrassed again," Milo answered. "I'll go put on my clothes. Would you both like that? It's the host's job to make his guests happy."

"As long as you're naked, I don't mind," Arnie said. He looked at Connie. "You?"

"Oh Christ, why make him put on that vest and tie? Let the man be comfortable, it's his home."

"I feel like I've known you both forever," Milo said. "I feel I could ask you for anything."

"Try us," Arnie said.

"Please feel free to say no, but I cannot tell you how much it would mean to me . . ." His voice trailed off.

"Say it, we can always tell you no," Connie said.

In reply, Milo said nothing, just put his thumb in his mouth, moved it in and out rapidly.

"You mean you just want me to blow you, that it?"

"You're not upset, Constance?"

"Hell, I blow Arnie all the time." She looked at Arnie. "You got any problems with that? I don't."

Arnie didn't either.

"Hell, Milo, I thought you really wanted a favor."

"Actually, my sweet, there's a bit more."

"We're listening."

Milo rubbed his hands together. "If you don't want to do this, even though it means a great deal to me, I'll die if you don't say no."

"You haven't said what you want," Connie said.

"All right. Here's everything . . . I want to sit on the couch and I want Constance to stimulate me, and when I am in the proper state, I'll bring her down into a sitting position and I'll penetrate her—I would put my hands on her perfect, as you call them, pillows, flicking away with my fingers—and that would take care of our activities, Constance."

"I'll just leave you till you're done, no big deal."

"Arnold, I could not let a guest of mine be bored, I've got someone for you too, that way we could all be occupied."

"Hey, Con, we never done that—swinging, you mean, right, Milo?"

Milo nodded.

"Great," Arnie said. "Who's this 'someone'? Is she beautiful, is she built?"

"The build is magnificent, but beauty is too personal for a definitive answer—my own feeling is yes." He clapped his hands then. Then there were footsteps on the stairs. Then an enormous naked black man filled the doorway.

"Holy shit," Arnie said.

"Is that a negative?" Milo asked.

Arnie hesitated.

"Feel free to say no," Milo said.

"Nobody's pushing you, Arnie," Connie told him.

"I never done anything like this before, I'd feel like a jerk, that's all." He walked to the bar, reached toward the ice bucket.

"Shall we get naked then?" Milo said.

Arnie put some ice cubes into his glass, drank some liquor, poured in some more, looked around. "Why is that whirring so loud over here?"

Milo smiled at Connie. "That man of yours, keen;

nothing escapes his attention.'' He looked at Arnie then. ''I've got sort of a machine rigged up—our pictures are being taken.''

''Now wait one minute—'' Arnie said.

''Moving pictures?'' Connie said, excited.

''—hold it, Con—I don't even know this black guy—you think I'm gonna want the whole world watching him cornhole me?—''

''—it's like a screen test,'' Connie said. ''Only it's free and everything. We could be stars, Arnie.''

''Who you gonna show us to, Milo?''

''No one you need worry about, Arnold; some friends of mine in Washington, perhaps.''

''Are they gay like you, Milo?—nothing against your friends or anything, but I've got my reputation at stake here—how do you think my mother would feel if she saw this?—''

''—you're an *orphan,*'' Connie cut in; ''what's this mother talk?—''

Milo shook his head then. ''This chatter is ruining the mood—you can't imagine how frustrating it is being so close to Constance here, trying to envision her splendors, with all this prattle destroying my concentration. I want this terribly, Arnold, but if a little stag footage is going to unsettle you, forget about me and my desires, forget everything, I don't care—''

''—Milo, I never said I wouldn't do this, of course I'll do this, a guy takes me into his home, offers me free booze and a screen test, I'm not gonna turn that guy down—it's just there's been a lotta surprises this last little bit, it took me a little to get used to it. But I'm with you all the way now, let the cameras roll.''

''Shall we get naked then?'' Milo repeated.

They got naked.

''Shall we assume our positions then?''

They assumed their positions.

''You know what I think, Milo,'' Arnie said, as he knelt.

"Your mind has unfathomable depths, Arnold; please tell me."

"I think it's new experiences like this that keep us young."

"The soul of a poet, that's you, Arnold," Milo said. Then he said, "I am about to enter ecstasy."

Arnie smiled at Connie. "Hey, sweetheart?"

She smiled back. "What, darling?"

"Some fun, huh?"

"Cat's meow."

# 3

# Uncle Arky's Champagne

Needlessly, Scout had set the alarm for half past four in the morning. He knew as he did it that he would never sleep, which turned out to be the case, but he did it anyway—he had never been self-destructive but this might be the first time, it was that important to him, the ultimate testing.

He lay in bed at quarter past four, lay in the darkness and stared up, trying not to think of his beloved Audible, but rather of the challenge that he would face in such a few hours. Every so often, it crossed his mind that his reputation would be forever ruined if any private detective burst in with a photocamera because what they would see was a six-foot-three blond kid lying in bed holding a basketball.

Well, that was life. At least his, anyway. The reason he slept with the thing—a Larry Bird model—was because one of his math teachers freshman year, two years before, was a gentle black man who had attended Tennessee State with Dick Barnett, the most underrated of the great Knicks, and the teacher told him that everyone always knew where Barnett was on campus since he bounced his basketball from class to class, held it during lectures, probably slept with it beside him at night.

If it was good enough for any of the great Knicks, Scout had no problem adopting the habit. He had read once that when Bradley was in high school he used to set chairs up in the gym and dribble at full speed in and around the chairs.

But that was no big deal. Anyone could do that. What made Bradley's chore special was that he wore glasses and taped the bottom half of the lenses so that he could never see where the ball was, had to find it by feel alone.

Across his room Scout had three pairs of glasses, all with the bottom halves thickly taped. He had not had to look at the ball for a year and a half now. He could dribble blindfolded if he had to, with either his right or his left (though he knew, deep down, that under severe pressure, the left was only maybe eighty percent as sure).

And of course, he could stick the jumper. He had read where the legendary Julius Erving had begun his pro career with all the equipment except the outside shot. So he developed one. By simply shooting thousands of times, thousands of times, until confidence came.

Scout had always had confidence in his shooting. His father had taught him when Scout could barely heave the ball ten feet up, much less aim it. But strength would come, his father had said, strength was never a problem. Form was the killer. You had to bend the knees just so. You had to release the ball not just perfectly but perfectly *every time*, to ensure the proper rotation.

When he was twelve, Scout began the practice program he still followed five years later. Start with free throws. No set number. That made it all mathematical. You just shot free throws until you hit twenty straight. (Scout led the conference in free throw shooting. Eighty-eight percent. Everyone thought that was fantastic, except Scout knew it had to be ninety, he was good enough to shoot ninety, and if he didn't it meant he wasn't concentrating.) Then, when the free throws were done, he started with layups. Just running toward the hoop, a perfect ten feet high on the garage in the back, and laying the ball against the backboard gently, his hands soft, gently up and in. Ten with the left hand, the same with the right.

Then he would move away from the basket. Eight-footers. From in front, then from both sides. Then twelve-footers. Then fifteen. Next eighteen. When he made ten in a row of each, it was on to the next. He was starting on twenty-footers now. He didn't like them much, they had an element of hot-dog in them and he was never a showy player. But he told himself that if he had the twenty-footer, if he got deadly with it, the other teams would have to honor him, and that meant spreading their defense, and that meant Scout could have an easier time hitting his teammates for easy shots.

Even Scout, with his desperate modesty, knew he could pass with anybody his age. He saw the whole court so easily, knew his teammates' strengths so well, would always hit them on stride for their best shots.

He could shoot. He could pass. He weighed a hundred and sixty-five pounds, no fat. He could run forever and not breathe hard. His coaches loved him, not just because he could follow instructions without complaint but because he had smarts on the court. He had, many said, everything on the court.

Scout knew different: he couldn't sky and he was slow.

Sure he could run forever and not breathe hard, but he couldn't run fast. And sky? David Thompson had a vertical leap of forty-two inches. *Measured* at forty-two inches. Scout was lucky if he could clear a ream of paper set on center court. He had done every conceivable thing to improve his weaknesses, but you couldn't practice elevation. It was like they said in the pros: you can't teach height.

Still, even with his flaws, he'd made all-conference junior year, had led the league in assists, come third in scoring. He was good, all right. It would be asinine to argue the point.

But was he good *enough*?

Was he or could he ever be what he wanted most: to be a *player*? (That was the ultimate compliment you could give another human: "He's a *player*.")

Scout got out of bed then. Held the basketball in both hands. Hugged it to his body. It was 4:29 A.M.

By noon he would know if he was a player or not.

Although they had agreed not to meet before Scout took the bus, Audrey—Audible was his private name for her, only his, a joke based on the fact that in class she always, whenever called on, spoke so softly and freshman year Miss Clemson had said, "You really must set your mind to achieving audibility, my dear"—was awake at four.

Not all that unusual for her. She had a lot of energy and she needed it, what with the chores. She tried to finish studying by midnight, always edged the ensuing dawn. Everyone in school thought she was just so smart and the endless *A*'s seemed to prove that, but Audrey knew the truth: she had no fear of working.

4:10. A moan from her mother's room. She quickly stood, hurried to her, trying to beat the next moan, because Aunt B., who took care of her, needed her rest. You needed rest when you were getting on.

Audrey opened her mother's door, flashed her best smile, crossed the room, kissed her on the cheek, whispered it was going to be a beautiful day, set to the task humming "Brighten the Corner," her mother's favorite hymn.

Her mother was incontinent now and in the beginning Audrey found it difficult, the cleaning and all. Not physically difficult but there was a terrible emotional pull, being, at seventeen, your mother's mother, so to speak. When her mother was clean, Audrey got her as comfortable as she could, whispered, "You sleep some more now," and left.

Audrey had deft fingers. Had always. Loved to sew. Crochet. Cook. Probably that was why she planned on being a surgeon. It was a silly dream really. Not much reality in that vicinity. Even if she was the brightest girl in town, you couldn't give much of a whoop and a holler about that since the town was that famous intellectual haven, Neptune, New Jersey, population in the low four figures.

No, Scout would be the doctor in the family. They'd planned it since they started going steady, freshman year. They would both attend Wagner State, just down the road, and Audrey would become a nurse and support Scout through med school. Just like in *Not as a Stranger.* Wagner State wasn't such a much, but with her mother's condition and Aunt B. of only limited help, Audrey had to live at home. And it wasn't that terrible a school. Some of their top graduates got into med school and Audrey was sure Scout would do the same there. He was the brightest boy around, and if his grades weren't quite as high as hers, well, they would have been if he had spent the time on homework she did.

The "Perfects" the other kids had called them when they first started going together. And Audrey could see how they might grate on the rest. They were tops in school, he was the best jock, she was class president. And although she would never admit that she was any more than average looking, the truth was she wasn't. They looked alike, her and Scout—both tall, blond, blue eyed—and Scout to her eyes was as handsome as anyone ever needed being and he told her she was the prettiest in the history of Neptune. (Once he said that anyway, but she hooted so he quit fast before it became a permanent part of his vocabulary.)

But then, midway through freshman year, the taunting stopped, no more calls of "Perfects" in the corridors. It had to do with their parents, obviously, or sudden lack of them. Scout's went together, in a car crash, and he moved in with the English teacher and her husband, who was athletic director. Audrey's went separately—a terrible way to think about it, Audrey realized, since her mother was still breathing. She wasn't "gone."

As good as, though.

And probably the deaths were what made her and Scout so close. They suddenly were all they had. When an affliction descends, you can give in to it or do your best to fight, and it turned out the two blonds were fighters. They maybe didn't look it, probably they seemed soft, spoiled even. But inside, inside they were tough down to bone.

4:50 and she heard it. From the sidewalk outside.

bounce—

bounce—

bounce.

That was all. His signal to her, three quick dribbles of the basketball, his most precious possession not counting her, his signal that he was off to catch the first bus to Manhattan.

For a moment, Audrey felt, and this surprised her, panic. She made it a practice not to let things creep up on her and go "boo" from the closet door; she was an expert at contingencies.

But now she wanted to run out after him and yell "It doesn't matter, it doesn't matter how you do, it won't change *me*." And of course that was true.

Lord only knew what it would do to Scout though. "Just do your best," she said in her quiet way, because that's all success was, doing your best, she'd read that someplace, nothing else mattered.

Except she knew that would never be enough for Scout. He *always* did his best. He needed a better send-off from her.

"Knock them dead, my darling," she heard herself say. Audibly.

Scout knew there were those who loved verse plays, and if they wanted to go shrining, Stratford would be their place. For others, depending on what you wanted most, it could be Kyoto, it could be Lourdes.

He reached his shrine before eight that morning. The bus to town got snagged because of an accident, so he didn't get to the Port Authority Terminal till near seven. And of course he had no idea where the IRT was or what it stood for, but finally he found the Times Square entrance, subwayed uptown. He had no idea if the express or the local was for him, but he chose the latter since he didn't want to miss the spot. But when he got to the right station, he still had to ask a couple questions before he had his bearings. Then it was a two-block walk.

And at a few minutes before eight he was there. To some it probably looked like just a playground. But he knew "a" was wrong, this was "the" playground. All his life he'd read about it. Jabbar had learned his hook here, someone said, when he was still Alcindor. And Earl Monroe when he was fifteen had come down from Philly, already with his own cheering section. Sure they knew their basketball in D.C.—Elgin Baylor didn't just materialize full grown. And L.A. had its hot spots.

But this place here, this asphalt-covered Harlem six-court spot was, if you cared, really *cared* about basketball, simply, the fastest track in the world.

Scout, the only white face visible, moved in past the fence, wondered if he could risk dribbling or taking a few shots, decided he didn't know protocol, so he sat with his back to the fence, his Larry Bird Special in his hands and waited for someone to ask him to play.

It was going to be hot but now the place was pleasant enough, if disappointingly empty. Only a couple of ten-year-olds at the far end shooting around. Scout, more conscious than he had ever been of his fair skin, sat hunched over, staring down with nothing much to listen to besides his heart.

"Whazzat?"

Scout glanced up, saw the dark druggie. Six three, wearing cutoff jeans and torn sneakers. Hard to tell the age. Twenty-five? A hundred and twenty-five? In there somewhere.

"Sorry?" Scout said, not understanding.

The druggie was pointing now. "Whazzat?"

Scout still didn't get it. "Is this what you mean?" He held up his Larry Bird Special.

"Riiiiiight."

Now Scout knew—the druggie was putting him on. He glanced around. Still pretty much empty. He decided to go along. No point in getting people upset. "It's a basketball."

"What it fo'?"

"You use it to play a game."

"Like dice you mean?"

"Well, it's a different kind of game from dice."

"What it do?"

"I don't get you."

"Kin I touch it?"

Scout tossed it to the druggie who almost dropped it. He

had very big hands, the druggie did, and he turned the ball clumsily around. Then he let it go, watched as it rebounded from the asphalt. "Oh, it bounce."

"It does, yes."

"You play a game like jacks with this?"

Scout almost smiled. "Well, it's kind of a different game from jacks too."

The druggie rolled the ball back. "You show me so I git it."

"You can't play the game with just one person."

"You show me," the druggie repeated.

Scout stood, decided the easiest thing was the easiest thing, a simple layup. He dribbled the ball a few times, getting accustomed to the conditions, then moved toward the nearest basket, left his feet a few inches, laid the ball up with his right hand where it angled off the backboard through the netless metal rim.

The druggie shrieked with glee. He pointed to the basketball, then the rim—"It fit," he said. "It fit right through."

Scout was aware now of half a dozen blacks, fingers through the fence, watching him.

" 'Mazin'," the druggie said. He turned to the half-dozen young guys hanging on the fence. "It fit right through."

Half of them looked away, the rest laughed.

Scout just stood still, bouncing his Larry Bird Special.

"What you be doon here?" the druggie asked then.

"I was sort of hoping maybe to play."

"You too good for these niggers," the druggie said.

"Don't I wish," Scout said.

"I think you better get out, you too good, you whup these niggers, they get mad maybe."

"I'm just here to play is all," Scout said. "I don't want to make anybody mad."

The druggie pointed to the tenements surrounding the playground. "Which you live in?"

"I'm not from around here."

"Oh, I bet you from downtown, one of them rich Jews."

"I'm not rich, I'm not Jewish, I'm not from New York at all."

"Where then?"

Scout pointed west. "New Jersey. I came from there this morning."

Now the druggie was practically hopping up and down. "He from *Jersey,*" he called to the gang that had filed inside the fence now.

Scout looked at them casually. They had a basketball. They weren't into trouble. Most of them were probably early twenties. They were all staring at him now. He decided it was best to smile. "Hi," Scout said, feeling like the fool of all the world, wondering when the druggie would get bored putting him on.

"He here to 'barrass us," the druggie said to the bunch.

"Hey, don't do that," Scout said. "That's not why I'm here and you know it."

"He made it fit right through," the druggie went on.

No response from the assembled.

"Do it again," the druggie said. "Do it again, they be crawlin' to play with you."

Scout hesitated.

"Go on, do it—don' make me out like I was lyin'—"

Scout sighed, bounced the ball a few times.

"He gonna do it," the druggie cried, moving off to one side of the basket. "He gonna make it fit right through. He from Jersey and they magicians there."

Scout, alone, twenty feet from the basket, hesitated only a moment more, because this was their playground, he was the foreigner, and probably what you did till you got your sea legs was humor them, so he began his slow approach to the basket, dribbling the ball hand to hand, not looking at it, you didn't need to look at it if you'd spent the thousands of hours he had with taped glasses, and as he got close to the basket he went a bit faster, getting his rhythm right, and when he had that he put the ball into his right hand—

—and at that moment, the black cloud began.

—Scout cradled the ball carefully, left his feet—

—and the black cloud began to rise, higher and higher in the still cool morning, and Scout, off the ground, felt his heart buck because the black cloud was the druggie only he wasn't a slurring awkward discard now, now he was something not to be believed as he skied higher and higher, his left arm extended, his big hand spread wide and with both of them in the air, Scout had his realization, he knew who the druggie was, it was The Stick, short for Pogo Stick, and Scout had read about him, he could jump over the moon and half a dozen years before he had been the most famous guard in all of New York's high schools, every college was after him, Indiana, North Carolina, Notre Dame, the *Post* wrote articles about him, there was even talk that maybe he was good enough to skip college and go right into the pro draft, such was his physical talent.

But then there was a drug bust and after that a short jail sentence and after that nothing until now, this moment here on this playground where The Stick materialized, soaring so high, so beautifully high—

—then it all stopped being beautiful. Because The Stick blocked the layup, his giant hand catching the ball before it even reached the backboard, and then he rocketed it back, dead at Scout, dead into his face and the ball careened into his mouth and nose and instantly there was blood but worse than that was the power of the block deprived him of any balance at all, and even though he wasn't high off the ground he was still helpless, and the force of the ball knocked him twisting backward and down, cartwheeling down, his head crashing into the asphalt and for a second he was probably out and for half a minute he just lay helpless, sprawled and bleeding, and then The Stick was jerking him up and shoving him toward the fence, slamming the basketball into his stomach saying, "Get the fuck out, motherfucker, this be for *players*," and then Scout was staggering outside, sitting down hard, and the blood would not stop pouring from his nose, and as he became more conscious he heard their laughter, all their black laughter, and yes, he wanted to die.

* * *

When the doorbell rang at ten o'clock, Audrey actually jumped. At first she thought it might be Scout calling except that couldn't be, they had agreed he would not do that, rather he would just return and come over. But she knew if it went badly, he'd call—he would have to tell someone and she was that one. And if she knew, it would give them each time to prepare for each other when he got back. Time to put on faces. "Who cares" faces. "It doesn't matter" faces. "In a year we won't remember" faces.

Then, when she realized it was the door, she wondered who it could be. There had been next to no visitors since her mother got bad.

It was, she saw when she opened the door, Uncle Arky, great white beard and all, with a wrapped gift in his hands. A bottle-shaped gift. He held out his arms and willingly she hugged him.

Audrey really didn't know much about Uncle Arky. Just that he looked like the Santa Claus in *Miracle on Thirty-fourth Street*, the movie that always made her cry come holiday time. And he was a famous something or other at Princeton, not that far down the road. A teacher, a researcher, she wasn't sure, but someone once told her he had won prizes, the international kind.

What she didn't need anyone to tell her was this: he was a hopeless basketball junkie. He saw all the games he could in Jersey, but for the last year or so, Scout had become his personal favorite.

"He went, didn't he?" Uncle Arky said. "Into the land of the giants."

"He did that."

"Here. For the both of you. You must promise me something."

"If it's not against the law," Audrey told him.

"You must both toast me with the contents of the bottle. And then you may toast each other. But first you must say, clinking glasses please, 'To Uncle Arky, who knew.' "

"Knew what?"

"That he would be their equal. No. Their better. That he would be carried home shoulder high with a winner's wreath around his head in a different world."

"We don't know how he did yet."

"I know. You can smile, Audrey." He handed her the package.

"What's it?"

"Small-town girls may be the end of me. Champagne, Audrey. What else would a civilized human gift another with when there was joy to be spread?"

"But we don't drink."

"Don't I know that? Have you heard of nonalcoholic beer? Well, this is the very finest nonalcoholic champagne. Tastes like the frogs themselves stomped the grapes. Just put it in the fridge and when celebration time comes, sip away. I have your promise?"

"You do."

He kissed her cheek. "If I were only eighty years younger, Scout wouldn't stand a chance." He half turned, stopped. "Please don't worry about today. I have specialized in studying guards for half a century and less. I have watched them all. Scout sees the whole court, Audrey. Only the true talents can do that." Now he laughed. "And just to cover all bases, I also prayed."

"But you told us once you didn't believe in anything."

"Maybe He doesn't know that. He's got to have more important things on His mind. Besides, maybe all this time we've had a dumb God—after all, how many really bright Messiahs decide to go into carpentry?"

Scout sat huddled where The Stick had dumped him for . . . he had no idea really. A long time, at least inside his throbbing skull, but was it ten minutes or two hours he really wasn't sure.

But the blood kept dripping from his nose and he could feel the right side of his face starting to swell. When he was able to look around, he spotted a water fountain not far away and he made up his mind right off that as soon as he was sure of being able to stand without his legs betraying him, he was going to head for it. He might have been a statue except for the tips of his fingers, which involuntarily pressed again and again into his Larry Bird Special. The playground was beginning to get busy now. Lot of people walking past him. Whistles and shouts. The thumping of a dozen basketballs. Laughter. Cursing.

All the happy sounds.

Scout took a breath, got up on his knees, then stood, picked up his ball, did his best to saunter as he made his way to the fountain. He took his handkerchief out of his back pocket, got it wet, wiped the blood from his face as best he could, then forced the cotton against his nostrils, applied pressure until the bleeding stopped.

Not far from the fountain was a bench which was mostly occupied by a sleeping wino but there was enough empty space for Scout to sit. He pretended to look mostly down, but in reality, he was clocking the talent on the courts. All kinds of games were going on, HORSE and twenty-one, these mostly with the younger kids in one corner, plus a bunch of two-on-two's, three-on-three's.

Scout could only marvel. The speed they had. The quickness, the jumping ability. He held his Larry Bird Special very tight, decided to bounce it once. He did. The noise bothered the wino, who kicked out in his sleep, by chance, knocking the ball away.

I can't even beat him, Scout realized, hurrying after his possession, picking it up, taking a last look at the playground. The Stick was in the midst of an argument, two other guys were yelling at him but he was yelling back, "Bullshit, you fouled me, you fouled me," and not a backward step was taken.

Scout left the playground then, began to wander. He had no idea where. He looked at his watch. 9:30. Five hours ago he'd turned off his alarm in New Jersey, set off like Prince Valiant.

Quit the whining!

At least he knew. He'd wanted to find out for how many

years? At least he'd sucked it up, sought the answer. So it wasn't the answer he'd wished. He was still plenty good enough to be all-conference in Neptune, plenty smart enough to get an academic scholarship to Wagner State and after that med school, plenty lucky enough to have his Audrey.

Audrey—blond and alone on a Harlem sidewalk, Scout could not prevent the sound of pain from escaping. How in the world would he ever be able to tell Audrey? They had talked about this day so much, had seriously discussed the possibility of its not going well, they thought they were prepared—

—except what The Stick had done to him wasn't quite "not going well" unless you were the kind who considered King Kong to be just a tyke.

I'll just never go back to Neptune, Scout decided, no big deal.

By eleven, the sidewalks were steaming and Scout, mindless, just kept moving along. He was aware that he wasn't exactly unnoticed, what with his pale skin and swollen face, but nobody hassled him. He turned a corner and stopped, because just up ahead was the subway entrance. He had a token in his pocket, to get him back to the bus terminal and he had a ticket to get him back to Neptune and he had two five-dollar bills for food and whatever else he thought he might need on the day.

And it was then he had his great idea—not going back to Neptune was ridiculous—of course he could go back to Neptune, and all would be wonderful—*because Audrey never had to know.*

What a fabulous notion. All he had to do was call her up and lie. He was a horrible liar but that was okay, because she never expected it from him.

He went into a bodega, bought a couple of Milky Ways, asked for as much change as they could spare, finally made himself understood, found a phone booth, soon was plunking in the change.

"Progress report," he said when she answered.

"Go go go."

"I'll give you the long version when I see you. But I thought you might be interested in a couple things."

"I might be."

Scout made his voice sad. "It wasn't perfect, Audible. It didn't start out quite the way I wanted."

"Well what happened?"

"—do you know Harlem isn't like the movies at all, there's lots of pretty houses, and—"

"—don't you tease me, what happened?"

Very soft. "I got humiliated."

"Aw no."

"I did. This guy—The Stick and he was a star a few years back—he didn't want me playing, he's got a color thing, he kept calling me 'Whitey' and pushing me around, embarrassing me in front of the others."

"Well, you couldn't fight him, not you all alone."

"That's how I figured. So I just took it while he shoved me and taunted me and made jokes about how my ass was probably covered with peach fuzz—"

"—did he *say* that?"

"Swear to God. And a lot worse."

"Well, darling, what did you *do?*"

"I tried keeping my head, and I told myself he'd get bored eventually and then I'd have a chance to show how I could shoot and stuff, and . . . and oh, Audible, I thought of you so much, it went like that, he got bored, he walked away from me for a little and I was maybe thirty feet from the hoop, way outside my range—"

"—*I* know that—"

"—well, I thought of you and would you want me to risk it and I knew the thing you cared most about me was that no matter what cards I get handed, I play them, I got fiber like you're all the time telling me so I shouted at Stick, *'Hey!'* and he turned and I fired off the thirty-footer and, Audible, it was like it had eyes, nothing but the bottom of the net except of course, they don't have nets here, and I could see he was impressed, this Stick, so I got the ball and shot again, banked it this time, a twenty-footer from the side and you can probably guess the rest.''

''How can I do that, *tell* me.''

Scout made himself sound as casual as he could. ''He asked would I be on his side for a two-on-two game. Against these two really big guys. And I'll never forget it, we cleaned their clocks, me and old Stick, he's almost like my pal now because we took on everybody who wanted a chance at us and they bet up here and we beat 'em all, he's up fifty bucks and he can't wait for me to get off the phone so he can make some more, so it looks like I won't be home for a while and I didn't want you worrying.''

''It's like a dream.''

''I love you.''

''Same only double.''

'' 'Bye.''

''I'm so proud, Scout—I always have been but you did it—what a perfect thing, when a dream works out, g'bye, my darling.''

Scout hung up. Inside the booth was like a fire. Scout closed his eyes and listened to her voice over and over. Going on about the dream. That was why they were so perfect together. They were so alike. She was every bit as rotten a liar as he was.

It was noon when the five-dollar bill fluttered to the asphalt. ''I can hit five straight off you,'' Scout said. ''If I can't, you can pick that up.''

The Stick bent for the money. ''All gifts greatly appreciated.''

Scout stomped his sneaker over the money.

The Stick stood. ''You almost hit my hand.''

''I tried.''

The Stick stared at him now. They were standing a few feet away from an unused basket. It was between games, and a bunch of guys were watching. ''You want to play, that it?''

Scout nodded. ''I'm a player.''

The Stick pointed to Scout's Larry Bird Special. "You want to have a game using that round thing?"

"Cut the shit—I don't need you putting me on anymore, all right?" He was maybe six feet from the basket when he shot. He could make that blindfolded. "That's one shot down, four to go."

"Wait a second—"

"—for what?" Scout said, and he put up a ten-foot jumper. Swish. "Two down, three to go."

"I ain't started, goddamit—"

From the crowd someone said, "*He* started, that what matter—" and when The Stick turned to silence the laughter, Scout stepped back, fired a fifteen-footer, another bottom-of-the-net beauty. "Three."

The Stick crouched, put himself between Scout and the basket. "Now I'm defending," he announced.

"You couldn't defend a tree."

Laughter.

"Do something, my man."

Scout released another fifteen-foot jumper before The Stick had finished talking. "Four."

"Man can shoot it," someone said from the crowd.

The Stick moved closer to the basket, gestured for Scout to do the same. "Any fairy can shoot it. Come inside, where us men play."

Scout hesitated.

"Motherfucker can't even make a layup," The Stick said.

Scout stood still, dribbling the ball.

"Come into my parlor."

"I will, don't worry."

"Today or in the near future?"

Scout stood very still, dribbling the ball harder, then backed off till he was thirty feet from the basket, staring at The Stick. The Stick moved off to one side a few feet, waited.

Scout suddenly was dribbling very fast, going all he had toward the basket—

—but the black cloud anticipated the movement.

Scout went faster, pounding the ball hard, feeling it rebound exactly where he wanted, into his right hand as he got near to the backboard—

—but the black cloud was nearing the backboard too.

Scout had committed himself for the layup now, the ball in his right hand, his body leaving the ground as his right hand extended up—

—and now the cloud rose gracefully into the air, so high—

—and Scout, with a move he'd done a million times before he was fifteen, brought his right hand down, carefully put the ball behind his back where his left hand took control—

—the black cloud flailed out helplessly.

An easy left-handed layup. *"Five,"* someone in the crowd shouted.

Scout went to the five-dollar bill, bent to pick it up, was straightening when The Stick, pissed, stood beside him. "You made me look bad," The Stick said.

Scout flicked his eyes toward the rim. That was really the essence of the game—eye contact—"Let me see your best," he whispered—"Jump over the moon," and he bounced the ball, flicked his eyes again toward the rim and he wondered would The Stick understand, and more than that, would he risk it, but Scout didn't wonder long, because in an instant The Stick had turned, was racing at an angle toward the backboard and when he hit the free throw line he got his balance and then he was skying and Scout arced the ball up above the rim and sure he was slow and yes he couldn't jump but he had a sense for the right strength on the right pass and now the man and the ball closed, The Stick's huge hands grabbing the ball and as he caught it with the rim far below him he had the glorious coordination still to time it so that his arms went up and he thundered the ball down, straight down through the hoop, a monster stuff, a stuff you had to be there to see, a stuff people would be going on about and on about and then The Stick grabbed the ball, fired it back at Scout, going, "Whhooooeeee, gimme five," and Scout got his right hand ready for the familiar congratulatory slap except The Stick said, "Gimme five *dollars,* asshole," and when Scout did, The Stick waved it high going, "Who want to take us on, two on two, we beat any motherfuckers on the playground, right, my man?"

"Any motherfuckers at all," Scout heard himself reply.

"Somewhere there must be a mother who could love a face like this," Audrey said, as she expertly moistened the cottonball with peroxide, cleansed the last of the area around Scout's swollen cheek, "but I'm here to tell you she's going to take some finding."

It was 9:45 at night and they were in the living room of her house, had been for the fifteen minutes since he'd knocked on the door, wondered casually if she was interested in the events of the day. She'd swatted his fanny in reply, and while he went on about triumph, she listened. Then, before she asked for a more detailed version, she got the cotton and peroxide, made him lie on the sofa, set to work ridding him of any possible infections. "Done," she said finally, put the bottle on the coffee table.

He reached out and held her then. "We did it, Audible."

"I was certainly instrumental, no doubt about that, all my clever coaching from the sidelines."

"No, it was the phone call. The way you handled it. I knew I had to go back and give it one last shot. When did you know I was lying?"

"When I picked up the phone and it was you."

"I tried my best to sound happy."

She kissed him. "No one ever has to 'try' for a thing like that, my baby. It happens. Like right now. I've never heard you so happy as right now, and you're not dancing up and down."

"You're happy too though?"

She nodded, stood. "As I've ever been." Then she disappeared from the room, came back a moment later with two glasses, a wrapped bottle-shaped package. She handed it to him. "From Uncle Arky. He had faith."

"He did? That made one of us." He pulled the wrapping off, looked at the bottle a moment.

"Nonalcoholic champagne," Audrey told him.

It was a small bottle and Scout opened it easily, poured their glasses full. "All I've eaten today is ten Milky Ways, this'll be different anyway." He started to drink.

She stopped him. "First we touch glasses, Scout; Uncle Arky told me that. And we're supposed to say something nice."

"God bless the faith keepers," Scout said, and they touched glasses, drank. He was thirsty so he drained his glass, poured a refill, did the same for her when she was ready. "Like a classy ginger ale."

"Um-hmm." She looked at him. "Truly ten Milky Ways?"

"We didn't break for lunch. The Stick was twenty dollars up by that time, so he sent some little kid for stuff."

"You didn't bet."

Scout smiled. "Stick sort of insisted. As a show of faith." He pulled some bills out of his pocket. "Can you believe this, Audible?"

She shook her head. "Ah me, corrupt at seventeen." There was a moan then from her mother's room. "Want some of my famous tuna salad?"

"You've got enough to do." He pointed toward where the moan had come from.

"It's *made,* Scout; I had to do something while you weren't here."

"Okay then, great."

She drained her glass, handed it to him. He finished his, took the empty bottle, headed for the kitchen while she went to her mother's room, stopping first at Aunt B.'s to check on her; she was asleep, as always, with the television blaring. Audrey knew if she turned the set off, the old woman would wake, so she closed the door and hurried to her mother's room, said, "Hey, Mama," as she began the work of cleaning and changing, all the while talking cheerily, even though more than likely her mother couldn't make total sense. Still, the doctors had said the sound alone was a plus, so Audrey never was quiet when she was with the helpless creature who had brought her red faced and angry into the world.

What was the reverse of anger? Whatever the precise word was, that was how she felt as she said "'Bye" to her mother, joined Scout in the kitchen where he was finishing his food.

"Ummmm," he said as she appeared, rubbing his stomach.

"Yes, Reverend, the first thing that made me fall in love with him was his unlimited vocabulary. Along with his ability to communicate."

Scout pointed to his mouth, managed "Full."

"And right after that his flawless table manners." She cleaned up then, washing the dishes, putting the bottle into the garbage bag, which was full, so she tied it at the top, carried it out to the big metal pail outside the back door, lifted the lid, dumped the refuse, returned to the kitchen where Scout, finished, was down on one knee.

"That was great tuna salad, Audible, marry me."

She didn't even break stride. "What would you have said if I'd made you my famous roast beef?"

"Hey!"

Now she stopped.

"I mean it."

"Scout, we're seventeen, what is this?"

He stood. "Okay—here's the deal—the way I figure things, I'll probably never find anybody a whole lot better than you and I'm positive you'll never find anybody half as great as me so why don't we just get engaged?" He reached into his pocket, pulled out a ring. "This here's from a Crackerjack box, I won't lie to you—we had a little Crackerjack toward the end of the day—and I figured me finding the ring was a symbol, I'll get you a better one when I can afford to, but why don't you wear this now?"

She squinted at him. "If you're teasing me, Scout, you will never be forgiven, believe that."

"I'm *not*."

"I think we just might be rushing into things, a little talk might not hurt, c'mon." She took his hand, they went to the living room sofa, sat close. "Listen, I love you and all, but I think maybe you're having a hyperventilating reaction to what happened in New York today, why don't we just get pinned like ordinary people?"

He stared at her. "Are you turning me down?"

"Of course not, I just think a little common sense never did a whole lot of harm."

"Where's the common sense to rejecting the person you love? Correction—*claim* you love."

"Oh, bushwah, give me the Crackerjack prize."

He slipped it on her finger. It didn't quite clear the first knuckle.

"Damn," Scout said.

Audrey had to giggle, it looked so forlorn, the ring, trapped near the nail like that.

Soon he was giggling too.

"Symbolically, we're engaged, all right, Scout? Now would you mind a little commonsense talk?"

He kissed her, then shook his head.

"All right, the reason I think maybe we're going a bit too fast is this: we've got senior year to live through and you've got to carry the team and at the same time not let your grades slip so we both get scholarships to college, and then there's four years of *that* and then—"

"—remember when I used to bowl?" Scout interrupted. "We weren't going together so much yet but I decided I wanted to bowl a two-hundred game so I set pins and practiced and got my form right and set some more pins and kept practicing and after a while, one day when I was all pretty much by myself at the alley I bowled two-oh-two which I figured was a lucky fluke so I tried again and made two eleven and guess what: I've never bowled since, never wanted to."

"And the point of that riveting tale?"

"I don't care about basketball so much anymore, Audible. Today I bowled two fifty so to speak. I'll play senior year, and I'll do fine, but the main thing is, there's more important events to me now in life, I've got to get good grades in high school, sure, to get a college scholarship but once I've got that, I've got to be a whiz there, Audible, because I need another scholarship for med school, so I'm not gonna play ball at Wagner or anyplace else. I just want to study and be with you until I hang out my shingle, and if that isn't all very riveting, well I can't help it, we neither of us have silver spoons, Audible, we're going to have to work to make it in this world."

When he was finished, Audrey began to cry.

"What's wrong?"

"Didn't you hear what you said?" The tears were harder now. "How can you expect me to behave any different?"

"Tell me."

"I don't need it on my conscience!"

"What—*what?*—"

"—you sacrificing yourself for me—now that after all these years you know how good you are—you don't need Wagner anymore—you can star in big places, you could have the best—St. John's or Georgetown—you know the only way we'll ever stay together is if you give up what you love and I don't need that on my conscience—"

Scout was weeping now.

"Aw, baby, aw, love, don't cry, I'm not worth it—"

"—yes y'are, yes y'are—"

"—it's true, what I said then?—"

Scout nodded, fought his tears.

"Well I release you, my darling—you go right on without me—"

"*—I need you though,* Audible—"

"—shhhh . . ."

". . . I do . . ."

She took him into her arms. "Aw, love."

He was sobbing now. "I never thought . . . never thought I'd want to . . . not twice in one day . . ."

"Want what?"

"Back in the city. When I had the bloody face and was sitting there, my brains all scrambled . . . I wanted to die, Audible, and now I do again."

"Let's."

"What?"

"Die."

"When?"

"Now."

"Yes?"

"Yes."

"How?"

"I'll get us some knives." She stood, started for the kitchen.

"Shouldn't we leave a note or something?"

"You're so sweet, Scout, that's such a sweet notion, you start in on it, paper's in that drawer by the phone."

He went to the drawer by the phone, got the pad, the pen, started putting words on paper.

Audrey returned with two butcher knives, the tears flooding down.

Scout was crying much harder too.

"Read."

Scout stared at the paper. " 'We just want to be together and this is the best way.' " He looked at her. "Enough?"

"I should add a note to Mama." She handed him the knives, took the pen.

"These are sharp, Audible, these are really sharp knives."

"If you're going to be a good cook, you get the best utensils. How's this: 'Aunt B.—tell Mama she's got a world full of friends.' Okay?"

He shook almost out of control.

"We better sign, Scout." Audrey wrote her name at the bottom of the page. Scout did the same.

They each took a knife now. "We're not making a mistake, Audible?"

"No, love; you're afraid of what leaving me would do to me; I'm afraid of what having you stay would do to you. Hold my hand?"

"Oh, yes."

They sat back on the couch then.

"Where should we do it, Scout? The wrists? I read that doesn't hurt so bad."

"The heart, Audible. It goes faster, and it's right for us."

"The heart, of course," Audrey said. "Of course. Perfect for us."

Now they were both in such tears it was hard to keep their hands controlled.

Slowly, they put the knives to their hearts. They looked at each other, each made a nod, pushed.

The knives were sharp, as advertised.

It was, for Neptune, a considerable crowd, especially for eleven in the evening. An ambulance, a police car, perhaps a dozen people standing in the darkness. Uncle Arky stopped his car, got out, went to the nearest uniformed man. "Officer?"

The policeman turned.

"What is all this, why all these people, I'm a friend," and he explained who he was.

"It's bad, Professor." A shaken, tired voice.

"It's the mother, isn't it? Another stroke?"

The policeman shook his head. "It's the daughter, Professor. It's Audrey and Scout. Double suicide."

Uncle Arky seemed to sag. "I spoke with the child earlier today. She was nervous, yes, but certainly no more. Suicide simply isn't possible."

"They both left notes. Signed notes. Nothing's impossible with kids these days, the pressures and all."

Uncle Arky shook his head, turned quickly, made his way to his car. He had seen Scout enter the house at half past nine so ninety minutes was all it had taken. Less. What a remarkable thing—it had never gone that fast before. Surely he was in the lead now, ahead of Standish, ahead of them all. He kept his head averted as he got in behind the wheel. No one must know that his eyes were dancing . . .

# II

# THE CONTEST

# 1

# The Testing

## 1

The helicopter pilot had obviously been smitten with Smilin' Jack when he was an adolescent and had never staged a recovery. Once the blades had quieted, he opened the door nearest him, jumped down. He wore movie star sunglasses, had a movie star tan. He looked at Scylla like he was from Mars. "You it?" the pilot said.

Scylla made no reply.

The pilot started toward him over the hard sand. They were in a clearing in the center of the island. The surrounding trees served to destroy the permanent breeze and the pilot was already starting to perspire, giving him a less jaunty appearance than he undoubtedly favored. "I've had some nutty assignments, but this is Twilight Zone time. I was supposed to fly to these coordinates and pick up a 'certain party.' How many's in this party? Or are you it?"

Scylla studied the younger man. Probably twenty-five to thirty with an IQ double that. "I'm 'it,' like you said." There—the first words spoken to another human in Lord only knew how long and what had he managed? Five one-syllable jobs. A step up from gibberish. Well, it was always nice to open on an intellectual note.

"Name's Kilgore," the pilot said. "You're . . . ?"

Scylla hesitated a moment, since he had no idea what his name was now. Sloppy that Division hadn't told him. Again, he made no reply, remained motionless in the heat.

Finally Kilgore said, "Well, if you're it, then this must

be for you," and he pulled an envelope out of his back pocket, handed it over.

Scylla took the envelope. Probably his new name was inside. So it hadn't been sloppy of Division after all, just incompetence from Kilgore. You *began* with information, never chitchat.

"You want some privacy for that?" Kilgore asked.

Scylla nodded, turned toward the palms, walked into their shadow, opened the envelope. It was from Perkins, no surprise there, in ink, the wording as flowery as his speech often was.

> *Go with this cretin.*
>
> *He will take you to a Captain Givens.*
> *Another missive awaits you there.*
>
> *If you think Kilgore is limited, wait until you meet Givens. The caliber of our employees has not been exactly skyrocketing of late.*
>
> *At least the disposable employees.*
>
> *Ah yes, I have given a good bit of thought to your name.*
>
> *For the nonce you are:*
>
> *MR. BEDE.*
>
> *First name:*
>
> *V. (Initial only.)*
>
> *Like it? I knew you would.*

Scylla had to smile. Perkins knew his father had been an historian and the Venerable Bede was a monk who had written, in the eighth century, *The Ecclesiastical History of the English Nation*, making him, as much as anyone, the father of all English history.

—the birds were suddenly crying out—

Scylla listened. Could they have sensed it, that their clumsy chaser, their darkening companion was leaving them alone again with their palms? What a wonderful parting gift that would be—the entire animal kingdom had a sensitivity we were deprived of. It was possible they knew. And were, in a sense, mourning, as surely as he would mourn their absence.

Scylla tracked the sound.

Not mourning; panic was the cause. Kilgore was whipping pebbles up at them, small stones, whatever he could scoop up and throw. Very softly Scylla said, ". . . you must stop that . . ."

—and Kilgore spun around, clearly afraid.

Christ, Scylla told himself, I must have shouted at him. Without knowing. He was not in practice at conversing, and what a good thing he realized it now, and not when a similar mistake might have caused a permanent departure. "Sorry," Scylla said; this time his voice was soft.

"You into birds, that it?"

"I'll meet you at the plane," Scylla said. When he was alone, he climbed skillfully up into the high branches, did his best to imitate the birds. What he wanted, of course, was to let them know he hadn't been involved with the throwing. But all he succeeded in doing was making himself feel very foolish—if they didn't trust him by this time, what the hell, what the hell.

Kilgore was standing in the clearing, dropping rocks on sandhills, making little explosive sounds as the rocks landed, shattering the tunnels so laboriously built. "That's what I'd like to do to those stupid Ay-rabs," he said. "Bomb 'em till there was nothin' but rubble and then bomb the rubble."

"Sorry?" Scylla said.

"The hostages, man. I'm gettin' tired of us having our nuts cut off by those people."

Christ, Scylla thought, how many days must they have been there now? Thousands. Probably they were insane by now, the ones the Ayatollah had allowed to live. No. Overdramatization. He had been a kind of captive for almost as long and probably he wasn't insane. "I don't think they're Arabs," he said.

"Hmmm?"

"The Iranians," Scylla said.

"The Eye-*rain*-ians?" Kilgore said. "Who the fuck's talking about them? I'm talking about the Beirut hostages."

Fool. *Fool!* "Of course you were—just making a joke."

Now Smilin' Jack was giving him a second Mars look.

"I'm ready," Scylla said, indicating the copter.

But the pilot would not stop staring at him. Finally he said, "You familiar with these babies?"

Under orders, Scylla had both murdered and made love in helicopters, neither very comfortably. He had even once, unavoidably, crash-landed one. "No."

"Well, they're noisier'n shit. They spent a fortune fixing this one up, extra power, extra fuel tanks, extra every you name it—but it's still noisier'n shit. So you got anything important you want to talk about, do it or be ready to shout."

"Nothing to say."

"You got it."

They both entered the helicopter, strapped themselves in. Just before the blades began, Scylla asked, casually, "What's the date, do you know?"

"Twenty-eighth."

"Of?"

"*Of?* You mean the month?"

"I just asked for the date," Scylla said.

"June twenty-eighth, for chrissakes."

Shit, Scylla thought, angry the idiot didn't see fit to include the information he was truly after: the year. Of course he could always ask, but the idea of a third Martian glance was something he really could live without. Besides, he had a fine mind, having, after all, graduated college with honors. With those qualifications, he felt sure he could learn the year, when they'd landed. He had been, once, a Yale man, and they rarely had troubles finding answers to questions of that magnitude.

* * *

It was four o'clock when Kilgore pointed, said, "Puerto Rico," probably a half hour later when they landed. An unpopulated part of the large island.

A small man with an Errol Flynn mustache was waiting for them by the hangar when they got out. "Captain Givens," he said and Scylla shook his hand, said, "My name is Bede."

"Got some stuff for ya," Captain Givens said, "luggage and a letter, but gimme a sec." He walked over to Kilgore. "I know you figure you're gonna relax now, don't you?"

"Not another job, shit," Kilgore said.

"Sorry," Givens said.

Kilgore sighed. "What?"

Givens smiled at Scylla, took a step closer to Kilgore. "I never had to deliver one of these before," he said.

"Deliver?" Kilgore looked confused.

"I got this X-rated message I promised to repeat, word for word." He paused. "You don't happen to know anyone named Ruthie, by any small chance?"

"Ruth the uncouth? You know goddam well I do. She's up in Jacksonville."

"Not according to my information. She said to me that she was wearing your shirt and nothing else. And she was waiting—where do you live, ten minutes from here?"

"You know goddam well where I live."

"Well, she said once you put your toys away—she meant the whirlybird—she might give you a shot. She was calling from your place and she said you better be ready for 'a real working over. No relaxing allowed.' Those are the exact words." He turned to Scylla. "Can you believe the things I have to do in my job?"

Scylla made no reply, struck mainly by the ineptitude of Givens' lying. But then, he had been away, perhaps he was wrong.

Kilgore seemed to think so. He made a masturbatory gesture, with great pride . . .

## 2

Cheetah was on the prowl. Silently. And that was a tribute to his greatness, that he could roam through this slime of an apartment without making a sound when his heart was raging. What he wanted to do was slam things, break them at the base. But no, that was not allowed. Not if you wanted a higher spot on the ladder. And if anyone deserved not just a more elevated position, but the highest place of all, it was he.

Modesty was never a strong point.

He continued his tour of the bachelor apartment. ''Slime'' was too strong a word for the place. ''Impoverished'' was better. And not in the sense of money lack—just that there was no taste on view here. It was, as much as anything, a *Playboy* magazine hole. High-tech this, hi-fi that, a well-stocked bar with almost nothing that came from America, a water bed, on and endlessly on—

—and how were you supposed to make this look like a robbery when there was nothing worth stealing?

He opened a dresser drawer, rummaged through, found what looked to be an old watch, some might-be-valuable cuff links, pocketed them, spilled the rest of the contents on the floor. The paintings on the wall? Leroy Neiman prints? One out of perhaps an edition of thirty-five million? No point in hustling them away.

He looked at his own watch. 5:22 and 30 seconds. A few minutes more till business. He quietly messed a few more drawers, spilled little piles expertly.

5:25. Claw time.

He had chosen his anonym with considerable care. Division let you do that, choose, and it was days before he decided to be Cheetah. The animal was, of course, the fastest four-legged thing on earth, and though he did not look that way—six feet plus in height, one eighty always, never more than a pound variance on either side—he had similar speed. Not with his feet but with his hands. They were his prize, not their power alone but the speed with which they could strike.

Only once, years ago, did Division supposedly have another with similar skills, the legendary Scylla. Cheetah had never met him but they had been in the same restaurant at the same time. A fancy French, a necktie place, in New York. They had screwed up his reservation, forgotten to jot it properly, and he was waiting at the bar, Cheetah was, angry but with a smile on, waiting for half an hour when this Scylla breezed in.

Big, dark skinned, the kind, probably, women rolled over for. But he wasn't with a woman now, just a tall, skinny kid. He had an arm wrapped around the tall skinny kid and you could tell, somehow you knew, they were related, brothers most likely.

And then the man who ran the restaurant came scraping out and Scylla introduced him to the kid, and the owner ushered them both into the restaurant without a pause while he, Cheetah, still did his secret storming at the bar.

So much for the great Scylla—but how great could he have been when he was killed, not long after, by some ancient Nazi? How fast could he have been with his legendary hands to be retired by someone like that, a decrepit? And yet Division had fawned over him, made him their top Provider.

Cheetah took his claws out, stiffened the fingers of his right hand, made the proper adjustments. The animal he named himself after also had nonretractable claws. His, he designed them, fit tightly over his fingertips, razor sharp, edged and pointed, extending no more than a half-inch.

5:29 and a quarter it was when he moved to the front door of the apartment, made sure it was unlocked, took a deep breath.

The first call of "Ruthie" came from outside no more than a minute later. And then the door was thrown open, and the young man filled the doorway. "Ruthie?" again, a question now. And then the claws flashed and the young man fell, his hands where his throat had been. Careful not to get any of the red stuff on his clothes, Cheetah removed the dying man's wallet, took the cash and let the credit go.

He looked around him. Sour taste in his mouth. Christ, was he always going to be this and no more, the remainder king, never the next step, the final step, a Provider? Work like this was insulting to him. He wanted to scream that at his superiors. He was a diamond, cut and glistening, and why did no one see?

Providers did more than slaughter. They moved in a splendid world, suites and caviar, women with hips like liquid. And where was he? In a shit suburb of a spick city, the home away from home of the beautiful people, San Juan. The sour taste in his mouth increased. He already had his next task and that ticked him too, no rest, no appreciation. Overworked, undercared—was that a word?—it should be, it summed up an attitude—he heard the young pilot die, then left, closing the door behind him. He had his plane ticket in his pocket. First class. New Orleans. He did not feel pity often, but he almost felt it for whoever was to be remaindered there.

## 3

The air conditioning in Captain Givens' car was driving the man crazy. Or lack of air conditioning, rather. They had no sooner begun to drive when it began malingering, which made the small man's Errol Flynn mustache twitch like crazy.

"I don't mind the heat," Scylla said.

"You don't understand—you know Cujo?"

Scylla indicated he did not.

"I don't mean Cujo, Cujo's the goddam dog, I mean Christine, you know Christine?"

Scylla decided he'd better say nothing.

"The one about the car. Christine's the car."

"Oh, that Christine," Scylla said, confident his reply was absolutely safe. Since his Ayatollah gaffe, he realized he had to side with Mies van der Rohe: less was definitely more.

"Greatest fucking writer since Mickey Spillane, Stephen King. 'Course, their styles are different."

"Their writing styles, yes, well observed," Scylla said. "Go on about Christine."

"Well, I don't have to tell you the goddam car was human." He opened his hand and slammed the air conditioner several times. "See, this miserable fucker's human too. I take it in to the garage, and tell them to fix it. They ask what's wrong. I say it don't work. They try it and it works. A charm in any garage. They all think I'm a head case, the spick mechanics. But it knows. Outside, when it's cool, like say, early morning, no problem. Purrs. *But let the temperature hit ninety*—" He banged the air conditioner again. Again.

Scylla decided it was time to read the letter Givens had handed him, along with the suitcase of clothes. He opened the envelope. It contained a plane ticket, a dozen fifty-dollar bills, and a letter from Perkins. He put the money and the ticket into his trouser pockets, began to read.

*My dear Bede,*

*Givens, as he may have told you, is to drop you at San Juan International. The enclosed ticket should pose, to one of your brains and accomplishment, little problem. You simply report to the proper gate when your flight is called.*

*This is my final note to you. ("Final" sounds so*

*final.) Fountain will have a message for you at the Continental Supreme Hotel.*

*If all this seems a bit overly furtive and cryptic to you, well, such is the nature of our occupation. (Actually, that is the purest bullshit, but people seem to expect it of us.)*

*Good luck with Fountain. You are a pearl of great price.*

*(I can hear you thinking now: was a pearl, etc., etc.)*

*Trust no one. Least of all me. The best minds in town are coming to the conclusion that E = MC squared. Do you think it possible?*

*P.*

Scylla was aware when he finished that Givens was watching him. "Everything okay?" Givens asked. "We should be at the airport by not much after seven."

"You've done splendidly," Scylla said.

"Must be important, I guess," Givens said, with a nod toward the letter.

Since it was such a titanically unimportant note, Scylla was at first tempted to just give the damn thing to the driver and let him learn its contents. But he realized if he did that, he would crush the man—Givens *wanted* it to be important. Here he was, a feeble operative in what must be among the least-valued posts in all Division. "I can't talk about it," Scylla said.

Givens was immediately defensive—"Christ, fella, I wasn't butting my nose in—just making conversation was all."

Scylla snapped his fingers. "A match. *Now.*"

"Will a lighter do?"

"It will have to—give it to me!"

Quickly Givens handed it over.

Scylla torched the letter till it was ash. Then he shredded

that. Finally he released the remains out the window. But slowly. Covering miles.

"No one will find *that,*" Givens said.

"I probably should have eaten it. You won't tell anyone I didn't?"

"Hey, Mister Bede—we're on the same side, remember?"

Scylla nodded even though years before he learned the most basic fact of life: sides changed. He felt, at that moment, almost sympathy for Givens. But not quite. For surely Givens had sent poor passionate Kilgore hot-pantsing off to his death. Just as surely as Givens would be going to his, and soon.

## 4

Truly, Hondo thought, as he sat waiting to kill Captain Givens, I am one of God's chosen. He stood, moved around the captain's office, shrugged his powerful shoulders. And powerful they were, along with the rest of him.

He just didn't look it. One of his gifts. He stood barely six feet, weighed an even two fifty, and his beer belly was the envy of many a football fan. He seemed slow, sloppy, the kind of enemy you might even enjoy having. Many had gone with that being their terminal error. Underestimation. Hondo exercised constantly, only never the kind that might make a show of his power. He squeezed rubber balls, did an hour of isometrics a day. True, he was not much on endurance, but in his work, that mattered not at all, everything ended quickly.

He loved his work and he loved lots of it. Pile it on, send him here, there, he accepted joyously. He had no desire to move on up the scale. The Jews had an expression, no, not an expression, a way of thinking really—if you stuck your head high enough above the crowd, surely someone would cut it off. He had every intention of keeping his thick neck foursquare on his shoulders. He was a team player, therefore his anonym, the great basketball player Havlicek's nickname. There had never been a finer team player than the legendary Celtic.

Hondo shared one other quality: he was versatile. That always surprised people too—by physical appearance, he seemed just your everyday hulk. But he had more than enough mind to get by. He could converse for at least a few minutes on almost any subject, and in his trade, a few minutes was more than enough to make the opponent relax. And when relaxation came, mistakes rode close behind.

One mistake was all Hondo ever needed.

He looked at his watch. Getting on toward eight. Hondo went back to the captain's chair and sat. It didn't take him long, not much of an office to traverse. Hondo was surprised to learn Division even had anything permanent in San Juan. And surely this wasn't much. A room, a desk, a phone, an importing name on the door, all in an unimposing building in an unimportant part of the sweltering city.

June in Puerto Rico. Not many love songs there.

Footsteps in the corridor now. Hondo put a smile on. He could have lurked in darkness, done his deed, but he was, in spite of his appearance, a fellow enamored of conversation, he liked the free-form twists talk sometimes followed. As the door opened he stood and said, "A genuine pleasure, sir."

Givens stopped dead. "Who the fuck are you?"

Stammered, confused: "Huh—huh—Hondo."

Still from the doorway: "How the fuck did you get in?"

Hondo pulled the small piece of metal from his pocket, kept the stammer: "Kuh—key."

"Where the fuck did you get it?"

"The thirteenth floor."

Givens relaxed a bit with that. The thirteenth floor was in D.C. All dispatching orders emanated from there. Now he closed the door, played with his Errol Flynn mustache. "Hmmm." Another pull. "The thirteenth floor sent you here?"

Careful, Hondo told himself, watching the other man's confusion; do *not* giggle. He was prone to that sometimes—silly in an adult, outlandish in an adult his size. "Yessir—they said many complimentary things about you."

"Sometimes I think they forget I'm even here."

"You're very well thought of, Captain Bradford."

"*Brad*ford?" Givens exploded. "Bradford? Who the fuck is that?"

"I thought you were."

"Oh, shit," Givens said, "it's just like I said, they do forget I'm here, they even get my name wrong." He gestured for Hondo to get out of the way, sat at his desk, grabbed for the phone. "A hundred and fifty Fahrenheit, my car air conditioner sucks, and now they've come up with a fictitious name."

"I don't think he's fictitious," Hondo said, watching as Givens began to dial.

"Who is this Bradford then?"

"Your replacement."

"Replacement? Re*place*ment? I'm not going anywhere." He turned to look up then, a bit too late to stop Hondo's fingers from attaching themselves to his chin and the back of his head.

Oh, but you are, Hondo thought, executing the quick double snap, letting the head crash to the desk top, wondering all the while who they wanted him to remainder on his next job, the one in New Orleans.

## 5

Calmly, Scylla entered San Juan International, prepared for the noise. He was not disappointed. Perhaps, he thought, it was cultural heritage, though that had a racial twang to it. All he knew was that more than their North American mainland neighbors, the Spanish visited airports. Was a third cousin going from Mexico City to Los Angeles? Fine. Twenty-two relatives would fit into a couple of vehicles and chug along. Was Aunt Consuela visiting Nueva York? Better to die than not be one of the fifteen who saw her off.

So he was well prepared for the noise. Still, he kept caution, pausing inside the entrance to take a breath, get his bearings, reminded himself that he was still but half a dozen hours removed from his island.

A pretty Spanish girl walked by wearing a T-shirt with another pretty girl's picture on it. Odd, Scylla thought. In the past, they did not flaunt sexual deviation quite so openly, not in the tropical countries he was familiar with at any rate.

The pretty Spanish girl smiled at him.

Of course, he had to smile back, and while he was doing that he realized that the T-shirt portrayed not another girl but a man with makeup. There was a name under the portrait. "Boy George," Scylla read. For a moment he was struck by how things had changed, but then he remembered Tiny Tim and along with that the realization that nothing truly changes. New twists on old twists, that was all the world provided. Boy George was cuter, that was all.

The plane to Atlanta was late.

How late? Scylla asked the girl behind the counter.

We're sure not very.

When will you know?

We expect soon.

God bless, Scylla told her, and headed toward the bookstore slash magazine stand. Planes to Atlanta were always late. Madison himself had written that into the Constitution. He entered the store with a strong sense of pleasure—he hated to fly and one of the ways he survived was to stock up on either writers he revered or trash. And the truth was he was like people interviewed as to what did they like on the tube and they always answered "public television," which made it odd that programs like "Beverly Hillbillies" or "Laverne and Shirley" were always the most popular.

The truth was, except for a very few writers, trash was a clear winner for him. Shelley Winters' autobiography. Glorious for a flight. *Mommy Dearest*. Nobel Prize stuff when you were five miles into the stratosphere. He picked up *The New Yorker* because it was the first printed matter he came to and more than that, you were *supposed* to pick up *The New Yorker* first. He flipped to the table of contents, put the magazine back: there wasn't a new John Cheever story and Cheever was the only one who could get him through even a shuttle. He bent down then, grabbed, for laughs, the *San Juan Star*—

—and the light-headedness came. He gripped the rack for support. Held it as tightly as he could, because Kilgore had been quite right, it was the twenty-eighth, the month was indeed June.

But 1985?

Not possible. '82, yes. He would have accepted that. Even late in the year. Early '83 wouldn't have thrown him. But *Christ!* Carter, the midget engineer, was finishing his first term, running against Reagan when he went to his island. Scylla loathed Carter, because he had voted for him, been suckered by the "I'll never lie to you" bullshit. Carter was going to get ripped by Kennedy before the Ayatollah had rescued him. Overnight Carter wrapped himself in the flag and ran from the Rose Garden and then, after the fiasco in the desert when our planes crashed, he had the fucking gall to announce that now that the Iranian situation was more "manageable," he was coming out of hiding.

If you had respect for the language, if you cared for the dead in the desert, you could not use the word "manageable." It was beyond pornographic.

Scylla glanced at a headline, saw the name "Reagan," realized the actor must have won. Then he thought a minute. More than won. This was mid-'85 now (it was, it was), which meant he must have been *re*elected. Scylla picked up the *Star* again, without wobbling this time, the

Miami rag, *Time*, *Newsweek* and, thank God, the last copy of the *New York Times*. Before he left he made a brief tour of the book department but there was nothing new by either of his greatest favorites, Irwin Shaw and Ross MacDonald, so he went to the counter, got a scowl for his fifty-dollar bill, waited while the girl who manned the counter went for change, took it, found a seat in an unpopulated area, and sat down.

Someone named Mikhail S. Gorbachev was now the Soviet leader. Which meant that while he was gone, Brezhnev must have died and this other fellow had won the power struggle. Scylla shrugged. It really didn't matter who ran Russia, they were all the same old second-raters who had lived through the revolutions and the wars, who were lacking in brain cells but strong on longevity. There was only one world leader worth admiring, at least to Scylla's mind, and that was Sadat.

He flicked briefly to the entertainment section, saw, with pleasure, that Mr. Eastwood was out with his annual summer action job, this a Western. Scylla liked action pictures and Eastwood was one of his two favorites, had been ever since his spaghetti Western days, but he had liked McQueen since *The Great Escape*, even longer.

There was an article he glanced at entitled "Five Famous Women" and there were photos of them with their names underneath and for the first time, Scylla began, just the least bit, to feel queasy—who was Sally Ride, who was Sandra O'Connor, who was Madonna, or Ferraro, or this Mary Lou Retton?

AIDS? "Desperate search for cure. Gene discovered in virus."

What was AIDS?

Or MTV?

Nothing ever changes, he told himself. New twists on old twists. Remember that. Never forget that!

And now his eye fell on a full-page ad with the screaming headline, "While They Last, Only $799.95." "Remote," it said. "Cable ready," it said.

What was remote and cable ready? He read the ad carefully, aware of the fact that he was in trouble, suddenly he was definitely not in a clean, well-lighted place, not anymore.

*A VHS VCR.*

He stared at the initials, and what made him more upset than ever was simply this: the ad didn't even bother to explain what the initials stood for. Which meant common knowledge to the masses. "Programmable up to fourteen days. Four events. Speed search. Front loading."

Scylla stared at the photo of the rectangular-looking machine. *What did it do?* It was on sale for a lot of money. A full-page ad was expensive. He was six hours away from his island and he realized to retrieve the calm he cloaked himself in just a few moments before when he entered the place, he had to take his mind back there. Yes. Where the world had no initials. Scylla closed his eyes, heard the wind and the birds and the trees creaking and the lapping of the waves and the screaming—

—but there was no screaming on his island.

He tried to keep his eyes shut but the screaming got only louder so he turned in his seat, stared as a hundred or more teenaged girls ran shrieking across the main check-in area, then stopped, milled, ran back, then stopped again where they were joined by what seemed like a hundred more teenaged girls and now in Spanish a voice began excitedly to talk on the loudspeaker and Scylla knew enough Spanish to get most of it—"It is a false rumor," the voice on the loudspeaker said—"Menudo is not here—Menudo is not here—please—young ladies—MENUDO IS NOT HERE."

Scylla stared at the madness and realized this: he was terrified. And he was not used to that. Even before the island, he was not used to that. He *inspired* terror. He handed it out like a Christmas turkey. His name—that alone petrified. But he, secure in his powers, was as immune as any man.

He was in another country now.

He suddenly had no idea of what he was capable of. But

as the girls continued to scream, as the girls, disbelieving the voice, started to half riot, as the initials taunted him—was it an MTV VCR?—was the gene cure to help solve VHS?—he knew he was not in a site of his dreams. And he wished for the Atlanta plane, wished for it hard, because once he was there he could make the transfer and reach whatever awaited him in his final destination of New Orleans.

## 6

If San Juan had surprised him with fear, New Orleans shocked him with sadness. He had been there only once, and then for not much more than a day, and that day had been two decades past, but as he waited for his luggage at the carousel, Scylla felt suddenly suffocated by a shroud. And he wasn't ready for the ensuing despair. But then, he had thought about so little for so long, probably he should have been. Ready.

It had not been, his previous time, your average day.

He picked up his blue suitcase, followed the signs toward taxis, got in line and, when his turn came, got in. He was rumpled from the flight—*flights*, more accurately, the first from San Juan to Atlanta, the connecting one from Miami to here. *Theoretical* connecting one, more accurately, since, because of equipment failure—where would airlines be without the enigmatic excuse of "equipment failure" to cover their fuck-ups?—a six-hour trip had taken double that time and a bit more. And since flying and waiting were two of the three things he hated most—chemistry class completed his dark triumvirate—he was more than rumpled at touchdown.

Try fuming.

He carried that emotion with him to the luggage carousel,

which, perhaps as much as anything, caused the surprise at the sudden onrush of despair; he thought his anger would stay with him a good long while.

It was just past nine in the morning when he closed the door of the taxi, expecting to hear himself tell the elegant, elderly driver his destination—the Continental Supreme. But instead, his rough voice said, "Is the Café du Monde still open?"

"If the world be turnin', it there."

"Then the Café du Monde, please."

"You a wise man." The cab began to move through the morning humidity.

Scylla sat back, wondering if the place had changed; probably not much, since he doubted it had changed much in the century or so it had been open before his one meal there. Scylla had eaten, during his Division years, at probably most of the world's—what was that insipid phrase? —yes, most of the world's "gastronomic palaces." Chauveron, when it was in New York, and Taillevant on Rue Lamennais, the Villa Lorraine in Brussels, the brilliant Swiss' place, what was his name, Giradet?

The Café du Monde was not a gastronomic palace.

And he had dined at many of the world's great bistros. Harry's in Venice, Durgin-Park in Beantown, El Parador's in Manhattan. He adored bistros, Scylla did.

The Café du Monde could not even qualify as that.

And since, when you Provided for Division living was always first-class, no wine list had ever daunted him. So yes, he'd had the '61 Palmer, many times, and the '47 Cheval Blanc, in magnum, if you please, and the '31 Noval, beyond argument the greatest wine of the century.

The Café du Monde didn't have a wine list. It didn't really have a menu. What it served was café au lait and beignets. Period. You could have milk if you wanted to. So why had it survived for so long with nothing but chicory coffee and crispy fried rectangular doughnuts, topped with powdered sugar?

Because it had weight. It was a *place*. When you sat and

stared at the brown Mississippi, you knew you were *there*. When you sat on your camel in Egypt and studied the Sphinx, you didn't say, "No, this won't do, show me a better one." And when you breakfasted at the Café du Monde you didn't say, "I wanted Instant Sanka and my Egg McMuffin, let's get out of here now." There was no replacement for the Café du Monde. It was that special. At least to Scylla, it was that special.

Besides, his parents had become engaged there.

Nineteen twenty-seven was the year. H.V. Levy, so brilliant, so poor, just starting on his doctorate, still a decade away from the fame he so coveted as an historian. Rebekkah Berger, as pretty as she was gentle as she was rich, all of eighteen. They had known each other for less than a week—H.V. had a cousin who gave him a letter of introduction to her family. And at the end of that week, so family legend had it, they sat at four in the morning in the Café du Monde, which never closed, and he asked her to wait and, when he could afford it, marry him. And she, of course, said, in a tone that included not just the affirmation but the exclamation point, "Yes!"

There is a story by Delmore Schwartz, a great story, Scylla thought, entitled "In Dreams Begin Responsibilities," and the narrator of it is somehow given the power to travel back through time and be present at the moment when his father proposed to his mother and just as the words are about to be spoken, from the yet-to-be-born son and narrator bursts this: "DON'T DO IT!"

How often in childhood had he wanted to scream those words? Scylla wondered, eyes closed now, as the cab made its slow way from the airport to the city. For the relationship, begun so romantically, had peaked before it truly began. H.V. Levy, so brilliant, so poor, was also so cold. Driven by career, climbing the complex facade of the Columbia history department with record-shattering speed. And Rebekkah, pretty and gentle (though after '29 no longer rich), turned out to be—just not bright at all. Scylla had been born, late, as an obvious attempt to prop up a crumbling building, but the building had all the solidity of a sand castle. And Babe had come a decade after that—Rebekkah was in her early forties—to the wonderment of all, the pleasure of few; none really, beside Scylla's.

"Tip up to you."

Scylla blinked. The cab had stopped, the motor running.

"Fare eighteen, but tip up to you." The aged hand pointed at the meter, then outside at the Café du Monde.

"I just wanted to see it," Scylla said. Had he dozed? He hadn't slept on the trip, he never did on planes. But dozing was a pastime for the elderly.

"You gotta eat—you got to have you a bahn-yeh."

"I just wanted to see the place," Scylla said again. "Now you can take me to the Continental Supreme."

The driver was studying him. "Ain't that much to see, the food what make it shine."

"Some people I know got engaged here."

"Sweet."

Scylla said nothing.

"They get married?"

Scylla nodded.

"Dumb."

Scylla nodded again, knowing that what had brought him to this place near Jackson Square was not the start of anything at all, but the final end, no redundancy.

The life of the family, H.V. and Rebekkah, the two sons, had seemed from outside, one to envy, the brilliant famous father, the lovely southern wife, the Louisiana accent permanently there, the boys no problem.

Then the bad patch started. (Sometimes Scylla wondered when would it ever end.) H.V. had always been absurdly liberal, and had done work in Washington, always in an advisory capacity, and when the McCarthy committee had the wind at its back, they worked him over wonderfully, made him seem the one thing he never was, absurd, and that broke him. Then Rebekkah paid the full price for ignoring the breast lumps, and when she was in the ground, H.V. discovered the bottle and when Scylla was a junior in college blew his brains away. Babe was alone in the house, found the remains, called the cops, who called the college, and when he got home it was night but Babe was there, bright eyes so wide, and when they embraced Babe said an odd thing: "Thank God it wasn't me spilled the paint."

Scylla saw the sense of it after he'd gotten Babe to sleep and went to the death room, studied where his father had fallen onto the rug, went to the doorway and realized that the body was hidden from sight but the red blood must have seeped into view, paint someone spilled on the rug.

College gave him an extension so he stayed home the next months, the two of them in the small Connecticut house, just Doc and Babe—their own sweet secret names for each other. To the world he was Henry or Hank, Babe was Tom.

The days following the funeral were normal, considering, but toward the end of that first week, Babe said it again: "Thank God it wasn't me spilled the paint."

And the next morning he said, "Doc?"

"What?"

"Promise you won't laugh?"

"Nope."

*"Please."*

Something in the tone made him promise.

"I don't think Dad's dead," Babe said.

The next morning he said it again. "I been figuring."

"Even though you're ten, you have no right to claim illiteracy. *I've* been figuring."

"Promise you won't laugh."

"Promise."

"He's testing us. Me, I mean. You, you're big and strong, but he's testing me, making sure I'm strong too, that's why he faked it all, the paint business, see, I think he's really watching, making sure, he loves me and he needs to know."

"He loved everybody—"

"—don't make it like it was past, Doc. Dad *loves* everybody."

Two mornings later: "Doc?"

"I won't laugh."

"Why didn't he come?"

"Dad?"

"Yeah. Last night I thought for sure he would. I haven't cried since the funeral or anything. Doesn't that mean I'm strong? How long is this test going to go on do you think?"

"Not much longer."

The next afternoon: "Babe?"

"Yeah?"

"Guess what's in this envelope?"

"What?"

"Plane tickets."

"*Plane* tickets? Where we going?"

"Surprise."

The next evening, inside an hour of getting to the Orleans Hotel, they sat in a corner table at the Café du Monde and the waitress brought coffee to Doc, milk to Babe, beignets to both. And while Babe devoured the hot doughnuts, Doc talked about H.V. and Rebekkah, and how they'd started off right here and Babe, all excited, stared around wondering aloud at which table and then Doc said it, very clear, just the one time, the words knifing: *"It wasn't paint, Babe."*

Babe blinked, blinked again, and then ran around the table into his brother's arms, crying as if his heart was breaking, which of course, it was . . .

"Tip up to me?" Scylla said as the cab reached the hotel.

Nod.

He doubled the meter, pleasing the ancient. He had always tipped well: it wasn't his money, but more than that, when you worked for Division, you went first class.

Which made the Continental Supreme Hotel something of an oddment. Judging from the accents of those strolling through and working in the lobby, it was certainly not "continental," and judging by the cigarette butts scattered near the standing ashtrays, supremacy was definitely in doubt. He shrugged. At least there were ashtrays.

"Bede?" he said to the room clerk.

The guy had him sign in, gave him two room keys, said, "Hold it," as he shuffled through some envelopes, took one out, flipped it over.

As he elevatored to the third floor, Scylla wondered if he would have a suite or not. In the old days, he would not have dreamt of wondering.

It was and it wasn't. It was two identical bedrooms with the connecting door unlocked. He could enter either door. He shrugged. At least he had freedom of choice.

The rooms were on the third floor and the air conditioning was powerful. He turned it off, opened the windows; he had learned these past years that heat could be an accomplice; your muscles were always loose in tropical climes; his were, at any rate. He looked out the window. There was a narrow decorative ledge that ran around the exterior of the building which was made of probably cheap brick. It would have made an easier climb than the trees on his island—

—for a moment, he missed the birds.

He opened the envelope. The message was signed by someone named Fountain. Concise, professional, standard.

3 pm

113 Jackson Ave

"Blistering."

At precisely 2:59 and 50 seconds, Scylla mounted the steps to the lovely old house in the Garden District located at 113 Jackson Avenue. There were two brass signs by the front door. The first announced that this was the NEW ORLEANS ARTIFACT SOCIETY, the second asked, PLEASE RING.

Scylla rang.

In a moment, a very large, permanently officious lady was in the doorway, eyeing him.

"I'm sort of an artifact freak," he said. "And I'm in

town for the proctologists' convention; is it all right if I look around?''

''Ouah pleas-jour,'' she replied, making a sweeping gesture for him to come inside. ''We ah maghtily proud of ouah koh-lec-shun. Look around, suh. Please. And be su-ah to take yoah tahm.''

Scylla entered the house, started to tour. The artifacts were all housed in cases on the first floor—a braided rope blocked the staircase with the sign PRIVATE OFFICES indicating, if the rope failed, that upstairs was not a place to go.

Tacky, tacky, tacky, Scylla thought, looking at the few dreary objects gathering, somehow, dust, even though the cases should have protected them. Louisiana had an extraordinary history—the flagpole at Jackson Square had flown the colors of four countries, if you counted the Confederacy, and he had no doubt that the locals very much did. There had been warriors here, and chiefs of great renown, and makers of quilts, braiders and carpenters whose work sold on many continents—a fabulous collection of artifacts was easily obtainable.

Here there was nothing but junk.

''It's hot,'' the officious woman said suddenly, waddling up beside him.

He hesitated. ''Is it all right if I just wander awhile by myself?'' he said. ''You did say I could take my time.''

An odd look. Then: ''Of co-ass.''

As he watched her walk away, Scylla realized he shouldn't have done it, but he could not help himself. The facts were simple. ''Blistering'' was the password and when she approached him and said, ''It's hot,'' he was supposed to reply, ''Blistering.'' He knew that. No pride involved. A two-year-old would have known that.

His problem was this: he *hated* passwords.

Always had. From the first day at Division, it was clear he was a rocket. None of his superiors found much to bark about. Except for that one peculiarity—he balked at passwords. Not so much balked perhaps as derided them. He treated them as jokes.

The truth was this: they embarrassed him. No matter how often he was lectured on their importance, his mind would always flash to the glorious Saturday afternoon serials of his childhood when the dastardly villains—villains *were* dastardly then, and more than that, easy to spot because they always wore villainous clothing—when these poor slob actors would whisper ludicrous words and phrases to each other, and he would sit hooting in the audience.

Ye Gods, how could anyone take them seriously?

Now the officious woman was back. "Ah don't know whah ah fand this heat so ay-maz-in', ah just dew. It is sew hot."

Scylla stood there.

"Yew dew agree?"

Scylla made a questioning look.

"The heat, the heat, ahm talkin' 'bout the heat."

She was beginning to get just a wee bit flustered. Scylla said, "Definitely."

"How would you descrahb it? How hot it is, ahm talkin' 'bout."

"Too?"

"There's a word—on the tip of mah tongue—ah just can't come up with it."

"If you could think of what letter it began with, that would be a help."

"Ah believe it begins with a 'b.' "

"Oh, sure," Scylla said, smiling.

She smiled, sighed back.

"Brutally," Scylla said. "I'm sure that solves your problem."

"It does not. That is a different word entirely."

"Bitch? As in 'hot as a bitch'?"

"You are drifting further an' further away."

"I *know* the word," Scylla said then. "Berry."

She just looked at him. *"Berry?"*

"Sure. Didn't there used to be a comedian on 'Saturday Night Live' who said, 'Baseball been berry berry good to me'? Well, I say, 'It's berry berry hot out,' are your problems solved?''

He watched as she stormed up the stairs.

Fountain sat at his desk as Miss Quincy hurried in. ''He's here?'' Fountain said, a nervous man, early forties, pudgy.

''I don't know *who's* here,'' Miss Quincy began, her accent for the most part gone.

''Perhaps a bit of explication is in order.'' He loved ''explication.''

''He came at three. This man came at three. Just like he was supposed to. Exactly as you told me someone would. Only—he won't say it—he simply will not say it—I tried—God *knows* I tried—'' She shook her head.

Fountain wondered if he had forgotten to put the password on his message. He knew the people in Washington did not consider him your crackerjack operative, but he was reliable. ''Why don't you just go on home,'' he told her. ''Slip on out the back. I'll handle the downstairs situation.'' When he heard the back door close a few minutes later, he got up from his desk, opened his office door, moved to the head of the stairs, cleared his throat.

A large, suntanned man moved into view below. ''It was 'blistering' wasn't it? The password?''

''Perhaps you might explicate.''

''I kept using it in sentences—to the nice lady—'blistering' this, 'blistering' the other thing. It's not a versatile word—I felt a fool. Had I got it wrong?''

''No—a communications mishap, nothing more, come on up, please.'' He watched as the large man gracefully obeyed.

''You're Mister Fountain?''

''And you're Mister Bede.'' They shook hands at the top of the stairs. ''In here,'' Fountain said, and they entered the office. Fountain sat at his desk, in front of the wall mirror. He gestured for Bede to sit across. When they were facing each other, Fountain reached for a thick yellow envelope, held it in his hands. ''I'm rather in the dark about all this, Bede. They give away ice in the winter, the D.C. boys do, when it comes to too much detail. All I know is you're interested in joining Division and apparently they have enough curiosity about you to have you tested."

"I was just told to come here."

"This is the mental part, Bede. You have to pass that to get a foot in the door. Here." He pushed over the thick folder.

"I'm to take this and?"

"Open it first."

The other man did as requested, pulled out the packet of stapled pages. "What am I to do with all this?"

"Read the data, do as required. Pretend you're in college and this is an open-book exam. I'm your grader. Get by me, it's off to Washington with you, I imagine."

Bede flipped through the pages. "There's more than a hundred pages here."

"Well, fret not—I should have explicated that you have the night. Twenty-four hours, more if you need them. Just so you're back here by six tomorrow. I'll be waiting."

"That's not much time, I better go."

When the dark-skinned man was at the door, Fountain said, casually, "May I tell you something? You're already making a mistake, applying too much pressure to yourself. Relax, Bede. Tell you what—do you like jazz?"

"In New Orleans there's only one answer."

"Good. I live above the store here, but I need to relax too—there's a lovely little place, Spanier Hall, not far from your hotel, meet me there if you like. Say around eleven. We'll both take a break from our labors, are we on? It's a five-minute walk from the Continental, no more."

"Thank you, Mister Fountain."

"Nothing at all." He got up, escorted the larger man to the stairs, watched as he descended, crossed to the front door, turned, waved, left, the door locking behind him.

Fountain went back into his office, said, "He's gone" to the mirror, which was actually a two-way glass, waited for Hondo and Cheetah to enter. "I set it up for you," Fountain said when they were in the room. "I'd guess he'll leave his hotel before eleven, walk to Spanier Hall."

"Who in Christ is he?" Cheetah said.

Fountain didn't like either of them. No. He didn't know them well, so liking was not the right word. Probably what he meant was they frightened him, only he didn't like to think about fear. He shook his head. "Some new recruit. Potential recruit. Washington wasn't rich with detail."

"He looks strong," Hondo said.

Cheetah whirled on the bigger man—"Then let *me* handle him—you piss in your pants somewhere and stay out of my way."

"Don't," Hondo said quietly, "use that tone to me."

"Gentlemen, gentlemen," Fountain said. "No cause for disputation. It's nothing we haven't done before. Just do your jobs."

"I'm very capable of doing *my* job," Cheetah said. "And I'm a good soldier so I'll do what I'm told—but they should have had more faith in me—me, myself and I. It doesn't show they have confidence, giving me an assistant."

"Don't," Hondo said, "ever refer to me as your assistant."

"*Please*," Fountain said. "I don't know why they sent two of you—I only know the decision was from the top. Policy himself."

"Perkins?" Hondo said.

Fountain nodded.

"And we're to do what?" Hondo asked.

"Test him. Check out his reactions."

"Can we cause him pain?" Cheetah said.

"How can you even ask such a question?" Fountain said. "Of course you can. But he's not to be remaindered. I'm to call Perkins with your feelings about this Bede. Top quality? Fair? Of no use to us at all? Just be quick but thorough."

Cheetah seemed mollified. "I can maim him then."

"But lightly," Fountain reminded.

## 7

It was really quite ingenious stuff, Scylla decided. Must have had top-quality minds to dream it up. All neatly categorized. He picked up the work he'd just completed. On breaking. A five-page single-spaced dossier on an imaginary enemy. All necessary personal data: parentage, childhood, education, quirks. Followed by a series of questions to be answered, both short essay and multiple choice. "How would you break this man if time were no problem?" "How would you break this man in a day?" "An hour?" "Could you break him in less?" "How much less?" "Precisely how much less and precisely how would you do it?"

There were a dozen such subjects to be covered. One dealt with detecting double agents. Another with the best ways of inspiring total trust. Yet another delved into the problems of how to best recruit the best potential candidates.

On and on.

He stretched, looked at his watch. Half past ten. Now he stood, got up from the hotel room desk, went to an open window, watched the night. On his island now, the birds would be asleep. Would have been for hours. As would he. From somewhere outside a car backfired. Or was it gunfire? Once he wouldn't have wondered.

He dressed, casually, shirt and slacks, socks and loafers, put some cash in one pocket, a handful of change in another. At quarter to eleven he asked the concierge (joke) if he knew where Spanier Hall was, and when he had the directions straight, Scylla moved out of the lobby into the New Orleans night. It was surprisingly quiet, but then perhaps Louisiana, like Miami, lost a lot of its allure once summertime came and the insects set up housekeeping. Plus, he had overheard a brief conversation in the lobby earlier that day about how the town had never recovered from the World's Fair (apparently there had been a World's Fair) which proved a disaster, and that, in turn, infected the city, business was off, hotels were empty, the whole town was like someone had thrown away the key. And before he had quite finished pondering the fate of the city, he was aware that the two men were flanking him so he whirled—

—too slow—

—too slow—

He caught a glimpse of the wide man with the potbelly but then the wide man had his arms pinioned, immobile, which made it easy for the angry-faced man to crash an elbow into his solar plexus.

Scylla gasped.

Then the angry-faced man brought a knee up sharply, ramming it into Scylla's stomach, and it all began getting blurry, he gasped again, his eyes began to slide up into his head and he wanted to double over, would have doubled over, but the strong arms kept him pinioned so the angry-faced man could continue tearing at his stomach.

"Spin him," Scylla heard.

"Why?"

"Fuckin' spin him!"

Scylla could feel his body being turned. Then there were blows into his kidneys, the small of his back, his body went limp.

"I'm letting him fall."

"Not till I'm finished."

The arms let him go, he fell, crashed to the sidewalk, listened to their footsteps retreat, then the word "Money," and the footsteps were back, hands were scouring his pockets—

"—he's got no wallet—"

"—gotta have cash—"

Now someone new was screaming, "Police—*Police*—"

"I got the cash."

"Let's get gone."

The footsteps retreated again.

Scylla lay very still. What he wanted more than anything was just to roll into a little fetal ball and lay still till dawn when the birds would start chattering—

—no, wrong, the birds were the old days, thirty-six hours ago.

Now the voice that had called "police" was standing above him. Scylla glanced up. An old man. "You okay?"

Scylla made a nod.

"You sure, mister?"

Scylla continued to rise. The last thing he needed was an encounter with the local law. Imagine their surprise, if they decided to fingerprint him, to discover he had none. They'd been gone for years, surgically removed.

"I do anything, mister?"

Scylla shook his head, muttered deep thanks, turned back toward the hotel. He had not been in pain for so long he had forgotten, if the beating was skillful as this had been, just how much pain hurt. Which was worse, he wondered, pain or fear?

Dead heat.

## 8

"Pie, I'm telling you," Cheetah practically shouted. "He was lemon meringue. Fucking schoolgirl would have given us more trouble." It was almost midnight, and he prowled around Fountain's office, wondering how Hondo could just sit in the chair like a clown when a job had gone as sweet as this one.

Fountain, behind his desk, said nothing, just waited for the prowling man to slow.

"He didn't even have the sense to know we were moving up behind. He just strolled like some asshole tourist. 'Course, that's all he is, an asshole tourist.'' Now he whirled on Fountain. ''I could have handled this easy alone—when you make your report, you be fucking sure the thirteenth floor understands what I'm saying.''

Quietly, Hondo said, ''You don't know that. All we know is *I* did the hard part, I kept him pinioned so you could toss a few punches. If I hadn't been here, he might have whipped your ass.''

Cheetah took a step toward the large man in the chair. He started to say something, stopped, finally muttered, ''Watch it,'' left it there.

Hondo looked at Fountain. ''Next thing he's going to be asking will I step outside. And me with a weak heart.'' He paused. ''This guy tonight wasn't meringue exactly; he was just real real slow.''

''Gentlemen,'' Fountain said, ''please don't make me put your personal antagonisms in my report. And I will. If they continue. I will explicate all, believe that.''

Cheetah started to say something again, stopped, this time remained silent.

''Nothing will show on Bede?'' Fountain asked.

''Ask him,'' Hondo said. ''He was the heavy hitter. All I did was the dirty work.''

''Why do you bother with a question like that, Fountain? 'Course nothing'll show. I'm no kid, I went for the gut and the kidneys, his face'll be as cute as ever in the morning.''

Fountain sighed. He hated what he had to do next, phone D.C., get Perkins. He'd only called that high twice before and both of those had been daytime. Perkins hated being bothered out of the office. Everybody knew that. Still, what had to be done needed his doing, so he unlocked the desk drawer, took out the Green phone, dialed 2, then the area code, then the number.

''Division.'' A female voice. Young.

''Perkins, please.''

''Call tomorrow.''

''This is Fountain in New—''

''—call tomorrow.''

"I have orders."

"As have I. Call tomorrow."

Fountain, nervous and pudgy, took a quick breath, went for quick bravery: "You get word to him—I'm phoning about Bede. And I *don't* expect Perkins to call tomorrow." He hung up hard, for the benefit of Cheetah and Hondo. Probably his entire bravura performance was for the benefit of Cheetah and Hondo. As a child, he had been a Conan Doyle fanatic and Perkins reminded him of no one more than Mycroft Holmes, Sherlock's older brother who was enormously fat but the brighter of the two. Perkins was enormously fat and perhaps brighter than anyone. Except Fountain had adored Mycroft Holmes and Perkins terrified him. He sat staring at the Green phone aware that Cheetah was moving faster and Hondo had gotten up, begun pacing too. Clearly, Fountain realized, he was not the only man in the room afraid of Perkins. The wandering continued for a time, stopping when the Green phone buzzed and Fountain grabbed it.

"This is Fountain speaking," he said.

From the other end now, the rumbling voice: "Since, Fountain, *I* am the one who placed the call to *you*, to *your* private number, the fact that it is *you* speaking comes under the heading of information I already possess."

"It's—it's about this Bede—"

"Now, Fountain, you are beginning to tax me—it is late and I am home, and one of my assistants contacted me that you had contacted the office 'phoning about Bede' is the quote I got, so you are again telling me information I already possess. Fountain, this conversation has yet to begin, now *get to it!*"

"Well—you see—we tested him—Cheetah and Hondo are here in the room—"

A deep sigh. "The way this all ought to have gone, Fountain, if I may try, however late the date may be, to get some logic into your fattening head, is thusly: 'Sir, I'm calling about the test and it went . . .' and then you would add one word, Fountain, to summarize the result."

"Disastrously," Fountain managed.

Silence from the frightening voice.

Fountain was totally unprepared for that. Perkins was not into silence, since it wasted his time, and for a moment, Fountain wondered if the Mycroft Holmes figure had heard him. "He was physically, to quote Cheetah, 'meringue.' To quote Hondo, 'real real *slow*.' "

"Perhaps . . ." The voice was more distant now. Hesitant almost. "I had high hopes for this fellow. He came wonderfully recommended. Yes. Perhaps there's a reason for his performance. Or lack of one."

"I wouldn't know," Fountain said, "but since I've got Cheetah and Hondo with me, perhaps they could go to the hotel and finish him now."

"Was that a thought I heard, Fountain, or has our connection altered? When did you take up thinking? I thought I did that."

"A suggestion was all, sir."

"I will cherish it forever, Fountain, full as I am with the knowledge that it is the *only* suggestion I will ever hear from you."

"Sorry, sir."

"Perhaps he has an excuse is what my mind had traveled to."

"Excuse?"

"Yes—perhaps he was ill, perhaps many things, when are you supposedly seeing him again?"

Fountain was quiet for a moment, because it was clear they were giving Bede a second chance and he wondered why, since they never did that for anybody else. "He's coming by tomorrow afternoon late-ish."

"Well, be surreptitious with him, as I know only you can be. Gently lead the subject to this evening's festivities and see if there is some explanation."

"And if there isn't?"

"I'm sure there will be. I genuinely want to take this fellow into the organization. I've heard such splendid things, I cannot believe they were all false."

Fountain felt he had to persist. "But if there isn't, sir. What shall I do?"

Again, the silence.

This time Fountain was sure he had been heard, so he waited, matching the fat man's quiet.

"... Do? ... Do your worst ..." came the soft reply.

Then the click.

Fountain held on to his phone a moment longer, trying to grasp the tone he'd just heard. So strange. Not that he talked all that often to someone at Perkins' exalted level. Still, they *had* conversed. Three times now.

"Do your worst" was said with such—upset? No. More than upset. And greater than disappointment.

Grief, perhaps?

## 9

"You missed some great jazz, Bede," Fountain said, as he ushered Bede into his office.

"Jazz?"

"At Spanier Hall. I was there waiting at eleven. I would have been there anyway, don't feel as if you'd inconvenienced me. I just love the place."

The bigger man shook his head. "My mind—sometimes I think I should just rent it out. Completely forgot." He handed over the thick sheaf of papers. "I was so caught up in this."

"You didn't go out at all then?"

Shake of the head. "I figured it was more important that I do well on the test papers than I listen to music. And then I got a bit, I don't know, obsessive. I always did well back in school. I wanted to do well now."

"You stayed glued to the spot the entire night?"

"Well, I did take a walk, just a head clearer."

"You had a headache?"

"No."

"You were overtired from your flight? Jet lag?"

Shake of the head. "Tip-top."

Fountain looked at his watch. A few minutes after six. It would be dark by nine. "You stayed close to the hotel on your walk, or did you ramble?"

"That is a great Dixieland song—"

"—what is?"

" 'Didn't He Ramble?' "

"Of course," Fountain replied quickly. "A favorite."

"I just walked around the block. Twice around, then back to my test." He pointed to the sheaf of papers.

"Sounds uneventful."

"In the extreme."

"Just as well. We have enemies." Fountain got out five photographs, the second was of Cheetah, Hondo the third. "Have you been followed at all do you think?"

"I wouldn't know how to tell."

"Well, look at these fellows, see if they're familiar." He turned over the first.

"No."

Now Cheetah.

Bede studied the face.

"Familiar?"

"Not at all; he just seemed so angry and I wondered why."

Now Hondo.

"Not your average matinee idol. No."

Four and five.

Shake of the head.

Fountain put the photos back into his desk. "Well, these five could cause trouble. Be on the lookout."

"From now on," Bede assured him.

"Bede," Fountain said then. "Sit down there." He pointed to the chair across from his desk.

Bede sat down. "You sound serious."

"Our work *is* serious."

"I didn't mean that, I know it is; I meant you sounded, I don't know, put out with me."

Fountain smiled. "Not at all. I just want to explicate something. Your test—" He rattled the sheaf of papers. "I need to know for final and absolute certain that it is your best work, that there are *no excuses*, no explanations if it isn't up to snuff. If there is, if you were nervous or for any reason whatsoever, not at your best, best you say it now, there will be no later."

"No excuses, no explanations."

Fountain nodded, made his fingers rat-tat-tat his desk top. "Good man," he said finally. "I'll run these through the computer, check it all out. I should be done by nine, that's three hours, should be plenty. I'll give you your grade then."

"You want me back here at nine?"

"I'll call you at the hotel. Be sure you're there. I'm prompt. You be too."

"I am."

"I won't call before so feel free to explore the city. The food equalizes the humidity. I can book you at Brennan's, you name it."

"I've heard of the Café du Monde."

"A bit limited, but lovely. Wander the French Quarter to your heart's content, be in your suite at nine." He watched the other man stand.

"I can find my own way out now, Mister Fountain."

Fountain nodded, listened to the footsteps descend the stairs, cross the foyer, heard the front door open and close. Then he took the sheaf of papers, put them into his shredder, turned it on and, a moment later, off. Finally he walked to the window, watched as the dark-skinned man moved slowly along the sidewalk. "He seems to be limping badly," he said to the two men he knew were now standing behind him.

"Miracle he's walking at all," Cheetah said.

Hondo said, "He wouldn't be if I'd done the hitting."

"Meaning," Cheetah said angrily. *"Meaning?"*

"Oh Christ, you two," Fountain said wearily. "I've set him up for you at nine, save your bickering for afterwards." He was already dreading the phone call he would have to make to Perkins after the deed was done.

## 10

At shortly after eight, Hondo phoned the Continental Supreme from across the street, asked for Mr. Bede please. The connection was made, the phone rang half a dozen times. Hondo hung up, left the booth, looked at Cheetah, shook his head.

Cheetah glanced at his watch, held up five fingers. Hondo nodded.

Precisely five minutes later, they entered the lobby of the Continental Supreme, went to the house phone. Cheetah took the receiver, asked for Mr. Bede.

Ten rings this time.

He hung up and they walked to the elevator, took it to the third floor. Bede was in two rooms, 305 and 306. 305 was nearest, so Cheetah picked the lock and then slipped inside.

"Hot," Hondo said, as Cheetah closed the door, leaving them in almost total darkness. "Weird he doesn't use the air conditioning. Maybe we should close the windows and turn it on."

"Very good," Cheetah replied. "Dazzling."

"You're being sarcastic with me, you do it so bad, it's easy to tell."

"No—I'm just in awe—I mean, why don't we close the windows and turn on the air conditioning and then put little signs on the doors that say 'Oh Be-eeede, we're in-siiiide.'"

"I hate it that we're with the same company," Hondo said.

"I mean Jesus," Cheetah went on, rolling now, "a man keeps his windows open and doesn't use air conditioning, and he opens his doors and what does he hear—goddam air conditioners blasting away—a thing like that wouldn't make him suspicious or anything."

"Okay, forget I mentioned the windows, I was only trying to make this easier, it's going to be a miserable wait, with this heat and no breeze."

"You ever wonder if you were in the wrong line of business? You might consider going to Alaska—I hear there's a real shortage of dog-sled makers—kind of an old-world craft and the young Eskimos, they're into computers—you could learn how, you'd be set for life, cold and breezy, perfect for a guy like you." He was in a rotten frame of mind because it was so goddam hot in there and what he wanted was to shut the stupid windows, blast away with the air conditioners.

Hondo wondered if it was worth getting pissed, decided no, that wasn't the best way to do business. Sweating already, he said, "We don't know which room he comes in."

"So?"

"You stay here in 305. I'll take 306. Whichever door he opens, that's it."

"What do that mean?"

"*It means it's my kill.* If he opens my door, I don't want you running in, getting in my way, claiming how great you were to Fountain later, like you already did when you hit him but I did the hard part."

It was a good idea, Cheetah realized. In the darkness, work was often cumbersome. And another person getting in the way could screw it up bad. Except, of course, he couldn't say anything to Hondo that might be remotely complimentary. "It's okay with me, but there's a problem—I don't think you can handle him alone."

"My only problem is I don't get to handle *you* alone."

"Get out of here."

"Oh boy is that my pleasure." Hondo made his way into 306, got into position near the door, took out his knife. Ordinarily he didn't much like them, but in the dark like this, especially when it was hot like this, you could lose your grip, your hands could get sweaty. No, when it was hot and dark, knives had their place. He looked at his watch. Twenty after. And Fountain would phone Bede at nine. It could be a forty-minute wait. Sweat stung his eyes. And he hated Cheetah. Still, he could not find it in his heart to complain. He really loved his work. But then, he would be crazy not to, glamour jobs were always hard to find.

Cheetah looked at his watch. Half past. Claw time. He made the fingers of his right hand stiff, carefully adjusted his weapon so the fit was perfect, almost tight enough to damage circulation, the points so sharp, the edges filed like razors, so he could slash or thrust.

Was anything better than freedom of choice?

At one point, when he first perfected his invention, he thought, only briefly, of the fortune he could make manufacturing them and selling them to mercenaries. A few discreet ads in *Soldier of Fortune*, and my God, would the money roll in. That he decided not to go into business was due to the fact that he doubted that Division would be pleased, they were paying him well enough, more than that, actually.

Plus this: the weapon itself was an aide, yes, but no more than that. It was hand speed that made it so effective, and no one could match his.

8:36.

Damn the humidity. How could anybody actually want to sleep in air like this? Relax, he told himself. Bede would not be bothered by such problems much longer. Cheetah took out his handkerchief, wiped his neck. Please, he almost prayed, make Bede the prompt type.

Answered prayers. At 8:47 there were soft footfalls in the corridor outside. A metallic sound then, the fumbling for keys. Then the key was in the lock. 8:48. And the door swung open wide.

## 11

Scylla arrived at the Café du Monde by seven, the almanac under his arm. He ordered coffee and beignets, stared off at the Mississippi for a while. He could not remember, ever, being in such a state of indecision. The testing was as good as over now, and he felt total confidence as to that outcome; he simply knew.

And with the world almanac open now, he knew so much more about the remains of the planet than he had in the San Juan airport. He had purchased the almanac that morning, had been studying it almost continually since.

He knew that Cheever was dead, so too MacDonald and Shaw. He knew what AIDS stood for and how many it had killed, how many more were likely to go in the near future. And he knew that Gorbachev had not replaced Brezhnev, Andropov and Chernenko came in between. And he knew that Sally Ride had flown very high, Menudo had sung far and wide, in front of one of the largest crowds in history gathered for performers, over two hundred thousand people. And he was sad to learn that Anwar Sadat had been assassinated, maybe the most important event that had happened in his absence. And he knew now that some giant brain had decided to play professional football in the spring and summer, that baseball players had actually gone on strike, that tennis players had replaced jockeys as the highest-paid athletes in the world. And he discovered the existence of something called "California Cuisine," surely an immortal contradiction in terms. And chefs were now stars, clothing designers now superstars; fortunes had been made in men's underwear.

He knew, really, an incredible amount now for being but one day older. What he did not know was this: should he rejoin Division or not? Flat and simple. Yea or nay? Had he the stomach for it anymore?

Of course, it wasn't as simple as all that. He realized he had let his coffee get cold as he sat muddling, so he raised his hand, ordered another cup, started sipping it immediately when it arrived. A clock on the restaurant wall read a quarter after seven.

Scylla opened his almanac at random, read that for reasons passing understanding (his interpretation) we, the entire United States of America, had invaded something called Grenada and, wonder of wonders, shortly conquered it. Was it a war, he wondered? Dubious. We didn't fight wars. We scuffled through "police actions," got involved in "incursions." ("Shakespeare, thou shouldst be living at this hour.")

What made his Division rejoining complicated was this: would they let him? He had no memory of anyone being allowed to leave. You could kick on duty, that was allowed. But of your own free will just walk?

Odds against. And for good reason really—if you worked for Division you knew things. And if you knew things you could talk, for money or drunkenly or you could be broken. His only advantage was that having been, to put it mildly, in the boonies all this while, no one could accuse him of being *au courant*. What could he blab? That Fountain was a fool? Not much shock value there.

Perkins liked him though. Maybe as a favor, Perkins just might allow it. Maybe as a favor, Perkins might just allow it if he did the job Perkins had recalled him for. When it was done, he just might ask.

Coming up to eight. He ordered another coffee, read a bit more in his almanac. (Mondale didn't just lose to Reagan, he was run out of the stadium—Mondale had promised to raise taxes early on in his campaign. Brilliant ploy that, probably thought up by the same boy wonder who thought up summer football.)

It was 8:30 when he paid, left, wandered the French Quarter till he found a cab, headed for his hotel, arriving at 8:43. There were no messages for him but it took the clerk a while before announcing the answer. 8:46 when the elevator opened on the third floor. He walked down the corridor, got out his keys, decided on 305. 8:48 when he turned and pushed, and the door went open wide.

## 12

As soon as he heard the door opening in 305, Hondo, in 306, knew it just wasn't his day. He had a fifty-fifty shot—one door was as good as the other—but Cheetah had fallen into it, and now, Hondo knew, he was going to have to put up with all the guff the smaller man had to offer. How *he* had done the deed, he, the great Cheetah, the king of remaindering as he fancied himself.

And yet, frozen in 306, Hondo had to admit a certain admiration for Cheetah's professionalism. He had heard, of course, all about Cheetah's skill with his claws, how quick and silent it went when Cheetah was on the prowl. But this, the action in 305, was remarkable. Not a sound.

8:49.

What the hell do the claws do? Hondo wondered. There ought to be some noise at least—no matter how sharp Cheetah filed the weapon, it still entered flesh, first passing through fabric if he went for the heart, though not, of course, if it was a simple throat grab, pull it out and done.

Shit, Cheetah wasn't even breathing hard. What kind of condition must he be in, killing was *work*, and no one in the field thought otherwise. Outsiders, sure, they might not understand, but a human life was not an easy thing to take. You had to be in shape, even if you used a weapon like Cheetah's claws.

It was almost 8:50 when it crossed his mind that something strange was going on in 305. Or, more precisely, that absolutely nothing was going on in 305. He crept to the connecting door. There stood Cheetah, easily visible in the corridor light the open door let in. "What the hell—?" Hondo whispered.

"—just shut up," Cheetah whispered back.

"Don't 'just shut up' me, for chrissakes—what's happened in here?"

"Even *you* should be able to tell that—nothing's happened in here."

"Where—?"

"—don't ask me where he is, I don't know where he is, the door opened only no one came in, maybe he went to the ice machine, who the fuck knows?"

"You must have done something wrong," Hondo said.

Cheetah whirled. "I didn't twitch."

"Then he woulda come in—you must have done some dumb fucking thing to alert him." He stared at the other man, who, with the useless claws covering his fingers and no enemy to dismember, looked pretty stupid. Of course, he probably looked pretty stupid too, standing in the doorway with a goddam knife in his hand. "Did you check the corridor?"

"Of course I didn't check the corridor—in the first place, I'm sure he isn't there and in the second place, if he is there, don't you think peeking out from his room might blow my cover, you asshole?"

"Well, I'm going to look in the corridor," Hondo said and he walked to 305, peered along the corridor, one way, then the other. "No one there."

"Gee, I wonder who predicted that?"

"What do you think we should do?"

"I know what I wish you'd do—go change your diapers somewhere and leave all this to me. He's got to come back here—it's got his stuff in it. Probably he opened the door and remembered he forgot something and went to get it."

"Oh, that flies, that's genius at work."

"Goddam you," Cheetah said, closing the door to 305 halfway, cutting out at least part of the light, "either get back to your own room or let me handle this alone."

"You've done great so far, I'll give you that," Hondo said.

"Why aren't you the enemy?" Cheetah said.

"Count your blessings, little man," Hondo said. He looked at his watch. 8:53. He dried his knife hand on his shirt, walked back into his room. It was precisely 8:54, hot and dark when he realized someone else was there with him.

. . . weird, Hondo thought, as the other figure came toward him . . . he slashed with his knife, didn't come close and that was unusual too, he had a way with knives . . . then the oddest thing of all began to happen . . . in the darkness, in the sweaty darkness, this thing that had come from somewhere, it couldn't have, the door never opened, it must have been there all along . . . wherever it had come from didn't matter, because the oddest thing of all kept going on and it was this . . . he was being lifted up into the air . . . Jesus, Hondo thought, I weigh two fifty, nobody picks me up like a rag doll . . . then he was thrown down hard . . . then his neck was limp, like a rag doll's neck . . .

In 305, Cheetah heard the gasps of struggle, the crash of Bede's body, the ensuing neck break and he was impressed because he had heard that Hondo was fast, he just didn't believe it, not with the gut he had on him.

Silence from 306.

"Okay?" Cheetah called.

Silence from the next room.

"No games, asshole."

Still the silence game from 306.

Ticked, Cheetah went to the connecting door, flicked on

the light, instantly blocked his mind against the surprise of seeing Hondo's dead body, raced to the closet door, threw it open, nothing, empty like the room was, and the door had never opened, which meant someone had come through the window so Cheetah went there and, with great care, studied the night from there, but no one could have come through the window, it was the third floor and, sure, there was a little ledge but it didn't look like the kind of thing you wanted to risk your life on, and yes the exterior wall was of bricks, but no one could clamber around out there unless they were some fucking chimp used to swinging in trees, and still not allowing surprise to get at him, he realized he was a dead open target at that instant, so he raced back across the room, flicked the light off, continued on into 305 and slammed the door so it was dark too and just before it closed he sensed, from years of labor, that a shadow had slipped through the window.

. . . great, Cheetah thought, as the shadow came right for him, nothing tricky, just head on, like the crazy killer always did in the *Halloween* pictures . . . when the shadow was close, Cheetah struck with his claws . . .

. . . too slow . . .

. . . too slow . . .

. . . impossible, Cheetah thought, as his wrist was broken . . . no fucking way this was happening, he thought, as he was spun and felt his back begin to go . . . this *thing* is faster with his hands than me, only nobody is, only Scylla was, once, and he's dead . . . no, Cheetah thought, his last, he's not dead, I am.

# 13

"You didn't call."

Fountain stood in his open front doorway, blinked at the large, dark-skinned man who stood outside.

"Hi. It's me."

"Bede, yes, of course," Fountain said.

"We're having a lot of trouble with connections, Mister Fountain. I miss you at the jazz place, now you miss me at my hotel."

"Your hotel."

"I figured when you didn't call—I waited almost an hour—maybe I should drop by and talk to you personally. I'm really anxious to know how my test came out."

"Come in, Bede, your test, yes, of course, come right in." He ushered the other man inside and from there they went up the stairs to his office. "You did fabulously," Fountain said then. "On your test papers. I got engrossed in going through them, that's why I forgot to call."

"You know what I think, Mister Fountain?"

"What?"

"Recess is over."

Fountain blinked again. "It's rare that anyone scores as well on our written exams as you, Bede, really quite unusual—"

". . . you must stop this . . ." Scylla said then, the same words he had said to Kilgore on his island when Kilgore was terrorizing the birds, and Kilgore had been panicked then, as Fountain was now. "You and your kindergarten classes down here—you set me up to leave my hotel and I'm beaten, but not around the face, the most vulnerable spot they leave alone, and you give me this bullshit sheaf of questions—Division never needed me for my brains, Fountain, I had other skills they valued more highly—and then you ineptly get me back to my hotel tonight at an appointed hour for our celebrated phone call—let me tell you something—something to always remember—"

"—what?—"

*"—you must never let the opponent know the extent of your capabilities!"* And he tossed Hondo's knife onto the desk top then, followed with Cheetah's claws.

Fountain stared at him. "Who are you?"

"What's that phrase the disc jockeys use, 'a blast from the past'?"

Fountain still stared.

"We're moving on, Fountain—what were you told to do in the event I didn't die? Who runs Washington—who's Policy there?"

"Perkins."

"Make contact," Scylla said, thinking sometimes events did go properly because Perkins should have been head of Division years ago, he was their best. He paced around the room, while Fountain went through some phoning mumbo-jumbo—special instrument, all that garbage. Pay phones were really all one ever needed. Their only flaw was they didn't cost the government enough. And who on Capitol Hill could face the public humiliation of coming out in favor of a thrifty intelligence-gathering operation?

"He'll call back," Fountain said, seated at his desk. "Perkins. It shouldn't take long."

Scylla was surprised at the expectation he felt of soon listening to the rumbling voice, mellifluous, the sarcastic tone honed over years of diligent practice.

When the return call came, Fountain grabbed it before the first ring had finished. "This is Fountain speaking," he said quickly.

"Fountain," the deep voice began, "where is your memory, man? We went through this yesterday: *I* phoned *you*."

"I'm sorry, I'm a bit flustered, I have Bede here with me."

Now a pause. Then: "Is he vertical or horizontal?"

"He's quite alive, sir."

"And the other two?"

Fountain stared at the knife and the claws. "They're in retirement."

Scylla had walked close to the phone now, stood behind Fountain, impatiently waiting.

"Let me speak to him."

"He wants a word," Fountain said.

Scylla clapped the other man on the back then, heard the exhale; after a moment, he picked up the phone. "Hello, Ma."

"So you survived."

"Apparently."

"Why don't you pay me a visit then? Washington in a heat wave should suit you, considering where you've been vacationing and all."

"Loverly."

"You realize all of your Louisiana adventure was done under my orders. There was no point in bringing you to D.C. until I was sure you were worth bringing."

"Understood."

"I had to try to have you killed is the subtext, and I hope you won't find it in your little hard heart to hold it against me."

"I like to think I'm bigger than that."

Now a long pause. "You realize your greatest virtue is your face, everyone's unfamiliarity with it."

"I do."

"We must protect your face, you see. Not from the world at large, obviously, but from those in our little covey who might talk. Obviously, Fountain has seen your visage."

"In all its pristine glory."

"May I give you a suggestion?"

"Please."

"Remainder him."

"I already did," Scylla said.

# 2
# Rules and Regulations

## 1

Babe left his office at the history department of Columbia University, walked across the campus toward Broadway. The late June sun was strong, but there was enough breeze so you didn't mind. The time was closing in on three and he looked forward to going home, changing, taking a leisurely five-mile jog along the Hudson. He had several magazine articles he was noodling with and he wanted to settle on one during the journey, pitch the others, at least for now, get down to some serious research.

Others found such stuff a bore, but he loved it, the research, the hours spent with aging volumes, the required Sherlock-like tracing through the arcane madness of the Dewey decimal system. The breasts on Emily Pritchard—

"Afternoon, Professor Levy," Emily Pritchard said, hurrying past him, heading toward Amsterdam.

"Emily," he returned, nodding to her as she went by, wondering, as he stopped and watched her for a moment, how one of his best graduate students had suddenly blossomed into something approximating a stunner without his noticing.

Babe resumed his Broadway trek, just the least confused. He had been, in his bachelor days, before Melissa had said, blessedly, "Yes," a better than average girl-watcher. And he wasn't old, early thirties. So could Emily have had a transplant since day before yesterday, when he'd most recently chatted with her outside his office?

Of course not. So how could he have missed the change? Perhaps she hadn't changed at all, it could have been the beauty of the day enhancing everyone. Still, it was a puzzler because he adored women, Babe did; all kinds. From a distance, of course. Growing up, he had been far too timid and gawky to approach much, and when he did try, more often than not, he perspired dreadfully.

But watching? Oh yes, yes indeed. There were some who attacked the problem scientifically, and he had once read a book where one of the characters graded women as if they were in school, graded them either *A B C D F* or *Incomplete*. Babe felt that was unnecessary; the main thing was simple appreciation, all done with taste and discretion and—

—and another pretty girl walked by.

Two? In one afternoon? At Columbia? Amazing. A*mazing*. At Northwestern, nothing unusual. At UCLA you more or less expected it. But here, at surely the ugliest of the Ivy League sanctuaries, cause for stunned rejoicing. He turned, studied the second pretty girl as she hopped into a run toward a young man who was waving to her from the steps of a nearby building.

Babe got to Broadway, waited for the light, crossed to the west side of the street, started downtown where the shops were—

—and then it happened.

A student walking toward him spun suddenly, stared after the girl who was half a block ahead of Babe, walking in the same direction, and Babe had to smile as he watched the kid, because that was the best way to girl-watch, he thought; to study the reaction of men coming toward you. Because if they ignored a girl up ahead, chances are she was no knockout, but if their heads turned, that told you something. And if several male heads turned, that told you a lot, and then you could, sort of casually, pick up your pace, gaining on the girl ahead they were stopping for, your expectation rising as you closed the gap, drew up behind her, pulled even, and then, still more casually, glanced over, noticing as you did the curve of her cheek, the quality of her skin, that sort of trivial earth-shattering thing.

Now a second guy stopped, turned, looked back.

Hmm, Babe thought, picking up his pace, but casually, casually studying, for the first time, the girl up ahead they were staring after, who wore a white blouse, had a slender figure, dark hair, a splendid—

—omigod, Babe realized, that's my *wife*.

For a moment, he was embarrassed by his prepubescent behavior, following Melissa. But that moment passed and he thought that it all might be just the least bit interesting. She didn't know he was there and if she did, he'd just feign surprise, wave, dash up to her, throw an arm around.

Of course, he'd better do that fast if she did spot him since, being the serious scholar that she was, she might take unkindly to his chauvinistic action and roast him pretty good when they went out with friends: "Hobbies? My cherished husband's hobbies? Oh, he has several. Skulking, mainly."

But she wouldn't be ticked for long, she couldn't be; she'd have to see it was flattering. In a fine mood, Babe watched a third young man turn and stare and for a moment he wanted to say, to the world at large, "That's my wife, you bastards, eat your hearts out . . ."

Melissa had spent a thrilling last half hour—at least it was thrilling for her—trying to place an accent. A new girl had come to work in the checkout counter of the bookstore and Melissa, browsing, about to leave, realized, once she heard the girl speak, that she was going noplace.

Now where oh where did that "r" come from, she wondered, flicking through her card catalog of a mind—at least when accents were the topic—and where did she find her "th"?

Melissa moved close to the cash register, seemed to lose herself in the books piled on the counter. She opened the nearest—a cookbook, no less—and pretended interest, all the while listening to the girl.

Well, obviously she had been brought up in Montana, any fool would know that. Melissa moved a step nearer, anxious not to miss a word. The girl was working the register, saying, "That will be five dollars, eleven cents, thank you." "That will be seventeen dollars even, thank you very much."

Melissa flipped to the section on sauces, trying to place the intonations. The girl was from Montana, yes, but her parents clearly must have been foreign. That would account for the special consonant emphasis. Italian? Likely, but what part. Southern? It would have to be very southern, well below Naples. Maybe even—a guess but not necessarily a bad one—Sicily. How can I ask her that without seeming nosy, Melissa wondered, and then she said to the girl, "Do you have the Puzo in hardcover?"

"*Godfather?* I don't think so, just the paperback."

"The newer one," Melissa said.

"Oh, you mean *The Sicilian*—"

"—yes, I hear it's good, very authentic."

The girl—probably mid to late twenties, Melissa's age—smiled and said, "My parents are from there but they don't read much so I guess I can't help you, would you like anything else, we don't have the hardcover of that one either."

In gratitude, Melissa bought the cookbook, which was a hoot, since she could manage to tense up when it came time to boil water. Feeling very on top of things, she left the store then, started walking down Broadway, conscious that a couple of young men found her attractive. Her first instinct was to wonder if she'd forgotten to put on a bra and was she bouncing?—her physical appeal was just not something she gave much mind to. She was dark, olive skinned, and her eyes seemed large and no one had ever complained about her face but that had to do with genes, not personal attainment, and—

—and glancing in an angled storefront then, she realized that her husband was behind her and that something unusual was going on. Oh, she realized immediately, he's trying to look *casual*. For a moment she was tempted to turn and greet him but clearly he was more interested in tracking than contact, so she decided, with no thought whatsoever, to give him something that would *really* interest him.

Up ahead, coming toward her, eyeing her, was a large young man, well muscled, wearing a Columbia T-shirt. Melissa, no expert when it came to wiles, wished for a moment she had a handkerchief, so she might adroitly drop it. Making do, she waited till he was just a few feet away.

At which time she winked at him . . .

Babe, trying to be inconspicuous, stood in front of the drugstore while this bozo in a T-shirt was occupying his wife. What the hell right did he have? Babe wondered.

He glanced quickly at them—

—and Melissa was giggling at something he'd said. Oh so shyly.

Melissa *never* giggled. Not with him. If he hadn't been following her, he'd have walked right up, but since he had been, he needed a moment or two to get his innocence back.

Now, in that moment, the bozo was offering her a cigarette—

—and she was *accepting*.

But you don't smoke, Babe wanted to shout. You never in your life smoked, you told me that.

Now the bozo was lighting it for her.

"Hi, darling," Babe heard himself call then, hurrying up to them.

Melissa looked at him blankly, then turned to the T-shirt. "Is he talking to you?"

"Melissa, stop this—"

"Why don't you just move on, fella," the T-shirt said.

"Yeah, fella, move on," Melissa said.

Babe stared at them. "I'm her husband," he explained. "And she's noted far and wide for her sense of humor."

"He was following me," Melissa said. "Does that sound like the kind of thing a husband would do?"

"A whim," Babe said. "And am I ever sorry." Then he saw what she was carrying. "What are you doing with a cookbook, for chrissakes?"

The T-shirt took a half step backward, was looking at them both now, from one to the other, back and forth.

Melissa brought the cigarette to her lips, tried an inhale, began coughing and when that was done, broke out laughing. "I'm sorry," she managed, to the T-shirt; "I truly am."

"This is very much like *Who's Afraid of Virginia Woolf,*" the T-shirt said. He took a step away. "And I think you two ought to work on your relationship, while there's still time." Then he left them, moved on.

"We better work on something," Melissa said, looking up at Babe. "Following your own wife. For shame."

"It's the day," Babe said. "I was just kind of enjoying watching people watch you. You're so smart, and every so often I guess I forget how lovely you are."

"I may bottle you yet," Melissa said, going up on tiptoe, kissing his cheek. "I'm off to the supermarket, stranger; the frozen food compartment. Any preferences for dinner or you want I should surprise you?"

"Surprise me."

Melissa kissed him quickly again. "I think I could have scored with that guy; you have been warned."

Babe smiled and they separated. He was in a wonderful mood now, really, and he turned, took a last glance at her departing form, thinking the words, "What a pretty girl, what nice legs."

And his mood was shaken.

Because that was a quote, from the end of an Irwin Shaw, "The Girls in Their Summer Dresses." His brother had gifted him with that story collection, his brother whom he alone called "Doc," whose employers knew him as Scylla.

Every so often—no, more than that, much more than that, the impossibility of Doc's being dead sideswiped Babe. He had loved only one woman, Melissa, had worshiped only one man, and that had been his brother. It was on days like this when Doc was most suddenly with him, on season-changing afternoons.

Doc seemed to ride in when the wind was warm . . .

## 2

Scylla arrived in Washington with his almanac in hand. It had kept him entertained on the flight north. It was eleven thirty when he picked up his blue suitcase from the carousel, sighed as he set out to follow Perkins' first instruction, which was to go to the bank of phones opposite the United area, reach under the third phone from the left, take the envelope that would be taped there.

The envelope contained a key to a locker on the far side of the airport. Scylla walked to the locker, knowing full well what would be inside: another key to another locker, this one at the train station.

He was right and he was wrong: it did contain another key, only to the main bus station. Scylla taxied there, in heavy traffic over rotten roads, knowing that the bus station locker would contain the train station locker key.

And he was right. Perkins was a wonderful man, yes, but he had this sadistic sense of humor when it came to Scylla's dislike of Division mumbo-jumbo.

On the way to the train station, half an hour wasted, Scylla sat back and tried to figure some minor revenge that would really get to Perkins, just rankle the shit out of him. Nothing came to mind. It was hard to think of ways of nailing Perkins. Hard for him anyway. Partly because the man was just so smart and, of course, partly because of the business at the Connaught Hotel.

Decades back. Scylla's first job. Ever. Not even a job really. All he had to do was book at the Connaught Hotel for dinner (he had never eaten there, had heard it was the best in all England, was excited by that as well as his work).

And at ten o'clock, precisely at ten, using pure deductive reasoning, he was to ascertain who the other operative was in the room, make contact via a password.

Simple enough.

Plus one final condition: he must not arouse suspicion.

If he could do this, they assured him, they would give him something a bit more complex in the near future. Something, they hinted, dangerous. He hoped so. He had not gone through their training program to end with a desk job.

He arrived at the dining room at eight, was given a table for two along the near wall. He gave the place a quick glance, was stunned at the elegance, the beauty of the aged, oiled wood, the serenity of the restaurant. Of course it was jammed, and trying to deduce who the contact was would be extraordinarily difficult. At least now. But at ten, traffic would have thinned, he would be able to do his job quickly and casually and to perfection. He was naturally gifted at reading faces; names he had trouble remembering, but that was of no matter tonight.

He had a glass of champagne while he perused the menu and the wine list. He decided on the quail egg appetizer, the grilled calves liver and bacon for a main course, accompanied by creamed spinach and *pomme soufflé*. For a wine he had limitations: not the list, which was vast, or the price, which mattered not at all to Division employees. But though he was a good drinker, he knew a full bottle of wine would dull him, so he had to pick a half, and the selection was, of course, smaller; he settled on a '55 Ausone.

Hey all you Ivy League assholes on Wall Street, I'm an undercover wizard, a secret operative, a confidential agent, a . . . a . . .

. . . fug . . .

Scylla could not believe his luck. Black and bleak and horrid: he *knew* someone else in the room. Some teacher (what the hell was his name?), some guy who had come to Yale and lectured on the future gains to be made by using computers to investigate history. Maybe eight years ago

Scylla had heard him talk, had taken a few meals with the guy—

—but what if the guy remembered? And came over? And in general made a pest of himself. He was eating alone too, maybe he was lonely, and Scylla's bosses had specifically said, *"Do not arouse suspicion."*

How did you get rid of a guy you kind of knew if he didn't want to be gotten rid of? Without arousing suspicion? Take it easy, Jesus, Scylla cautioned himself. You've seen him but he hasn't seen you. Don't sweat it.

He got up, quickly took the other seat at the small table, so his back was to the professor. He could feel his tension ease. He signaled for the sommelier, requested more champagne.

By 9:45 he realized, sadly, that the finest *de luxe* meal of his life thus far was ending—he had only two spoonfuls of *crême brulée* left.

Ah well, take the bitter with the sweet.

He expertly scanned the room without seeming to, immediately knew who his contact was—a small man with thinning hair who was just too careful not to glance in his direction.

At 9:53, just seven minutes before the successful completion of his first task, a couple of things happened that more or less displeased him. The small man with the thinning hair finished paying his bill and left abruptly.

And the professor descended—"How *are* you, odd I didn't notice you before—"

Scylla stood, stammered, "Hi, Professor, this is sure a surprise—"

"—and a pleasant one," the professor replied, sitting at the other seat without even being asked, "—and pleasant surprises must not go unnoticed, have you had the port? —they've got some '31 Noval, legendary, legendary," and he quickly gave the order to the sommelier, who scurried off.

At 9:57, Scylla, thoroughly unnerved, came unglued. It

began quite innocently when the other man smiled expansively at the emptying restaurant and said, "I prefer this room."

Scylla nodded. "Fabulous food," he agreed, but as he said it, the thought crossed his mind that the professor had said "prefer," which meant "like better than something else." "Prefer it to what, sir?"

"Why, the Grill, of course."

"Of course," Scylla said quickly. "The Grill." He was finding it very hard controlling his tone. "Which grill exactly do you mean?"

"Why the other dining room, that grill."

*Shit,* Scylla thought, nobody told me there were two rooms, and here it was two minutes before contact and he was in the wrong place—"Off to the loo," he managed, wanting to run, except jogging through the dining room of the Connaught Hotel was not exactly your best way of not arousing suspicion, so he kept his speed under control, asked at the desk where the Grill Room was, made his way there at precisely ten.

Which was when he realized in his panic he had forgotten the password.

Did Division draw and quarter incompetents? What would they do? Chain him up someplace where he couldn't do any damage. *Stop this,* he commanded. Use logic. If you'll just use a little ordinary logic, you'll come up with the password, any fool could and you've just proved you're not just any fool, you're *special.*

But then what difference did it make?—no one in the Grill Room looked remotely like a contact. It was emptying, and there were two only large tables left, both occupied by formally dressed couples.

When he sat back down in the restaurant, the sommelier was finished pouring the port.

Could the sommelier be the contact?

*Stop doing this to yourself*—think!

"So what are you doing in London?" the professor asked.

"Thinking."

The other man looked at him rather strangely.

"Think-tank work, sir, that sort of business."

"Taste this, please," the professor said, and as they raised their glasses he said, "I'm not unfamiliar with that field, which particular think tank sent you over?'

"I'd rather not say, sir, if you don't mind."

"That sounds rather suspicious, doesn't it?"

*Jesus Christ, now you've aroused his suspicions*. "Delicious port," he said, "fabulous." It was, but he wasn't truly concentrating because a lone woman had entered the room, sat across the room, looked quickly at him, even more quickly away.

So his contact had arrived. Late though. Should he report her? No. Everybody made mistakes. The important thing was she was there. If only he could remember the password.

"They say only the English truly appreciate great port, but I dispute that," the professor said.

And right then Scylla wanted to hug the intruder, because the password had to do with things English. English what though? A town? Was "village" the word? No. Shakespeare was English though, that's what it was, something from Shakespeare. Yes—*The Merchant of Venice!* No. "Venice" was the town. That was the word.

Except "Venice" was a word, and it was certainly a town, but it was not now and never would be English.

Double fug.

The lone woman smiled as three men arrived, kissed her cheek, sat with her, asked for menus.

Scylla finished his glass of port, realized several things by the time he was done with his second: (a) he was a bit beyond tipsy; (b) he had no idea what the password was; (c) it was almost ten thirty now; (d) he had totally, totally failed.

"'Hamlet,' you asshole," the professor said then.

"Sir?"

"The password was 'Hamlet.' We often use it for first-timers because, well, *it's fucking impossible to forget*."

"I was close," Scylla said. "You've got to believe me."

"I do—no one could lie about a thing like that." He shook his head. "I am here because we often like to throw a little bit of adversity in the way of our beginners, check their reactions. Before we make our report."

"What's the grade below failing?"

"Don't be silly, I'm going to give you a rave, you fool, an all-out vote of confidence."

"Why?"

"Because you've done so extraordinarily in training. And because I believe in second chances. But mostly because I haven't enjoyed anything as much as these last forty-five minutes in years. I have been honored with attending the greatest balls-up since Chamberlain believed Hitler. If you continue work of this caliber, we'll make you a double agent and let you ruin the Russians. Have some more port."

"Thank you, Professor."

"My name is Perkins, you drooling fool. Alfred Perkins. My intimates call me 'Ma' but you will never be an intimate, since they all must be able to read and write at the very least at the kindergarten level."

Then they both broke out laughing . . .

It was close to one when Scylla entered his suite at the Madison Hotel. The locker at the train station contained a smaller matching blue suitcase and a piece of paper with the word "Madison." Scylla was pleased. Though he'd lived in Washington for years—it was his main base as a Provider—he liked the Madison. Set diagonally across from the *Washington Post* it was, to his taste, the best D.C. offered.

When he checked in—Bede no longer; Perkins had informed him at the end of their New Orleans call that he was "Richard Blaine for the nonce," Bogart's name in *Casablanca,* Perkins' favorite film—there was a message for him in Perkins' hand. He did not open it until he was alone in his suite. The writing was flowery as ever, not so the words: "Pick me up at seven." That was the entirety.

Six hours of freedom. He decided to visit the Four Seasons Hotel set at the edge of Georgetown, on Pennsylvania. He had heard it was supposed to be a lovely place. Where lovely women lunched. He had been away now for a long time. And he was hungry. For food too . . .

## 3

Martha Anne sat amidst the greenery of the Four Seasons Hotel, sipping tea, dreading what was certainly to follow: sitting alongside her on the banquette, Colby would not stop flirting—eye play only thus far—with the handsome suntanned man two tables away. And when Colby flirted, success was a certain by-product. Colby was now, at thirty-two, what she had been at ten, an empty-headed knockout.

Martha Anne had been in this position before, she knew the steps in the charade. Soon, the man would make his approach. Colby would engage him in double entendres, inflaming the man's interest. Chitchat would go on and on—and she, Martha Anne, with her wonderful figure but poor plain face, might just as well be on Saturn. Then Colby would turn and say, "Martha Anne, you're going to be late for your appointment and we don't want that, do we?" and Martha Anne would feign surprise and leave.

Humiliated.

Again.

Why am I here, Martha Anne wondered. Whatever the reasons for their friendship once were, they no longer computed. Colby was elegant, twice divorced, rich forever from alimony, with no interest in anything she couldn't buy. And she, good old plain old Martha Anne, was a reasonable success as a businesswoman, she had a fine antique shop on Madison Avenue in New York but better than the shop was her lease: she had signed a twenty-year job when the city was going bankrupt in '76, already had rejected an offer of over half a million cash from her dyspeptic landlord. She came to D.C. twice a year, to see what was going on at the Hirshhorn but more than that, to check out the furniture at the glorious antique shop just !ross the way from the Four Seasons. And every time she came, out of duty or guilt or some other sickness, she saw Colby for lunch or dinner and enjoyed it not at all. Their parents had been friends. Was that a good enough reason to be miserable? Probably.

Oh God, here he came, growing more attractive as he approached. Martha Anne had not realized, while he was sitting, the obvious power of the body inside the clothes.

"May I rely on the kindness of strangers?" he said, smiling at Colby.

Colby flicked a smile back, turned to Martha Anne. "Up to you."

"Sure," Martha Anne said, knowing Colby would kill her if she'd said anything different. She gestured toward the empty chair across from them, watched as he sat.

"I've only the afternoon," the man said. "If you only had an afternoon, what would you do in a city you've never been?"

"What do you want to get into?" Colby said, casually emphasizing the final word.

"Again?"

"What are your interests?"

"Beauty."

"Old or young? Martha Anne here is into old beauty, antiques; I'm not like that."

They talked on and on, and Martha Anne listened and watched, and the more she did, the more she realized she could not help blushing, because—was she going crazy? —the more they talked the more she became convinced of one lunatic wonderful thing: this suntanned creature who had appeared before them was interested in *her.* At two thirty she took a deep breath, did perhaps the bravest thing she'd ever done, risked all: "Colby," she said, "you're going to be late for your appointment and we don't want that, do we?"

* * *

"You just permanently altered a decades-old relationship, you know that?" Martha Anne said. It was two forty-five and they were in her room at the Four Seasons. "Here I am in a room with you and I don't know that I want that."

"Then you must ask me to leave."

"You know damn well I won't."

"Come here then."

She moved to him by the window. They embraced. He kissed her several times. All so gently.

"I don't even know your first name," Martha Anne said.

"And I don't know your last. Nor do I want to."

She pushed away. "This is just a one-night stand, that it?"

"If you don't relax it won't be that. A one-afternoon stand sounds better, don't you think?"

"Why didn't you take Colby? Everybody always has."

"I didn't fancy combat."

Martha Anne thought about that for a moment. "Good point, she can be a bitch. But then, so can I."

He shook his head.

"You don't know that."

"From your face," he said.

"My beautiful face reveals all, that it?"

"Your body is beautiful, your face is kind."

"Can you ever talk—has anybody turned you down?"

"Not in recent years."

"Why are you smiling?"

"No matter, please come here."

"I don't want to sleep with you."

"Fine. But lie with me. We'll undress each other and slip between the sheets and hold each other and sing sad songs."

"Can I do you first?"

"The order doesn't matter, just so we both end up naked."

She took off his jacket, undid his tie, began to unbutton his shirt. "Your skin is warm."

"It's been in the sun."

"Where?"

"I really don't know. South somewhere."

"I want to sleep with you, I lied before."

"Probably we can work that into our agenda."

She pulled his shirt out from his trousers, carefully laid it across the back of a chair. While she was turned away, his hands began unbuttoning her dress. She moved sharply away. "I'm not good at sex," she said.

"You do have an exalted opinion of yourself."

"This is all going to be a disaster—I haven't been near anyone for a year—why does *that* make you smile?"

"A year is not such a long time for some people." He moved toward her. "Now finish up."

She took off the rest of his clothes, stood very still while he undressed her. While he was taking off the bedspread, she said, "I'll just be frigid, you'll hate it."

"It's all right, I won't be able to get an erection, happy?"

She started to laugh.

He lifted her easily, set her down between the sheets, moved alongside, began to massage her body, whispered: "Years from now, when you talk about this, and you will, be kind . . ."

"Damn," Martha Anne said. It was five thirty, and she lay in bed, watched him start to dress. "And I was supposed to have this really exciting afternoon antique shopping."

"Sorry about that."

"I'll forgive you, I'm not into grudge holding, McGivern."

"Again?"

"That's my last name—you can maybe call me sometime if you're in the city—if you phone long enough in advance, I think there's a good chance I might make myself available."

"You're very sweet, but I won't call."

"Why?"

"Best."

"I don't mean anything serious—we could just go out as, don't get sick on me now, friends."

"I don't have friends."

"Why?"

"Best."

She got out of bed then, came into his arms. "I don't want to bug you or anything, but what the hell do you do?"

"Terrible things."

"And people do that to you too, don't they?" She indicated his scar.

"I got that out of love. Someone was menacing someone I cared for. I stopped thinking for an instant, and it cost me."

"Was she beautiful? The one you cared for?"

"Six feet plus and skinny."

She looked confused.

"Kid brother."

She started to say something, stopped, kissed him.

He held her awhile. Then they broke and he continued dressing, more quickly now.

"Do me just one thing: say you *might* call."

"Okay."

"You mean it?"

"Do I have to mean it?"

"Yes."

"Then I do."

"I just *knew* I was irresistible," Martha Anne said. When he was dressed she said, "Are you off to do terrible things now?"

"Probably not till tomorrow."

"But you never would to me."

"No, you're safe."

"Why?"

"Because you're gentle."

"Is that so important?"

"Gentleness is next to godliness. Never forget that . . ."

## 4

Since Division Headquarters was not called Division Headquarters, and since the organization made every attempt to seem inconspicuously down at the heels, renting a foul building on the outskirts of a black Washington slum, Perkins' limousine was not a limousine. He had a driver, certainly, and the driver was always properly turned out, but the car itself was an old station wagon, the backseat customized for strength, in consideration of the amplitude of its chief passenger.

Promptly at seven, his soft-sided briefcase, as always, crammed, he waddled to the street, looked around for a moment, another moment, then got in the back unaided. He was convinced the car was bugged so he said, "Fuck Communism," and waved to the driver to get going.

He opened his briefcase, took out some papers, began speed-reading. He was always able to do more than anyone, making up in mental quickness for his slowness afoot.

At ten after, he raised his head, said, very loudly, "All pinkos are pork packers," thought about that briefly, then said to the driver, "Do you know what a pork packer is?"

"I've no idea, sir."

Perkins shook his head. "Slang is in a sad way, I fear; since it's now indistinguishable from everyday speech. A 'pork packer,' " he said, again loudly, for the benefit of the bug, "is a person with a morbid fondness for dead bodies, a common pinko practice—after all, what else have they got to do?"

He reached into his case for a thick folder, licked his thumb, began his attack. It kept him occupied until half past, when the car turned into the gravel driveway of his house. The place was small, relatively desolate, the nearest neighbor being a quarter mile down the quiet road. There was a small apartment over the two-car garage, and the driver went there after he'd parked, closed the garage door while Perkins entered his house through the kitchen doorway, called out "Little Orphan Annie has come to our house to stay," as he made his slow trek to the stairs, took a deep breath, slowly mounted.

Edna awaited him at the top. He kissed her cheek, then asked his older sister how the day had gone.

Edna, vigorous as ever as she approached eighty, made a "*comme si, comme ça*" wiggling gesture with her right hand.

"I'll take over," Perkins said.

"Don't overdo now."

"You mean give up my triathlon training? Never."

"I mean sleep. At least some."

"Oh, shoo."

She nodded, smiled, descended the stairs, began the brisk quarter-mile walk to her place.

Perkins entered his wife's bedroom—once it had been *their* bedroom, but that was before the accident. "Felicity Perkins," he said, approaching the bed. "You here. Fancy. Such a surprise." She was your basic vegetable but that didn't stop him from prattling on as he circled the bed, his tone like a ten-year-old's addressing a beloved doll or pet. "And looking so pretty, but then when weren't you? Want to hear about my day?" He paused a moment. "Okay, now tell me about yours." He paused again. "Okay, now get yourself all comfortable; let me help." He walked to the bed, moved her heavy body gently, fluffed her pillows. "Any favorite programs on tonight? Which station?" He waited. "Okay, why don't I just put it on two and you holler if you want me to change it." He fiddled with the sound. "Too loud?" Pause. "Okay, you're right, too loud." He tuned it softer. "I'll be just next door in the study, if you want anything, give a holler, promise?" Pause. "Oh, stop it, how could *you* ever be a bother to *me?*"

He left her then, dumped his case next door in his study

where he slept now, waddled to the kitchen, flicked on the intercom, buzzed the chauffeur's apartment, said, "Get over here," and when the uniformed man appeared, a few moments later, Perkins scowled and grumbled, "You drive putrescently."

"Sticks and stones, Ma," Scylla said.

"Pickles, shall I have pickles?—decisions, decisions, yes, of course I shall." Perkins hovered over the kitchen table which was literally covered with sandwich makings. "How does this sound to you, Scylla? Envision it as I speak."

Scylla, a cold bottle of beer in hand, lounged against the stove, closed his eyes.

"On three pieces of seeded rye bread, I propose the following: corned beef, pastrami, tongue, cole slaw, Russian dressing."

"I see you've got your anorexia well in hand."

"It's a constant battle—please answer."

" 'Heavy' on the Russian?"

"But *naturellement*."

"Then you have my permission to proceed." As he watched Perkins set to work on his creation, Scylla said, "I find one thing bothersome."

"Ease your mind."

"Since we seem to have eradicated half the civilized world in getting me secretly to town, why is it safe, my being here, in your home, chatting away."

"Because it *is* my home. Because if anyone tried photographing us from outside, they would find my abode comes outfitted with distortion windows. And they wouldn't get here easily—my elder sister lives down the road, along with several of our people. The entire area is more or less wired. This is not a heavily populated part of the countryside. Strangers would be noticed. All kinds of other precautions go with the territory. If someone came for me here, I might not defeat them, but they would not take me unawares. But you of all people should know why it's safe *only* here—we do not, except when things get out of control, involve family. Once I leave my office, at the end of the day, until I return the following morning, there is relatively little surveillance—and we honor our enemies similarly. I've never done business personally here until tonight. They bug my car only because I know it and that it infuriates me. I, in turn, have bugged my Russian equivalent's office washroom. He hasn't got much positive to say about democracy." His fat hands moved with surgical precision, as he piled the meats one atop the other, making sure the center of the sandwich didn't get too high. He added the second piece of rye, began spooning cole slaw, when he cocked his head, muttered, "Excuse me," hurried away.

Scylla watched from the kitchen door as Perkins huffed up the stairs, entered the room at the top, spoke a few muffled words, exited, closed the door behind him, came back down. "Felicity unwell?" Scylla asked.

Perkins stopped, stared. "Omigod, you don't know, do you?"

"I think Gore Vidal it was, made a wonderful remark. He and Tennessee Williams were talking and Williams said, 'I was drunk all through the sixties,' and Vidal said, 'Don't worry, you didn't miss a thing.' I'm sort of behind on the eighties, Ma. Catching up hourly, but I doubt I qualify for expert yet."

"I was driving us home three years ago. Five minutes away. Pissed out of my skull. Things went a bit awry. I suffered scratches, Felicity, everything—please don't feel compelled to say you're sorry, I'm sorry enough for all of us." He walked back into the kitchen, completed the cole slaw sculpting, added the Russian, then turned to Scylla. "Envision this now please: two pieces of lightly toasted white bread, between which I propose to place white meat of turkey, chopped liver, bermuda onion thickly sliced, lettuce, tomato and Hellman's mayonnaise."

"I prefer your first concoction."

"You know the most disgraceful thing about the accident, from my point of view?"

Scylla shook his head.

"I still drink and drive," Perkins said. He busied himself

then, made a second perfect sandwich, went to a cupboard, got out two large plates, put both the sandwiches on the first, handed the empty one to Scylla. "There's yogurt in the fridge if you prefer," Perkins said.

Scylla laughed, grabbed some bread, got busy. "Why was I brought back?" he said then.

Perkins surrounded his sandwiches with a ring of half-sour dills. "I'll get to that in time."

"Thumbnail it at least."

"I don't know, to save the world, I suppose."

"Oh, ho hum, that," Scylla said.

"About your brother," Perkins said, rubbing his stomach. They were upstairs in his study, he was working on his second sandwich, Scylla his third beer.

"I didn't ask about him."

"But you wouldn't mind hearing, would you now, 'fess up."

"No, Ma, I wouldn't mind at all; is he happy, say yes."

"My data comes from our computers—I read about him this very afternoon—I couldn't risk a printout, it might have seemed odd if anyone had seen and fully a tenth of our people also work for them—at least we're *sure* of a tenth—we have that many and more of their people working for us—you'll have to trust my memory. Computers aren't much into happiness, I'm afraid, but he's certainly doing wonderfully well."

"Teaching? Writing?—"

"—both, and hush, I don't want to forget anything." He closed his eyes a moment, then looked at Scylla, started to talk. "Thomas B. Levy. Associate Professor of History at Columbia. Two books, both well received, one on McCarthy, a second on the failings of the Supreme Court over the years. Numerous articles in dreary learned journals—'dreary' is my own interpolation, not the machine's. And I suspect—another interpolation of my own coming up—that his wife may be brighter than he is—"

"—no shit," Scylla said, raising his beer bottle into

toasting position. "The kid went and got married, son of a bitch, fantastic, who is she?"

"Melissa Biesenthal, daughter of the *head* of the history department—no fool he, your brother—"

"—fuck you," Scylla said, "he doesn't need help to get where he's going."

"The reason I suspect her brightness is that your brother was mid-twenties before getting his Ph.D., whereas she got hers at twenty-two. A philologist. Teaches in New York, travels all over on various consulting jobs, California, Illinois, recently to Europe. Home: 465 Riverside Drive, near Columbia, I forget the zip code, you'll have to excuse me." Then he paused, cocked his head listening, said "Excuse me" again, paid his wife a visit down the hall.

Scylla went into the corridor. "Can I help?" he asked when Perkins emerged.

"Nothing much to do, really. I keep thinking I hear her calling. Probably the television. It *is* the television. Felicity does not verbalize much these days." He looked at Scylla now. "And you stop what you're thinking."

"Computers read minds now?"

"No—but it's so obvious—the only time your eyes have truly come alive is when I was giving the résumé. You're thinking of paying him a visit, aren't you?"

Scylla shrugged.

"Well, don't—don't ever—unless you want to kill him. Kill *them*, he has a wife now."

"Bullshit."

"He was *involved* with us—not through his doing, but he knows things—unimportant things—why do you think he's alive?—only because you're dead. You are an important thing. If you visited, if anyone saw or found out, they would, I assure you, also pay him a visit—and find out where you were and under what name—and once they had forced it from him, or her, they wouldn't leave much to incriminate them. If you visit him, you risk killing him—"

"—Jesus Christ, I wasn't planning to move in—"

"—if you visit him, you risk killing him. Say 'bullshit' again, why don't you?"

Long pause. Then, quietly, sadly, ". . . no . . . no bullshit, Ma. I'm not about to put him at risk, believe that."

Perkins draped an arm around the bigger man's shoulders. "I said I wanted you to save the world, I never said it was worth saving." He started back into his study. "Come, let's switch to Scotch and go to the movies . . ."

"Why you dirty pudgy old man," Scylla said, staring at the images coming from the television screen in the study.

"Hush, this is serious business, you fool."

On the screen now, in badly lit black and white, a muscular Negro was cornholing a smaller white man, while on a sofa nearby, all but out of focus, a large-breasted woman was sitting on a fragile, gray-haired effeminate man, sitting, more precisely, on his organ, raising her splendid body up and down.

"What happens next?" Scylla asked. "When does Candy Barr come on?"

"These are hot off the presses, as it were—the tape quality can be accounted for that Standish's apartment isn't set up to be a movie studio."

"Standish?"

"The humper on the couch. Quite remarkable performance from him actually; his inclinations tend more toward the dark-skinned gentleman." Now Standish was in close focus and Perkins pressed a button on his remote, froze the picture. "Remarkable machines, these."

"That's a VHS VCR, I take it," Scylla said.

"Don't sound so proud about it."

"I saw an ad in a paper that resembled yours, just checking, go on."

"Milo Standish. Remember him."

Scylla nodded.

"Fifty-two, lives in the Village, independently wealthy, inventor, scientist, internationally acknowledged as totally loathsome, equally brilliant." He changed cassettes then, and the sex scene was gone, replaced by a funeral. "Our men took these, better quality, don't you think?"

Scylla nodded, studied the color picture on the screen. It seemed to be a very well attended funeral in a tiny cemetery. Most of the mourners were young. Except for one, the most distraught, a bearded sweet-faced man.

"Two children were just buried," Perkins said, his voice beginning to strain. "The boy was a wonder, the girl a glory, she had a sick mother, she tended to her needs, not an easy task for a child."

Now the camera was on the weeping sweet-faced man. "Grandfather?" Scylla asked.

"Murderer," Perkins said, freezing the picture on the tear-stained face. "Remember him too: J.F. Vaughan, known to the world as 'Arky' after the great Pittsburgh baseball player. A sports fanatic, retired science professor, Princeton. Still lives there, has his own lab in the basement of his house, works alone, relatively weak heart, improbably strong mind."

Scylla was about to speak when Perkins was on his feet with remarkable speed, because this time it did seem as if a sound had come from the adjoining bedroom. Scylla went to the hall as Perkins hurried to his wife.

Even in the hall, the odor was strong.

Scylla moved to the doorway, saw the elephantine Perkins doing his best to maneuver his immobile wife, but he had already downed one large Scotch, and his hands were not as nimble as they might be. Scylla entered, started to help.

"Please," Perkins said. "There's no need."

"Just trying to speed things, Ma." He turned her body, took off her gown, set to work cleaning her.

"I can do all this, Scylla, I do it every night."

"Get me another diaper, why don't you, and a towel and gown."

Perkins got them.

When he had cleaned her, the odor was gone. He handed the soiled material to Perkins, quickly got her back in order, did his best to make her comfortable, all the while thinking of the tone in Perkins' voice when he was describing the girl who had been buried, of the weeping bearded face of the murderer that was still frozen in close-up on the foul VHS VCR.

"Most people don't like going near her when she's like that," Perkins said as they began to leave. "Just my sister and myself."

"I count that good company," Scylla said.

"Go on ahead, why don't you?"

Scylla nodded, left, tried not to listen as Perkins whispered, ". . . I'll just be in the next room, give a holler if the fancy strikes, okay . . . ?" A pause. Then, ". . . yes, it is Scylla, but I don't think we ought to tell anyone . . ." Another pause. ". . . yes, it's amazing the difference, but then, surgery is amazing these days . . ." A final pause then: ". . . of course you'll be fine, you'll be wonderful, you're getting better each and every day . . ."

In the study, Scylla got tired of looking at the murderer, played with the remote until the picture went away. "Good of you, that," Perkins said on entering.

"Stop it, just pour." He indicated their Scotch glasses.

Perkins refilled their glasses, took a long pull on his. "There's so much to cover, I'll try to be brief, if you have questions, ask, but the subtext of everything is this: there's going to be a world war, America is going to start it, and counting you, three of us know."

Scylla was about to ask who the third was, decided that could wait, gestured for Perkins to get on with it.

"Actually, the beginning came at a rather remarkable meeting in the Pentagon during the peak of the Ayatollah hostage thing. We were all there, those of us who counted, to hear the Pentagon's plan for rescue, which was roughly this—there was a football field next to the embassy, and they proposed to land a shitload of marines, all heavily armed, who were to quickly surround the entire area, field and compound, and begin a murderous field of fire—that was the exact quote—and while that was going on, others were to storm the embassy, get as many hostages out alive as they could.

"There was the usual burping and farting you get with the military and then someone familiar with Iran said this—that the area was very heavily populated, that the entire population was very heavily armed, and a horrendous bloodbath was certain whereas this person—it was, I must admit, yours truly—asked why, if we had to abandon diplomacy, why didn't we simply use a nerve gas we have which does nothing more than put everyone to sleep and gives them terrible headaches for the next day or two. And the Pentagon spokesman said—and I quote: 'We can't do that—*it's bad for our image.*'"

Scylla broke out laughing. "You really mean that?"

Perkins nodded. "The reason that was the beginning of where we are today is it became very clear that the military was not as interested in fighting enemies as in public relations. All the branches are jealous of each other, as are all the secret forces. From that meeting forward, Division has become really extraordinarily powerful. The CIA's budget is one and a half billion. National Security gets ten billion. I needn't deal with mathematics but we are not in financial need."

"What are you spending it on?"

"Do you know what the Black Goyas are?"

Scylla nodded, said he thought they were the only reason for visiting Madrid.

"Then you know that that is the one time in all of art history when a genius allowed himself to deal solely with the darkest sides of our nature. In our own way, that's what we're doing too. What do you know about weapons?"

"I know that wars don't kill people, weapons do."

Perkins smiled, drank. "You know of my interest with computers and history. I've done rather a lovely bit of research on killing power. Giving a sword, for example, the power number 'one'—which is arbitrary but allow me that."

"You're allowed."

"Well, if a sword is 'one' then the power of the flintlock

rifle is 'five.' And a modern assault rifle approximately 'two hundred.' Zooming up the scale, a light machine gun is 'one thousand,' a multiple rocket launcher with nerve gas rockets rates 'one million,' a Soviet ICBM with a twenty-five-megaton warhead is a billion times as powerful as our once lethal sword. Pretend you're not a dunce—what's wrong with weapons of such magnitude?''

"Obvious—we ain't the only ones what has them."

"Smart lad. And all the current talk of weapons systems—you don't know about it but take my word—has the same problem. All useless once the enemy has it, all such Star Wars talk is bullshit. But, what if we had something no one else had?''

"We did. Back in the forties—the bomb. We didn't use it after the war was over and I don't think we'd act any differently today."

"Six months ago you would have been right. Even three. But now, right now, at this precise period, the pendulum has swung. And I alone am here to tell you."

"How can you be so arrogantly sure?"

"Toy dolls," Perkins said. "Toy dolls are the tea leaves of war. And only I can read them."

"Fantastic," Scylla said, suddenly excited, out of his chair—"I'll blast Barbie and Ken, and once they're gone, I'll attack all our teddy bear factories."

"Ye of little faith."

"Come on, Ma, Jesus, Timothy Leary used to make more sense than you do."

"Are you aware that, etymologically, the word 'doll' connects with the word 'nightmare'? Thus linking dolls with magic and superstition."

"Don't you use a word like 'thus' to me." He went to the Scotch bottle, poured them each some more.

"I do tend to be pompous on occasion, probably because I'm so much brighter than anyone else."

"At least you're humbler."

And now Perkins was excited. "Listen to me—this is the

most extraordinary thing—all my life, I've been wondering if there was a connection between war causes. Because, everyone knows wars are not healthy—even the lowest in intelligence know you can get hurt in a war. But they happen and they happen. Why? Was there a single connective? I ran computer tests on everything conceivable. I'm talking years, Scylla. And then I stumbled onto this: the rising tide of patriotism in America paralleled a phenomenal growth in toy dolls—*action figures*—*male* dolls."

Scylla sat back down.

"Historically, female dolls have a twelve-to-one ratio over male dolls. But last year, the most successful industry on the stock market was the toy industry—almost twice above any other—and the most successful segment of the toy industry was action figures. Males over females. This was not true in earlier years. So I began to research. And it's rough, yes, but it worked in every case I could sample—in Germany in thirty-six, in Japan in forty-one—the action figures boom in popularity, they're surrogate fighting men, only soon they become reality. I've researched dozens of wars, believe me. It's true—it's always true. It's not by accident the words 'doll' and 'nightmare' are joined at the hip. America will start a war soon."

"Then why don't we just sit back and enjoy it?"

"There are—to use present Pentagon terms—two kinds of people in the world: 'Godists' and 'Bloodies.' Godists, of which we are two, believe that the best way to improve existence is slowly, with mutual assistance, one person helping another, one nation doing the same; in other words, Godists believe in some kind of gradual decency. The Bloodies don't, they want quick change at any cost. Fortunately, the Godists are in control almost all the time. But there are windows—windows of danger—when the doll sales soar, when the Bloodies lead, when the wars begin. But those windows are small. If you can delay things, the Godists regain command, the Bloodies lick their wounds."

"And I'm to delay things?"

"That is our hope."

"Our?"

"Yes, Beverage is in on this too, of course. He's the third of our trio that knows."

Scylla blinked, his mind back in the airport as the hundreds of girls chased screaming across the check-in area, chasing the imagined Menudo, for surely that was as shocking as this: no one alive hated him, not as much as Beverage. Probably not ever.

"Why did you say, just now, 'of course'?"

"Beverage is Policy, Scylla; he heads Division."

"But . . . in New Orleans, Fountain said you were Policy here."

"I am. But once we began to swell, it was determined to move headquarters far away, not draw attention. Beverage has lived in England for four years. Actually, he was all but overjoyed when I suggested you return."

The girls were screaming in the airport again. "The Prick? Overjoyed? Not possible."

"I know. It's strange—perhaps he's mellowed toward you—I never realized quite how deep your dislike went for each other until he began so passionately to court your lovely wife before the divorce was final."

Scylla said nothing for a while.

"What's on your mind?"

"The birds on my island. I used to chase them through the trees. I miss that." He rubbed his eyes. "Who am I to delay?"

"We have so many experiments going on. One group in California is trying to make cancer contagious. Another group in Oregon is convinced they can make people burst into flames. A sweet group of doctors in Maine is attempting to make all children girls. But these are years away."

"And our two film stars?" He pointed to the VCR.

Perkins handed Scylla a breath atomizer. "Standish uses one identical in every way to this, keep that as a gift if you like, the only difference being that this is a breath atomizer and no more, whereas Standish has developed a substance that causes compliance. Whatever he asks, you do. That man you saw in the homosexual act—the white one—is a homophobe—Standish squirted some of his elixir, asked very hard for compliance, you saw the result."

"And the bearded one at the funeral."

"He has a liquid that causes suicide."

"Jesus Christ, Ma, do you like your work?"

"*It doesn't matter,* don't you see?—it only matters now, because of the window for war. I'm in charge of all the experiments, everyone reports to me, and I say 'Good work, carry on,' but secretly I know it's meaningless—we won't ever use them. Except in the last days, both Standish and Uncle Arky have developed adherents. It's madness, because both their ideas are so flawed—if we used Arky's, we'd have to dispose of a quarter of a billion Russian corpses. And Standish is splendid except no one has the least idea how long the compliance lasts. The only good thing is, they work alone. If they're gone, there aren't an army of assistants ready to step in. Time will pass. The window will shut, we'll all be safe till the next time."

"What the hell did you bring me back for?"

"We hired these people—Division pays them—and now we want them gone—but we can't be connected with such actions in any way—we're going to continue working on weapons, Scylla, whether you and I like it or don't like it—we *need* the scientific community—and if they know *we're* killing them, well, it won't do much for our reputations as equal opportunity employers, you see that, I assume."

"I still don't know what you brought me back for. There must have been others."

"Everyone else has a past. Pasts can be traced. You've none. Now, shall we get on with specifics, or do you want to keep asking me why we brought you back?"

"You're the boss—no, you're not, The Prick is. Beverage is."

"You two will have to deal with your own demons face to face—he wants you in London once you finish here."

"*If* I finish here."

"I have total faith in you on that score—you can kill any man in the room, and you don't care much if you live or die." Perkins smiled. "That gives you an advantage over most people . . ."

# 3

# Midterms

# 1

Uncle Arky sat high in the Princeton gym, as close as he had been, of late, to ecstasy, a word he connected with sex, but when you reached postretirement years, sex seemed as important, at least on some days, as whether or not to have Post Toasties or Raisin Bran for breakfast. Except now, at not much past nine o'clock at night, fortune was smiling.

Because one of the greatest assemblages of young basketball talent—one hundred and ten in all, most of them high school juniors—was on display in his very own hometown. Not South Philly or the steaming playgrounds of D.C. In his Ivy League atmosphere, this nonmirage existed. And not just your ordinary basketball camp, where they did nothing but run and shoot ten hours a day. This was a camp beyond all that—an invitational for the best America possessed, a camp to prepare them not just for sport but for Life. Academic classes in the morning, personal counseling and lectures filled the afternoon—the great Michael Jordan tomorrow or the next day. And then, oh then, with dozens of coaches and college scouts in the stands, and gym rats like himself, the young men were allowed to play in the evenings, free to float and score and perform miracles of their improvisatory devising.

As he watched the splendor unfolding, Uncle Arky was as totally carefree as one with his preoccupations could ask.

"Fuckin' niggers," he heard from behind him.

Uncle Arky whirled, saw the suntanned newcomer sitting in the row behind him, a big man, powerful, with a look of disdain. He turned to Arky. "Can you believe they let those gorillas loose at night?—lock 'em up and lose the key, give the game back to guys what know how to play it."

"Who might that be?" Uncle Arky asked, playing with his Santa Claus beard to hide his irrational irritation.

"Oh, cut the shit."

"I assume you mean Caucasians," Uncle Arky said.

"Are kikes Caucasians?" the suntanned man asked. "Are they like you just said?"

Uncle Arky scowled, turned abruptly back to the gymnasium floor.

"Who are you, Princess Di?"

"I happen, sir, to be a sports fan, which clearly, you are not."

"Bull*shit*—I know everything—and I know ain't no kikes play basketball—the one good thing the niggers have done is run 'em out. But they play other sports, and there's never yet been a good one."

"Sid Luckman was the greatest quarterback the world has ever seen." And now there was an "ahhhh" from the crowd, and Arky whirled, but too late to see what must have been a magnificent dunk. He moved away down the bench.

The suntanned man followed him. "So they can jump," he said. "Kangaroos and frogs do it better. But they got no brains like kikes got no guts."

"Koufax? Koufax was the greatest pitcher in history. I met him. He was a true gentleman—I revered a talent tied to such modesty—"

"Sure—and he chickened out of playing in a Series game on account, he said, it was some kike holiday. The truth, which every sports fan knows, is he knew he was gonna get his socks knocked off."

"Please," Uncle Arky said; "I'm trying to watch."

"How long can you stomach this crap?"

"Till they finish. However late they play—"

"—they go till up to eleven."

"Then I shall be here till that time."

"You're gonna stay put till eleven with nothing but apes for company?"

"Please," Uncle Arky said. "Let's terminate our relationship before you begin giving me your philosophical thoughts concerning those of the Spanish persuasion." Uncle Arky stared at the court for several minutes, before allowing himself a quick turn.

The suntanned bigot was gone.

A relief. Below now, a black giant was blocking a shot with such grace. The dark athletes ran back and forth, and he watched intently until it crossed his mind that the bigot certainly had more than a little interest in learning his whereabouts for the evening.

Odd. Or was it?

Scylla left the gym, went to his car, a red Chevy, drove into the western section of Princeton, passed Uncle Arky's dark house, turned the corner, parked. In the backseat was a holster which he quickly strapped on. Alongside the holster was a wrapped Magnum. He put on a pair of thick gloves, unwrapped the gun, slipped it into its holster, grabbed his blazer, a strong flashlight, went outside, put the jacket on.

He walked to Uncle Arky's house—the mailbox name read, as Perkins had told him, J.F. VAUGHAN. He moved into shadow by the house, waited a moment. Nothing moved. Then he did, quickly, picking the front door lock with no trouble, entering, turning on the flash. Not a terribly impressive living room. The house was a bungalow, on a decent-sized lot, not much character. He crossed to the basement steps, flashed the light ahead of him as he descended, found the laboratory with no trouble at all.

Christ—the bottles. In the center of the large room was an enormous desk and on it, at least a hundred identical glass bottles, all clear liquid inside, all with stoppers, all possessing similar labels. Scylla ran the light across them.

Each label was a typed color. There was "Blue" and

"Thalo Blue." "Amber" and "Burnt Umbre." "Sandy." "Yellow Ochre" and "Indian Yellow" alongside that. "Lavender," "Turquoise." "Gray" and "Lemon" and "Copper" and he was transfixed for the moment, or more than likely he would have been, had he not become instantly aware when the floor he stood on began to crackle, it was electrified, now there was light coming from beneath where he stood, he could feel heat, there was growing heat and the crackling sound increased and he was no beginner, he knew when he was trapped and surely he was that now.

"I'm a very good shot," Uncle Arky said, standing suddenly in the doorway of the glowing room, an almost dainty pistol in his hand. "And you're a very bad thief. If you care to dispute either of those statements, make a move. If not, I suggest you form a cross."

"Jesus—"

"—out fucking wide with your arms!"

The arms went out wide.

Uncle Arky flicked on the lights, flicked off the glow from the floor. He moved quickly toward Scylla and when he was close paused, then grabbed the Magnum from the holster inside the blazer and stepped back. "If you are blessed with a 'next time,' young man, don't be so anxious to nail down your potential victim's plans. What have you stolen?"

"Nothin'."

"Empty your pockets."

"I started down here—I was going for the silver and the VCR after."

Uncle Arky started to laugh.

"What's so funny?"

"Your panic or your ineptitude, I'm not sure which I find the more amusing." He opened his tiny pistol. "Empty, as you can see. I keep it just for show, I'm a scientist, not a gunslinger." Now he pointed the Magnum at the larger man's heart. "But I am, believe me, a very good shot indeed.'' He lowered the gun somewhat, aimed for the testicles.

''Christ—lemme get out—''

''Not until you tell me what you were going to rob.''

''Just shit—you know, whatever goes for cash on the streets, I got a habit, I need cash—''

Arky stepped outside the room again, flicked the floor switch so that the electricity crackled, the glow got stronger and stronger. ''I can fry you through your shoes, if you want that, *now get on with it.*''

''Some fag wanted a bottle!''

Uncle Arky felt, for the second time that night, near to ecstasy. Standish. It must have been a panicked Standish, trying to delay him. *Glorious*—what further proof was needed that Standish was far behind. He flicked the electricity off, watched the glow die, turned the light back on, cocked the Magnum, moved closer to the fool. ''You should have asked.''

''Huh?''

''Take the bottle.''

''Which?''

''Ah—that does present a problem.''

''I didn't know there was gonna be a lot—this guy, he said he'd gimme two fifty if I'd drive up, grab it, drive back to the city. I thought it was going to be a snap.''

''Oh, it is,'' Uncle Arky said. He gestured with the Magnum. ''One of those bottles is what you're after. I swear to you—if you pick the right one, my blessings.''

''But there's gotta be a hundred.''

''And then some. Pick.'' He watched as the suntanned man looked at the labels.

''They're all labeled with colors.''

''True.''

''But they all look the same.''

''Keen mind—I understand Standish's selection.''

''Look, let's be honest, I'm not probably going to get it right off, what happens if I'm wrong?''

"I'll tell you later—for now, just make your choice, pick it up, unstopple it, sniff it, put it gently back down."

"Gimme a chance for chrissakes—"

"—all right I will—if our positions were reversed, I'd guess correctly."

"A *chaaance*—"

"*—pick!*"

He watched as the man hesitated, selected a bottle, put it back, picked up another, half put it back, then unstopped it, sniffed, put it back. "Okay—I made my guess—what happens now?"

"I'm an inventor—all the bottles but one are filled with a little something I invented. A gas in liquid form. You should have . . ." He looked at his watch. ". . . a good five seconds left alive."

"You son of a bitch!" the big man said, starting toward Arky, charging the gun. Halfway there his legs went and he fell hard to the very hard floor. Arky watched with great interest. A hand twitch. Another. Then no motion at all. He stepped over the corpse, moved to his table where his most precious invention of all was so well protected by its hundred-plus sentries. Out of curiosity, he picked up the bottle the dead man had chosen, was stunned to find the dead man had guessed correctly, was stunned again to hear, over the pounding of his heart, the corpse's voice saying casually, "Even my enemies admit I die superbly . . ."

Scylla stood gracefully, brushed off his clothes, stared at the reddening face of the bearded man.

"You knew already—you must have known—"

"—nonsense—you told me this evening—all that Koufax worship—the bottle I picked was the only one named after a sports legend—'Sandy.' "

"You guessed?—"

"—of course—"

"—you could have been wrong—"

"—of course—"

''—how could you risk your life on a guess?—''

Scylla just shrugged.

Uncle Arky aimed for the testicles again, fired two bullets.

''Blanks,'' Scylla said. ''Play with the rest if you like.''

Uncle Arky slipped sideways, went to his knees.

''The gun handle was also covered with a glorious poison—seeps through the skin for the weak parts—is your heart pounding?''

Uncle Arky fired till the gun clicked.

Scylla stood still, waiting.

''. . . why . . . why are you doing this . . . ?''

''Why did you kill the two children?''

''. . . for . . . the good of my country . . . I'm . . .'' The voice was fading now. ''. . . I'm . . . American . . .''

''Don't think Jefferson would agree,'' Scylla said.

He spent the next little while tidying. Then he gathered up the required debris, put it in the red Chevy. He looked at his watch. Not quite half past ten. Standish usually didn't get to the Blacksmith till two thirty or three. It was all scheduling as he'd planned.

He started the car, began the dull drive to New York. It really had been stupid of him, picking the bottle. Especially when he knew he had only to wait another few minutes for Arky to go.

But to hell with logic—if he was still the best—no, wrong, if he was again the best—and he wasn't remotely sure yet if that was true or not, the competition had been less than top grade thus far, just watching an ancient die of poison was no sign of quality or . . .

. . . where was he? Yes. If he was still top, it was only because he accepted the possibility of losing. He never dreamt of retiring unbeaten, untied and unscored on. He felt at home riding the tail of disaster.

He drove out of Princeton, gunned toward the turnpike

when it was safe. Wondering more than ever why they had brought him back. *Why?* All so simple so far. Well, perhaps it would get dicey later on. He hoped so. Fervently.

It was close to two when he parked on Riverside Drive, across from number 465. He could be making a mistake but he didn't care. No. He cared. Terribly. But who knew if he would ever be in the city again, and alive.

The doorman woke to his knock and he said, "Levy live here?"

The doorman, sleepy eyed, nodded.

"Apartment?"

The doorman, a kid, college soph most likely, summer job, gestured up. "Fifteen in the front. But it's awful late."

"Oh, Mark's expecting me," Scylla said. "You know us bachelors."

"This isn't a Mark Levy, this is Tom. Thomas. And he's married too."

"Oh, thank God you caught it, I must have the wrong building, 'scuse," and he smiled, left, hurried back across the street by his car.

Now he counted up the flights. Fifteen was at the top. With a terrace. Babe had a terrace with maybe the best view in the city. What a thing. Just to make sure, he counted the floors again. Had it right the first time.

Scylla stared up through the night. Only a couple of lights on, in the lower floors, "lit in lust or illness" as Irwin Shaw used to say.

Dark on fifteen.

Then, standing alone by his car, he could feel his heart, just a little. Because he couldn't be sure but it looked like someone was moving up on that terrace. At this hour. Could it be Babe? Pacing. The two of them so close in the night. What if it was Babe? Scylla continued to stare up.

Wouldn't that be a thing . . . ?

## 2

Babe came awake with a shock, not just because of the dream but more importantly, he had lain down as one convinced sleep was out of the realm, at least this night. Even though he was exhausted. Even though he had left their place before eleven and run Riverside Park down to 72nd and back, then crossed the West Side until he reached his beloved reservoir, circled that awhile, knowing it was not just an unsafe thing to do but major league dumb—you could shatter an ankle running in the darkness, but he figured, racing on, that an injury like that would have upped his feelings.

Once he had fancied himself a potential marathon man, and he used to dream about battling legends, Nurmi, his idol, and he would make up scenarios where he caught Nurmi in the stretch of the Marathon, passed him while the millions lining the course screamed his name in rhythm, "*Lee*-vee, *Lee*-vee." But he was early thirties now, he fantasized less, listened to his Walkman instead, Bach, Vivaldi, occasionally, when he felt secure no one would catch him, Neil Diamond.

He'd gotten back to 465 after midnight, showered, read a little, realized he was going to read a lot before the night lost out to dawn, promptly zonked, came awake with the shock. He looked across the bed. Melissa was out, her back to him; he listened to be sure he could hear her breathing. Then he got up, made himself a strong Scotch and soda, which he didn't do often, once, maybe twice a year, threw on a robe, wandered out to the terrace, rested on the balustrade, stared out.

All this because he and Melissa, at shortly after seven,

after four years of what he was sure to others in their vicinity was unseemly happiness, had not just their first bloody combat but a doubleheader.

And, an hour earlier, such things weren't clouds on any horizons.

He had finished work at Columbia, it was a terrific early evening, the first heat wave had yet to flatten the town, and Melissa was struggling with her Pittsburgh heiress when he entered the apartment. He waved, went into his study, but left the door open enough so he could hear because, sure, Melissa was making a hundred an hour for her work, but it was hard cheese.

The Pittsburgh heiress flew in twice a week for lessons, flew back home the same night, practiced diligently on her own. She was a sweet child, seventeen, whose father had, three years before, gotten terribly rich on what was probably an illegal real estate deal. And he realized that his beloved, then-fourteen only child, was a lump and a loser and would never crack Pittsburgh "society," something Babe thought had to be a contradiction in terms. So the father had gone to the best doctors, and Willie's ears had been flattened, the nose made straight. Wilhelmina was still chubby, but eventually that was gotten rid of: Weight Watchers, diet camps, medical specialists. What eventually worked was the promise of a Porsche.

So Willie was no longer a lump. She had hairstylists, skin experts, clothing consultants. The outside was as good as it was going to get.

But she still had this incredible Pittsburgh accent. This incredibly awful Pittsburgh accent that no one in "society" would ever listen to without laughter. So the father had asked around, heard of a Melissa Levy in New York who had a better ear than Henry Higgins, and so, for three months now, the biweekly lessons had gone on.

Moving his chair close to the door, Babe eavesdropped. Melissa was so smart, so brilliant at what she did, but she had never before encountered an ear quite as leaden as Wilhelmina's. And it was tough sometimes to keep the despair from her tone.

"All right, Willie," Melissa said, her voice bright and sprightly. "Where do we put the cows at night?"

"In the born, Mrs. Levy."

"I've told you, Melissa, not Mrs. Levy. Now think. How do you spell that word where we put the cows?"

"B-a-r-n."

"Do you hear the problem, Willie?"

"I'm sorry."

"You're doing wonderfully, you're going to speak beautifully, it just may not happen this evening. Please don't say you're sorry anymore, I'm the one that should be sorry because I'm working so badly but I'm doing my best so I shouldn't be sorry either, what do you drive to school?"

"My Porsche."

Melissa sighed. "What is it that you drive, Willie—a horse and buggy, a scooter, tell me."

"My core."

"Let's leave the *a*'s to fend for themselves awhile, shall we. Have you worked on your *o*'s?"

"Oh yes."

"Good. Tell me what Harvard is."

"Cawledge?"

"Right. Except why don't we try making that first syllable sound like this: 'Coll . . . coll . . .' Try that."

"Cawl."

"Coll."

"Cawl."

"Coll—coll—watch my mouth, Willie, *coll.*"

"Coll."

Suddenly Melissa was singing, "The rain in Spain stays mainly in the play-hain."

"You want me to sing, Melissa?"

"No, Willie, to these ears, you *are* singing," and there was no despair, none whatsoever, in her tone.

When the lesson was done, the front door closed, Babe danced out of his office, doing his best Donald O'Connor imitation: "Hoo-ray for *Hawly*wood, twah-twah-twah-twah-twah-twah *Hawly*wood."

Melissa made no reaction at all, simply walked past him into their bedroom, began to undress.

Babe followed. "Yale is a cawledge in Cawnnecticut."

"Yale is a university, and I really do not appreciate my husband behaving like a feep, snooping while I'm trying to work."

"You never minded before."

"Well, I do now."

Babe said nothing, watched his beloved's slender naked body. Olive skinned, large dark eyes . . . He never dreamt, gawky klutz that he was, at least on the outside, that anyone as bright and sought after as Melissa Biesenthal would find it in her ample heart to care for him. He went to her, wrapped her in his arms.

"Nawt interested," Melissa said, pushing his arms away.

"What's up?"

She shook her head.

"What going on?"

"Nothing."

"Don't lie."

"I'm telling the truth!"

"Do you have to tell it quite so loudly?"

"I don't want to talk about it."

"There is a split in your logic, my dear—if there is 'nothing' wrong, then there would be 'nothing' to talk about. Since there is—I suspect we ought to get it off our collective bosoms and since yours is by far the more delectable, why don't we begin with you."

"You'll laugh at me."

"I won't."

"I know you."

"I swear."

Melissa hesitated, then softly said it: "I saw her again."

Certain of the answer, Babe asked, "Saw who?"

"The droopy-eyed woman. She was tracking me."

"Where was this?"

"The supermarket."

"Did you go up to her?"

"She was in a different aisle. She never got close."

Babe shook his head. "Melissa—listen: two minor points to be considered. One—this apparition would only be following someone if there was a reason for that person to be followed and since you are that person and there is no reason, we can kind of chalk off your worries. Two: if there *was* a reason, the person they would get—don't ask me who 'they' might be—would be innocuous in appearance. A woman with a droopy eye kind of stands out in a crowd, at least she does to you. So I suspect you're getting yourself worked up over a comparison shopper."

She just looked at him, said not a word.

"Honey—I've had Andre the Giant dogging my tracks all week but you don't hear me saying he's following me—we just have been more or less heading in the same directions is all, the library stacks, the history department offices, the—"

"—you—swore—you—wouldn't—laugh—and—now—you're—laughing—"

That was the beginning of fireworks. Escalation went on for perhaps ten minutes, she held off tears until near the end when she locked herself in the bathroom and Babe stormed out, so steamed he couldn't trust himself to say more, the anger all inner directed because there was a chance, small but present, that she might be right. Someone might indeed be on their trail. Or, much more likely, his alone . . .

"Apawlogies," Babe said from the pay phone on the corner, at a quarter to eight.

"Me too."

"I just hate it when we fight."

"What a blessing we don't do it often."

"You're my blessing," Babe said.

"More, more."

"Don't want to spoil you. What do you feel like cooking, the soft-shell crabs look fresh at the market," a feeble enough joke.

"If I'd started sooner we could have had my *daube* but who wants to eat at midnight?"

"Throw on some clothes and I'll meet you at the Hunan place."

"Tom—I've been crying *hysterically*—I won't be presentable to the outside world until next year at the earliest."

"Okay—how about if I come home and we make love and then order pizza?"

"Have you got a deal," she said and they hung up, and in five minutes he was back, and in an hour they ordered pizza and in the time between they gentled each other, soothed, and usually Babe got aroused first, and he did now, but he had caused the upset so he did nothing, waiting for a sign from her that festivities might commence; when she gave it they were both, at the start anyway, awkward, not such a terrible thing.

When the pizza came they split it, along with a couple of bottles of Miller Lite, Melissa's favorite, not so much because of the taste as because she loved listening to the commercials, guessing where the athletes came from, Spillane's accent was the purest, she thought, his or Heinsohn's. Then they both worked, Babe taking notes for an article on forgotten men of history that he was outlining, Melissa reading up on some recent studies on phoneticism, after which she made a list for the trip that was coming up for them—Babe just threw in clothes, men could do that, get by on gray slacks and a blazer, but women had to plan, coordinate outfits, not easy for her, since she cared slightly less about clothes than she did about cooking.

At ten thirty they got ready for bed, turned out the light, held each other. "What?" she said then.

"I didn't say anything."

"I can sense your tension."

"We can't have that, can we," he said, rolling over to his side.

"Methinks something's gone awry."

"Imagination."

"Fine. Have it your way. 'Night."

"Same."

A long silence. Then he said it: "Okay, but you've got to promise not to laugh at *me* this time."

She rolled up on one elbow, flicked on her reading light.

"I never went into it much in detail with you, but once, years back, there was that trouble."

"When you lost your brother, you mean."

"I didn't 'lose' him, I hate euphemisms, they cloud things, he was killed and the guy who did it was a German, Szell."

She waited.

"He was Mengele's protégé, Szell, and it crossed my mind, don't think I'm crazy, I'm not saying this is happening or anything, it's just that with all the Mengele publicity the last weeks, him being found, his bones I mean, well, who can tell what that might have stirred up, there are a lot of weird people in this world, who knows who might be following who?"

And suddenly she was shouting at him—"Christ, Tommy, how could you sit quietly and let me think *I* was crazy—how could you not tell me what you thought?—I've been thinking paranoia and you could have stopped it but you didn't, so how could you think I'd *laugh*—that damn woman with the droopy eye *is* after me and—"

"—*me*, for chrissakes—nobody's after you—"

"—you don't *know* that, you son of a bitch—"

"—Melissa—you listen to me, the first fight we had was my fault, but this is *yours*—"

These fireworks were briefer, more explosive, and he was in his running gear and out the door inside five minutes, beginning his lunatic dash through the night.

Now, at going on two, he drank from his Scotch and soda, stared out at Riverside Park. Not much traffic. A car was parked across from the building. Babe had been good at cars once, when he was a kid, and this was maybe a Chevy, probably red and he wondered why it was there, why was the guy standing alongside it, and from this distance it was hard to tell but was the guy looking up?

"It *was* my fault," Melissa's voice said from behind him.

"Ancient history."

"I was just so relieved by what you told me."

Babe smiled. "If that's what *relief* brings out in you, I'm not looking to be around when someone makes you happy."

"Oh, hush, you make me happy every day."

"Some days twice."

"Ancient history." She was barefooted in her nightgown and she shivered.

"Warmer in here," Babe said, and he held out his robe; she moved to him, he wrapped it around her. On the street the red Chevy drove downtown.

"You cried out, you know."

"You awake?"

"It's been a terrific night for all concerned."

"It's just the whole crummy Mengele business, talking about it. It brought back Szell and I dreamt about Doc."

"Hmm?"

"We had secret names for each other, I was Babe just to him, he was Doc to me. In the dream I was chasing after him along a river. He kept gesturing for me to hurry and catch up. He was a fabulous-looking guy. With this wonderful smile. He was smiling at me and it was all so real, I thought he was alive. *Knew* he was. Till I woke up."

"You don't give up easily, do you, Tommy?"

Babe shook his head. "For a long time after his funeral, I knew my father was alive."

"You got over that."

"I had help," Babe said.

## 3

It was half past two in the morning as Standish studied himself in the mirror, buttoned his vest, and contemplated again his singular problem: would pure and total happiness eventually become boring?

He didn't expect such happiness overnight. Certainly not in the next day or two. But surely it would come, and surely, he deserved it. The atomizer was an undisputed success. His adherents in Washington were growing in power. Only the old Princetonian, Uncle Arky, had a similar group of endorsers. But Arky's position was static.

Standish expected the military to give a go-ahead to the manufacture of his atomizer formula soon—one of its greatest values was the simplicity of manufacture. Of course, he alone knew the formula, at least for the moment. But once he divulged it and it was used on an international scale, he knew the results: he, Milo Standish, would be the first and only human on earth to win a double Nobel *the same year:* one for chemistry, the other, obviously, for peace. So careerwise, things were humming right along.

But he had always done well along that line. He was too gifted a scientist to ever be less than successful. His sex life, alas, less so. At least in the old days.

The first person he ever loved, craved, would have killed for, was James Dean, they had been born the same year. Standish had seen him as the Arab lover on Broadway, had waited at the stage door night after night thereafter, always wanting to find the courage to make an introduction, knowing he never could. Dean was too beautiful, he was only brilliant, with the added virtue of inherited wealth, nothing when beauty was what mattered.

Not anymore, sweetheart.

Now he'd just walk up and say, "Hey, Jimmy babe" and then, with a little squirt from his atomizer, they'd be romping together till sunrise.

Standish adjusted his tie tight to his throat, put his suit jacket on, his wallet in one pants pocket, his keys and change in the other.

And last, his beloved atomizer in the right jacket pocket.

Armed for anything, he left his Village penthouse, elevatored to the street, walked awhile. His problem was becoming bothersome. Could he, Milo Standish, soon to be the most famous scientist in history, not to mention the most beloved man of his time, not to mention a human sex machine able to have any man he fancied, could he juggle all that and stay interested in the world around him—

—or would it pall?

Would he find himself wearying of the adulation? Would he be annoyed at the intrusive, adoring public? Would the most beautiful men in the world, always anxious to do what pleased him, eventually deprive him of zest?

And if it did, what then? Surely there could be no greater achievements left. What, oh what would he do if, say, in a year, he woke with a frown?

Well, he had always been strong of mind. Perhaps pure and total happiness was not meant till heaven. At any rate, all he could do was let it happen. And it would. He knew that. Just as surely as he knew that the most breathtaking hunk in the Blacksmith would soon be naked in his apartment, begging the Great Milo Standish to do his worst.

Which was very naughty indeed. He had been using his atomizer for over a month now, in various bars, picking and choosing, bringing them back. And in a week if he wanted, all he had to do was phone them and ask, if they wanted and he would never dream of putting them out but would they feel like visiting him. And they always ran to him. And begged for his treatment. (Standish scowled for a moment—

Arky's adherents claimed no one knew how long his atomizer would last—anything to stay in the race. He knew, of course, the answer was forever; he simply couldn't prove it yet.) And there were those who might claim he was using his invention for personal gain, spraying beauties for his personal pleasure.

Standish sighed; all that he did was for scientific research, he was just a man who loved his work, no more.

The Blacksmith was filled with the standard leather crowd, and not as packed as usual. He made his way toward the bar, got halfway there when the drunk sprawled into him and they both fell hard, tangled up on the sawdust floor. The drunk, not so inebriated he wasn't embarrassed, rose first, put his hands on Standish, lifted him to his feet, said "Sorry, sorry" as he ran his hands over Standish's elegant suit, getting the sawdust off.

"Enough," Standish said.

The drunk muttered "Sorry" again, stepped back, almost bowed and scraped.

Standish studied him. He was suntanned, decently dressed, blazer and slacks. Stunning looking really. No child, but clearly a powerful body. And the hands, as they had ranged across him, were good hands, strong. Big, too. Thick in the shoulders.

But there was something a bit off: yes. The man was petrified.

Standish turned sharply, went to his pet seat in the corner of the bar. Eventually the bartender brought him his regular summertime libation, light Puerto Rican rum, soda, lime, in a tall, ice-filled glass. When Standish got out his wallet, the bartender shook his head. "Comped," he said, gesturing across the bar where the drunk sat staring down at his glass.

Milo took a sip, circled the room, sat down next to the drunk. "Do you know who Florence Foster Jenkins was?"

"No."

"A creature beyond legend. Wealthy, a singer, with a great love of music and possessed, most critics agree, with absolute lack of tonality. She would give an annual concert in Carnegie Hall and pack the place. Madame Jenkins was, you see, a forerunner of high camp—most still feel she was the worst singer who ever lived."

"Don' get it."

"You're about that bad an actor, you're not drunk, we both know it." He held up his glass. "By the way, *gracias.*"

*"De nada."*

Standish watched as the gorgeous suntanned man turned his glass around and around. "I've been here an hour," he said, his voice sober now.

"And how many of the assembled have you knocked over?"

"You were the . . . the first one who looked like . . . I don't know, is 'class' the word I'm looking for?"

"You like your mates with class, do you?"

The speed of the turning glass increased. Standish reached over, put his hand on top of the other man's, brought the glass to a stop. "I did have a few drinks," the suntanned man said finally. "I just can't get drunk."

"Ever or only tonight?"

"Only tonight."

"Tell me your first name, I'm Milo, we'll never see each other again, but if we don't know too much, we can't blackmail each other, can we."

"We haven't done anything, my name is Richard, what else do you want to know?"

"I don't need to ask. Your nerves betray you. Shall I guess? You don't do this kind of thing."

"It's that obvious?"

"How many children?"

"Two boys and a girl."

"Same wife?"

Nod.

"Does she know?"

*"Know what?"*

"Touchy, touchy."

"Sorry. No, she doesn't."

"How long have you known? I knew about myself before I was eight."

"Older. In my twenties. Maybe. I'm not even sure."

"Oh, come now, Richard."

"I've never looked at anyone."

"Till tonight."

Nod.

"When I came so deliciously into your vision."

"Cut that elegant talk."

"Touchy again."

"I just hate that."

"Such a macho figure. Where do you live, Richard?"

"Chicago."

"And you're here on a convention?"

"I guess."

"Let's go to my place, it's much more comfortable."

"I'm not sure I want to do that."

"What are you afraid of?"

"Who the fuck's afraid?"

"Spunk. Good. I like that in a man."

"You talk like that again, it's done."

"We haven't started. And if we do or don't, it's up to you—" Standish smiled. "After all, you're big and strong, I'm neither, so how in the world could I force my attentions on you?"

"I guess you couldn't."

Standish stood. "Shall we visit my abode, Richard, from Chicago? It's just a short taxi ride. And I'll make you two promises: First, the view is spectacular. Second: so am I."

In the elevator up to Standish's penthouse, Scylla tried not to let his excitement show. But it had gone so well, as perfectly as any job he could remember. Maybe he was as good as ever, as good as anyone, ever. You didn't want to stand on a soapbox orating that fact, but still, it didn't damage your confidence, knowing that you were the best. Just your standard brand legend, invincible as always—

—*Jesus*—what kind of nut thinking was that? "Legend."

You start believing that, people started knifing your insides for a foot or so. And Standish was alive, bright and dangerous.

And smiling at him now. "Your body moves beautifully inside your clothes—"

"—knock that off."

"Richard, we're *alone* in the elevator."

"Well, I think it's good to be careful. You never know when someone's waiting to get on."

"I shall lock my mouth and throw away the key until we're safely inside." He mimed the gesture.

Scylla watched the numbers over the elevator door. When they reached PH the doors opened. Standish bowed, allowed him off, then led the way down the hall, got out a key, unlocked his door.

The view was as advertised. Scylla went to the picture windows, was impressed. Most of the Village was low houses, so being high gave a startling sweep to one of the prettiest parts of the city, a way of seeing it most were not privy to.

"Shall we get comfy?" Standish said.

Scylla, who had been watching him cross toward him, shook his head. "I'm fine the way I am."

"Scared of little me?—oh, I forgot, he doesn't find that kind of talk appealing, does he?"

Scylla took a step away.

"Why do you watch me so closely? You haven't taken your eyes completely off me since we left the Blacksmith."

"Maybe this wasn't such a hot idea, me coming here."

"Oh, stop that juvenile panic."

"Well, what if, you know, something did happen, between us, and then, you decided to blackmail me?"

"An easy chore." Standish couldn't help laughing. "I'll just rush out to Barnes and Noble, purchase the latest Chicago phone book—what's the population nowadays, four million, five? And I'll grab a cup of coffee and call the few Richards who live there. There can't be more than what, fifty thousand? I admit I'll have a tidy phone bill but it will be worth it because—What do you do, Richard?"

"Construction business."

"How many employees?"

"Well, it's seasonal."

"At your peak, dear heart."

"Maybe twenty-five."

"Well, now I understand why you're right to feel threatened—I could blackmail you for, oh, hundreds of dollars easily."

Scylla looked at the elegant little shit smiling at him. "You like embarrassing people?"

"Fools. Silly frightened fools, yes. Come here."

"Not in the mood."

"Well then, by all means, let's get in one." He pointed to the bar. "Make us something strong."

"What do you want?"

Standish moved close. "Surprise me."

"Rum and soda, like in that place?"

"Not just rum and soda. *Strong* rum and soda. Strong like you are."

"It won't work; I can't get drunk, I told you that."

"Hush, silly, just give it a try."

Scylla walked to the bar. All the ingredients were perfectly set out. He filled two glasses with ice, poured the rum, careful not to spill, poured the soda, then grabbed the lime segments, concentrated not to make a mess, and while he was doing that, he heard a sound, whirled, but too late, to stop Standish from squirting him with the atomizer he held in his right hand . . .

"What is that shit—why are you smiling that way?"

"You looked so surprised—and I'm embarrassed—I apologize, but I have a cleanliness fetish—"

"—and that's perfume?—"

Standish smiled. "Odorless, I promise you. Just don't get upset with me, beloved Richard—and stir the drinks, I like my liquor cold and my men hot."

"I'm not gonna warn you again about that kind of talk."

"How forgetful I can be in moments of triumph." He

walked across to his view while the other man finished making their drinks. "Come here."

"I told you. I'm not in the mood."

"Well, at least bring my libation."

"Sure, I can do that." He crossed to Standish, handed him one glass, kept the other.

"To our future."

"Milo, once I'm done with this drink, I'm gone."

"Of course you are." He held out his glass, touched the bigger man's, smiled and they drank. "You should be a bartender, Richard."

"You think?"

"You have the talent, but have you the power—you have to have endurance to stand those long hours. Why don't you get comfortable, Richard."

"I am comfortable, Milo; who wouldn't be comfortable in a spread like you have?"

"Well, at least take off your blazer."

"Oh, that, no problem." He took off his jacket, slung it over a chair.

"Richard?"

"Yes, Milo?"

"I know we don't know each other well, but it would mean a great deal to me if you'd—please feel free to say 'no'—but I wish you'd put your glass down and take me in your arms."

"That's not much to ask, Milo, considering the free booze and all." He took the little man, held him. "I never held a man before. My kids, sure, all the time, but never a grown-up."

"Have you ever kissed a grown man?"

"Are you serious?—never."

"Try it—you'll like it."

"I don't know, Milo."

"I'm rushing things, I have a terrible habit with that, and please, if you don't want to, don't do it, but I'd feel ever so much closer to you if you'd kiss me—like you meant it. Shut your eyes, my lionhearted Richard."

The big man closed his eyes.

"Who did you dream of when you were younger?"

"Jean Simmons. And Elizabeth Taylor in *Ivanhoe*."

"Well, make believe I'm one of them—just for now—we'll deal with reality later—but to ease into things, pretend. I'm Elizabeth Taylor, Richard. And I'm twenty years old and more beautiful than any woman in the world—kiss me."

They kissed.

Milo was the one who had to break it. He could feel himself beginning to harden. He stepped back. "Dear God, what a piece of work you are. Don't do this if you don't want to—promise?"

"Word of honor."

"Take off all your clothes."

"Huh?"

"It would just mean the world to me—but I would never dream of risking our relationship. Forget about making me happy. Just do what you want."

"Socks and shoes too, Milo?"

"They're clothes, aren't they?"

"Point me to the nearest bathroom."

"Here will be fine."

"You want me just to strip right here?"

"So very much, but as I said, it's entirely up to you."

"It's just a body, Milo, but if you want to see it, I don't see any problem."

"You're perfect," Milo whispered when the other man was naked.

"Don't I wish—this scar's not exactly great."

"I love it. I'm going to tongue it later."

The big man took a step back. "That's disgusting," he said.

"I can't help it, I have a sadistic streak. Show you what I mean. Clasp your hands behind you."

The big man did. "Like this?"

"Perfect. Now stand with your legs wide apart. Make kind of an inverted 'V.'"

The big man did. "Have I got it right?"

"Two perfects. Now, I know we've only met, but please, it's so terribly important to me for this next event to happen, but as always, the final decision rests with you. I want to knee you as hard as I can in the testicles, Richard."

"Milo, that's going to hurt like crazy."

"Only for a few minutes."

"You sure about that?"

"Five minutes of intense agony, then it lessens, believe me. In half an hour you won't probably even remember."

"Couldn't you just hit me or something? I wouldn't mind that quite so much."

"Richard, I don't have to do anything, if that's the way you're going to behave—I mean I did say how much it meant to me, but if my happiness is unimportant, you can get dressed and we'll talk about your wife and family."

"Don't get mad at me like that."

"I could never be mad—I just pride myself on being a flawless host and I was afraid I'd upset you—"

"—hey, I'm not upset even a little."

"Then you don't mind if I knee you?"

"Well, I can't say it's going to be the highlight of my day, but give it a go if it makes you happy."

"It does, it truly does. Are you interested in why I want so to do it?"

"To satisfy your sadistic streak like you said?"

"Partially that," Milo replied, and then he moved in swiftly, kneed the suntanned man with all his power, watched as the man gasped, covered his testicles with his hands, lost color, reached for a chair, missed, fell to the floor and rolled into a little fetal ball. "But the fuller truth, my dark beauty, is that I do not for a moment believe that my 'class' drew you to me. I think someone *sent* you to me. And guess what: you're going to tell me precisely everything. And I pray, beloved, I like your answers. For your sake, not mine . . ."

"Why don't you just spill all the beans you like," Standish said, a few minutes later, sipping his drink, sitting in the couch across from the naked man, the glorious naked man, who was slowly regaining color.

Silence.

"Oh, this means more to me than anything, Richard, please don't grow all shy and silent. Is your name Richard, by the by?"

Nod.

"Why are you resisting me over a simple thing like your name? Don't answer if you don't want, forget about my happiness."

"Today."

"What 'today'?"

"I've had many names. Richard is the one today."

"Oh, goody—tell me some of the others."

"Well, I was born Henry David. In honor of Thoreau. My father was an intellectual."

"Well now, that was neither painful nor revelatory, so why the resistance?"

Shrug.

"There's that resistance cropping up again. I think, frankly, you are the rudest creature I have ever come in contact with. Here I'm practically begging for tidbits that would bring me *such* joy and you do nothing but hold back on me."

"Scylla."

"Come again?"

"Scylla was my anonym."

Standish just stared.

"I picked it myself. You see, Scylla was a giant rock off the coast of Italy. I liked to think of myself as that, a rock. There was a whirlpool nearby. Charybdis. It was dangerous, when you were near Scylla."

"So you're dangerous?"

"I don't know anymore, I think so sometimes. I did earlier tonight, coming up in the elevator. But I've been away. For so long. When I got this scar, I died. Everybody thought I had. But the decision was reached, if I could be saved I might be useful. My eyes are the same. But my fingerprints were removed. And my vocal cords were thickened so my voice is hoarse. And my lips were thinned and my forehead built up and my cheekbones flattened and my eyebrow ridge altered. No one knows what I look like now. No one that knew me before would know me now. And I've been away on an island gathering strength for when I was needed."

"And you're needed now?"

"Yes."

"By?"

"Division."

"You work for them too?"

"I have, yes, for twenty years."

"And they wanted you to check up on me, is that it, use your beauty to insinuate yourself, an inside man, yes?"

Silence.

"How can you be so cruel, Scylla, to withhold the juiciest parts? What did they want you to do?"

"Kill you."

Standish got up, made himself another drink. "Does Perkins know?"

"Perkins gave me the job."

Standish whirled. "That does not compute. Perkins hired me."

"I know. But you're doing too well. You and Arky. The Bloodies are in control. If I can just delay you two, the Godists can take over, at least he hopes they can. I can't say for sure."

"Have you visited Arky?"

"I've delayed him, yes."

"Oh, you glorious creature," Standish said. "You wonderful man, how can I ever repay you?" He crossed to the chair, knelt in front of the big man. "I tell you what let's do. Let's go to bed together, you and I. I'll tie you up—I mentioned that sadistic problem I have, well, I wasn't inventing anything—and I'll cause you great pain and suffering, and then I'll repent until orgasm and then we'll go for a swim."

"Swim?"

"Yes, you'll be all sweaty, I promise you, and we'll get

dressed and stroll to the Hudson and then would you do the single greatest favor I've ever asked of another human? Would you take a little dip?''

''The water's all dirty and cold, isn't it, Milo?''

''I said 'little' dip. Just a few strokes, and that's all. Then you stop.''

''But if I stop, won't I sink?''

''That's a very strong possibility.''

''Then wouldn't I drown?''

''The odds would favor such an event, yes, Scylla.'' He stroked the other man's powerful legs. ''God, you're an animal, feel those thighs.''

''I want to hear more about the drowning than about my legs.''

''Well, you see, with Arky gone, the battle's done. I'll have to ruin Perkins' power base, of course, but you'll help by leaving a little note—or you can dictate, whatever you prefer—explaining this horrid and unpatriotic plot—and I can't leave you around, I don't like leaving enemies around, it's messy.''

''Will it hurt?''

''The drowning? No. A trifle chilly but that will be over quickly. Now, what I'm going to do to you in the bedroom, *that* will hurt. You will lose, by the time I'm finished, more blood than I suspect you knew you had.'' He smiled, stood, took the big man by the hand. ''Come along, come along, let the festivities begin.'' He stopped, turned. ''Could you love this face?''

''I don't know.''

''I've never been this happy. I'm going to win a double Nobel Prize and make love to a god. Scylla was a god, I trust.''

''Actually, a female monster. In mythology.''

''Perfect for me, the monster part. And earlier tonight I worried about dealing with happiness. 'Never trouble trouble, till trouble troubles you.' Remember that, Scylla. Now kiss the fingertips of the happiest man alive.''

Scylla touched his lips to Standish's fingers.

Standish began to cry.

Scylla said nothing.

"All my life I've prided myself on decency and goodness." The tears were pouring down his face. "And here you dispose of my bitterest rival, assuring me immortality, and what do I do: I decide to abuse you and then murder you. What kind of horrid creature am I." He was sobbing now, and he made his way blindly to the chair Scylla had been sitting in, collapsed and wept until he could make words again. "What's happening?"

"You're dying, Milo; you're about to commit suicide."

"But I was so happy."

"Trust in me."

"How can you be so sure?"

"I took the bottle of suicide liquid from Arky's laboratory. I put a drop in your drink when I stirred them."

"But I sprayed you."

"I know. But Perkins gave me an identical atomizer bottle to yours. I switched them when we collided and fell. When I helped you up, more accurately. I've got relatively deft fingers, it wasn't much of a chore. You just sprayed me with ordinary breath atomizer, that's all."

"How long will it take before I die?"

"I suppose that depends on how you decide to do it. Perkins wants me to stick around and note things. He's interested; good scientific mind, Perkins."

"I really want to die, Scylla."

"I know." Softly. "Shhh. You will."

"But I don't like *receiving* pain, you see my problem? I like to make other people suffer." He took out his handkerchief, blew his nose, cried again.

Scylla walked to his clothes.

"Don't leave me, Scylla."

"I wouldn't dream of it, I just want to get dressed, Milo." When he was done, Standish was still weeping. "I think you better get on with it, Milo; you're just suffering unnecessarily."

"I'm anxious to end things, Scylla, truly, but I like to

think I'm not just a common slug, so I don't want to go out the window and let strangers peer at me as they walk by and I've got an electric oven so I can't very well stick my head in it without feeling like a fool. *Help* me."

"Didn't you tell me you were going to tie me up?"

"Ropes! Yes. Sashes more precisely." He began to grow excited. "Beautiful paisley patterns. I've got an enormous collection." He looked around the room. "No place in here." Then he snapped his fingers. "The dining room chandelier. It's strong and I don't weigh that much. I'll just move the table out from under, make a knot—oh, you'll see, it will be a magnificent knot, delicate but strong, the envy of all—*thank* you for helping me, Scylla."

"That's why God put us here, Milo, to help each other when we can."

"What a good good friend we have in Jesus," Milo Standish said, as he went scampering off to die.

The rest was simple carpentry. Scylla got Standish's key, a bottle of whiskey, elevatored down to where he had parked his car, got Arky from the trunk, poured liquor over him so he smelled very drunk indeed, went staggering back up the stairs, chatting with Arky as he passed the half-asleep night porter.

Upstairs, he settled Arky into a dining room chair where he had a clear view, or would have had his eyes been working, of Standish's body turning slowly, slowly, in the wind.

Then he picked up the phone, dialed the most secret number in Washington Division had—or so Perkins claimed. A crisp male voice answered, and Scylla could envision the automatic taping equipment and other scientific bric-a-brac looming around.

He began speaking French then—once he had been bilingual—his voice hoarse and, he hoped, triumphant. Then, before the crisp male voice could begin querying him, he hung up. They would trace the call in minutes, so he had no time to rest. At least not there. It was still the middle of the night, not quite four, and he wondered as he had so often in the last days, why had they brought him back for child's play. The only truly interesting part of the Standish scene was when he was kneed. Years before, his first trainer at Division had told him an important secret: enduring pain was a great weapon, especially if your enemy knew he could inflict it. It built your character, and made him uncautious. Twice recently he had suffered, the beating in New Orleans, and now this. Twice he was the last man standing. Not ever the worst thing to be.

## 4

The crisp male voice that received the odd message in the foreign language belonged to a very crisp young man named Mullin, who had become, in not too many years, Perkins' chief assistant. The call, of course, struck him as two things: legitimate and serious. There were no crank calls, not on that number.

Mullin alerted several of his assistants, and while they set off on their appointed chores, he phoned Hough in New York. Hough, a large well-conditioned man in his fifties, did the bulk of the troubleshooting in the Manhattan area. He was not glib enough for corporate success, but Perkins trusted him, had for decades.

Hough was thrilled when the call came, even though it was still the middle of the night, because, although he looked as impressive as ever, his body had begun to betray him, sleep to visit less and less often. Once Hough could simply put head to pillow and be gone. No more. Mullin suggested Hough might make a quick trip to the Village where Milo Standish lived, and call back when he got there.

Hough did call back from Standish's, reported on the two men who seemed to be almost eyeing each other in the dining room, suggested Mullin might rouse Perkins, while he, at the site, summoned as many technicians as he deemed necessary. Mullin agreed. The technicians came, dusted and clicked and probed, after several hours left, leaving Hough and Boynton, the chief medico, to await the arrival of the Washington contingent.

That group, consisting solely of Perkins and Mullin, arrived by ten in the morning. And the six men, four still living, gathered in the dining room of the Standish penthouse, talking softly, at least at first, all of them ignoring the view.

At the initial sight of the dead scientists, Mullin thought, feared rather, that Perkins might collapse, he seemed that distraught. Not only had both men worked, in a sense, for Perkins, not only had they reported directly to him; more than that, Mullin knew that in the battle between the Godists and the Bloodies, no one was a more vicious supporter of the Bloody point of view than Perkins, and surely his cause was wounded now.

Perkins, in fact, did sit heavily down. He looked at Hough. "Anything?"

"Not a print," Hough said. "Nothing for even the remotest lead. All very odd."

"Odd?" Perkins said. "Shit, man, we've been baffled before."

Mullin watched as Hough stepped back a pace. Hough was afraid of Perkins too. That rather pleased him.

"Odd in that the glasses weren't wiped clean, the room wasn't fixed. Lots of prints of Standish. It's as if whoever he or they were who did this had no fingerprints at all, which, I must admit, to me is odd."

Perkins nodded, muttered, "Sorry," rubbed his eyes, looked at the doctor.

"Can you help?"

Boynton shook his head. "It's top-quality work really. I mean, medically speaking what we have is an elderly man with a record of heart problems whose heart seems to have failed him. And a younger man with a brilliant mind but swings of emotion committed suicide. His prints are all over the sashes. His alone. So, if I were to give a medical report on the evidence, I would say a heart attack and a suicide, without the least doubt."

"Even though we know it's a double murder," Perkins said.

"Even though," Doctor Boynton said.

"What about the phone call?" Perkins looked at Mullin.

"They were just getting the final data together when we left for the airport, shall I call them now?"

And now Perkins' voice had its energy back. "No, Mullin, why should you dream of getting the facts? I suggest we all four darken the room and hold hands and have a séance."

"I'm sorry, sir, I just—I didn't know if you wanted to make the call or should I do it?"

"Clearly one of us must, Mullin. And since you answered the fucking phone, you might have some intelligent questions to ask, though to believe that requires a mighty stretch of the imagination."

"I'll just be right back," Mullin said, and he hurried to the living room where the nearest phone rested.

The three live men sat quietly amongst the dead until Perkins said, "Hough?"

"Sir."

"Why are we sitting in this room? This room must have surely the most depressing view of any in the vicinity. I don't like looking at corpses, do you?"

Hough shook his head.

Dr. Boynton seemed to flush. "Actually, I don't mind so much."

"You should have been a doctor," Perkins said, and he stood slowly, moved his weighty body into the living room, where he found the softest couch, collapsed into it.

"I've got everything now," Mullin said, hanging up.

"Then you must speak," Perkins said.

"The voice prints don't tell a thing—it's no one we have on file at any office. It could have been disguised, it was thick and hoarse and almost glorying in its tone—but we have nothing to go on. The words of the message were these: 'Arky is dead. Madame Standish also. Our scientists can lick your scientists.' All, of course, in well-accented French. We're working on trying to find something from the use of the colloquial, but, again, nothing.'' He looked at Perkins, was surprised because for a moment, he thought the old man was almost smiling.

''Mullin,'' Perkins said then. ''I have a question for you.''

''I'll do my best.''

''Since, in your brilliant report, you have just told us twice, you have 'nothing,' why did you hang up and say that you had 'everything'? I am asking, Mullin, in my well-accented English, to fucking make sense.''

''I know who did it,'' Mullin said then.

Perkins waited.

''The Blond,'' Mullin said.

Perkins looked shocked.

Hough said, ''Shit.''

Boynton wondered who The Blond was.

''He's their best,'' Hough said. ''Top of the line.''

''There's an illegal gambling casino on Third Avenue in the eighties. The Blond loves roulette. He was seen playing there at five this morning. Apparently in a splendid mood.''

''Fucking horrorist,'' Hough said.

Boynton wondered what that meant too.

''It's the next step in our splendid evolution,'' Perkins answered. ''Terrorism is theater. Terrorists love fame. Horrorists are silent, they believe in the grisly. Their opponents are so dread filled, they tend to do less than their best.''

Suddenly Hough said, ''I wish Scylla were alive—I'd have bet on him against The Blond.'' He looked at Perkins. ''Yes?''

''I don't gamble,'' Perkins replied. ''But I would have paid to see it.'' He looked at Mullin. ''The Blond did not do this, I don't care how cheery his mood at the roulette table.''

''I think we should check every lead.''

"Mullin, I would never deprive a drone from checking leads. But if I remember his dossier, The Blond does not speak 'well-accented French.'"

"He could have learned just those few words," Mullin said.

And now Perkins was roaring as he got slowly to his feet. "Look at their faces, man—go in the next room and look at their faces—*they've still got them*."

Mullin hesitated, then made a nod. "I'm sorry, I wasn't thinking."

Perkins started slowly for the door. "I think we should get Arky back to Princeton, yes?"

Hough nodded.

"And then let our public relations people handle the rest."

Mullin nodded this time. "Anything else?"

Perkins smiled. "What's that wonderful line in *Casablanca* at the end when the villain has been shot? 'Round up the usual suspects'? I think, considering our salaries, we should, at the least, look busy. But it won't come to anything." He paused by the apartment door. "Someone new has entered the equation, gentlemen. And I, for one, am frightened."

"Why?" Mullin said.

"'Our scientists can lick your scientists'—that's *funny*. Don't you understand?—if the Commies ever developed a sense of humor, America wouldn't stand a chance!"

Perkins slammed the door, he hoped not too hard, ordinarily he didn't overact. He went to the elevator, looked at his watch. Plenty of time. Too much really.

His daily call to Beverage, the unofficial one, took place at precisely 11:25 A.M., eastern standard time. And that was forty-five minutes away. He didn't feel like just waiting around so he decided to brave the problems of finding a pay phone in the Broadway area—and Perkins was very brave when it came to the Carnegie, not just New York's but the world's greatest deli. He taxied up through the garment district traffic, got to his haven. There was a line but it was still only a quarter after. The line moved slowly and Beverage would be angry if he was late.

But what was anger compared to such pastrami as this?

When his turn came, he ordered, in all, ten pounds of cold meats, a pound of the cole slaw, a dozen half-sours, paid, had them double-bag it because the odor could cause attention on the shuttle, even through his briefcase.

Which he opened as he left the deli, put the bag in, took out the quarters, turned around, spotted a pay phone which was not only vacant but worked, dialed the country code, the city code, waited for the operator to come and tell him it would be "fi-uve dollars and fifty cents for the first thuh-ree minutes," laboriously dropped the coins, heard the ring, and then Beverage's regular "Wot?—wot?" which always opened things.

Beverage, when he had been promoted over him to run Division, had not been one of Perkins' favorites. But since the move to London, their relationship had become workable. Beverage was a remarkable organizer, had a chess player's mind.

The connection was one of their less good ones. Beverage had several pay phones he used, and they switched, according to the day. But this was going to be one of their less discursive chats. "Bad connection," Perkins said.

"Wot?—wot—?"

"Hard to make you out," Perkins said.

"Can't fucking hear," Beverage replied.

Perkins had to laugh. Here they were, the cream, at least in theory, of the world intelligence community, shouting at each other over pay phones like fishwives over clotheslines. "The grade is *A* plus," Perkins said loudly.

"Hooray for us Godists—no slip-ups at all?"

"Nary a one."

"Top form then? As he was?"

"Let's put it this way—I don't want him angry at me."

Now a pause. "But is he angry at me? Does he still, do you think, have a negative opinion?"

"You mean does he still use the 'P' word? Yes, the word

'Prick' usually follows the mention of your name. You two will have to work that out when he gets there."

"We're both professionals."

"You should be getting the official news about Arky and Milo shortly."

"I promise to be both horrified and grief-stricken over the fate of our late colleagues." A pause. Then: "Ma?"

"What is it, Malcolm?"

"We may just win this after all . . ."

## 5

Scylla was in his suite at the Madison late that afternoon when the bell desk said that a package had arrived. He asked for it to be sent up, tipped the bellboy, locked the door to his suite, began to open the plain brown wrapper with "Richard Blaine" written in Perkins' flowery hand.

Inside, it was like a treasure hunt. The largest package said "Open me first," so Scylla did. It was all new money, crisp and bundled, a small fortune, tens of thousands of American dollars, tens of thousands of British pounds.

The middle-sized package said "Me next" so he tore that envelope open. It contained a passport with a letter wrapped around it reading "Read me before peeking." In Perkins' hand, he read:

*I have put a great deal of thought to this.*

*Your name, I'm talking about. No more "Bede's" or "Blaine's." This one is forever.*

*But it couldn't be ordinary. I wanted something that would be as romantic and dangerous a figure as you are. I wanted a name that would strike, if you will, fear. I wanted a name like D'Artagnan, like Captain Blood.*

*If you think it's easy, try it sometime. Hope you approve. You may peek now.*

Scylla opened his new passport, looked at his permanent name—

ELMER SNERD

Revenge would be his. Someday, he would get back at Perkins, do something heinous, hide his mayonnaise perhaps. "Elmer Snerd." "Full marks, you old fart," he said out loud, unable not to laugh.

The last envelope was the thinnest. On the outside were the words: "Open me if we're still speaking." Scylla did and began to read:

*Well now.*

*Frivolity in our line of work? I suppose you think it's funny, "Our scientists can lick yours, etc." Well, it is, but you should let a man know when you're going to let fly with something like that.*

*When the message was translated, I came near to barfing out loud. Not an adroit move when I was supposed to be heartbroken and striving for shocked surprise.*

*Your work, by the by, was slovenly, totally inept, and only a man of my generosity would find it in his great heart to forgive you.*

*You're off to London soon and we have much of import to discuss. There's a restaurant I've heard of and I want your opinion, it's in the Connaught Hotel. (There is a rumor current that there may be two places to dine in that elderly establishment, but I have my best men on the case and should have it tracked down before your arrival.)*

*Come visit when it's dark. I was, as you may remember, in New York earlier, and managed to nip up to my mecca—I have in my possession acres of cold meats from the Carnegie. You can watch me eat.*
*Lucky you.*

*Ma*

Scylla knew, at half past eight that evening when he took his first step into the Perkins house, that there would be no luck for them, not that night. The place was fairly dark, but he could make out the body slumped on the stairs, facedown. He turned her over, almost lost it, because her face had been all but torn away, but he assumed this was Perkins' older sister, Edna.

And he knew Perkins' wife, Felicity, was upstairs in bed, because the odor was stronger than it had been on his previous visit. Scylla knew no one was going to answer, but probably because he cared, because in spite of all he was still a sometime romantic at heart, he called "Ma?" several times, then ascended through the ensuing silence.

Perkins was dead, horribly savaged, his face all but taken away, his arms wide across Felicity's bed, as if trying, in those final moments, to protect her against a force of panicking power. Scylla studied Perkins a moment. One hand was strangely clenched. Scylla opened the fingers. A few blond hairs were stuck under the nails. Short blond hairs, likely too short for a woman. Felicity, also faceless, lay sprawled, her odor truly unsettling.

Scylla left the room, because this was not news that was going to stay undiscovered forever—he had to get out if he was to have safety, so he raced down the stairs and was almost to the front door when he stopped, trying to remember what Perkins had said to him, about his protection.

"... if someone came for me here ... I might not defeat them ... but they would not take me unawares ..."

Those were his words. And clearly he had defeated no one. But just as clearly, he had not been taken unawares—because whoever had come for him had more than likely destroyed the sister first, the old one on the steps.

So.

Scylla tried very hard to think without emotion. Once he had excelled at that. Except where Babe had been concerned, he had always excelled at that.

So.

As he stood very still he became convinced of one thing: had he wanted, Perkins could have left a message for him. Somewhere in this dark house, there might well be a piece of information meant explicitly for him. From the dear dead man. For him alone. But it would take forever and then some for a thorough search. And he had considerably less time than that.

So.

Where?

If Perkins had indeed left a message, where in this entire edifice might he hide it? With a blond monster in the vicinity, where would Scylla and Scylla alone know to look?

He closed his eyes, concentrated on how Perkins' mind worked.

All so easy.

The kitchen. More specifically, the refrigerator with all Perkins' beloved fattening glories. Scylla raced to the kitchen, stopped dead.

Someone had gone mad there—cold cuts had been crushed underfoot, chopped liver was smeared on tabletops, flecks of once glorious meat still clung to walls.

Scylla stared at the room. And he felt such fury. He had not been possessed for so long, but a friend had been slaughtered and there was no time, but in the house—not here but somewhere—there *had* to be a message. And if he was ever to extract retribution, he would have to find it, would have to *think*. With *insight*. And *clarity*.

And so he did.

Properly confident, Scylla went back up the stairs, back into Felicity's room, walked to her body—he had cleaned her, Perkins had seen that, her odor meant nothing to him—and lifted her.

And there, beneath her, was a small mashed piece of paper. Scylla read the frenzied writing, no flowery curlicues here. The last word Perkins had written, five letters long:

"Tring."

Tring, the little town not all that far from London. Tring, which had a nice restaurant, a good wine list, all located by a winding river. Perkins had taken him there for lunch once, when there was a Perkins.

He had, of course, not the least notion why "Tring" should be important. But clearly it was. Something was happening there and he needed to find out what. And he would. He was certain of that. He would go to England and meet the man who so hated him, and he would hope someday to meet a monster with blond hair, and that was certain too. Scylla felt, as he stood in the dark death house, that it was all coming together, it was all getting sort of just the least bit interesting and he wondered, with a surprising amount of excitement, if he would be around for the outcome. Right at that moment, again to his surprise, he very much wanted to be.

(And he would be.

He would live.

Proving there was no God.)

# III

# ACTION FIGURES

# 1

# The Gathering of the Clans

## 1

When the final form had quieted, he relaxed, sat, lit his pipe, closed his eyes, and allowed the lines of the nursery poem to occupy his mind.

> . . . Between the dark and the daylight
> When the night is beginning to lower
> Comes a pause in the day's occupation
> That's known as the children's hour . . .

How he loved those lines. Not that they were perfect. He always wished, whoever the poet had been, that a finer rhyme could have been found than "lower" and "hour." In point of fact it wasn't a rhyme at all. Lazy work. Sloppy, sloppy. Too bad.

Still, what he felt most drawn to, the reason for his deep affection, was because they could have been written about him. The dark part of his work was completed. Daylight would arrive soon, symbolically, yes, but whenever another chore was successfully done, he felt as if he was walking into daylight.

And, of course, right now, right this moment as he sat and smelled his glorious pipe mixture, he was in his happiest time, that pause in his occupation. When he was able to quietly reflect on his abilities, and where might there be improvement room. Pele, a hero, he had seen many times, in many countries, and he wondered, after the black

Brazilian had scored yet another goal, as he raced back upfield, safe within the thunder from the stadium, did Pele reflect on his day's occupation, on how he might, even though great, become more perfect? Was there a dip, a hip shift that might have been more adroit, was there wasted movement before the scoring kick or header? Could he have made an even more accurate pass?

He inhaled on his pipe, felt the rush of warm air on his throat, reveled in it. He knew that pipes gave you lip cancer if you didn't inhale, all the others if you did. He inhaled constantly. He knew what alcohol did to your liver. He drank whenever he wanted, in whatever quantity. He knew what cholesterol did to your innards, he gorged on beef. Especially American beef. He had worked in Japan and they raved about Kobe, American was better. He had worked in Argentina and they were so proud of their cattle, but then, Argentinians were, in general, not the brightest of people.

But not just American beef captured him. He loved more than the prime ribs and the hand-sized filets. The Maine lobsters, the soft-shell crabs, the corn on the cob, cold even better than hot, cold, smeared with rich Wisconsin butter, pepper twisted on top. Americans ate better than any other nation. And when he was there, he outdid himself in what he could down.

And now, as he sat amongst the forms, he tapped out his pipe and felt, as he always did, shame. Because just as some were peepers, he had his own vice, silly as it seemed. He loved raiding people's iceboxes. Especially in America. Especially in nice American homes such as this one, where who could dare guess the riches held behind the refrigerator door.

His stomach rumbled.

It was odd, but he was never as hungry as when he had finished part one of a chore, with just the scraping left to do. If he had to work in a hotel room or on the street, of course, there would be no chance at refrigerator raiding, but still the hunger was there. In the beginning he would stuff his pockets with food, to give him sustenance. Later, when there was money, he would always go to a fine restaurant after leaving the hotel.

But this could be a memorable time for him. Fat forms meant food intake, and nice houses meant money to buy delicacies. Once, one fabulous time in Massachusetts, he had come across three large lobsters on a platter. *Three*. He wasn't sure, at the sight, if he could do them all justice. But he was a hard worker when the cause was great, and he finished them all, sucked the last particle, left nothing but the shell mountain.

No question, that had been a high point.

He stood, stepped over the form, went to the stairs, made his way around the other, entered the kitchen.

He could feel his heart—the refrigerator was enormous, the commercial kind. And this was early summer so surely the soft-shells were in season. He remembered his first one—it looked so odd he didn't know quite what to do with it. But something, his carefully honed instinct probably, made him try to bite a leg. And of course it was like butter. He put the whole into his mouth, crunched to glory.

The excitement and the shame were mixing now as he stood in front of the large chilling machine, threw the door open and—

—and yogurt?

It was like a slap. Half a dozen yogurts stood like sentries on the top shelf. He looked down to the next shelf. American beer—worse—no body, any of them. Abominations.

Then he saw the large brown bag, all but filling the bottom shelf, and he knew, from his perfectly honed instinct, that he had entered Valhalla. He took the heavy bag, put it on the kitchen table, reached inside. Pulled out a wrapped package, opened it, smelled it, came close to gagging—tongue. The next package open—chopped liver. And after that came corned beef and the disgusting odor of garlic attacked him—

—jewfood—

—the entire bag was jewfood—

—the excitement and the shame were blinked away, with

disappointment and anger moving in—he grabbed a packet of pastrami and balled it up and threw it against the wall—and then he smeared the chopped liver across the tabletop—and then he set to wild work, ripping at the rest, tearing it and throwing it and crushing it beneath his shoes and slapping it on walls until the kitchen was nothing but a reeking garlic slum—

—he wanted to make someone *pay.*

Of course, those upstairs had already done that.

He left the kitchen, started back up the stairs. So disappointed. Crushed, truly. It was never wise to expect too much from life—there were jabs and sadnesses lurking for you everywhere.

The garlic smell followed him. He stopped. Had he gotten it on his own clothes? That would have been the final demeaning straw. He hated that smell. Hated it worse than—

—than . . . ?

Now another smell attacked him. From above, from the crippled woman in the bed. She had evacuated. Disgraceful, degrading.

And he had been so happy with his poem just a few moments before. He took a deep breath, reached into his pocket, got out his scraper, and since the old woman on the stairs was the first he came to, he set first to work on her, taking her face off.

It was strange, really, the way secret fame came calling sometimes in ways no one could have expected. His first job. A decade and more ago. He had no political interests, had gotten involved with the political group for but one reason: the girl who ran it. Anna. Not that she was so pleasing aesthetically. But he wanted her for her fury, for what she considered injustices. He himself had begun with beautiful girls. The first time when he was barely thirteen but already big, and so fair, with the hair almost white blond, the eyes so blue. Women seemed to need him to complete their days.

But he attracted dumb ones, pretty yes, round yes, sought

after, definitely yes, but they provided no task. They were available and then they were soon naked and sometimes it was like plugging lard.

He knew if he ever was allowed into Anna, it would be electric. But she had no interest in him because he had no interest in her causes so he feigned enough, got her trust, agreed to do some work for her if, later, they would have their time.

The first form he created was a young man. Of no import but Anna said his father was rich and evil and if the son went, the father would prove more malleable so he traveled to the son's apartment, and it was quick and as he was about to leave the dread took him, the total conviction that he would die for his deed but what if no one knew, he thought—what if no one could identify the form, and he had a pocket knife with him, primitive, and half in tears he destroyed the form's face, or most of it, before fleeing.

He could never have guessed the reaction. The condition of the body shocked the city. Anna, proud of his strength and fearlessness—he never disabused her—became his love, and she was electric, everything he wanted, until a silly attempt at a bank ended all her relationships.

He was sad, of course, but also by that time famous.

Later, he read about an American cowboy, the greatest American cowboy, Horn his name was, Thomas Horn, and he had captured Geronimo and been a range detective and no one could ride or shoot or fight at his level, and toward his end he bounty-hunted, and each corpse, under the man's head, he would place a rock. It was Horn's sign. A corpse with a rock would empty an area of outlaws, such was their fear.

He bought himself a utensil and got it so it would shame the finest razor and used it for his scraping. He had the same effect as Horn. Horror preceded him and his fees were the highest in the trade, but that was fair, he was legendary long before thirty.

"... Between the dark and the daylight ..." he thought,

only he used different words, more applicable words: "...between the death and the scraping..."

He worked like lightning. He was like an outdoorsman scaling fish. The old woman on the stairs was done and then the smelling cripple was done and for last he saved the fat man who had so foolishly defended the cripple, had fought, had actually had the gall to even attempt an attack, grabbing and pulling some hair.

Finished, he took a breath, went to the bathroom, washed his scraper. He would take the shuttle to New York, roulette the night away, then Concorde to England, get a day's rest. The jobs were coming faster now, the money too. That was good—he needed money.

Everything was good. Except for the shame he felt at the hunger. If he could only get rid of the shame. Nothing wrong with eating after a job. Everyone had his peculiarities. There were even some in his line of work that experienced orgasm after a kill.

He smiled. At least he wasn't sick.

## 2

Melissa would never know for sure, but probably her hated birthmark was what saved her.

"Hated" was actually far too weak a word but English was—at least according to French philologists—a second-rate impoverished language, and perhaps in this case, Melissa felt, the frogs just might be, in their own uniquely arrogant way, right. Hate was insufficient, but the best she could come up with.

What her birthmark was was this lump. On her right side. A few inches below the level of her right breast. Orangish in color. The size to her of a watermelon, in actuality, a plum halved. In the beginning, it was fiery in color and, according to the doctors, nothing unusual. Many children had similar markings. It would absolutely, with time, disappear. And besides, who would notice, the rest of her was so lovely.

In time, the mark changed not in size, just in color. And Melissa noticed. Every naked second of her growing up. She hated showering with other girls, got very adept at keeping her right arm hanging down, masking the thing, soaping only with her left. When other girls did find out they, sweet young things being sweet young things, taunted the shit out of her.

When she was closing in on seven, Melissa talked with her father about it. She had no way of knowing then that Mark Biesenthal was as famous as any American historian, not to mention more successful. He was just this perfect man that appeared for dinner and wore a necktie. It was early December and bedtime when they had their conversation. He was where he always was after dinner, in his study. She crawled up into his chair and he held her, as she kissed his cheek, whispered "'Night," then, very softly, "I know *just* what I want for Christmas."

"Perhaps if you tell me I might remember."

"I read about it in one of Mommy's magazines."

"Then I trust it will be expensive."

Melissa pointed to her right side where "it" was. "Plastic sugary," she said.

"Hmmm." He smiled and held her for a moment. "Now this plastic sugary, what does it do?"

"Well, it takes away things, Daddy."

He looked at her then for a long time. "Melissa, are you smart?" he said then.

"Dunno."

He sighed. "My darling, you have a remarkable ear for language considering your chronological state of advancement, so you should know, without my having to tell you, that 'dunno' is not, in this or any tongue, a word. Banish it as of now. All right?"

She nodded.

"Let me put the question differently: how are your grades?"

"Well, you want me to get the best."

"I don't think it makes you unhappy either, does it?"

"No."

"And you don't seem to work so much you haven't at least a little time for television."

Another nod.

"All right. Are you—I know this is difficult but try—are you attractive to look upon?"

She squinted. "You mean pretty? No." (Not so much a lie as a fib. She was. Everybody knew it and she had hopes. But it was another decade before she was able to think in the affirmative.)

"Well, I tell you you are. But are you athletic?"

"I run fast."

His voice began to rise in mock anger—"Do you beat me at jacks? I, who in my time, was a champion?"

"Well, I practice more than you."

"Let's total it up—a pretty, bright, athletic creature—if she's not careful, she could become very arrogant."

She looked confused.

"A bragger," he said.

She hated braggers. "I would never."

"You might. But I think the lovely birthmark—which all the doctors have promised us will go away as you well know—is just something put there as a reminder that we are none of us, excluding myself, perfect. So I think we should come up with an alternative to sugary for Christmas."

"No?"

He kissed her cheek. "Perhaps when you're in your dotage, my darling. But for the moment, the answer is a definite negative."

Her mother entered the study then. "I'm going, I'm going," Melissa said before her mother could tell her to scoot. She dashed out of the room, hesitated a moment, listened to the talk inside.

"A definite negative to what?" her mother asked.

"She wants her birthmark removed."

"Why does it bother her that much?" her mother wondered.

"Dunno," her father replied . . .

Probably that night was the peak of her obsession with the red-going-orange part of her. Not that she didn't wish it away at night. Not that she didn't peek at it first thing most mornings to see if her wish had been granted or that she didn't measure it from time to time, carefully, both height and circumference, and if it wasn't making plans for a departure, at least it wasn't growing, and perhaps that, as much as anything, freed her good mind for more profitable pursuits.

But even though the obsession ended, she was constantly ambushed by wisps. She never, even though her body had been splendidly shaped for it, ever wore a two-piece bathing suit. Or swam naked, no matter how secluded the Caribbean beach. Or made love with lights on. At least until Tom Levy came cantering into her life, gawky and smart enough to not take a back step from her father. The first time they slept together, his long fingers were caressing her and they lay with no clothes on in his pit of an apartment and his fingers touched it before she could glide them away. He sensed her tensing, asked the problem, pursued past her "nothing" reply, forced it out of her, flicked the bed light on, flipped her body so that the mark was *there*. And then he said the most wonderful thing: "I wish I had one," before kissing it and again before returning them to darkness. Melissa had been pursued by men for more than a good while, but after that night she knew that this skinny one was not about to get away.

Now, on a late June afternoon, four years into their marriage, she lay on their bed, reading an article in a British medical publication that dealt with some new work on larynx surgery that had remarkable results on children with certain speech defects.

Melissa licked her thumb, turned the page. Licking her thumb was a habit she could not break. It drove her father mad. "My books are covered with saliva, you must stop this on threat of being disowned" and she tried, but she couldn't, she just couldn't, most likely because it was such pure reflex she wasn't aware she was doing it, like McEnroe sticking his tongue in his cheek when he served.

Melissa was very happy as she lay there. She was married to the man she loved, she was reading an article that fascinated her and, to tell the truth, she also was not doing the ironing. She loathed it, but felt obliged, since she couldn't cook, to do something housewifely; she believed in it, no matter what the feminists said.

The first time the doorbell rang she ignored it. Then, a moment later, it came again. Melissa got out of bed, smoothed her skirt, tucked in her sleeveless blouse, went to the front door, didn't open it, said, "Yes?"

From outside she heard, "Groceries, lady."

Melissa judged the voice. Late teens, certainly Spanish, but probably a bright kid, the accent was almost totally gone. "I'm sorry?"

"Gristede's, miss."

"I didn't order anything from Gristede's. I don't even shop there."

From outside now, a sigh. Then—"Isn't this the fifteenth floor? 465?"

Melissa opened the door carefully, but left the thick chain lock on. The young man was small, well groomed. He carried a cardboard box filled with groceries. "I'm sorry," she said. "Maybe the other apartment."

"I tried—no one there."

"Well," Melissa said again. "I'm sorry; obviously there's been a mistake."

The young man looked genuinely upset. "My second day on the job and this happens. I get paid mostly on tips; damn."

"I'm not going to tip you," Melissa said, "you can't expect me to, it wasn't my mistake."

" 'Course it wasn't, it's just, damn, now I got to waste time getting this delivered right and time is money, in my line of work.'' He smiled. ''That's what my old man always says: 'in my line of work.' You know why that's funny? He don't do anything. You see the humor?''

Melissa nodded. ''You see the humor'' was advanced speech for this one. Definitely a very good mind inside, perhaps looking for a way out, however unlikely the odds.

''Can I use your phone to call the store? Please?''

''No.''

''I'll be one sec and I'm gone—it'd clear this up and I wouldn't have to go all the way back to the store.''

''You don't have to go all the way back to the store—there's a pay phone two blocks up.''

''It's probably broken and *it costs a quarter.* Really. Please.''

''No. I hope you understand.''

He nodded. ''I do. I understand, believe me.'' He started to turn away.

Melissa watched, and when the pivot was half done he was back looking at her, only now without the smile, now there was just the hopeless ghetto stare. ''If I was one of you you'd open the door, that's what I understand, lady.''

Melissa was instantly ticked. Because in the first place she came from a liberal family, had been strictly brought up. And dumb she wasn't, you didn't let strange kids into your apartment, black brown white or green.

Except he would never in this world have believed that. And, in truth, she didn't blame him, if it had been the reverse, she wouldn't have believed either, and angrily she worked the chain free, gestured sharply for him to follow her into the kitchen, pointed to the phone. The iron and ironing board were set up by the sink, along with a pile of Tommy's shirts. The kid carefully put the groceries down on the board, making very sure he didn't muss the clothing. Then he reached for the wall phone, took it off the hook, muttered, ''Thanks,'' dialed quickly until he whirled and smashed her alongside the head with the instrument and she went down flat, her head hitting hard, the stinging tears filling her eyes and she hoped he didn't think for a minute she was some weeping lady full of hysterical fear because she wasn't, the tears were involuntary, there was not much fear at all, only anger at her own liberal stupidity, until he brought the sharpened screwdriver into his hand and jammed it toward her face. Then there was fear enough for all.

"—gimme—"

"—huh—?"

"—gimme, goddamit!—"

"—give you what?—"

"—don' fock around—ever'theeng—"

Melissa stared at the young man with the screwdriver held close to her throat and where her mind went was to the odd fact that, under stress, his accent was infinitely more accessible, and she wondered why, perhaps it was like some well-bred Englishmen she had met once who it turned out were cockneys hiding their origins, but that was unusual for a young man such as this, for he was so clearly Hispanic, whereas there was no physical way of knowing the Englishmen weren't from where their accents pretended, and it crossed Melissa's always enquiring mind to ask him why he was dropping consonants now, stressing different vowels, but because her mind was also keen as well as enquiring, she decided against any cross-examination just now—"Jesus, shut up, Melissa," she told herself—"just do what he says, *he's not here to help you, he doesn't want to be your friend.*" She started to turn then, but he stopped her, shoved the sharp end of the screwdriver into her side.

"Who tol' you could move?"

"—my purse—it's in the foyer—I was going for my money, that's what you want, isn't it—?"

"—*we* go get it—you don' go noplace weethout me—"

They went to the foyer, where she pointed and he took it, dumped the contents on the table by the door, grabbed her wallet, opened it. "Feefteen fokking dollars?"

"—I'm sorry, I don't carry much money, but—look, I've got two credit cards, take them—"

"—focking women's credit cards don' do me sheet—I look like a woman to you?—"

"—no—no, of course not—"

"—jewels?—"

"—I don't wear them—"

"—gimme your fokking jewels, lady, you wanna be smart—" and he jabbed her again in the side.

"—that *hurts*—"

"—supposed to, now hand over your jewels—"

Her voice was starting to tremble now. "I swear to God—I wish I had some so you'd take them and go—"

"Show me where you dress—"

They went into the bedroom and her dressing table. He opened the drawers, dumped them, found nothing, cursed.

"You see? I wasn't lying."

He whirled on her. "You better fokking not be. Gimme your CD."

"My what?"

He jabbed her harder. "Gimme."

*"I don't know what it is."*

"You ain't got no compact disc?"

Melissa shook her head.

He stared around the room. "Okay. I'll take the TV."

Melissa closed her eyes. ". . . please . . . I'm not lying to you . . . believe me . . . but . . . we don't have one . . ."

*"Ever'body got fokking TV."*

She looked at him now. "We had one but it broke and we didn't watch that much, just 'Cheers' and Ted Koppel—"

*"—I don't care what you watch!"*

"—of course you don't—I'm sorry—the point is, we haven't gotten around to buying a replacement yet—"

He glared at the money in his hand. "Feefteen dollars?—I work my ass off for feefteen dollars—?"

Melissa studied him. He looked confused, a spoiled child who didn't get enough presents at his birthday. He glanced around, stared through the room across the foyer to the front door. And she realized that what could have been a horrid confrontation was ending, he wanted out, it was over, she had won, and just to give him an additional reason for going, she said, with as much strength as she had in the vicinity, "You're lucky you got that much, you better go now if you're smart, my husband will be home soon."

Such a mistake, oh, such a one.

Because first of all, he didn't believe her, and he looked at her differently now, because now he knew she was totally alone, helpless and alone, and he saw a chance to cut his losses, get his manhood back, make it a birthday party to remember. "Real soon?"

"Yes."

"Like right away, you mean?"

"That's right."

"So I better take off, you think?"

She nodded, watching as he took the screwdriver, put the sharpened end in his hand, pushed the round handle against her privates.

She brushed it away.

"He's one locky fokk."

She said nothing.

"You a pretty thing, y'know?"

"Look, you—" she began.

He pushed her in the privates again, harder. "I don't wanna look—except maybe at you." He pointed behind her, she knew where; to the bed. "You two light the lights? You and your locky man?"

She could think of not a thing to say.

"C'mere," and she thought he was going to try to kiss her so she bent her head to one side, pointless—it was her skirt he was interested in; he ripped it off her body.

"STO—" she began, but his hand went hard over her mouth and he whispered, "—thass the last time you try that, or I rip you up very bad, you believe me?"

She nodded.

"Step out of your panties."

Melissa could not move.

"Oh, come on, bitch, just do it, don' make me, all right?"

In a moment she was naked from the waist down.

He took the screwdriver handle, touched her again.

*"Please . . ."*

". . . women like that . . . tough stuff . . ."

". . . no . . . they don't . . ."

"Gentle then. You want it gentle?"

". . . I don't . . . neither . . ."

"You will—when you see this—" and he began unzipping his pants. Then he held it in his hand, began manipulating himself as he moved toward her, shoved her back on the bed.

Melissa fell, trying to keep control, trying to remember, what did you do in a situation like this—of course no intelligent woman would ever find herself in such a situation, but still, she'd read articles, and now as he knelt over her she tried so hard to recall—did you fight?—did you submit?—did you try and talk your way to freedom?—

She could not, not for the life of her, find the answer. And that was such a waste, answers were always second nature to her in school, college, grad work, nothing if you applied yourself, and now, when it *mattered,* when it wasn't studying a book for a meaningless grade, she failed. Think please, she told herself—fight? yes?—but then something echoed that if you did and you angered the man he might panic and kill you—of course he might panic and kill you if you tried to talk him out of it, and submitting seemed so disgraceful but maybe if she made her mind a blank, that was best, forget the creature above her, make believe he was a Sendak vision, scary yes, but with a comic intelligence enlightening it all—

—there was no comic intelligence in the face coming down toward hers.

He kissed her. He shoved his tongue into her mouth, with one hand on her head so she couldn't turn, with the other touched her nakedness, which meant he must have put his deadly screwdriver down, which meant he was moving into action so she closed her eyes, kept them shut while he kissed her again, and then his hands, both his hands were on her blouse over her breasts—

—"think of a field of yellow daisies"—someone had told

that once to a child when something unpleasant was about to happen—"think of a field of—"

Now his hands were tearing at her blouse.

Snow. White snow, that was always a favorite. Think of that, she told herself, and think of being pulled on a sled, think of that too, and ice cream after her tonsils were taken, cool and white, and Snow White and being loved by a prince and being fairest, and—

—and suddenly there was such power in her arms, such shocking brute strength in her slender legs, because she realized, as her blouse was ripping that he would see it, he, this brown-skinned thing would be able to see her orange shame, and no man had done that since she was grown, no man but Tommy, and that was right, that was fair, and that was also the way things were going to stay—Melissa twisted suddenly, twisted her body, pushed with her arms, kicked with her legs, and he wasn't ready, lost balance, and her fingers went for his eyes, missed, but as he toppled she saw his screwdriver, grabbed for it, didn't miss, flailed out at him with it, struck a blow, not much of one but enough for him to recoil, which got her to her feet, off-balance, yes, but moving, and he was behind her quickly, diving, his hands catching her heel and she went half down in the doorway, scrambled up, and she could have tried for the front door, but it was closed, she never could have gotten it open in time so she opted for the kitchen, because there were knives in the kitchen and when she got there she grabbed for one, missed, but she still had the screwdriver so she whirled, jabbing with it as he advanced, wondering if she could seriously use it, blind him, stab his throat, could she perform such a thing?

It wasn't an answer she needed to find immediately, because her Tommy came rushing in behind the other man then, her beloved husband, such tears of anger in his wild eyes . . .

Babe never knew why he cut his run short. Often he circled the reservoir for an hour, especially on pleasant late afternoons, such as this one, but today, twenty minutes in, before he could even work up a decent fantasy—Edwin Moses, the undefeated hurdler, had challenged him to a marathon, the whole of it to be televised live worldwide, for charity of course, and the sports pages were filled with controversy: could a half-mile hurdler never known for endurance defeat a great marathoner even though Babe had not trained seriously for a decade?—it was as if Bobby Fischer were coming back—Babe had been a history professor for years, and no matter what his former unquestioned greatness, could he return to anything resembling form?

Jerk, Babe told himself, slowing down, stopping. What a half-assed daydream. He liked to fiddle with reality when he ran, but this—this was the dumbest he'd come up with since . . . maybe the dumbest ever.

He leaned against the reservoir fence as the masses passed in review. When he'd begun running here, nobody knew about the reservoir. Just a few other nuts like him. Now it was a meeting place for Dalton mothers. It was no fun running today. You could have made better time jogging through Bloomingdale's.

And he missed Melissa. Not that they'd been apart, he just missed her. Breakfast had been mostly silent, not out of anger but she was beginning to read this fabulous piece on larynxes and it was tough getting her attention. Babe smiled, pushed off from the fence. There were those who might have found her weird—how many pretty young women *liked* riding the subways alone so they could pretend they weren't paying attention staring idly out the window or not reading a paperback, all the while listening passionately to the way people elongated their vowels, violated their consonants?

I guess she is weird, Babe decided, heading out of the park, running up to 116th, then crossing the West Side to 465, then up the elevator and he was surprised the front door was unlocked and as he opened it he could hear skirmishing sounds from the kitchen and as he ran in he saw it all so quickly, the short powerful brown man, fly open, his wife, ripped blouse and naked from the waist down, and as the tears came he went straight at the enemy, long thin arms outstretched, fingers tense, set to strangle, but the guy ducked, lashed out with a fist in his stomach and Babe, no Golden Glover, gasped, staggered back and the guy was on him, this time punching at Babe's face, landing, and Babe felt his balance going fast, reached for the ironing board to stop his fall but it collapsed and he was down, hitting the floor hard, and the guy dropped on top of him, knelt over him, smashing down with both hands now, as Babe's mouth began filling with blood . . .

Except for movies, Melissa had no knowledge of violence, and on celluloid it was always so precise, so choreographed, and besides, sitting there in the darkness, you knew there was no pain.

Now, standing there in her kitchen, seeing the blood smearing her husband's face, watching it spill along his chin as the smaller man continued his assault, she was frozen. It was so ugly and graceless and even though the last fifteen minutes had not been pleasant for her, they were nothing compared to watching her husband's pain. Suddenly she rushed forward, swung the screwdriver at the intruder's neck but he sensed it, quickly whirled, ripped it from her feeble hands and as he did she realized she had only made things worse and yes, her birthmark had saved her from a rape back on the bed, but what was going to save them now . . . ?

As the Spanish guy twisted, ripped his weapon from Melissa, Babe knew several things, two most notably—first, that the guy was going to return to his onslaught, probably with the weapon now, and second, it didn't matter. Nothing the guy did mattered. There were some truths that held, in earthquake or firestorm, no matter how the earth might tilt. Gravity you could count on. That the poor would suffer you could count on. That the wrong guys would enter politics you could count on. And that he, Thomas Babington—

Babe to his dead brother only—he, Tom Levy, was not going to lose this skirmish. Not with the sight of Melissa battered and shaken, her eyes glazed with fear. No. He could remove that look. He could make her Melissa again.

The Spaniard slammed him in the mouth.

Big deal.

The guy crashed an elbow against his neck.

It didn't matter. Because the guy didn't know one crucial thing—that the man he was on top of was capable of terrible violence; not often, not on the streets when people bumped him. He always said, "Sorry," and showed good-boy manners. When others were rude or insulting, he bore it with a smile. The grievances of the day washed off him.

Just don't come near his family.

And so, coughing blood, he reached around, scrabbled with his fingers for something to clutch onto, found the iron, gripped the handle, swung it up toward the Spaniard's face, where it connected, not much of a blow, a glancer at best, but it wasn't a fist, it was metal hitting flesh, so there was some power, even if Babe was not in a good position to get much leverage. He swung it again, backhanding the edge of the iron against the brown guy's temple and this was better, because the guy lost his balance, fell sideways, and they were panting terribly, exhaustion racing in to work its alterations, but not before Babe got to his knees and slammed the iron into the enemy's face, flush, sending him back and down, blood spurting and eyes starting to daze, and the next time Babe swung the iron he was over the guy so this was a cruncher, the metal cracking the spick's chin wide open, revealing bone, and he was unable to retaliate anymore, and the next time Babe swung he went for the nose and broke it and now the guy was next to unconscious, a trip he completed with the sixth swing, and Babe, over him, looked down at his senseless foe, raised the iron high and began the strongest blow of all until Melissa was screaming, screaming please for him to stop, backing up her words with actions, throwing herself at him, knocking him off balance, the blow aborted, the two of them most strangely in each other's arms . . .

The cops were terrific. They arrived within ten minutes, went at their jobs with wonderful efficiency. Led by a lithe black detective named Rory Baylor, they cuffed Ramiriz—the intruder's name was Jaime Ramiriz—took him away. Then Baylor led Babe and Melissa through a well-organized question-and-answer period, everything tactful and quiet. When he had what he needed he made his good-byes, said he would be in contact and please be sure to contact him if for any reason they felt the need. Babe accompanied the man to the front door and when they were alone wondered quietly if Baylor would be on duty later. Baylor did not ask why, simply replied that he most definitely would be, gave Babe the address of the precinct house. Then he was gone. Babe returned to Melissa.

She was terrific too. She had held together wonderfully during the questioning, now, alone, broke only briefly, sobbed into her husband's neck, took a deep breath, said that was more than enough of *that,* wondered next if her meringue soufflé had been damaged by the recent activities in the kitchen, which got a relieved laugh from Babe, because when she had her humor, you didn't have any cause for worry.

What she wanted was a bath, she said, and went to the bathroom, turned the tub spigots on. Then she undressed in the bedroom, was touched when she went to the tub to find that Babe had added some bubble bath to the water, making it even more inviting. She got in, closed her eyes, let the water heal her. After perhaps ten minutes she called for Babe and when he came, asked didn't he want to get the blood off his face too and of course he did, but he could wait, take your time, he told her.

She told him he was a nerd.

He didn't get it.

She pointed to the tub. Now. The water, I'm here to tell you, is fine.

The tub, he pointed out, was barely big enough for one.

His brain, she told him, was smaller than that.

Finally, *finally,* it crossed his mind she wanted him. But she'd been through a lot, he wasn't sure, so he asked.

She hid her head, saying please don't make me answer, I'm embarrassed enough as it is.

He stripped, edged his bony body in alongside hers. The water slurped over the sides, flooding the floor. It didn't matter a lot. She took a washrag, gently dabbed his face free of the dried blood. He took the rag when she was done, massaged her breasts. She talked then, quietly, about how the birthmark had given her strength. He answered quietly, truthfully, that she was what gave strength to him. They got out of the tub, dried each other gently, went to the bed, gently made love in the darkness. Then fatigue hit her. Her eyes half closed. He wondered if she minded if he left for a little, he didn't feel like sleeping and there was some work he'd left at his office at Columbia, would she mind being alone just for a bit while he went for it.

Not as long as you promise to come back.

He kissed her neck, massaged it. She rolled over onto her side, brought her legs up, breathing deeper. When she was asleep he dressed quietly, got to work. Because just as he knew, back in the battle in the kitchen, that he was not going to lose, he also knew there was more to the Ramirez business than simply robbery and attempted rape. There was information in the area, he was positive, he just had to find it.

It took him even less time than he expected. The second guy he talked to in the building, the first after the super, told him what he needed. It was a kid, a summer doorman, who usually worked nights.

"Anything unusual," he replied to Babe's question. "You mean like in the last little while?"

"Anything at all," Babe said.

The kid thought. "Nope." He shook his head. "Sorry."

"Take your time," Babe told him.

The kid smiled. "This isn't exactly an action-filled job, Mister Levy. I'd remember if there was anything."

"Sure you would," Babe said. They were standing in the foyer of the building. Outside, the summer night was darkening.

Then the kid remembered. "Would you include a mistake as unusual?"

"I might. Who made a mistake?"

The kid dropped his voice. "Don't tell the super, all right? But I was asleep here the other night when some drunk came by asking for you."

Babe had to force himself to take it easy. "For me?"

"Yeah—except that was the mistake—see he asked did a Levy live here, said you were expecting him, wondered what floor you lived on—"

"—and you told him?"

"Was that the wrong thing? I'm awful sorry—"

"Just go on, you didn't do anything wrong. Why didn't he come up?"

"Because it was late and I said so and he said not to worry, that you were big buddy bachelors and you, Frank or Mack, I can't remember what name he said wouldn't mind. That was the mistake, see? I told him your name was Thomas and you weren't no bachelor and he got embarrassed and went away."

"Tell me what he looked like?"

The kid shook his head again, made a face. "I can't, I don't much remember, I'd been asleep and he was in the dark and I was in the light. I guess he was big, but that's about it."

"This is the most important thing of all—try and answer this—did he have an accent?"

"You mean like a foreigner?"

"Like a German, for example. Was there any kind of German accent?"

"I don't remember. I don't think so. But then—"

"I know," Babe cut in. "You'd been asleep." He started

out then. "And don't worry, I won't tell the super—the *New York Times*, maybe, other than that, you can relax."

The kid smiled, waved, and Babe took off into the night.

Baylor, the quietly efficient detective, was working at his desk in the precinct house. When he saw Babe, he gestured for him to come over so Babe did, shaking hands, sitting in the chair alongside the desk. "She okay?" Baylor asked.

"Sleeping."

"You can never tell—after an experience like that, some women don't sleep for a good long while."

"I have to talk to you about something important," Babe said.

"I know—otherwise you would never have left her alone."

"Right." Across the room, a thin man with heavy make-up began to shout, "Here she is, boys, here she is, world, here's *Rose*," then started a mock striptease.

"Don't let that bother you," Baylor said. "He's harmless. It's just that he's convinced he's Ethel Merman and sometimes he loses control." Baylor stood, escorted the man back to the bench he had vacated. "You're in good voice tonight, Ethel."

"Thank you, Rory. With the cost of voice lessons these days, I can't study as much as I might want to."

"We're a little overworked tonight, Ethel, so if you'd kind of keep it down till we book you, I'd appreciate it."

"You really think I'm in good voice?"

"I do, yes."

"Then I shall be mum," he whispered.

Baylor came back to his desk. "Sorry."

"I have to tell you a little about myself before I get into it—believe me, I'm not into self-aggrandizement."

"Thank you."

"What?"

"Most civilians wouldn't assume a policeman would know a word like that. I appreciate it, go on, I won't interrupt again."

"Okay. I'm a college graduate, a Rhodes Scholar, I got a

doctorate at Columbia, I'm an associate professor there now in the history department, I've only been married the one time, to Melissa, for four years, we're going to have a baby next year, according to our master plan." He paused. "Know why I *spieled* on like that?"

Baylor shook his head.

"Because I want you to know I'm a very normal person, I'm not into oddball schemes, I don't send money to the Flat Earth Society, so please believe what I'm here to tell you."

Baylor gestured for Babe to go on.

"What happened today—in our place?—I think that was planned. I know it was. I just do. Someone sent, what was his name, Jaime Ramiriz to terrorize Melissa in order to get at me."

"Who?"

"I don't know—but this gets more whacko sounding—I think it might have been a bunch of Nazis or maybe even a government."

"You're telling me you think Ramiriz was in the employ of some very important people who are out to get you."

Babe nodded.

"You don't happen to also think you're Ethel Merman? —if the answer is yes, there's someone here I think you ought to meet." He shook his head. "Forgive that—really—apologies—okay?"

Babe nodded again.

"Frankly, Mister Levy, I'm grateful for the background you gave me, because otherwise these would be very deaf ears."

"What I want you to do, if you would please, is check his background. I think you might find some stuff to substantiate my story. Training overseas, maybe, I don't know. Would that take you long to do?"

Baylor flipped a folder across the desk. "That fast enough? It's Jaime's record. I know it damn near verbatim. I've arrested him twice before myself. He's twenty-eight, looks ten years younger, been doing the same dodge since he was fifteen. Cases a building, spots a security weakness, has his box of groceries, worms his way in if he can't find an unlocked door, steals. Sometimes he does what he tried on your wife. Look, Mister Levy. Jaime's been on the street maybe six months the last ten years, the rest in jails, check it out."

Babe opened the folder a moment, then closed it. "I believe you." He leaned forward. "Maybe he hasn't been in those jails—maybe they just marked it down that way to make it seem he was there."

"Who's this 'they'?"

"I don't know."

"What would be their motive?"

"I don't know."

"I think you're kind of wrong, Mister Levy."

Babe rubbed his eyes, wondering should he tell about the guy who asked what floor he lived on. No point. Not concrete enough. Baylor wouldn't buy it. Then he wondered about mentioning the droopy-eyed woman Melissa had seen following her but no point to that either. What did it substantively prove? Then he got the notion that maybe Ramiriz was a twin and the twin was the guy who got caught today and at that point he realized he was in very considerable danger of leaving reality behind. "No, I'm not wrong—there's *something*—but probably I'm just wrong on this, I'm sorry for bothering you."

Across the room, Ethel began belting, "Let me entertain you, let me make you smile."

"You're the nicest bother I've had today, Mister Levy, stop by anytime." He stood, they shook hands again, Babe left.

Out in the night, heading home, Babe realized how tired he was, and what a good thing Melissa had the job in England so soon, they could both use the vacation, especially after today.

Then he angrily kicked out at a Diet Pepsi can on the sidewalk, sending it half flying across the street—there *was* something going on, goddamit—he *knew* it. Just like he knew nothing better ever happen to Melissa. His brother was killed by Szell, and Babe had shot Szell dead. If anybody went after Melissa again, he would kill them too. He began to run home then, his mind full of murder...

## 3

As he stepped from the plane and entered London's Heathrow Airport, Scylla was reminded, as he always was here, of the infinite greatness of the mind of man. For surely, just as today we conjecture as to the beauty of Babylon's Hanging Gardens, future millenniums, he knew, would wonder about the greatness of Heathrow.

And how did some legendary architect manage it so perfectly, manage the seemingly impossible task of making every arrivals gate, no matter where in the world you came from, a good minimarathon away from the customs area. Somehow, you would imagine, there would have been a single slip, one gate where you could just smile good-bye to the stew, then a quick hip-hop and there you were, giving your passport.

But no, Heathrow was sublime in its total disregard for human comfort. As he walked briskly along, the trek was starting to take its toll. To his right, two American women were getting light-headed and he heard, "I've got to rest, Florence, you go on ahead if you want." Scylla continued on. Now a group tour was beginning to list, and their leader was saying, "No hurry, why don't we all slow down."

Scylla sped up. It really was remarkable. First-timers to Heathrow all experienced the same feeling—they had taken a wrong turn, it must be a mistake, customs had to be back there somewhere, they had passed it.

Alas, no mistake, customs was far far ahead, beyond the walking sidewalks that didn't walk, the WELCOME TO BRITAIN signs you wanted to deface, the permanent printed announcements of "temporary" improvements, all in the interests of a "better" Heathrow. A little girl sat down on the floor in her pink dress, and started to kick her heels in justified frustration. Her mother pleaded, "Honey, I'm tired too." Scylla envied the child for a moment—she was expressing all of their feelings, pink and kicking—but was the only one honest enough to truly let fly.

He moved on, passing all kinds of winded Orientals, puffing burghers, until at last—roll of drums, the customs area appeared. And now Scylla smiled, because the makers of Heathrow had their final fillip ready. Your heart rose in expectation as you entered the hall—and then they had you.

It all involved the number of passport clerks. This was a busy Saturday morning. Logically, the largest contingent of clerks with their rubber stamps should be yawning their way through. But no. The largest number were only on duty at night, preferably late, when there were few passengers. At busy times, only a skeleton crew worked. The hall was jammed, the lines curved and sagging, the passengers tired, beaten, all eyes bloodshot. No question, Scylla thought, as he took his place at the end; man can, when pushed, accomplish miracles.

Two hours later he was in Tring.

A perfect British summer day, and as he wandered along the single shopping street of the tiny village thirty-odd miles northwest of London, he totaled up what he knew. Specifically, the answer was nothing. On a more vague level, he was quite sure that since Perkins had chosen to end his life writing the village's name on a piece of paper, that something was very much going on here. And that something was undoubtedly not visible to the casual viewer. And involved either Division or enemies of Division, whoever they might be these days.

The shopping street seemed as normal as one might wish. A cleaner, a video recorder store (even here), a pub, a sweet shop (recently gone out of business), a tiny florist, a wine emporium (they seemed a bit small to call themselves that), a greengrocer, butcher, a large stationer's, that was pretty much all.

Scylla stopped at the end of the street, began to retrace his path, ask himself the odd question. Was it logical that a town so small would have its own florist? (Probably not so much odd as a less than sound business decision.) Was it unusual for a town so small to have such a large stationer's? (Same answer, Your Honor.)

But the sweet shop. Abromson's Sweet Shop, to be more specific. With its shelves still filled with delicious-appearing bon-bons. And the scrawled-pencil sign taped to the window. "Open no more. Without Max, my heart ain't in it. Thanks be to you all." And then the weak signature, "Mrs. Abromson."

The shop was flanked by the butcher and the wine emporium, and he hesitated, wondering if he should pay a visit to either place. No point, he decided. If you were seeking answers, you always did better, at least it had been his experience, if you had some idea of what your questions should be.

At the other end of the street was a small post office, a similarly sized library, beyond that, the commercial district gave way to residences. Well-tended homes, blocks of them. Scylla began to stroll. And look. For anything, anything at all. The streets had such wonderful British names. Drummond Ride. Meadow Close. Betty's Lane. (An immediate favorite.) Mortimer Rise. (Another.) Barber's Walk.

It took him over an hour to cover much of the residential part of the town. And of course it was pleasant, all of that. But such a waste. All of it. Everything. Until he saw the burnt-out shell of a house. He checked the address. He was on Tring Mews, the destroyed home had been number sixteen.

He glanced at it only a moment before turning, going quickly to the library, asking for and quickly receiving the last month's issues of the *Tring and District Gazette,* going to a quiet corner, commencing to turn pages. It would never give the *New York Times* cause for worry, but probably the paper did an excellent job of pleasing the local populace. There was a lovely headline article in one issue about the area band going on tour. And that space in the next issue was taken up with the great good news that the playgroup had been given a year's reprieve. (Scylla wasn't interested enough in finding out what the reprieve was for to read deeply into the article.) And many articles about land for sale. The next issue had a well-written piece on a major local problem, the widespread destruction of carrots by the badger population.

And then there were the photographs. Two Tring residents had been killed in a freak boiler explosion. One of the residents was a woman, a char who had been cleaning. Scylla looked at her picture. It meant nothing.

The other deceased citizen was the man who owned the house, an American businessman named Webster. Scylla stared at the photo, not a clear image, probably not that accurate either. But years ago, a decade and more, he had seen that face, or a much younger version. Once. Briefly. Somewhere. Only the man wasn't American, wasn't named Webster, wasn't a businessman.

Perhaps it would come to him sometime, the specific information. Surely not now as he sat, tried to remember. The best he could do at present was a hunch—he had seen "Webster" in Europe, perhaps in Germany. And he was wearing a white cloth coat over his clothing. Such as a doctor might wear. Or, in a laboratory, a scientist . . .

Scylla sat in the pub on Tring High Street, finished his luncheon of bangers and beans, all washed down with a Guinness. Delicious. Probably someday, an astute publicist/hustler/chef would decide that there was such a thing as nouvelle British, and then we would all get to dig in to Scotch smoked salmon with kiwi fruit, not to mention warmed salad of dover sole with walnuts. But at least for now, as long as pub food survived, there was hope for the Empire.

As he sat alone in a corner table, he was tempted to end his visit for now, head back to his suite in the Savoy. He had flown all night with nothing but Lana Wood's autobiography for company, was unquestionably weary. His mind was not functioning full out, and if it hadn't been for Perkins' message, he would have known that nothing untoward was happening in the bucolic village. A boiler had exploded. A man was using a false name. There had been some kind of sadness in the sweet shop. Absolutely no logical reason to assume the remotest connection between events such as these.

Except, because of Perkins, Scylla knew there had to be. Perhaps if he slept for a while, he would have more sense of confidence in his ability to think. But what the hell, he was here, why not try a little more, so he paid, wandered outside, stared at the closed sweet shop, crossed and entered the florist next door, expecting nothing. A cherubic, dimply-faced man was putting things away.

"Excuse me," Scylla began.

"We're closin'," the cherub answered, his Irish brogue fresh and pure.

Scylla said, "I was hoping to buy a gift, some chocolates, is Abromson's closed permanently or—?"

"—don't ask me nothin', if you can't speak well, don't speak a'tall, 'tis a motto o' mine."

"You weren't friends, then?"

"He was a fat nosy fella, what happened we all seen comin'."

Scylla gave a confused look.

The cherub became exasperated, pounded his heart. "The ticker, man, you keep stuffin' chocolate down yer throat, yer ticker's bound ta give."

"Yer wrong an' ye know it," came from a female voice, another Irish cherub, this one female, who entered from the back.

"Anhh," the man said, made a disgusted exit.

"It wasn't chocolate killed him, it was the strange children."

"Children?" Scylla said, casually, all the while knowing somehow he had struck gold.

"The invisible ones, them children."

"I know you're about to close," Scylla said, "but I'd love to buy some flowers," and he handed her a bill.

She looked at it. "For twenty pounds, ya kin have the shop."

Scylla gave her his sweetest smile. "Just some flowers an' conversation will be fine."

"Mrs. Abromson?" He knocked lightly on the cottage door.

From inside: "Who?"

Good question. Who indeed. Probably the world was his to choose, so, perhaps because it had been so long, he decided to string along with truth. "My name is Levy."

"Wanting?"

Just the trace of an accent—he wondered how many decades it had been since she left central Europe. "I'm here on behalf of the Webster family. I know this is a difficult time for you, but it isn't easy for them either."

"I got to?"

"No. Of course not. But I've some flowers here for you—perhaps they might be cheering."

Now the door opened. A pinched ancient face. He held out the enormous bouquet.

She hesitated. "They didn't have to do all this."

"Take it. Please."

She did. "You got nice eyes."

"My parents had something to do with that. But thank you."

"An' you talk good."

He knew she was measuring him in her mind, that she had already decided, in the affirmative. He stood quietly in the doorway, waiting.

"In, in." She gestured. He followed her to the tiny living room. "Sit, sit."

He found the sturdiest chair, sat.

"Anything?"

"No, thank you."

"These go to the kitchen, won't be long." She shuffled away, he counted the steps. Ten. Then ten more and she was back. She sat across, studied him. "Married?"

"Divorced."

"Children?"

"No."

She nodded her head awhile, going, "Um-hmm, um-hmm."

Scylla looked around the room. Wonderfully well kept up. A few photographs. One of two young people on their wedding day. It was clearly this same sad lady, her face was pinched and old even when the rest of her was young. The groom was already overweight. The other photos were of children.

"So?" she said finally.

"I'm told your husband was a witness to the explosion. Why don't you tell me how that happened to come about?"

"I told before."

Scylla smiled. "But not to me. Please."

Again the "um-hmm, um-hmm." Then soft. "Two weeks was it? Saturday was it? I think. He was in the shop. A bad mood he was in too. No business. Closing up thoughts in his head. Then the blessings."

Scylla said he didn't quite catch her last word.

"He called them that—later—'the blessings.' These little children. So adorable you wanted to . . ." She took her own cheeks, gave them a little shake.

Scylla nodded, smiled.

"But spoiled, he thought. All this I'm telling you—I wasn't there—he told me about it. At first, spoiled brats. Little—six, seven, maybe eight. Good clothes. Good manners. But at first he figured they was looking down, you know? Snoots."

"But they weren't?"

"No—that was the big surprise—sweet they turned out. And good behaved. Lot of talk. A birthday. A pound to spend. They bought. Max—he said he wished he could have brought them home. He gave white chocolate to them—expensive, but what is that when you can make children smile?''

Scylla waited.

''They left. He felt bad. Our kids—we got kids—not such a close family but that's the way now. Anyway, these blessings, when they was gone he got down in the dumps. So he quick made a couple of bags of more chocolate—presents in addition to the white—but what he wanted was more to talk. So he filled the bags and locked the shop and hurried up after the way they went. He got to the Mews corner and saw them way up ahead and started toward them. They were stopped near the Webster house and maybe one of them was crying. He huffed and puffed after them until the explosion blew. It knocked him off balance. He fell but got up and then he started crying. The shock. The boiler goes crazy and disaster, so fast, he cried from the surprise. Then he got as close as he could but the heat was terrible. Others came after the sound. Then the police and ropes went up. Craziness. More and more police. More and more people. Firemen. Nothing like this in Tring before. Never once a disaster and we been here thirty-forty years. Max waited. Till the very end. To see if he could help. It was late when he come home. I made him tea and he told what I'm telling. So upset he was. But nothing near as bad as the next morning.''

''What happened then?''

''The papers. Little articles was all they had. And . . . of course . . . they said only two died, Webster and the lady who cleaned, they never mentioned the boys. Brothers they were. The blessings. Max didn't understand. He called the police, he went to the police, he told about them—he even knew the names—Stan and Ollie—but they weren't found, no bodies, the police said he must have been wrong, just the grown-ups died.

''Max went crazy. He didn't believe. So close to the house they'd been standing, and even though he was knocked down he knew they were there—he didn't actually see perfect, but he knew. But no one believed him. He went to all the other shops in town and asked, did they see the brothers? No. No was the answer. They didn't shop noplace else. Over and over he pestered. Some of the others began to laugh and at the pub—sometimes after the day was over he stopped in—they'd ask him about his invisible kids."

"But he knew they weren't."

"He knew. But he couldn't convince no one. It was all he could think about. He went back and back to the police and he wrote and wrote all the papers and the television. Telling them. He phoned and phoned too. It got so I had to tend the shop to give him extra time. People was laughing louder at him; after a lifetime, in a week he's the joke of the town but he don't care, my Max, he was stubborn, so he kept on and he never would have stopped if the heart attack hadn't snuck up and he dropped." Now her eyes closed and the "um-hmm, um-hmm" was back.

Very quietly, Scylla said, "Didn't he know he was endangering himself, his heart, working himself up this way?"

"He wasn't endangering nothing—yes he was plump, yes he ate rich food, but the doctor, not six months ago, said he was still an ox. But I wanted him to slow down, not go so crazy too, he was worked up all the day about the blessings. Not a week ago. In this room. We're having almost a fight—we never really did but this was an almost. I told him, 'Look, your eyes ain't that good, maybe they went across the street,' and I told him, 'Look, you was knocked down, you can't see everything when you're knocked down,' and he said, 'You don't believe me either?' and I said, 'I always believe you, when did I never, but there's got to be other answers,' and then the dumb messenger came—he rang like you rang with a package for Max and Max took it and looked at it, he held it awhile till he got his glasses and then told the messenger, 'I ain't your guy, you got the wrong address,' and the messenger, so sweet and embarrassed he was, he apologized and went away and Max came back and begged I should this once not doubt him, he was right, he was right, and his voice, yes, it was loud, like I said it was almost a fight, and then he reached out a hand to me and falls dead. The doctor said heart. He's a good doctor. It was heart."

Scylla, knowing exactly what it was, seeing Uncle Arky fall dead in the laboratory of his Princeton house, the poisoned Magnum in his hand, asked, "Was the messenger wearing gloves?"

She nodded. "Very fancy he was, gloves and a tie all the way up to the throat. Such good manners. And so embarrassed at the trouble he caused."

"I'm sure," and he smiled across the tidy room, and they talked a few minutes longer, and then he thanked her and left and walked back, stood across the street from the wreckage that had once been sixteen Tring Mews. He hadn't unraveled a mystery, but at least he knew on his own that there was one, and at least some of the dramatis personae. Abromson had seen something he wasn't supposed to see. And he would not stop talking about it, to the papers, the TV. And someone who wanted him to stop must have found out.

But the brothers, the blessings, Stan and Ollie—they had to be the key. The key to what, he had no idea, but he would return to Tring, and when he did, perhaps he would know.

He was terribly tired now. And that condition had to be tended to. He had to be at his best tomorrow. Because that was when the hated Malcolm Beverage would come back into his life.

## 4

*Control it,* Beverage told himself, as he studied the unsatisfactory way his latest suit jacket looked in the three-way tailor's mirror. He seemed, as always, calm. If you took a poll of the people he knew casually—he only knew people casually—almost none would have commented on his having a particularly harsh temper.

But inside, the tides were always pounding the barriers. He had a dislike for shoddiness, for the ordinary, for the barely better than competent. He sometimes wished he had a comic book zap gun so he could disintegrate those who displeased him. If ever he had, the earth's population would go into a very sharp decline.

Beverage had a flattering face. People, on first meeting, liked him. He was clearly intelligent, he listened well, had wonderful smile lines. And his physique was as well muscled now in his mid-forties as it had been half a lifetime ago when he excelled as a gymnast. He still carried himself as the athlete he once was. Alas, he also had a gymnast's height, five six and a half, though the half was pure affectation.

His tailor hovered alongside. Beverage wanted to disintegrate him. Quietly he said, "I wonder if the shoulder is quite right." And smiled.

"It seems so to me, Mister Beverage. But of course, you're wearing the garment." A returning smile.

Beverage moved his body a few times. "Tight. Feels a bit tight. Can't have that now, can we, Freddie?"

"Not in my shop, sir."

Beverage made an almost imperceptible gesture. Instantly the tailor's assistant moved forward, took off the jacket, helped him into his blazer, brushed it, stepped silently and quickly back out of the way.

There, Beverage thought, that was the way the world was meant to work, each in its ordered place; he had no ear for music—the hum of efficiency was his favorite sound.

Outside, on Sloane Street, he looked at his watch. Close to five. He worked till seven at the very least, even on a Saturday, particularly this Saturday, since Scylla should be calling in. Should have already called in, hours ago, and they both knew it, except Beverage also knew that Scylla, with his prepubescent sense of humor would make him wait and wait, hope he would lose his temper.

Control it, Beverage told himself. Let Scylla hope in vain.

His office was across from Harrods, in Hans Court, so he turned off Sloane Street, moving gracefully through the crowds. He glanced at himself in a store window and was pleased at what he saw: a smartly dressed man out for a Saturday stroll, successful, probably not a care.

It took a lot, to make that appearance. Because now was perhaps the most trying time. His home life was a disaster and it was his fault, and probably there were some that would have buckled under that. And Perkins' death, reacting to that, not easy.

It was no surprise of course, quite the reverse; he knew that Perkins was due to die, just as he was, they all were in their line. Still, he would miss Ma. He cared for the fat man. With the home life that was also a disaster and it had been Perkins' fault the car crash, and he had buckled under that—the eating became increasingly compulsive, he looked at times like an aging opera star.

In fact, the phone call about Perkins had moved him terribly—and that had not happened to him in recent years. Not that he cried, far from that. But he and Ma had been locked together for so long now—the world thought them Bloodies when they were the total reverse, secret Godists, in this terrible time. The Bloodies were stirring confidently now, more so each day. But they would lose. That, as much as anything, was what supplied him with the confidence to keep control, Beverage knew. He had to stay in control, total, now.

Because, with just the least luck, peace would break through, and for a long time. Lifetimes. He more than anyone now had to see to that. Yes, he was a cold and hopeless husband; true, he was a cold, uncaring friend. List his vices, fill notebooks with them, it was, in the end, inconsequential. He loved peace more than any lush loved sweet wine. Whether the world knew it or not, Beverage knew this fact: he was the greatest Godist. That would have to be enough for any man.

Beverage was not much enamored of his office space. The location, Knightsbridge, Harrods, Sloane Street—impeccable. But when it had been decided, four years earlier, to move the head of Division abroad so as to avoid suspicion, the "avoiding suspicion" aspect was taken really much too far. The building was shabby, the space cramped, the rooms bone cold in winter, and when Beverage had suggested air conditioning for the occasional summer scorcher, it was decided to be a bad idea: air conditioning in Britain was showy, and went against avoiding suspicion. So on warm summer days, such as this warm summer day, the staff suffered.

His male secretary shook his head when Beverage walked in. Meaning no calls. Beverage looked at his watch. Five fifteen. He went into his private office, opened the windows, stared down at the well-dressed crowds still pushing their ways either in or out of the famous store.

Deservedly famous. Beverage rarely felt like disintegrating anyone that worked in Harrods. Oh, occasionally during their biannual sales, they would get in some young Sloane Ranger types who didn't know the stock, but on the whole, Harrods was an oasis for those who thrived on efficiency. If only the U.N. worked as well.

His private phone rang then and he wondered what his wife might want, since they rarely spoke at home, much less in his office, but he picked up the receiver without anger—he had, on occasion, allowed his control to go when they were alone, had hurt her, physically, made her cry out in pain. What could she want?

"Hello, Prick."

The sudden rough voice made him sit. The sound was different, changed along with the rest of him, but the tone and vocabulary were unchanged from decades past. Only Scylla called him that, at least to his face. And in that special way, the emphasis, with such contempt, on the "k."

"Now, Scylla," Beverage replied, "I want you to know there are those who might consider such a greeting insubordinate. I am not among them. I take into account your feeble mind and limited vocabulary."

"Beverage?"

"What?"

"We've detested each other a quarter century—let's not change a winning game. In other words, I hope that was your last attempt at charm."

"So be it. When do we meet?"

"Tomorrow. Noon. Speaker's Corner."

"Done."

"And come alone."

"And just what is *that* supposed to mean?"

"It means no bodyguards."

"You've become even more paranoid."

"It's a quality you bring out in people."

"I do my best."

"Good-bye then, Prick—try and sleep tonight. Don't fret. I won't hurt you." A pause. "No. I might hurt you."

Click.

Beverage sat in his chair, perspiring lightly. Probably from the heat. At least partially the heat. He wondered how many bodyguards he would need tomorrow. Scylla was prone to violence. Two. Two good surreptitious men. That should be more than plenty.

Beverage closed his eyes, contemplated just who it was he was meeting. Decided four bodyguards would make him feel more comfy . . .

Perhaps every century, Scylla reflected, as he walked into Speaker's Corner late the following morning, God shows His presence. For where else in the world but here, on Sundays, in the northeast corner of Hyde Park, was any human allowed to put forward any argument on any subject, no matter how distasteful or insulting, without fear of physical retribution?

If only every town had a Speaker's Corner, what a world this would be.

There were thousands of visitors strolling in the sunshine, dozens of speakers vying for their attention. Socialists and Communists and End of the Worlders, believers in Vitamins, devotees of Free Sex, British haters of America, British haters of Britain, Indians, Africans, going at it as long as their vocal cords could survive. And the crowds would flow, from one to the next, success depending not on which speaker had the most cogent philosophical position put most articulately, but on the quality of hecklers the speaker attracted.

It was the hecklers that made Speaker's Corner special. God alone knew what they did during the week, but on Sundays, the hecklers converged with only one intent: to destroy the speaker's attention span. Scylla had seen frustrated speakers actually burst into tears, which, of course, only made the hecklers hoot the louder. They were a special proud breed, merciless, giving admiration only to those few with sufficient power to maintain their sanity midst the din.

Oh, to be a heckler, Scylla thought.

In years past, this was where he always spent his Sundays. Admiring the skirmishes. It was a remarkable place—all the crowds, all the clashing points of view, always the heckling—and the whole of it controlled by just a few London bobbies, with their domed helmets, their uniforms of midnight blue.

Scylla paused briefly by a feeble speaker, standing, as most of his peers were, on plastic milk crates, going on passionately on the subject of how we must avoid nuclear winters. A fine subject, yes, but the man, clearly well informed, had a stammer which made him so pathetic not even the hecklers would bother with him. Scylla started next toward an elegant Oriental man who held a sign saying YELLOW POWER and was speaking intentionally just above a whisper, a Speaker's Corner ploy to draw the crowd in closer, and then, behind him a huge voice began going "Nipples, Nipples, Nipples," and a large man mounted a milk carton, continuing with his "Nipples" chant. The man had huge gaps where most of his teeth had been. Scylla, being so close at the start, decided to keep his position, at least for a moment. As he glanced around, he realized he'd made a wise choice—several hecklers began elbowing their way close.

"My subject," the speaker began, "my subject for today is: *are women human?* I say they are not. They are good for breeding, but there it ends. Women are weak, they snivel and whine, and they are stupid—"

"—your mother was stupid, that's plain, George—" a tiny heckler burst in "—she forgot to take the pill—"

The speaker ignored him. "Breeding farms are my solution for mankind. We should place all women in breeding farms—"

"—when they circumcised you, George, they threw away the wrong bit," the tiny heckler said.

The speaker, evidently named George, eyed the small tormentor, pointed down at him and said, "Everyone has a right to be stupid, my pygmy friend, but you abuse the privilege."

Now, another heckler burst in—"Why does George laugh on Wednesday mornings?—Because he understands the jokes we tell on Sunday."

And now another heckler—"George's dentist went on strike and his teeth walked out in sympathy—"

"—I would like to be a pigeon and shit on your head," George said to the latest intruder. "Now, these breeding farms, which I feel are the only hope for mankind—"

"—I had a shower this morning," the tiny heckler cut in. "Please stop spitting when you speak—"

As Scylla listened, hearing the crowd's enjoyment, watching the size increase, he wondered, did he have the strength of will to heckle? In the past, he never had, but now, after the years away, he wanted to, except all the hecklers were locals, would they resent him, jeer him into humiliation? Suddenly he was speaking loudly, using a Texas accent—

perhaps that would please them, "Dallas" was popular here—"Knock knock—"

No one answered him.

He looked around at the other hecklers.

Silence.

"Knock knock," he tried again, his courage waning.

Finally, from the tiny heckler, a quiet "Who's there?"

"Shirley."

"Shirley who?"

"Shirley George is an idiot."

And they laughed. The hecklers laughed. Not uproariously, but they never did, and in any case, it didn't matter, the decibel level. What counted was he was, for the moment, accepted, and louder, he did it again, "Knock knock—*knock knock*—"

Heaven.

Beverage entered Speaker's Corner at five minutes before noon. He crossed Park Lane on the run, very clearly alone. He intended the entrance to be that way, putting Scylla at his ease. His four men were, he noted, near enough if they were needed, not close enough to draw attention.

He stared at the milling thousands. He hadn't been here in years, loathed it, could easily have incinerated them all, the locals with nothing to do, who seemed to be half the gathering, the tourists from literally everywhere, the other half, each, it seemed, with a Nikon clicking away.

He migrated toward the biggest crowd, where a gap-toothed man held court trying to deal with some fool of a Texan telling knock-knock jokes.

Beverage wheeled away. Had he ever told Scylla how much he disliked Speaker's Corner? He must have, which was why Scylla insisted on meeting here. No one could possibly like it.

He glanced at his watch. Five after twelve. Scylla had said noon. Which meant he would probably appear at three. Beverage was fully aware of the wait ahead of him, had spent the morning making sure he could control it, the idea of giving Scylla pleasure anathema. Scylla would appear at three; Beverage would be all smiles. Scylla would say that he was sorry he was late. Beverage would reply, "Late? I just got here, I thought the meeting was for three."

Beverage almost smiled in anticipation.

At the least, it was a perfect English day. He walked aimlessly from group to group, glancing from time to time to make sure his four men were tracking him. They were, but no one could have known. Several Iranians ran by, chanting, "Death to Khomeini." Beverage walked on. A very fat woman walked by carrying a sign, I'VE LOST EIGHT STONE, YOU CAN TOO. Beverage always had trouble with the English weight system. How much was a stone? Twelve pounds? Did that sound right? If it did, how much had she shed? He was close to getting the answer when he froze, feeling the great killing hands on his neck, heard the rough voice whispering, "I said to come alone, Prick."

"I am alone," Beverage managed, but then the pressure increased on his neck, the pain was sudden and for a moment he began to black out.

"I enjoy hurting you," Scylla said, standing close behind the smaller man. "Take as long as you like, it's fine with me."

"All right," Beverage whispered, and he made three gestures with his hand.

Scylla glanced around, saw the three men peel away, begin their slow journey out of the park. He released his hold.

Beverage turned, stared silently at the large man with the skin so dark from the sun. Finally he shook his head. "Nothing recognizable at all. Amazing."

They began to walk. Ahead of them, a large nearly bald woman mounted a milk carton, began beautifully to sing "Danny Boy," eyes closed, as the crowd slowly began to move toward her.

"It's good to see you, Mal," Scylla said, putting an arm around the other man's shoulders.

"Affection from you? Hardly expected. But then perhaps you've mellowed over the years."

"I haven't."

Beverage felt the strong fingers then, pressuring into his shoulder joint. He gasped in pained surprise.

"Do it, Mal."

Beverage could hardly speak. "Do . . . what?"

*"Do it, Mal."*

Beverage again almost blacked out, managed a gesture with his hand.

Scylla glanced back as the fourth guard turned, quietly walked toward the nearest park exit.

"Silly of you, bringing them along."

"I suppose, I suppose."

To their left now, a speaker was losing his composure, screaming down at a heckler, "You speak two languages, crude English and bloody rubbish."

They continued their walk in the midday sun.

"About Ma," Beverage said then. "I want you to know—"

"—don't you ever call him that!—his friends called him Ma, you call him Perkins, you were no friend—"

And suddenly Beverage lost brief control, grabbed the bigger man—"You don't know that—you don't know shit—you've been vegetating for the last century—we were close—we were deep friends—"

Scylla took a step back, stared at Beverage; there were almost tears in his eyes. "Sorry. I don't want you getting human on me. I apologize."

Again they walked.

A Billy Graham type held court on their right. "Are you weary of the sadness of the world . . . ? Jesus is standing right beside you . . . Jesus is knocking this moment on the door to your heart . . ."

Beverage pointed to a bench and they sat.

"Let me be brief with this—the less we linger in each other's company, I'm sure the better off we'll both be."

"Go," Scylla said.

"Ma was murdered by a figure called The Blond. I hate

flattery but what he is, more or less, is the new you. You know about the Godist–Bloodies struggle?"

"I do."

"The Blond has been decimating our side."

"And you want him remaindered?"

"No, nothing that simple. Killing is never a problem, you know that. We need to know who our enemy is—in other words, who he works for. But there's a problem."

Scylla waited.

"He won't talk. He's been captured twice in the past decade, once in the Middle East, once in Central America. Both times he was rescued, but before that, he was also expertly tortured. And the man is impervious to pain."

"Or has been up till now."

Beverage nodded. "Or has been up to now."

"Do you know where he is?"

Beverage nodded again. "He's very open about that. Doesn't use shadows, evidently feels capable of surviving without the need. He arrived in London yesterday and was seen last night playing roulette at one of the better gambling clubs in Belgravia. He fancies roulette. Bets heavily. Loses a great deal more than he wins. I would think he'd need money, but whoever employs him obviously pays him very well."

They stood then, began to walk again.

Ahead, Scylla saw the saddest thing: a black garbage man resting wearily on a bench, his broom alongside him, staring glumly at the throng. Why sad? Because for him, this was not a place of joy, an oasis for the exchange of ideas. It was just mess. Bales of ice cream cups and shredded newspapers and cigarette butts. Mess in quantity, and he would never have surcease, it was infinitely replaceable.

Ahead of them, a heckler was saying, "As an outsider, what is the speaker's opinion of the human race?"

"We also have a good idea as to why The Blond is here. One of our chief allies, an eastern senator, is arriving tonight for a week, and he's bringing his two young sons. There are rumors of a possible kidnapping."

"Won't the children be guarded?"

"Guards don't always work," Beverage said. "I knew a man once—you won't believe this but it's true—who had four guards and they weren't much help at all." And then he smiled.

"Please don't try turning human on me again."

Beverage's smile only broadened—"Have no fear—I hate you much more than you detest me—"

"Music to my ears," Scylla said . . .

## 5

The croupier at the roulette table was confused. It was three in the morning, business was slow, he had but the one player, the large dark-skinned Frenchman. The croupier was also French, and they conversed easily, had done so for more than an hour. And the man bet fairly heavily.

But still, two things confused him. First, the man had no interest at all in the game. He would ask the croupier how many children he had, and when the croupier answered "three" he would bet three. Or he would ask the month the croupier's wife had been born or the date and bet those numbers. Nothing unusual in that—everyone had a system. But the suntanned man, win or lose, clearly didn't care.

The second confusing thing was this: the lone player was also not French. Oh, the accent was flawless, the vocabulary clearly that of an educated man. But there was something odd. As if it was a stored gift, the French, something placed in an attic and forgotten and only now being restored to use.

In French, the large man asked, "What year were you born?"

"Nineteen forty," the croupier replied.

"Not a good year for Paris," came the bettor's reply, as

he put ten pounds on the one, nine, four, the zero, watched the wheel spin, stared down at his hands until the ball landed in the "four" slot, only looked up again as the dealer pushed his winnings over.

He bet the same numbers again, watched idly as the croupier gave the wheel a counterclockwise spin, started the ball on its clockwise journey. Then stared down at his large folded hands.

The croupier smiled then as a familiar face approached the table, sat across from the dark-skinned man. "You've been away?" the croupier asked.

"Business trip in America," came the smiling reply, followed by the nod of the handsome, blond head.

Scylla hated roulette, it bored him probably as much as summer football would have. And the odds against The Blond showing, although not impossibly long—there weren't *that* many gambling casinos in Belgravia—still they were against. But he wouldn't have minded a sizing-up period before they went to war. He liked to know as much as he could about any enemy, and he'd done well enough in the past.

He decided to at least practice his French, which he hadn't used for a very long time and it was clear that something in his speech confused the croupier, still he was doing well enough, as he sat, hands folded on the table, staring down at them, listening as the "Business trip in America" was spoken.

And then the blood urge was on him.

The Blond felt the blood urge as soon as he sat, and it surprised him; not that he hadn't felt it before, but never this sudden, never with such potency.

He had been in a good mood when he came to the table. Because he had his next job, and it involved kidnapping two very rich young children, and if he handled it right, it could make him his fortune, let him gamble forever if he so desired.

He looked at the dark-skinned man sitting across, staring down at his large folded hands. Who in the world could that be, he wondered? It didn't really matter. He rarely wondered, he knew answers, just as he knew that he would undoubtedly have to kill the dark-skinned man, and soon.

The croupier, of course, knew nothing of any blood urge at this point. Any more than he knew that there was a terror scale which covered the facets of human behavior during, say, an earthquake. The lowest stage is not felt by people. Liquids sense something, and they may, if encased in a container, gently begin to sway. And the second scale might trouble some birds. And then horses become agitated. And dogs. And hanging objects begin to swing.

And finally, people become aware, and the blood urge works on the same level as the terror scale.

And the croupier finally became aware of something, as suddenly his mind was full of past slights, embarrassments, and he began to breathe more deeply, because he felt a terrible need for air, and if his dead father had been standing alongside him now he would have done what he always wanted, kill the man, just do it—

—and as his breathing became more audible he stared at the table where the most astonishing thing took place: the dark-skinned man stopped staring at his big hands, raised his head, stared instead across the table. For a moment there was nothing, just the two large men, eyes locked.

And then The Blond reached out, suddenly slapped the dark-skinned man across the face. Not hard. But with such contempt. And the dark-skinned man whirled and stood and fled, leaving his chips behind him.

## 6

Grumpy was the Switzerland of privileged information. A bril-liant sidewalk artist, a dwarf with a foul disposition, he spent all afternoons, Christmas included, in a quiet cul de sac off the King's Road. He appeared promptly at three, no one knew from where. He chalked till six, then left, to a destination unknown.

He would draw whatever fancied him at the moment. If a famous person had died or been involved in a scandal or whatever Grumpy might consider noteworthy, he would do a portrait, to the life, perhaps six feet high. Sometimes he would copy old masters, most usually Van Gogh. He worked furiously, his chalk box open as he darted around the sidewalk, grabbing one color, replacing another. That was all he had with him. The chalk box.

The hat he carried on his head. Put it near the box upon arrival, dropped a few pound notes inside, so passersby would know this was commerce as well as art. Sometimes children would watch, but his surly temper and fierce misshapen form frightened them; they rarely lingered. Other times, tourists would pause to watch, and he would scowl at them, glance at his hat, and if they dropped nothing in, he would stop working and stare at them, embarrassing them into either a tip or a departure. On occasions, men or, less often, ladies would pause, drop a folded-up bill into the hat. And if you were close enough and your eyes were very sharp, you might see there was a note folded inside. This was information, given for some future return. But usually this was superficial stuff—no one knew how his significant channels worked. But his information was limitless. He worked for no side—everyone used him, the decision having been reached sometime in the past that a figure such as Grumpy would be useful to all concerned. So like Switzerland, he had no enemies, was free to function as he wished. A figure of considerable mystery—gnarled and gifted, greedy, and always silent—no one had ever heard him speak . . .

The afternoon following roulette, Scylla entered the cul de sac, unsure until he saw the tiny figure that Grumpy was still operating. He had been away for so long, and Grumpy, though his age was difficult to determine, was clearly not young when Scylla had used him in the past. He paused, studied the portrait that was emerging, almost half-finished—it was after four. A dazzling likeness of Boris Becker, the young German who was terrorizing Wimbledon, coming from the pack with upset after upset.

Grumpy glared up at him, glanced at the hat.

Scylla, prepared, had brought money. "I need an answer to a question."

Another glance at the hat.

Scylla could not remember what the opening fee was. Before Grumpy would even allow for the possibility of your existence, money had to change hands.

Scylla put fifty pounds, folded neatly, into the hat, assuming that was enough.

Grumpy went to the hat, took out the note, looked at it, pocketed it, glanced at Scylla—then spit with clear contempt near Scylla's shoes.

Clearly not a gesture of satisfaction. Scylla took out another fifty-pound note, let it flutter hatward.

Grumpy worked on Becker's hair for several minutes, mixing his chalks, getting just the proper shading of red. Then he stretched, crawled around his work to the hat, took out the second fifty, looked at it, pocketed it, made a quick mark on the sidewalk with a piece of chalk: "*"—which he then quickly erased.

Evidently a hundred pounds was the opening price now,

inflation had infected everything in his absence; the asterisk mark meant this: "go ahead."

"The Blond? Do you know of him?"

Another mark: "+." The plus mark meant "yes."

"Has he a weakness?"

"+."

"Do you know his weakness?"

"+."

"Tell me."

"$."

Scylla put another hundred pounds into the hat.

"$$$$$."

Scylla wadded two hundred more.

Grumpy spat again, this time not missing Scylla's shoes.

Scylla reached into his pocket again, stopped as a little girl said, "Oh, look, Mummy—Becker."

"And rather good too," the mother said. They stood in the sunshine, smiled at the dwarf. "Go ahead," the mother said. "We'll just watch for a while."

"Oh, good, yes," the child said.

Grumpy shook his head.

"This is public property," the mother said. "And I warn you, I can be stubborn if the occasion warrants."

Grumpy scowled at her.

She folded her arms in front of her, firmed her stance.

Grumpy grabbed some chalk, began drawing something phallic, stopped when the mother said, "Come along, dear," and dragged her child away. Grumpy erased his most recent effort, looked at Scylla, drew "$$$$$" again, erased it too.

Scylla went to his wallet, counted out a thousand pounds, hesitated. Whatever it was Grumpy knew was information he had to have; when he went against The Blond, he was going to need any edge, however slight. But Grumpy had a temper. If you gave him too little—or at least what he considered too little—he would pocket your pounds and give no answer at all. Simply stare at you with scorn until you realized you had lost.

Scylla dropped twenty-five hundred pounds into the cap.

Grumpy counted it, pocketed it, studied Scylla for a long time, as if trying to remember. Finally he made a mark: "*." Go ahead.

The weakness obviously was either mental or physical. Scylla hoped it was physical. He had confidence in the power of his hands. Years of his life had gone into that confidence. "Is it physical?" he asked.

Grumpy stared at him still, that same studying look on his face.

They had done business, but years ago and not often and Scylla began to get angry waiting—Grumpy would never guess who he was—and he needed his answer. Louder: "Is—it—physical?"

Grumpy made a mark: "–." The minus sign. The minus sign meant "no."

"Mental then," Scylla said. "What is it?"

Another "–."

"It has to be mental if it isn't physical!"

"–."

*"What then?"*

Grumpy's hands flew, in an instant there was a cross, a man nailed to it.

Scylla was angry now, angry and frustrated. "A religious weakness? What the hell kind of an answer is that?"

Now the Christ was gone, and a stick-figured man was robbing another stick-figured man, and then that was gone and then—

"—*Moral*," Scylla said loudly. "The man has a moral weakness."

"+."

"Draw it!" He knelt now, got close as the dwarf made a chalk cloud, only a strange one, with a mouth, and after it, a running man.

Scylla shook his head.

Grumpy pointed at the cloud with the mouth, the man following.

Scylla just stared.

Grumpy scowled at him.

"Is this a game?" the first of two teenaged boys said, stopping, staring down, and Scylla whirled on them as he stood and his voice must have been the same as it had been back on his island when he frightened the helicopter pilot because what he said was, "No, not a game for you," and the teenagers just looked at each other and ran.

Grumpy had drawn another cloud, another, an entire string of clouds with mouths and the man chasing after them and—

—and Scylla realized they weren't clouds, what they were was a depiction of wind, the man was chasing after wind and enough of the Bible quote returned to him so he at last knew the weakness, said the one word: "*Vanity.*"

Grumpy nodded, erased, aimed one final shoe spit, then returned to Boris Becker . . .

# 2

# The Man in Lincoln's Nose

# 1

The brothers—they must have been brothers, though except for size they looked like twins, pudgy, reddish hair, freckled, the one an irresistible nine, the other an endearing seven—the brothers, excited, walked close together through the early evening Oxford Street shopping crowds.

"I wanna boiguh," the older one said, his accent very obviously New York.

"I wanna boiguh too, Clark," said the younger. The clouds were thick and low, fat with impending rain.

"Nyah, nyah, Spencer is a copycat."

"Not, not," Spencer claimed.

"An' frize."

"Me too."

"Wid unyuns."

"Me too."

Clark hugged his brother. "Yer not a copycat—yew just want the same as me."

Spencer smiled, took Clark's hand, started to cross the street.

From close behind them came the quiet admonishing voice of the black-haired man with the limp. "Easy, lads. Wait for me. Let's cross together."

The boys slowed.

The black-haired man said, "Good lads, the both of

you," took them by the hand, carefully guided them across the dangers of Oxford Street.

Once the trip was done, the brothers skipped on ahead again. "I keep forgetting his name, is it Mister Atkinson?" Spencer whispered.

"*Park*inson, think of the carousel in Central Park and that'll help."

Spencer hugged his brother now. "Parkinson, Parkinson, Parkinson," he said, plainly overjoyed with his new possession. Then, softer still: "Why does he have to follow us?"

"He's not *following* us, he's *guiding* us—so we don't get lost or nothin'. We never been to London before."

"Well, I wish he wouldn't look around all the time."

Clark glanced casually back. "He does look around all right. Maybe that's what a guide does—check things."

"Nothing could happen to us, could it, Clark?"

"Not before we get to McDonald's," Clark replied.

"I wish he'd stop limping like that."

Clark slugged Spencer on the arm. "He can't help that, dum-dum."

"Oh." A pause. "Maybe we should."

"Should what?"

"Limp?"

"You'll drive me bonkers—*why?*"

"So he won't feel bad about it."

"You're very sweet, Spencer, you really are."

Spencer had to smile.

McDonald's was jammed. They stood in line, the dark-haired man between them, and finally when their turn came, they ordered and he paid. "Aren't you gonna eat?" Clark asked.

"Later," the man said.

"But Mister *Park*inson," Spencer said proudly with a quick look at Clark, "you gotta eat, this is Mc*Don*ald's."

"Perhaps I'll pick off your plates," Mr. Parkinson said, carefully looking around. He located a table in the far corner that was empty, led them to it, sat them with their backs to the room, so that he had the view of whoever came or left. "Quite a day you've been through, laddies; the zoo and the cinema and now this. Are you happy?"

Clark nodded.

Spencer shook his head.

"What's wrong?" Mr. Parkinson asked.

Spencer had his mouth full so Clark said it for him. "He misses Dwight Gooden."

"Who?"

*"Who?"* Spencer said, amazement in his tone. "The Doc. Doctuh K. He's the greatest pitcher I ever seen in all my life."

"Spencer's in love with Dwight Gooden," Clark said.

Spencer took another bite, nodded.

"This is baseball now?" He reached out across the table. "May I?" He was pointing to the french fries.

Clark nodded.

"What's so special about this fellow?" Mr. Parkinson asked.

And suddenly the words came pouring out of Spencer's mouth—"He's eleven and three an' it's only Joo-lie—he's whiffed one-three-seven in one-three-eight innings, he's—"

Mr. Parkinson laughed. "I believe you, I'm sure he's very special." He stopped now, looked at the door where a blond man entered quickly, looked around, took his place in line.

"You haven't heard the worst—he's pitchin' today—if I was home I'd be by the tube and I could count his strikeouts an' everything. But you don't have baseball in this stupid country."

"It's not a stupid country," Clark said. "Apologize."

"It's not a stupid country," Spencer echoed. "It's just stupid they don't have baseball."

Mr. Parkinson said nothing, stretched, watched as the blond man changed his mind, left the line, hurried out of the restaurant, ran after a disappearing bus. "We have baseball," Mr. Parkinson said then.

Spencer took a breath—"Ya doo?"

Mr. Parkinson smiled. "In the autumn we televise a

professional football game each week and we do the same in the summertime with baseball.'' He looked at his watch. ''It starts in just a few minutes, in point of fact.''

''Can we see?'' Spencer asked. ''Can we, can we?''

''By the time I returned you to your hotel, what with the traffic and all, you'd miss a good bit of it.'' He paused. ''But I don't live far from here, finish your food and we'll taxi right there. Won't take but a moment.''

''We can always have McDonald's,'' Spencer said, standing immediately, pulling Clark along. And then a moment later they were outside in the darkness where Mr. Parkinson dashed for a cab, got it, and a few moments after that they were in an elevator going to the top floor where he stayed, and then they were in his living room, Spencer kneeling by the tube, getting it on, fiddling with the dials while Clark opened the windows because it was stuffy inside and while they were occupied Mr. Parkinson excused himself, went into the adjoining bedroom, closed the door, lay down on the bed, reached for the phone with one hand while with the other he threw off the well-fitting but uncomfortable black wig, mussed his blond hair, getting the tousled look he sometimes favored . . .

The job had a stink to it from the beginning. The Blond had his instructions, oh sure, and they seemed logical enough—pick up these senator's kids at the Connaught Hotel, take them to the zoo, a movie, a fast food meal, then bring them back early evening.

Except you didn't hire someone like him to baby-sit.

He could have kidnapped them right off, never gave it much of a deep thought—but the stink told him to beware. For all he knew, others might be following him.

So he decided to wait, be careful, look around all the time, just making sure he was alone, and then, when it was dark, whisk them away. He hated the black wig but it had cost a fortune, altered his look greatly when he coupled it with the limp. He could have been a great actor. If you didn't know for sure it was him, you'd have sworn it wasn't.

He hadn't expected the brothers to be chatting it up with the doorman when he got there. Their rooms, sure; the lobby maybe. But there they were, outside, making the doorman laugh. He introduced himself, and they were cute enough, and their manners weren't bad for rich Americans. But he sensed right off that the smaller one was bothered by his limp.

Well, he wouldn't be bothered for long.

It was a humid day, and he wore a blue suit, a white shirt and tie, so he wasn't comfortable. But then, that wouldn't bother him for long either.

The doorman hailed a cab and they got in and headed for Regent's Park Zoo. They sat in the rear and he faced them from a jump seat, looking around constantly as they drove, making good and damn sure no other car was happening to be going their way.

It was twelve thirty when they reached the zoo, and the movie they wanted to see—*Return to Oz*—started at four in the Oxford Street area, so that meant he had to fake looking interested for a good three hours. He had never, even as a child, liked public places; probably it was his light hair, his blue eyes. People were always touching him; that was a chief childhood memory, strangers, fat old women mainly, coming up, touching his pale-colored hair.

The movie was worse than the zoo. About how Dorothy wants to go back to Oz and see her friends but everyone thinks she's crazy so her aunt and uncle take her to an asylum where they put electrodes on her head—

The Blond looked away during that sequence. It wasn't that he was squeamish so much as he hated killing children, and if things didn't work out well after the McDonald's meal, these two beside him in the darkness were going to be forms.

He latched onto the idea of telling them there was baseball on the telly no more than ten seconds before he said it to them. It didn't matter really what story he used.

They were kids, they believed things. The baseball story happened to fit in so he used it.

The suite was in the residential hotel he had booked that morning, two rooms, along with a bath. High floor. The building was big, run-down, it didn't matter, he wasn't planning to stay there long. He stocked it with a little food, a few more violent supplies, then dressed and went to the Connaught . . .

"Oh, I hope we haven't missed the baseball," Spencer said as he dashed across the living room as soon as the front door was open. He knelt by the set, turned it on.

"Can we open the window, it's stuffy," Clark asked.

He smiled. "Whatever you fancy, lads, make yourselves to home," and he left them, closed the connecting door, lay down on the bed, took off the cursed wig as he dialed the phone and when it was answered he spoke with great quickness and clarity: "I have Clark and Spencer, never mind where. If you ever want to see them again, and this is, believe me, your only chance, I want a million pounds for each, I'll tell you where to deliver it later, but first, are we in business, your only chance, yes or no."

A long pause, then: ". . . no . . ."

The Blond sat up, shocked. He shouldn't have been, but he wanted the money so badly—there were cities in the world where he'd never played roulette, and he wanted to visit them, visit them all—"You understand you're killing them, I mean this, a million for the pair, *yes or no?*"

Again the pause. Then: ". . . no . . ."

He was about to lower his price still further when he was overcome with contempt for himself, either you were a man of your word or you weren't, either what you said meant just that, what you said, not half—*how could he have caved in like that, lowered his price like that, humiliated himself like that?*—

He slammed the phone back into its cradle, lay still, eyes closed, wondering what to do next. No, not what. Who? Spencer, the smaller, was the more adorable of the two, the most difficult to end, so Spencer had to go first—that way, ending Clark would be almost enjoyable. "Spencer lad," he called out. "Come here a moment, would you please?"

From the next room, muffled: "I'm looking for the baseball." Sounding upset.

Christ! The last thing he needed was tears. "Clark, tear yourself away from the set a moment and lend a hand to me, there's a good lad."

Clark came in the doorway. "What do you want, Mister Parkinson?" He pointed. "What happened to your hair?"

"Come in, come in, close the door."

Clark came in, closed the door. "Your hair, though."

The Blond pointed toward the dresser. "Bring me the bag, son. I wear the dark sometimes, makes me look younger." He pointed again.

Clark said, "There's two," and looked in the nearest. "You want fruit and cookies, Mister Parkinson?"

A smile. "The other."

Clark crossed the room, handed it to the man, who stood, took off his coat, took off his tie, unbuttoned his shirt, then took some rope and some tape from the bag. "I thought we might play a game with Spencer, does he like games?"

"Oh yes, he loves them, we both do, what game?"

"How does hide and seek strike you, lad?"

Clark made a face. "We played that a lot."

"Not my way."

"What's so special about your way?"

"Well, the trouble with hide and seek is that sooner or later the one who's hiding makes a noise and is found out."

Clark took a step backward. "I don't think I want to play your way," he said, the last words he got out, because suddenly the tape was slapped across his mouth.

The Blond was surprised at the weight of the child; heavier than he'd imagined as he spun him, expertly tied his hands tight behind his back, tied the legs at the ankles, carried him to the large bedroom closet, dumped him inside, shut the door. Then he went into the living room, studied the perfect freckled face playing with the dials. No question he was right—Spencer had to go first; after that Clark would be pie. "Spencer lad?"

"Yessir?"

"Clark said he wanted a bath, I'm going to run the water, how do you boys like it, hot, warm, tepid?"

"We don't like baths."

"I didn't either when I was a child; but if you had to have one, how would you like it?"

"Not that last thing and not hot."

"Warm then, fine." He moved to the bathroom, turned on the spigots, got a nice warm temperature, let the water flow. When the tub was half-full—that was all his needs required—he turned the water off, went to fetch the youngest.

"I can't find the baseball, there's only cartoons."

"Life has its ups and downs, Spencer, come along," he said, and then he lifted the child, clamped one hand across his mouth to stop the scream, carried him to the tub, spun him again, facedown into the warm water, and held him there . . .

It wasn't till he saw the dark-haired limping man all but sprint for the cab outside the McDonald's that Scylla realized that The Blond wasn't going to overpower the children's bodyguard, he *was* the bodyguard.

He had been alerted that the children were safe and well at the movie theater, and he picked them up there, sitting many rows behind them and their guard, watching as the bleary film unfolded.

They really should pass a law, he thought, as he sat there: No Movie Sequels. Ever. Under threat of death or worse, banishment from Chasen's. Other arts didn't do it to this degree—Leonardo never made a Mona Lisa II. Michelangelo had a smash with his Sistine Chapel, but once was enough for him. Why would anyone feel the need to sully Judy Garland?

He shifted in his seat, decided to try being cheery: there had been no *More Singin' in the Rain*. Or *Return to the Battleship Potemkin*. Bergman, his favorite, had not been tempted to direct *The Eighth Seal*. Wilder had not done *Some Like It Cold*.

Now he was sort of amused. He half shut his eyes, coming up with more sequel titles. *The North Philadelphia Story. Two Flew over the Cuckoo's Nest. Gertrude, Queen of Denmark. It Isn't a Wonderful Life. Fresh Strawberries*—no, not right, "fresh" wasn't the opposite of "wild," he was getting silly now.

Besides, blessedly, the movie was over.

He walked up a different aisle from the trio, the two cute kids, the dark-haired guy with the limp who was clearly doing his job, looking around constantly, eyes flicking.

He kept that up on the street in the darkening early evening, always on the lookout; Scylla hung back a good distance. The guy was doing his job for him—no point to being closer, if The Blond was going to make a move, the guy with the limp would be ready. The three crossed Oxford Street and later found the McDonald's and sat in the window corner, eating. Scylla stayed across the street, watching whoever entered or left until suddenly his three were moving toward a cab and the limp was gone.

He ran the first half-block, trying to keep them in view, looking for a taxi of his own, and just when it looked like his luck was bad it was good, a couple got out of a cab and he got in and he was behind, sure, but he knew the direction the other cab was going and he did his best to keep it in sight which he did, until the very end, and when his cab turned the final corner the one he'd been following was empty and there were two buildings on the block, residential hotels, both big, one called the Wellington, the other the Saint William, and he gambled—he knew there might not be much time, wasn't sure why he knew, he just did—tried the Wellington first, and the seedy desk clerk shook his head at his description of the three, at least he did until Scylla flashed a bill, and then he knew his quarry was in suite 1010, and he had to wait for the slow elevator and it was irritating as hell but it came and after that he was on the tenth floor and he found 1010 easily, but first used his lock pick to enter 1009, which was empty, and he crossed it, threw the window open, saw the six-inch-wide ledge just a few feet down that circled this, the back of the building, and then he was out of 1009, hurrying next door, expertly raking the lock, throwing the door open wide . . .

Spencer was kicking as he lay, facedown, in the tub. He was doing it clumsily but with unexpected power, and the water splashed all over the bathroom.

The Blond had not expected the resistance, surely not the ferocity of it or the water hitting his eyes, making him blink, and probably that was what loosened his grip, at least for a moment.

The moment was enough for Spencer, who wiggled loose, got his head up above the water level, gasped at the air.

Then The Blond had him again, this time one hand at the neck, the other on the boy's face.

Spencer bit the hand.

The Blond pulled back a moment, then grabbed the boy again, half lifted him, pushed him back down under the water, faceup this time, held him tightly.

But not tightly enough, Spencer slipped free, again gasped for air, this time made a clumsy swipe at the man's face.

The Blond turned his head in time, the blow grazed him with all the force of a spring raindrop.

Spencer tried getting out of the tub.

The Blond shoved him back and down.

Spencer clambered to his knees.

The Blond began to get angry at himself for the wastage of time.

Spencer got one foot on the floor outside the tub.

The Blond pushed him back, or tried to, but he slipped on the wet bathroom floor.

Spencer had both feet on the ground now.

And now The Blond realized his trouble—it was always hard doing this kind of work, it wasn't what he enjoyed, debasing children, especially sweet children, but he was a man of his word with a great and greatly earned reputation and that was important if you wanted to succeed in this world, so he grabbed the child, lifted him, threw him down to the hard floor, lifted him again, so the adorable face was staring at him and he let fly with an elbow smash that all but turned the child's head around and then he lifted him a final time, plunged him back facedown into the water, applied all the pressure he could, one hand on the head, the other holding the feet, no kicking this time, not allowed, and he began to count to himself, a thousand one, a thousand two—

—it was over before he reached a thousand two hundred but just to be sure he counted another sixty seconds, then left the still child in the tub, exited, headed into the next room where Clark was tied in the closet, started to open the closet door.

Stopped. His stomach was rumbling.

It was a good thing he'd thought to bring some food; he went to the dresser, reached into the bag; chocolate cookies, a favorite. And several Granny Smith apples. In England, they were among the great tastes. Tart and green, they whetted his appetite. So he put the chocolate cookies back, settled for just the apple. He took it to the bed, lay down. When Clark had joined his brother—and that would be soon and would take no time at all—he would have a real meal. Perhaps the rack of lamb at the Capitol Hotel.

He crunched into the apple.

And almost blushed as he did so, such was his embarrassment. You must stop this, he told himself. It's really silly, these hunger pangs. He had never made a form after a full meal and he wondered if he did, when the corpse was still, would these hunger pangs come then? Maybe that was an answer. Only work after eating. That might take away the humiliation.

Another delicious bite. He'd picked a good one, the white insides crisp and exceptionally juicy. Another bite. Hungrily now, another and another. The juice of the apple was running down his chin when, to his quite genuine astonishment, the door to the room opened and the fellow he'd slapped at the roulette wheel the night before last stood there, surely not by accident.

Then The Blond did two strange things. First, because he felt so sheepish, lying there eating, he threw the apple core at the intruder; it didn't land close but what damage would it have done if it had? Second, he threw his body off the bed and charged the suntanned figure, straight-out charged, no feints, just bull in and close and then their arms were locked around each other and their bodies fell against the door, slamming it, and then The Blond broke the hold, pulled away. He knew what he had to know now: yes, this stranger was big, and clearly a man of great power. But not great enough. He was also too old. Not quick enough, strong enough, fast enough, young enough. Oh, he would pose problems, but that could sometimes be pleasurable.

His scraper was where it always was, resting securely in his right-hand pants pocket. In time it would be in his hand. And that would certainly be pleasurable. Scraping this one would work up a wondrous appetite indeed.

Scylla was startled when The Blond charged. It was such a dunce move, surely he would alter it, and he prepared himself for those contingencies, but the man surprised him again when he came straight in, and their bodies locked, a strength test surely, and he gave his best.

But it wasn't quite enough. The younger man had an edge there. And surely a larger one in more recent experience. And give him quickness too.

Not to mention he was armed. Whatever he used to disfigure the dead, surely that weapon was on his body.

Then they began to circle. Scylla made a slight move, almost imperceptible. The Blond made an equally imperceptible counter, came back with the swift start of motion of his own which Scylla dodged. If you were watching from on high, what you would have seen was nothing. A scorpion dance. Two lethal creatures minueting, a safe distance away. Nothing.

But of course everything was going on. The Blond didn't know who Scylla was but Scylla knew very well who they both were. And the number they had disposed of in the past. And all these tiny feints, if not countered immediately, were death blows for the uninitiated.

The Blond began initiating more moves now and Scylla, crammed in the bedroom, edged toward the other room, hoping it was bigger, was pleased when he got there to find it was. It was also quite dark, the only light coming from the dancing cartoon creatures on the color TV.

Somehow they were fitting witnesses for the bloodbath that was sure to come.

The Blond did not like the larger space of the living room. He preferred it close, where he could simply close, not use up energy stalking. But they were in the living room now, it was a condition you had to use to your advantage, a different battlefield than one he might have chosen, but not to worry. He never worried, not when his hands could speak for him.

The cartoons caught his attention briefly, and even though it was but a brief eye flick, he paid for it: the suntanned man got a fist into his rib cage, no damage, he sensed it quickly enough to dull the blow—

—but cartoons were for later. Now it was time for the scraper, his versatile tool, it could slash throats as easily as take faces. He turned his body slightly left, freeing his right hand to grab it from that pocket—

—but again he paid for it, and this time it hurt, for the other man feinted toward the rib cage again, then surprised him with a sudden kick to the right wrist, numbing it. He wanted to curse but that would be giving satisfaction to the enemy. He bit down on his lower lip, feeling an anger begin.

Good. Very very good. Anger had long been a friend to him.

As soon as The Blond began to turn his body at an angle, trying to free the right side, Scylla knew what he was up to.

The man was right-handed, his scraper had to be in that trouser pocket.

And it had to be kept there.

The first kick, after the rib fake, worked well, it had to hurt, and more than that, The Blond had not known he could use his feet till that moment so that gave him more to worry about.

The enemy body again began to turn now, the left prominent, but Scylla circled quickly, giving nothing away, he had to keep on top of the right, crowd it, cripple it, keep this hand-to-hand not hand-to-blade. Whatever the scraper was, he had seen what it had done in Perkins' house and he knew it was extraordinarily sharp.

Still the circling; Scylla pressed, ducked when The Blond tried a right swing, could have gone for the midsection, might have landed a hurting blow, but not a crippling one, so he kicked again, got the fingers of the right hand this time, saw the look of pain in the other man's eyes.

The Blond was whipping his right hand now, flapping it, trying to get circulation back, and Scylla was in control—as long as the enemy had only one move you were always in control. And suddenly he lashed out with his own right hand, the edge of it, slashed the wrist of The Blond, saw the pained look again, a sweet expression in the dark room, the cartoon brighter now as the characters chased each other, and even though they had been at this for but a few minutes, he sensed that The Blond was losing either confidence or energy, he would have loved both, settled for either.

The Blond was a tennis fan, and he knew that Jimmy Connors had a great weakness: his approaching forehand. Usually, when he hit it on a rush, he would net it. Sometimes he sent it long. Rarely did he win a point when he had to hit an approaching forehand.

So why had Connors won more championships than any other man? Was the weakness a secret? Of course not. It was simply that few other players had sufficient talent to force him to hit a hard approaching forehand.

And the parallel to his position? Yes, it was difficult to have to grab your weapon from your pocket. But no one he had ever gone against had sufficient talent to make him pay for it as he was paying now, as his right arm, numb and damaged, seemed helpless in its reach for salvation.

But if you were very great, as The Blond was, you always sought improvement, and there was a system of violence that emanated from Denmark, Maso it was called, after the word for people who want pain, and the secret of Maso was this: you accepted pain, put yourself in a position to have it inflicted on you.

Stupid. Yes. But not if there was a greater good behind it.

So now The Blond made his move, started to repeat his earlier attempts of leading with his left side, then dropped his left arm and twisted his body and for an instant he was vulnerable, his rib cage was revealed, and the suntanned man filled the instant, elbowed him there, and he knew several ribs were cracked, and of course the pain was considerable, but the diversion worked, his scraper was in his hand . . .

As soon as he saw the opening Scylla went for it, had to go for it, cracked or broken ribs took a toll, an increasing one if a struggle was long, and he had the blow half delivered before he realized he'd been trapped, and there was nothing he could do but complete the blow, hear the bones give, see the bright eyes of the enemy as the weapon he'd sought so desperately appeared clear and deadly in his right hand.

It resembled a straight razor, except clearly it had been specially made—there was a curve to the blade, a face-fitting curve, and now he began to retreat as The Blond led with his right, his weapon hand, and Scylla kept his body in balance, awaiting the first blow, and when it came he blocked it, only to discover too late that he had been fooled again.

* * *

The Blond, hurting, knew he needed to end it quickly so he did the obvious, slashed with his scraper, except when the enemy came up to block the blow he dropped the weapon, grabbed the wrist, grabbed it with both of his hands and, using his muscular body as a fulcrum, flipped the other man across the room, spun him with all his power across the room where he slammed into the wall and slipped down, stunned.

He got up quickly, but not quickly enough, as The Blond was on him again, leveraging him again, only this time he took aim at the open window and spun the other man dead at it, got him half out, but his arms saved him.

Not for long, as The Blond grabbed the arms, and the other man kicked and fought but The Blond was relentless, he was always a great closer, and now he forced the dark-skinned man out of the window, and down into the night, and—

—and *SHIT*.

He stared down at his victim and cursed the fates because the man was clinging to a fucking ledge, clinging not very strongly, he was battered and stunned, but both of his hands held to the ledge and he hung there, ten stories up in the dark night, *alive*.

The Blond reached out the window, tried to smash the other man's hands with his own but it was just too far. He yanked off his shoe and slammed down onto the ledge with that but just before the blow struck the other man saw it and managed, weakly, to clamber a foot further away.

And now he seemed to be resting, shaking his head, trying to think.

Then he was going, slowly, to the neighboring window, but before he was halfway there The Blond raced to the bedroom where the next window was, threw it open, reached out, stopping the other man's progress. The man began to move back toward the living room window, but when he was too far away to be reached, he stopped and hung there.

The Blond was back in the living room window now,

staring down, waiting for gravity to take its effect. The man had to be exhausted. The ledge was rough, made of sharp brick as was the side of the building, and it was perhaps six inches wide, no more, not a place where a man could linger long and—

—and *SHIT!*

The man was trying to force his body up to the ledge. The Blond watched the feeble efforts, no more than eight feet away. He was actually trying to get a strong enough grip to swing his body up so he might actually stand on the ledge.

The Blond had no fear of heights, only a hatred of waiting when sudden hunger hit him, as it did now—he wanted an entire leg of lamb, a side of beef, he wanted to gnaw through bone. The hunger increased as he carefully stepped through the window, got the feel of the ledge, kept one hand on the sill, kicked at the enemy's fingers—but the man evaded the kick, moved a yard further away.

The Blond followed him and in the darkness the two men were both on the ledge of the tenth floor in the rear of the Wellington Hotel, on the face of the building—the battle was finally joined.

But only for an instant. The man moved away, The Blond followed, the man moved away, The Blond followed—and then, just then, The Blond knew his mind had snapped because there, there in the darkness the dark-skinned man swung his body quickly like a gymnast and then they were both standing on the ledge. But again only for an instant, because now the dark-skinned man began to climb, yes climb, up the face of the building, climbing quickly and surely, first up above The Blond and then sideways, so he was over him, and then he began kicking down, and The Blond could do nothing, couldn't risk reaching up because he knew his balance would go, and the kicks continued, not trying to force him out but down, and down he went, trying at first to sit on the ledge but it was too narrow, it wouldn't work, and then he was hanging, his fingers holding to the ledge, as his enemy had been a few moments before, and he liked it better the other way, when he could look out hungrily, not now, when he was clinging with diminishing strength to the brick ledge, all appetite gone.

Scylla, as he clung in space to the ledge, kept thinking of *The Man in Lincoln's Nose,* the original title of *North by Northwest,* one of his favorite movies, which climaxed with Cary Grant in danger on the face of Mount Rushmore.

Not that he felt in any particular danger. Oh, he wouldn't have wanted to spend his summer vacation here, but his arms were strong, and the brick, though rough, the same. The problem he had was to make himself such an alluring target as to get The Blond to come out on the ledge to finish him. Because once that happened, it was game, set and match—climbing this building was nothing compared to chasing the birds on his island.

He tried tempting the other man by drawing close, then decided to pretend he had a sudden resurgence of energy and would make it back to the ledge safely.

It worked. When The Blond was far enough out on the ledge for him to move, he did, getting first quickly to the ledge, then climbing up and over, starting to kick down, but carefully, he didn't want The Blond falling, so the blows came sideways and down, and the other man tried to sit on the ledge but that was impossible, and then he was hanging tight as Scylla moved down to the window, stepped inside.

The Blond was within reaching distance.

"Who ordered you to kill Perkins?"

Shake of the head.

"Who?"

Shake of the head.

"No way to make you change your mind?"

Shake three.

"Want me to step on your fingers?"

"Do what you want, death doesn't bother me."

Scylla stared down at The Blond. His grip was weakening. He reached out, took the man's hands, raised him a few inches. "What if I let go now?"

"Death doesn't bother me, if you want to, let go."

"Maybe I'll use your scraper—maybe I'll take your face off."

"I don't care if I die."

Scylla looked confused. "Oh, listen, I think you've got it wrong, I don't mean to imply you'll be dead when I use the scraper. I would never do a thing like that, not to a handsome man like you."

"What . . . are you saying?"

"Well, just listen—I'll break your shoulders so your arms won't feel like much, and I'll sit you in a chair and then I'll get your scraper here from the floor and I'll just, you know, go to work."

"Work?"

"Sort of work, it's hard I'd guess, I've never done it so probably I'll be clumsy but I just thought eventually I'd scrape your face all away, and you'll be beautifully alive while I do it, and you'll be alive when I'm finished but maybe not so beautiful anymore, what with the skin gone and your other features too—probably you'll have a hard time meeting girls at first—"

"—don't talk that way—"

"—why? You think I don't mean it? I mean it. Look at me. Nice vain fellow like you, you'll love what I'm going to do."

The Blond looked up into Scylla's eyes.

"I saw what you did to Perkins, you better believe I mean it!"

The Blond, when he crumbled, went quickly, the sudden burst of tears coming from his eyes and then he was screaming, *"Beverage, Beverage, I work for him,"* and Scylla found that interesting, and they chatted for a few moments more until Scylla pulled the sobbing hulk inside, did what scraping needed doing, and then, thinking very much of Ma, pitched his killer out the window.

He needed to find the children, or what was left of them, and since The Blond had been in the bedroom with the apple in his hand, he decided to begin there, tried the large closet right off, saw the large bundle on the floor.

Carefully he lifted the heavy child, took the tape off his mouth.

"Don't do no more, mistuh," the kid said.

"Shh," Scylla said, "it's all right now."

The kid looked at him. "You shuah?"

Scylla smiled. "Shuah." He got the ropes free of the child's hands, started to work on the feet when the boy hugged him, gratefully; he was a brave young man, not trembling, no tears. Scylla got the ropes off his feet.

"Spencer okay?"

Scylla shook his head. "Not sure yet."

"He was watching the cartoons," and with that the child turned, raced into the living room, going, "Spencer? Come on now, it's me, no games."

No answer.

Scylla stood in the doorway, turned on the lights so the television no longer supplied the sole illumination. He went to the nearest closet.

Empty.

Now the kid was hurrying ahead of him, throwing open the bathroom door. No sound. Then, softly: "Aw, Spence." So sad.

Scylla moved to the bathroom then, peered inside. The room was a shambles. The tub was full of water. Huddled in a corner was a smaller version of the child he'd just rescued.

"Ya got all wet, Spencer," the larger child said.

"It wasn't my fault, Clark, I didn't mean to," Spencer said.

Scylla watched as the two brothers embraced, and now there were tears, Clark picking up his smaller sibling, holding him gently. Then Spencer saw him, gasped.

Clark glanced around, then back. "Don't get upset, dum-dum, he untied me, he's a good guy."

Spencer wasn't so sure. "You positive?" he whispered.

Clark hugged him all the tighter.

"You better be right," Spencer said; "I don't want to get drown-ded again."

"Izzat what happened?"

"You betcha. He put my face in the water and held it down but I kicked and I kicked and then he got real mad and held me down for forever and then he left me and I didn't know what to do so I just crept out of the tub and hid in the corner. There was a lot of noise, outside, Clark, it sounded like a fight."

Clark looked at Scylla. "Was there? Did you win? Is he gone?"

Scylla nodded. "Cross my heart."

"Who are you anyway?" Spencer asked.

"My name is Mister Snerd," Scylla said.

That got a giggle. "Snerd?" said Spencer. "*Snerd?* Oh, I hope my name is never Snerd."

Scylla smiled, took a towel. "Let's get you dry, Spencer. You grab a towel too, Clark, we'll both attack the problem."

"It's not gonna be easy, he's awful ticklish." But he took a towel and they did their best to get rid of some of the dampness, trying to ignore Spencer's sometimes hysterical laughter, and in a few minutes, he was as dry as he was going to be. They walked back into the living room where Spencer ran to the tube. "Oh, the cartoons are over," he said sadly.

"Come along then," Scylla told them.

They looked at him. "Where?" Clark asked.

"I'll take you home."

"Oh, you don't have to do that, Mister Snerd, you done plenty for us already."

"Don't be silly."

"We mean it, don't we, Spencer?"

"Yup, yup, yup."

"Well, I don't care what you mean, I'm going to see you get home safely."

"Please don't, Mister Snerd," Spencer said. "We been so much trouble." He walked over to Scylla, hugged him around the waist. "Just let us alone now."

"Stop this."

"But you've saved us, that's enough."

"Come on, Clark, I mean it. Now, where were you picked up today?"

"Connaught."

"Then that's where I'm taking you back."

"But—" Clark began.

"No 'buts,'" Scylla said.

"Please let us be, Mister Snerd," Spencer said.

"At the hotel, Spencer." He reached out his hands, one for each.

They hesitated, looked at him, then, for a long moment, at each other. Then they took his hands and started out.

But not before they looked at each other again . . .

## 2

You could never tell with trouble, Parkin realized, at close to eight that evening. A dozen years on the force and that fact still, and it shouldn't have surprised him. Trouble often had a build, it was tactile, you just knew sometimes it was coming up on the outside.

And other times, it was just, well, on you.

Like with the kids.

7:48 and it was just another cloudy London night, he'd known enough of them, he was a local. And then up ahead, rounding the corner toward him came the big gent with the kids, holding hands, one kid for each. Ordinary scene. Father out for a stroll with the family perhaps. Your usual.

Quiet place, some few others out walking, not many. He was heading for the station house, perspiring too much, because it was muggy and his blue uniform wasn't the thinnest of fabrics and also because, he'd put on a few pounds of late, the wife's cooking, he had the beginnings of a bulge now where his waist once had been.

Parkin was thinking about what to cut out of his diet, the beer, the potatoes, the beef, when one of the kids went limp, surprising the big man, and the other, the smaller kid broke free and ran toward him going, "Officuh, huh, please, help."

"What's the matter, son?" Parkin said, kneeling as the adorable, perhaps seven-year-old hugged him, shook his head, unable to speak for the tears.

"I'm sorry, Officer," the man said, bringing the other child over, holding tight to him. "Spencer's tired, and he's got a flair for the dramatic." He reached out for the smaller child. "Come along now, Spencer, we don't want to keep people waiting."

And now the bigger kid was crying. "He ain't no one we know, Officuh—"

"Clark, come on now," the man said.

"Why don't we all just take it easy," Parkin said. "Us grown-ups as well."

The dark-skinned man smiled. "I just didn't want to cause you any trouble."

"If there wasn't no trouble, I'd be out of a job now, wouldn't I?" Parkin said.

"Of course, it's just that it's late and I want to get them home."

Now the smaller one looked at the larger—brothers, freckled, very American—could have been twins save their size—and the larger one looked at Parkin, said, "I wanna tell you somethin'."

Parkin stared at the other man. A pause.

"By all means," the suntanned man said finally, releasing the child.

"What is it? Clark?" Parkin said.

"I wanna whisper."

Parkin put his head close to the child's mouth.

"We don't know him—we wuz—we wuz havin' a boiguh and frize and he said, since we wuz Americans, and his kids were back in the States, could he buy us the boiguhs, and we didn't know what to do but we said 'sure' . . ." He was sobbing again.

"Come on now," the man said. "Stop this."

". . . he touched us . . ." Clark whispered when he could. He looked down at himself. ". . . there . . . After the food he took us to the bathroom—he said to clean our hands . . . but when he had us he touched me and Spencer . . . there . . . and now he's taking us someplace to touch us again."

Parkin stood quickly, because he had a thing against people who went after kids, who the hell didn't have a thing against people like that, and he shouted, "You two stay right here," and the brothers nodded and said "Yessir" through their tears, and then Parkin was running, running full out because the other guy had taken off for the corner and before they'd gone half a block Parkin knew he had no chance at all, the big guy ran like an athlete, and he shouted for help but too late, the guy was gone, the night had him. Parkin went back fast to the two kids.

The night had them too. They had said they would not move but they had disappeared. Parkin called their names once—"Spencer—Clark," but he knew it was useless. He turned around in the dark. A dozen years on the force but never an incident like this. The brothers, the suntanned guy—it was all crazy, strange, it was as if it hadn't happened at all. But it had.

Something had, anyway . . .

# 3

# The Little Bang Theory

## 1

It was half past two the following afternoon when his male secretary buzzed, told Beverage a package had arrived. A moment later, a brown paper bag weighing surely not much more than a pound or so was deposited on his desk. The secretary left. Beverage stared at the thing. He'd been expecting it, or at least some communiqué, so he wasn't surprised.

Queasy, yes.

Clearly, it was from Scylla. Scylla must have killed The Blond. He'd heard no more since the ridiculous phone call demanding ransom for the children. The children had returned safely to Tring, talked of their physical maltreatment, their escaping the suntanned man. The Blond's body would likely turn up soon, but Beverage had no way of knowing what identity The Blond was using, so it might take days before he was unofficially notified of the why and how of his demise.

Meanwhile, the package.

Beverage stared at it, wishing for a moment he could incinerate Scylla several times, slowly. He let his fantasy run. The ultimate toy. To be able to eliminate your enemy whenever you felt the need. Much better than working off aggressions on a punching bag.

Still, the package.

To hell with it, Beverage decided, I'm not going to let him terrify me, so he reached for the bag, ripped it open, fell ill as the contents spilled on his desk top, a blond scalp, bits of lip, parts of a nose, all of it smeared with dried blood.

And a note. He unfolded the single sheet of paper, read it quickly: "Ma died in great pain. I don't see any reason why you shouldn't."

Beverage took a few deep breaths, got control. He shoveled the contents of the bag into a larger bag of his own, buzzed his secretary, told him to incinerate the lot. Then he tried to figure where Scylla would strike. The logical place would be his apartment, which meant, of course, that Scylla would never dream of attacking him in his apartment. Still, covering all possibilities, he picked up the phone, got security, ordered half a dozen guards to 50 Belgrave Square where his top-floor flat was located, put them on twenty-four-hour call, three in the back of the townhouse, three in the front, all suitably disguised.

Then he ordered Hayward.

Hayward, though physically undistinguished, was the only member of his employ he had never wanted to incinerate. The man, small, tending to flesh, married to a simple-minded woman with a drooping eye, was permanently loyal.

His first week in England, four years before, Beverage had made a very strong though unofficial suggestion to his underlings that they all consider being, to use his terminology, "baned." Nothing original in the suggestion—many of the top German intelligence people did, and that back during the Second World War. Of course, Division would pay for the work. It was really very simple. You went to a special dentist who hollowed out a tooth, inserted a tiny vial of deadly enough poison to kill within minutes, had the bottom of the tooth covered so that you were totally safe, even if you were a world-class teeth-grinder while asleep. Nothing unintentional could break the bottom coverage. You had to slam your jaws together, crunch down, to bring death.

The reaction of his men was hysterical, as if he, Beverage, had suggested something from the Dark Ages. Panic ran like a virus through his troops. Disgraceful. Naturally, Beverage, to avoid a fuss so soon on the job, withdrew the suggestion.

But not before Hayward had had himself baned.

When Hayward arrived, Beverage asked that he take a permanent seat outside his office door. Because, he knew, that was where Scylla would come for him—it was the least expected, therefore, at least to Beverage's mind, a certainty. Once Hayward had settled in his post outside the office door, Beverage sent his secretary across the street to Harrods to buy a small tape recorder, a single blank tape, and when the man returned, Beverage made a brief but, he thought, pungent recording, sent his secretary to the Savoy with the recorder, the tape still inside, with very specific delivery instructions.

He jumped when his phone rang.

Damn Scylla and his games. He hesitated before answering, hoping the call would be from his wife saying she was bored and going off somewhere to visit for a day or two. This was not a time to have to fray his thoughts; he didn't need her around distracting him.

He could sense his luck turning when she spoke. Would he mind, she asked, if she went up to Edinburgh for a bit, her friend up there, the teacher, had had a love blow, was forlorn, needed cheering, was it a problem if she paid a visit?

Beverage lashed out at her, vilified her for trotting off at the least opportunity, reminded her what a dreadful wife she was, dreadful and deteriorating, ended by saying of course she could go, at least he wouldn't have to try and force his way through another one of her ineptly prepared meals, hung happily up.

He worked till close to nine, then, with Hayward close by his side, they strolled to Belgrave Square. One of the most beautiful and prestigious in all the city. One of his favorite parks. Not many lived on the square anymore, mostly it was embassies, the spiritualist society had the whole of number 33. Inside the square was a tennis court, glorious trees, benches, immaculately kept up, and Beverage wondered, as they turned the corner of West Halkin Street and the square came into view, if Scylla himself was lurking there, watching him.

Possibly, but unlikely. He noted the security men placed close to the entrance of number 50, enquired of their chief, was assured three more men guarded the rear. Beverage, of course, believed him, then walked with Hayward around to the back to make sure. The men were there.

The homes along the square were in crescents, attached one to the next except where the streets divided them. Traffic, clockwise, was usually heavy well into the night.

The bottom apartments of Beverage's building were similar to his, one apartment per floor, populated by wealthy Europeans, all of whom he'd had vetted, so although it was possible Scylla had invaded one of their homes and was waiting his chance to spring, it was highly unlikely.

He and Hayward walked up to the top landing. He unlocked the front door, he and Hayward went inside briefly where they checked his security—it worked flawlessly—if a door was pressured or a window nudged, the ensuing racket would signal half of Belgravia.

Then he got Hayward a chair, set it outside the front door, apologized that it wasn't more comfortable. Hayward said it was fine and the way he said it made Beverage realize the man was probably not going to sit in it much anyway. You lost concentration sometimes when you sat. Hayward took out his pistol, showed it to Beverage, told him to rest well, and they parted.

Beverage entered his flat, went to the bar, poured himself a single-blend malt with just a cube of ice. Then he went to the bedroom, undressed, hung his clothes with extreme care over their hangers.

He stretched, yawned. It was a tribute to his ability to control himself that now, on this night of all nights, he would actually be able to sleep. He went to the bathroom next, brushed his hair, checked, as he always did, a silly habit, to see if his hairline had disobeyed since morning, begun a minute retreat.

No. He was as he always was, in control, the same weight now as in decades past. He took a sip of the whisky, put the glass on the sink, turned on the shower; it was pathetic, a permanent tribute to the ineptitude of English plumbing—but then, who was without flaw? He stepped under the dripping water, soaped his body, let the water take it away, reached for his shampoo, from Trumpers, his barber, the finest in the land, in any land, got a rich lather, massaged his scalp, feeling, all things considered, on top of the situation, that is, until the lights went out in the room and he knew at once it was not a power failure, no fuse would fix this darkness.

And Beverage, naked and wet, began to tremble then, because Scylla was there, in the bathroom with him, except it wasn't possible, he couldn't have gotten in, slipped unnoticed past the guards—unless Perkins had lied and Scylla was dead, and this was his apparition, risen from somewhere, come across the world to torment him now...

## 2

Fifteen hours earlier, the day had begun in that apartment with Sally Beverage feigning sleep. She lay motionless on her side, her slender body covered by a sheet, while her husband finished getting ready for work. She knew the sounds—the soft ringing of coins going into one suitcoat pocket, the similar ringing as the key chain was deposited in the other. Then the quiet whisper of fabric as he deposited his wallet into his rear right trouser pocket.

She also knew that he was perfectly aware of her wakefulness. They had been through all the fabrications these last dreadful years, dreadful for her anyway, though she sometimes thought that if Malcolm were ever asked he'd reply, "Oh, it's been a bit ragged on occasion, but you know Sally, good stock, rises to the moment, all in all I'm sure she'd say she's happy on the whole."

Now the final sound, the click of the front door and she was safe. Safe from his emotionless stares, his distant voice tone as she tried to make what passed for interesting conversation, safe from the odd violence he would mete out—was "mete" the right word? Once she would have known.

Out of bed, she glanced at the paper—a summit meeting was really an exciting prospect, you had to have hope the way the world was hurtling now—went to the kitchen, took her vitamins, the multi and the C. (She believed in Linus Pauling, no matter what the medical establishment trumpeted.) Then she finished the pot of coffee Malcolm had made, sipped it black along with a piece of toast, wondering if she would be lucky today. It seemed to have deserted her of late—she had purchased nothing in over a week, and that was a disappointment, considering the hours she tromped, the countless stores she had entered.

For that was what she did now with her life: shopped. Bought gifts. Remembrances. For friends.

And it was the thing she took most pride in, the single activity that gave her most pleasure, that she liked to think she did truly well.

Oh, it wasn't the buying—anyone could buy. And it certainly wasn't the spending—Malcolm was always after her about throwing good money after what he called bad, but he didn't understand; and more than that, she wasn't spending his money, never had, or would. She came from a semiwealthy background, the cash that flowed was leaving her account, not his.

The secret of a proper gift was memory. The present should touch a past chord. And remind the receiver of two things: better days and the good thoughts of the giver.

But before she could get at the daily task, there was the

apartment to put in order. When they had lived in Washington they'd had a house and servants to help. But in London these past years, with just the few rooms, outsiders weren't necessary. Sally enjoyed the labor. It took her hours, yes, because she was a cleanliness buff, but it made the shopping all the more delicious when its turn came.

And there really wasn't any need for a servant. They never entertained, not at home. She wasn't specifically sure what Malcolm did; she had asked in the beginning, and he had said exporting, and she went along with that as long as she could. Certainly he was in government, more than likely in some form of intelligence on a highish level, but the few times she'd pressed he'd angered, so she let it alone. It didn't really matter what he did "out there." What he did when they were alone was the important thing, and what he did there was glacial. Or angry. She had failed, failed as a wife. Again.

By nine the apartment was done and she was ready. She wore a sensible tan dress from Marks and Spencer. Her long brown hair was in a sensible bun. She had on flat, sensible shoes—she was tall, five nine, and never wore heels except on those rare occasions when he took her out for an evening, and then he insisted on the highest she could manage—she towered over him flat-footed and in the heels she felt a fool but he liked it, joked about it. Once, when she had been able to turn him on, she suspected it turned him on.

Sally gave herself a final glance in the mirror: what a bore that woman looks, she said of herself, and with that she was out the door, destination: King's Road.

A favorite. London had so many for her. Islington, of course, and often, the street markets, Portobello Road, Bermondsey, the others. And some days she traveled Regent Street, another might find her on Picadilly. Oxford Street, where so many of the big stores were. Or Jermyn Street, with so many small delicacies.

Hard work it was, at least if you shopped Sally's way, truly concentrating, not just on the merchandise displayed, but on her list of old acquaintances and matching the gift with the friend with the celebration at hand: Christmas meant a different giving than a birthday, and they both varied from private times, such as the date her Wellesley roommate senior year confessed she was no longer virgin.

Sally loathed showy gifts—such as the dozen-acre plot bought in secret for his wife by the Texas millionaire, who spent three years building and outfitting a mansion and when he drove her past it and idly asked her opinion she said she found it cramped looking, so they continued their drive and never set foot inside. Or the Hollywood director she'd read about who for a child's third southern California birthday had imported truckloads of snow.

Money itself was not an evil—she found it acceptable for J.P. Morgan to keep a tailor at his Scottish hunting lodge so that each of his guests might have a shooting outfit—gaudy, perhaps, but there would always be the memory every time you saw those clothes in your closet.

Not gifted with the ability to create humor, she appreciated it greatly, and she loved when the playwright Charles MacArthur met Helen Hayes at a cocktail party and gave her a brown bag of peanuts and said, "I wish they were emeralds," which spurred their courtship, and years later, rich and returning from travel, he gave her another brown bag and as the emeralds spilled into her hands he said, "I wish they were peanuts."

But perhaps her favorite gift involved gold and the greatest Scrooge, Jack Benny, whose dearest friend was George Burns. Benny gave Burns a gold money clip, with caricatures engraved on each side, one of himself, one of Burns, and Burns had used it every day for half a century. Thoughtful, the gift was. And personal. And the memory was there. More and more, Sally realized, as her life continued its steepening downhill curve, as her shopping became more and more important to her, she had a terrible fear of disappearing, not so much from the earth, we all did that, but from the minds of those she'd known.

She sensed, the moment she left Peter Jones' and started

along the endless line of King's Road stores, that today was going to be unusual. The third place she entered had a lovely new supply of sachets; they were the size of a paperback book, liberty print fabrics, tied in a white bow, and with a vast number of fragrances, honeysuckle, rosemary, on and on. Sally started out of the store, a few moments later turned; something was drawing her to the perfumed sachets.

What and why?

She put her good mind to work. Even though she carried a diary, she rarely needed to use it—she had all her friends' crucial dates memorized. All the July birthdays trooped by; friends, relatives, their offspring.

Then she had it.

It was the scent of honeysuckle. Her baby brother's wife, a delicate tasteful girl (who would love the liberty print), had said, oh, years ago in passing, that when she was a child growing up in Virginia, the honeysuckle had been her favorite flower.

And she had a birthday on the twentieth of July.

Sally asked did the store ship?

They did, the saleslady said.

Credit cards?

Yes.

Elated, she paid, wrote a sweet note, said to be sure please to mail this right away to America, it had to get there by the twentieth.

The saleslady assured her.

Elated, Sally smiled and continued on down the King's Road, secure in the knowledge that luck came in threes so twice more she would be anointed this day, the time still being before ten.

The second piece of fortune came by eleven.

At a junk shop, would you believe. A large, dirty, three-sectioned painted screen. Sally took out some Kleenex, worked at the dust, got a better look, thought then of her beloved ailing aunt in Poughkeepsie, who had been so essential to her upbringing. How often had she been rocked to sleep to the sounds of her aunt's soft singing, "Red sails in the sunset, way out on the sea, oh carry my loved one, home safely to me."

And this screen was filled with painted red-sailed boats. Her aunt had already had this year's birthday, and Christmas was too far away, so Sally decided to make this screen one of her "Because it's Monday" gifts, the name coming from an anecdote she cherished about Mark Twain, who gave his daughter a music box once and when asked why shrugged and said, "Because it's Monday."

Ship? the junkyard man said, almost scornfully. Then he shook his head.

Sally didn't bother enquiring about credit cards, simply asked the price of the screen, paid cash. Now came her problem—the screen was heavy and bulky and yes, she *could*, more than likely, find a cab, get it home herself. But that would break her day, and she was riding so high, with a third gift surely in the offing. She didn't want to change her luck. And that was that. Would you deliver? she asked.

He cocked his head.

Fifty Belgrave Square, it's not that far.

When?

Sally calculated—by two thirty or so she would be done for the day, the third gift safely in her possession. Some weeks she didn't find three gifts. Some months even, not as fine as these. She stated the time.

For a fiver.

Sally gave him five pounds.

That's for my efforts, understand; I'll have to close here to find someone. You'll have to take care of whoever delivers.

Aware she was being taken, Sally agreed. And packing the screen would be a chore, mailing it another. Still, she knew if she got it to her aging aunt in time, she would be remembered. I'll be home at half past two, she said, and moved on down the road.

She was home at two fifteen. Disappointed. No third gift. Nothing. At promptly two thirty, the buzzer sounded from the street. She spoke into the mouthpiece by the front door. Yes?

Screen delivery? Beverage? Fifty Belgrave Square?

Sally said yes again, pushed the button, unlocking the front door of the building. Then she opened the front door of the apartment and waited, hearing the footsteps coming up the stairs, and, a few moments later, a man lumbered up carrying the screen, carrying it, she was pleased to note, with some care.

Just in here, she told him.

He put it down where she'd indicated.

One moment, she told him then, you've come a long way, and she opened her pocketbook, took out her money purse, opened that, began taking out some one-pound coins, trying to decide how many would be just and fair.

It was during her deciding that she felt the back of his hand softly on her cheek. The tips of his knuckles. Grazing her skin. Circling.

*"Stop that!"* she almost said, as she almost moved away. *"Get out of here or I'll report you!"* she came close to yelling.

He continued silently as before, his body close to hers, the two of them standing in silence. And it was amazing what the mind could do, the jumps it could accommodate, because suddenly she was twenty years younger and on an early date with a dangerous young man, he'd been engaged three times, twice to classmates of hers, and she knew what he wanted probably was the physical Sally, not the whole package, but something about him invited trust, and as they sat together on her sofa, half-drunk, she started talking about something strange, because he reminded her, somehow, of her father, and her father had done this wonderful thing to her when she was young, had touched her cheek with his knuckles, so softly, and their next date, when she knew they were going to sleep together for the first time, before that happened, he touched her gently on the cheek with his knuckles, circling, and he always did that after, even when they were married, before they made love he touched her cheek in that way, their secret, and now, as his movement continued she whispered, "You're dead," and he whispered "I'd like to think otherwise," and in a moment the door was shut and a moment after that her legs were open as they lay naked in their favorite way, he beneath, she straddling, he hard, she moist, and Sally realized she had been right before, because luck did come in threes and surely this was the greatest of the trio, her ex-husband, her own Lazarus, rising beneath her now . . .

"Not your everyday afternoon," Sally said, as they sat together in the living room, half-dressed, sipping tea.

Scylla smiled.

She pointed to the teapot. Yes?

He nodded. Please.

She stood, poured, sat.

"You're still so lovely."

"You don't have to flatter me, we've already bedded down."

"You still take compliments well."

She smiled now. "We've both weathered the passage of time better than some, let's put it that way." She gestured around the room. "I suppose you've come to take me away from all this."

"No. What I'd like, actually, is for *you* to go away from all this. Now. Is there anyone you can visit?"

"David, this is really incredibly bizarre—you appear after damn near two decades, take me totally against my will"—she tossed in a smile—"and now want me to leave my own home. All without an explanation."

"You don't want one, believe that. Who can you visit?"

"I don't know. I've a chum—five years in England you call girlfriends that—teaches at Edinburgh University, I visit there a lot."

"See if she's free?"

"I don't want an explanation, but a hint wouldn't hurt."

"I have to chat with your husband when he gets home

from work tonight and you don't want to be here when that happens."

"You don't mean 'chat,' do you."

"Discomfort; does that upset you?"

After a moment, Sally shook her head. "It doesn't, really. Isn't that a terrible thing?"

Scylla stood, reached for her, pulled her to him. "How in the world could you marry him?"

"Besides to spite you, you mean?"

Scylla said nothing.

"Malcolm has a lot of energy—he overpowered me, overwhelmed me actually, and I was low on self-esteem at the time, being, thanks to you, damaged goods—"

"—oh, stop it—it wasn't you caused the divorce and you know it. I was entering a high-risk occupation. It didn't do to have emotional encumbrances. Why have you stayed?"

"He was very against my leaving. Wouldn't have looked good on his job record, I suspect. I'd failed once, I didn't much want to fail again." She touched his scar. "How did you get here?"

"I was waiting in a cab when you left this morning. I was outside when you bought the sachets. When the delivery man left the junk shop I stopped him and gave him ten pounds not to deliver. Then I took the screen, dropped a package at your husband's office, came here." He kissed her, pointed to the phone.

She kissed him, stood, started for the phone saying, "At least we don't spend so much time together we bore each other." She picked up the receiver, put it down, faced him. "Just what exactly do you want now?"

"I want you to call your friend and make arrangements to visit. Then I want you to call your husband and tell him you're going north."

"And you'll touch my cheek again?"

"Oh yes."

"One more thing?"

He waited.

"You won't let me disappear?"

He looked at her.

"Promise I'll be a memory?"

He crossed his heart; she dialed.

## 3

In the darkness: "Hello, Prick."

"You don't understand—"

"—that's right, I don't, but I will." Scylla flicked the bathroom light back on, gestured for Beverage to move.

"Let me put a robe on." His voice was calm now.

Scylla shook his head. "No. I'd like to remember you just like you are, all shriveled and shivering." He gestured again, and when Beverage approached, he pushed him ahead of him into the library, closed the door. Beverage sat in a chair, Scylla across from him. "Why did you hire me to find out who was paying The Blond when *you* were paying him?"

"I wanted the two of you going against each other. If he killed you, well, of course, I would have wept for days. If you'd killed him—well, I thought he was becoming untrustworthy. And when someone knows a great deal, it's dangerous if he can't be trusted."

"But he incriminated you."

Beverage nodded. "I never thought he'd talk—I thought it would be over quickly and one of you would be dead before any chance at conversation. I thought he had no weaknesses."

"We all have weaknesses."

"That's right, even you, your brother, as I remember."

*"What's that got to do with anything?"*

"Nothing. I just never thought he'd talk—I wanted to test his reliability, so I arranged for him to shepherd the children."

"All a setup."

Beverage nodded. "I'm surprised you didn't suspect."

"I didn't suspect—I *knew*—Perkins told me you wanted me here but that was before he was dead, so obviously you didn't want me to find his killer when there wasn't one. I don't want to shock you, Mal, but I don't believe a lot of what you say; as far as I'm concerned, the truth is a foreign object in your mouth." He stood, moved behind the naked man. "But not tonight."

Beverage smiled. "There's no need for lies tonight."

"Why did you kill Ma?"

"I hated doing that—such a bright dear man."

Scylla wondered if he should break a knee or a shoulder.

Beverage turned, saw his face, said, "*Don't*—don't do anything, I promise there's no need. Ma must have found out about the Webster business, and stopped trusting me."

"Webster? The guy whose boiler blew in Tring?"

"You've been doing very good work, Scylla; truly, top of your game."

"Who was he?"

"A Canadian scientist who worked in Europe; I brought him here, set him up, gave him funds, he was a very brilliant man and someday the world will know that—"

"—shut up about him, tell me about the children—"

Beverage smiled again. "Special creatures, aren't they?"

"I don't know what they are—but last night when I got away from this fat policeman who was after me I lucked into a cab right away and paid him a fortune to get me fast to the Connaught and he did—they couldn't have gotten there before me. I waited. They never showed."

"Of course not. They weren't told to."

Scylla waited.

"Can I at least have a drink?"

Scylla poured two Scotches. "Go on about the children."

"May I make a sports analogy? Joe Louis, when he was forty, could still hit as devastatingly as twenty years before. So why was he through? Because his reflexes were dulled. He could hit, but he could not position himself to *deliver* the blow. The power of a weapon is truly inconsequential, if you can't deliver it. *Delivery is all.*"

"What's that got to do with the children?"

"Mandrakes. That was Webster's word for them. After a comic from his growing up days, a magician named Mandrake. So he called them that."

Scylla waited, staring across at the small naked man.

"They're bombs, Scylla. They liquefy when they go off, so they leave no trace. And they are the ultimate weapon because they can go anyplace they want in this world: no one yet born can find it in his heart to deprive a poor lost child. A helpless Disney child. They got away from you last night easily enough, didn't they?"

"As if I wasn't there."

Beverage nodded happily. "And those were simple instructions to follow. They were to meet The Blond in front of the Connaught, I'd told him they were rich children, I thought he might try and extract money for them, his roulette losses were getting dangerously high. If he tried to kill them, they were to feign death until he left, and then return home. If you found them, they were to try to have you leave them, and if you wouldn't, get away from you, then return home." His voice began to rise. "They *are* magical. They can go wherever they want, explode whenever they want, take whomever they want with them—"

"—where are they?—"

"—it doesn't matter—you're too late to do anything about what's going to come—the bombs will flame and no one can stop them—"

"—you fucker, you want that—"

"—*wrong!* I want the world at peace—"

Scylla grabbed the other man, threw him across the room. "*Goddamit, where are they?*"

". . . Tring . . . the academy at Tring . . . and you can do . . . precisely . . . zero . . . you're too late and it's too well guarded . . . how does it feel, at this most important time, to be helpless, totally helpless, with not a thing in the world to do—?"

"—you forgot one thing."

"Doubtful."

"I can kill you," Scylla said, and he started toward the other man, stopped as Beverage slammed his jaws together brutally, and Scylla knew what it was instantly, the Germans did it, some at Division did it, and then there were droplets of moisture in the corners of Beverage's mouth. And the droplets foamed as Beverage began to die. He looked at Scylla. "Anything to deprive you of pleasure . . ."

## 4

The guard who stood inside the enormous gate of the academy was a huge man in a surly mood. He stood in the entrance to the rectangular guardhouse, stared through the darkness at the figure that had suddenly appeared outside. "No one gets in till morning," the guard said. His name was Hoffer and he hated working nights; sleep had always been a pal of his, except it was hard nodding off in daylight, sun always seemed to creep in by the corners of the shades.

"This is important," the man said.

"I got my orders," Hoffer said.

And now the guy exploded: "What's your goddamned name?"

"What do you care?"

"So I can have your ass, obviously. Look—I'm new to London, new to Division, I didn't ask to get transferred here, I didn't ask to get sent out here in the middle of the goddam night with some note I've got to hand personally to the chief guard—Beverage doesn't tell me anything but what I've got to do and you say I can't so I need to know who's screwed up, it wasn't me, you're gonna take the fall."

"Beverage?" Hoffer said. "He gave you the note for Tomkins?"

The guy waved a piece of paper through the bars of the locked academy gate.

"I'll take it."

"No you won't, nobody's going to, I've got to deliver it personally, you won't let me in—so it's over, and you still haven't told me your name."

Hoffer could sense the other guy staring at him now.

"Never mind," the guy said; "I'll describe you well enough." And he turned away.

Hoffer left the guardhouse, went to the gate. "At least let me see the note, check it out, make sure it's legit."

"Horseshit I will."

Hoffer hesitated. He was armed, he had size on the other guy, had everything, except he wasn't sure if he was in danger of getting reported or not. "Hoffer's my name, and if you show me the note, I might let you in."

"You can't open an envelope from Beverage."

"Just the outside, for chrissakes." He waited as the other guy turned, hesitated, finally came slowly toward him, held out his hand with an envelope. It was after midnight and there wasn't much moon but the guy had one helluva suntan. So maybe he was new to London. The guy passed the envelope through the bars of the gate at waist level, so Hoffer had to look down to grab it, and that, he realized immediately, was a mistake, to take your eyes away from a stranger, because suddenly these hands had him, these incredible hands were spinning his body so his back was imprisoned against the gate, and then he began getting light headed but he could feel his keys being taken, and then the gate was opening and he was helpless on his knees.

Scylla had made good time in getting to Tring. Leaving Beverage's apartment was no problem, Sally had shown him earlier that there was a security system, how it worked, so all he had to do was, since the apartment was on the top floor, lift himself to the roof, then hurry along the row of connected houses, vaulting the brick walls that were low but provided separation, and when he reached the end, jump to a fire escape, from there the ground came easily.

And he had no trouble, in Tring, locating the Academy, a giant ancient structure a mile from the center of town; dirty brick, with a high wall surrounding it. Probably it had been built in another century to house the children of the rich, teach them enough so they wouldn't make fools of themselves when they took their grand tours of Europe years later. He could have climbed the wall easily enough, but information was crucial to him now, so he hoped the large guard was as dumb as he looked, tried the envelope gambit, was not displeased when it worked.

"When will you be replaced?" He lifted the large man from the ground, shoved him toward the guardhouse.

"One."

Almost an hour away. Too long. "When will they contact you?"

No answer.

*"When?"* He applied pressure to Hoffer's shoulder till the man began to pale.

". . . soon . . ."

"How?"

Hoffer pointed to a buzzer. "They buzz me, I buzz back."

They waited till the buzzer sounded then. Scylla nodded. Hoffer pushed the button, buzzed, dropped his hand.

"How many are you?"

"I don't know exactly. A dozen maybe, at nights."

Scylla hesitated. Beverage hadn't lied when he said the place was well guarded. "All armed?"

". . . yes . . ."

"Authorized to kill?"

". . . of course . . ."

You're not the only ones, Scylla thought, and he made his hands dig at the proper spots in Hoffer's body, and when it sagged, he carried him behind some bushes near the guardhouse, left him there, began to move silently toward the gigantic house.

Before he reached it he heard laughter. Coming from a building off a short distance from the main house. Perhaps the place had been used for major storage once, now it had a table and chairs and a coffeepot and a stove and some sofas and a refrigerator—Scylla stopped, crept to an open window.

And best of all the room contained half a dozen guards, just below window level, all sitting and eating snacks and drinking tea.

Great good fortune had come calling.

He made his moves, hoped they hadn't heard him, stared in to see if they had, but they hadn't, they were laughing too loudly, talking rough barracks talk. Transfixed, he studied them, studied their faces, studied too deeply, was unaware when great good fortune turned, because when he finally turned it was too late and the guard with the mustache already had his rifle in clubbing position, the blow was crushing, Scylla fell . . .

Fogerty was out of grass. And yes that was irritating but you couldn't get mad at the world when it was you screwed up. This guarding shit upped his intake. Ordinarily he didn't use grass except when he was on his own, off duty, but since he'd been at this dump he was stoned pretty much all the time, what the hell else was there to do?

So he decided to pay a trip to Hoffer at the main gate. Hoffer had supplied him since they started working here, and although he knew Hoffer wouldn't have an ounce or anything with him, he'd sure have at least a joint and that would get Fogerty through the next period till Hoffer got relieved and he could make a major buy. He hated having to hustle joints, but sometimes you had to, so he crossed toward the guardhouse, taking a shortcut by the rec room where the guys were eating—

—and there, *right there,* was this guy, this intruder, this whatever the hell he was, standing there, staring down at the guys eating inside. Fogerty moved fast, raised his rifle, slammed the guy hard enough to brain-splatter, grabbed the still body, dragged it inside the rec room where Tomkins and the others stopped their chatter, muttered "Jesus" or "son of a bitch" and looked with surprise at the suntanned guy, then, Fogerty realized, with admiration at him; they all knew a hero when they saw one.

Scylla sat weakly in the chair, arms held, while they beat him across the face. Not accurate. "They," two guards, only held him; it was the leader, Tomkins, who whipsawed him.

"More?" Tomkins said.

Scylla licked the blood from his mouth, shook his head.

Tomkins whipsawed him again.

Scylla blinked.

"Okay? We'll cut the bullshit now. Who do you work for?"

"I told you a minute ago—you didn't believe me—I don't want you to hit me again—"

*"Who do you work for?"*

". . . Division . . ."

Tomkins took his rifle, jammed it into Scylla's stomach; Scylla gagged, doubled over, tried to breathe.

"How'd you get here?"

"I told you . . . Hoffer let me in . . ."

"We'll find out about that in one second, my man," Tomkins said. "As soon as Fogerty gets back." He went across the room, grabbed a mug of coffee, drained it. He looked outside, saw Fogerty hurrying toward the rec room. "Well?" Tomkins said.

Fogerty was panting and scared. "Dead in the bushes," he said.

Tomkins blinked, went back, got his rifle, cocked it, aimed it at the man's bloody face. "Last requests?" he said softly.

Even though he was in charge of security, Tomkins didn't like the Tring assignment. Probably it was important; Beverage himself had called him in, told him he was his best guard, implied that on the far side of the job was a promotion. Still, it was miserable work. They didn't go into the main house much, just kept track of who came, who went—usually, at least until the last couple of weeks, it had been the boss, Webster, who was on vacation, somebody said, now.

It was boring work, that was the crux. Boring and frustrating not being allowed really on the inside. Oh, the kids were pleasant enough to talk to, and it was fun with the different languages you'd hear.

But Tring was not a place anybody ever returned to. It was a place you left, and he couldn't wait to leave when his duty was up. He had never been as bored, which is why he could have almost kissed Fogerty when he turned up with the suntanned guy. It gave you a chance to get back into action, ask questions, strike blows, if necessary, blow someone away; which he never much minded, even though in the movies people always kept having their conscience bother them.

Tomkins slept like a baby.

Now, with his rifle pointed at the suntanned man's face, he wondered if he should kill or not. He wanted to, but would his superiors complain that he might have wiped out a useful informant? He looked around at the other guards. Probably they'd do what he said, so if he said the guy was breaking for freedom, that was why he shot him, they'd go along.

"Last requests?" Tomkins said.

"Let me," Tomkins heard.

He turned. It was Fogerty. "Hoffer was *my* friend."

Tomkins hesitated. If Fogerty did it, they couldn't blame him for taking an informant away without milking him fully. "You man enough?"

"Give me my shot."

Tomkins moved a step back, still holding tight to his rifle while Fogerty moved in, pointed his. "Last requests?"

The suntanned guy nodded.

"Say it fast."

Tomkins watched as the suntanned guy looked at him. "I want you to kill Fogerty," he said.

"*Whaaat?*" Tomkins said.

"Well, at least take his gun away from him. I'd really appreciate that a lot."

"No big deal," Tomkins said, and he smashed down with his rifle at Fogerty's hands, made the gun drop, picked it up while Fogerty, stunned, stared at him.

"What is this shit?" Fogerty said. "I'm your buddy, I'm the hero of this gathering—Christ—who spotted this guy—me—I see him squirting something from what looks like an atomizer through the window all over you only you're all such blabbermouths you don't pay any attention, then who captures him—me. And who goes and scratches around in the woods to find poor Hoffer? *Me*. And now you listen to what this guy says?"

"It's just it would mean a lot to me," the suntanned guy said.

"What would?"

"Having Fogerty taken care of. I'd just appreciate it so much. But if you don't want to do it, by all means, don't, but if a couple of your men would take him outside and do it quietly, I'd be so much more at ease."

Tomkins gestured and three guys grabbed Fogerty, one stopped his screaming while the other two dragged him outside into the night. In a few minutes, they were back. "Anything else?" Tomkins asked.

"I'll think of something," the dark-skinned man said.

Scylla was not happy taking the beating. But he was not totally sure how long it took for Milo Standish's atomizer to take perfect effect, so the best thing was just let the sadists work on him, keep them happily occupied as long as he could, until he was sure.

He sat in the rec room alone now, sipping coffee, while the six guards under Tomkins were off taking care of the other half dozen who were out stalking the grounds. Probably he could have let them all live—except they had been perfectly willing to dispose of him; and many of them had seen his face, and no one knew how long the effects of the atomizer would linger. No, tonight was not a time for worrying about the sanctity of Division's employees—if he had ever lived through one before, he knew this: tonight was a night for obliteration.

He had seen the children, had chattered with them in the hotel after the business with The Blond, had seen how tenderly, how irresistibly they hugged each other, how they cared. And he knew how quickly they had gotten rid of him when they wanted him gone. Webster, like Arky and Milo, was clearly a brilliantly gifted man. And Beverage had, in those children, a terrifying weapon.

"All done," Tomkins said, puffing back inside.

Scylla finished his coffee. "How many scientists are inside?"

"Just the two."

"They will be my pleasure. Is the door to the main house locked?"

Tomkins nodded.

"It looks quite dark too—I don't want to impose, but if you give me the key and a flashlight, I'd truly be appreciative."

"I wish you'd ask me something hard," Tomkins said, going to a locker, getting out a flashlight along with a set of keys he kept on his belt.

"I don't know whether I'm imposing or not," Scylla said then.

"You aren't, I swear, I really don't mind doing stuff for you, please."

"Well, can you get your hands on some kerosene?"

Tomkins laughed. "Are you serious? That's not hard. Kerosene, gallon cans of gasoline, the works, we're really well supplied here."

"Now be sure and tell me if this bothers you, because I would never want that, but what I'd like is for you and the remaining men to get all the kerosene and gasoline you can and go to the basement of the house, and spread everything flammable around you can find."

"I like fires," Tomkins said. "When I was a kid I was a whiz at building them." He looked at Scylla. "And then what?"

"Well, when I give you the signal, I want you to light everything."

"And then what?"

"Just stand there and watch it."

"Won't we die though?"

"I thought you just told me you liked fires—I thought you'd get a real kick out of being right up close to a genuine conflagration—but if the answer is no, it's no—"

"Hey, it's never no, not to you."

"Good man," Scylla said. "Now let's both get busy," and he left Tomkins, moved past the other guards who were bunched outside the rec room door, started to the giant old house.

There were lights burning on the top floor, but only there. He unlocked the thick wooden door, stepped into the dark house, closed the door, took a step forward, tripped over something, fell. He turned on the flashlight, and in the beam, walking aimlessly, was an adorable Disney child, saying "I wanna boiguh an' frize—I wanna boiguh an' frize," and now, as he got to his feet, Scylla was aware of the soft babble of sound. He threw the beam to his left and several chubby-cheeked children were talking in Italian, though not to each other, just walking aimlessly, speaking the language. Then he heard a Boston accent—"Pahk youh cah in Hah-vahd Yahd" as another cherub brushed by.

He was standing amidst the bombs, praying only that they had not yet been programmed to detonate, and as he slowly made his way to the grand stairway, he realized the entrance to the house was filled with dozens and dozens of children, chattering away, speaking mindlessly, bumping into each other, moving on, and he was reminded of the last scene in *The Birds* where the hero carried his wounded love through a mine field of killing birds, all of them cooing softly as his trousers brushed their feathered heads.

The stairway was a dozen feet away now, now ten, and he was, no point to lying, frightened as suddenly, as if by signal, they all began to laugh, happy laughter, and then, a moment later, the area was filled with tears.

Now the children were talking again, in their many languages and accents, and he was on the stairs, starting up toward where the two scientists were.

The first lit room he came to on the top floor contained the first scientist, an overweight man who was concentrating on some papers so he heard nothing as Scylla moved in behind him, did what needed doing, left. The second scientist was a sudden problem, because of sex, Scylla had never liked taking women, and this one, working with a recording machine, had a nice face, and just before he reached her he must have made a sound because she turned, staring up at him, eyes so bright.

He dulled them, turned, quickly left the room, the floor, made his way back down, slowly when he passed into the realm of the children because he had no idea when one of them might go off, or if, but in any case, this was not a happy vicinity, and Tomkins was waiting in the basement, the place smelling of gas, and the other guards who Scylla had used the atomizer on were all grouped around him, smiling and awaiting instructions, so Scylla told them to count to fifty and have a ball and then he was up the stairs and out the front door and racing across the lawn because he did not know how fast the house would burn but from the looks of the timbered interior that he'd seen, his guess was fast.

At the gate he turned, saw he was right, there was already billowing smoke emptying from windows. Another thing he did not know was would the children burn or, better yet, when confronted with extreme heat, explode, and if they did, how large would the explosion be.

The answers were yes they would, and gigantic, because

the house seemed to suddenly rise in the air as the blast attacked the sky...

## 5

It was after three in the morning when he reached the Savoy, went to his suite, undressed, lay down, far too exultant to sleep. Ma would have been proud of him. Not that he gave himself highest marks—only an amateur would have gotten clubbed the way he had—still, the job was done. The window would close. The Bloodies would shuffle like hyenas into the darkness again.

As he lay still, he realized he could not keep his eyes open. Surprising, that. Then again, as his breathing deepened, perhaps not—it had been a full last few hours, what with The Blond and then Sally and then Beverage and now Tring. His body drained of energy. It was as if he was back on his island after a swimming day. Ten hours sleep. At least that. He was that tired. The last thing he heard was the birds high in the trees, saying good night...

The sharp knock on the door came again and again—he knew it was there but couldn't fight his way toward it. Again and again. He blinked, his brain would not work. Again and again. Finally, he stumbled to the door, saw an embarrassed bellman. With a package. They mumbled at each other. The package passed. The bellman went away. He closed the door, unwrapped.

It was a tape recorder. His first temptation was to just drop it on a table, head for bed. Except he was far enough from sleep now to know he mustn't do that. He pushed the PLAY button, was astonished to hear Beverage's voice from the dead.

"...I made this this afternoon and had my secretary

bring it here. With the most specific instructions. If you arrived here early morning, it was to be delivered at this hour, precisely half an hour before dawn. If you did not arrive, it was to be sent back to my office. If you're listening, you must be very proud of yourself. Believe me, you've no reason. What this is is a triumph not for you, but for me. A double triumph, both professional and personal. My first over you. All things come, they say..."

Very dull stuff so far, Scylla thought. He was tempted to turn the machine off and pitch it—that would certainly be a triumph for him. The ultimate conquest of the bore: to stop listening. Except he knew he couldn't do that. Beverage with his chess player's mind, his ability to make moves ahead of the enemy; Scylla knew he would improve, once he'd gotten warmed up.

"... a quick aside. Probably you wonder why I've loathed you all these years; was it some childhood slight, some psychotic urge on my part? Really very simple. I am a totally competitive human being, and from the beginning, it was clear you were better than I. Better at work, at play, in life, in bed. When a totally competitive human being does nothing but lose and lose and lose to another, it does not create an atmosphere for friendship..."

Snooze, Scylla thought. Get to it. Beverage did.

"I assume you've destroyed the children in Tring. Let me assure you you've destroyed precisely nothing. Those were expendables, extras, defectives. The day after Webster died—that was our test run—we began shipping. There are perhaps five thousand children now, in every country of consequence, all programmed, waiting now in closets and boxes and cases, in ditches and woods. We go today at dawn..."

(It was seven hours earlier outside of Denver. Two little chubby children knocked on the door to an unpretentious house. One of the children began to cry. The other consoled. "C'mon now, Meathead, don't do that," and the weeping one managed, "Aw, Archie, I can't help it," and then the door opened and a woman in a nightgown said,

"Yes?" and the larger of the two brothers—they must have been brothers though they looked like twins, except for size—replied, "We went off the road, our daddy's trapped by the wheel an' his heart, he's had trouble before and we need someone to help, please, please, please," and the woman said, "I'll get my husband," and a few minutes later a man came down the stairs, hastily dressed and he knelt by the brothers, began to ask a few questions, his voice reassuring. His name was Arthur Minnifield and he was a general, third in command of NORAD, his immediate superior lived just across the road, and as he knelt, General Minnifield was shocked to see the house of his superior explode. Nothing ever shocked him ever again.)

". . . we would rather not have gone so quickly, to be totally honest, because additional experimentation is always an aid, but we've been overtaken by events here—do you know of 'the British Disease'? It's how the Europeans refer to the violence that has begun to insinuate itself in England. The Bloodies are rising here too, Scylla, here, in the last place on earth where civilized behavior is still regarded as an asset, thought of as a way of life. Enough to break the heart . . ."

(It was one hour later in Paris where, on the Champs Élysées, two stocky men walked briskly along in the early morning light. One was Russian, the other French. They were both leading nuclear scientists. Two little chubby French children came running up toward them, all smiles, babbling with joy. The scientists stopped. It was difficult not to smile at such children.)

". . . The Little Bang Theory is now in operation, Scylla. Within an hour, it's my fervent hope that most of the crucial figures alive will then be dead. As you might expect, there will be more than a little chaos. And from that chaos? Peace. Truly, Scylla. Webster did not believe me when I suggested it to him, suggested that his wonderful children could bring peace, so I experimented with getting rid of him. Successfully. And do you know why there will be peace? . . ."

Scylla listened. Obviously Beverage felt in full control now, taking his time, like a Baptist minister working his audience, voice rising and falling with differing passions.

". . . Because England will rule the world. Every other country's leaders will be decimated. And of course, a few here will go, some doddering ministers and a sacred monument or two. But England will survive virtually intact, as it must. The only chance for peace is that a peacelike country have control. America, China, Russia, any of the emerging nations, they know only blood. The world was at its height when England was in charge—they did it better than anybody for centuries, Scylla, it's in their makeup—they did it best before and they shall again . . ."

(It was nine hours ahead in Tokyo where, not far from the Ginza, half a dozen important bankers and businessmen were in the midst of a meeting. An embarrassed female secretary knocked discreetly, then apologized, hands clasped together, muttered that one of the children outside, one of their waiting sons, was having a fit, was in terrible pain, needed a doctor, needed something, and the man chairing the meeting said, "Sons? Whose sons?" but then as he watched two enchanting little Japanese boys were in the doorway, one of them holding his stomach, the other hugging the secretary so tightly, and the boys smiled, and the men looked at them blankly, then at each other, then came the flash.)

". . . the world will flock to the British for leadership, Scylla, first because it will be the only country with established leadership in place. And they will keep flocking because of the skill with which the British lead. You have no children and neither have I, but what a gift to leave to those that do. I am the Greatest Godist. The only one with will enough to make it happen. And you? Probably smirking as you listen. You are going to suffer. So dearly and so long. My personal triumph is on the horizon. It should be dawn now. Have an interesting day . . ."

The gloating tone came to an end as the recorder hissed into silence. Scylla flicked it off. Outside now he heard a distant, dangerous sound. He rushed to the window, stared out at the Thames, glistening in the morning sun, saw, beyond, that Big Ben had burst into flames . . .

**. . . after the end . . .**

Clearly, it was the first organized worldwide terrorist attack, said the pundit on the BBC at 6:30, when the explosions had been going on for half an hour. Scylla, watching the television from his suite, could not believe the arrogance of the man, who went on to say that, again, clearly, Arafat and Khomeini had joined with Khadafi, that much was obvious.

At 6:40, when three of Khadafi's top men were bombed and Khadafi himself nearly incinerated, the pundit's theory lost a bit of its credence.

Riveted, Scylla watched as the news came pouring in—no one mentioned children, no one mentioned the possibility of empires toppling. Casualties were all they counted, and then, at 6:45, the first American cabinet member died in a bomb explosion, shortly followed by an old Supreme Court justice.

Then a new pundit came on as the news grew worse, and this man said although this was not a time for chauvinism, it was clear that Britain, by virtue of its many precautions, had evaded the terrorists better than anyone.

Then, at seven o'clock, came the news that the White House had been damaged as a bomb went off there, but the president, helicoptering in from Camp David, was nowhere near the place.

The calamities were being reported ragtag now, horror jumping over horror—the chief military minister of France;

four members of the Politburo who were getting out of their limousines in Moscow; a dozen scientists were wiped out in a single explosion at a convention in Switzerland; on and on—and at 7:20 the chaos was building in an unprecedented degree, the BBC was connecting with American television, then on to Madrid, and now there were the first photos of the destruction, and the announcers were panicked, you could tell it, because three thousand bombs had gone off by seven, four thousand in the following fifteen minutes, and with seven thirty coming up the total should be close to five thousand with who knew how many more to come.

Scylla knew. Many things. Most notably this: yes, there would be more havoc, but in the end, Beverage's notion hadn't worked—too many crucial people were still alive. Fourteen senators were dead in America but that left eighty-six to fumble on. Those percentages held more or less in many countries. Destruction beyond anything yet known, in recent decades, certainly. But Beverage had rushed it, had sent the children out too soon, before all the kinks had been smoothed, because there were reports now of an explosion in a cornfield in America, a cornfield a mile from a governor's home.

The children were going off too quickly or too late, not all of them, but enough. The hysteria was still building on the tube, but Scylla, knowing how many bombs there were, knew it was all but done—the rising tide of violence in Britain had rescued them all.

He stood, went to the window, saw the fire under control on the face of the great clock. But the next time, the flames would not be controlled—technology would win out the next time, or the time after the next time, when the window was open and the toy sales soared and action figures were in demand. The Bloodies would rise and curdle the atmosphere with their long-stifled shrieks of triumph.

Fuck them, Scylla thought, because that was out of everyone's control, all anyone could truly do was gather your loved ones around and hold them so tightly they could never get away, and he had but the lone loved one, and yes,

Perkins had said it would be dangerous to Babe if he ever contacted him, but the world was dangerous enough just now, thank you, just breathing was an act that required courage, so he went to the phone, got New York Information, asked for his brother's number, Thomas Levy please, on Riverside Drive, and when he had the number he phoned and when Babe answered he was momentarily unable to speak—and glad of it.

It wasn't Babe, it was just his voice, going on with the most wonderful message, that he and Melissa weren't there just now, thank you, they were at the Bloomsbury Hotel in London—

—in London!

Scylla would not have to pack and dash to hateful Heathrow and sit for hours in a plane reading Jane Russell's autobiography—all he had to do was shave and dress and check the address and get in a cab—

Fuck shaving, Scylla thought, as he threw on some clothes, went to the lobby, got a cab, gave the address of the Bloomsbury, stood in front of it, a dump of a place but with character, by 8:35.

At 8:40, he was standing outside Babe's door, hand raised to knock. Then he hesitated a moment, wondering for a final time, was this reunion going to bring grief to his beloved? No. *No*. No one knew his face. No one knew his name. He had the small fortune in money, dollars and pounds that Perkins had given him back in America.

He was as safe as anyone these years. Maybe they'd all go on a trip together, Babe and his *frau*, charter a boat, take off into the Caribbean, maybe he could find his island, show them the birds, teach them how to chase through the treetops—

—he was drifting, because he was, truly now, frightened. What if it went badly? What if Babe had forgotten? What if the years had etched him out of Babe's life? "Oh, hi, sure, of course I'm glad to see you, glad you stopped by, no, we can't chat with you now but give us a call why don't you, we'll be glad to work you in . . ."

He was drifting again. Simply because he was afraid to knock. What should he say? He wanted something that would cut through the surprise, the minutes of "My God, I thought you were gone" crap. He wanted to just slay his brother with kindness, say something only they would know.

Finally he knocked, and a moment later, a tall, tousle-haired man in his middle thirties was looking out at him curiously, saying, "Yes?"

"You got so big," Scylla wanted to say. "Look at the way you filled out. You were so skinny before, you were just a student before, now you're a professor and you've got a wife and maybe kids on the way soon and—"

—and *"Yes?"*

Scylla stood there trying so hard to think of what to say. Here he was, helpless when it mattered. Here he was, a weapon who could climb and run and bleed and kill, who could outsmart chess-minded monsters and survive, who could—

"—I think you've got the wrong room, mister." And the door started to close.

Scylla pushed it open, said four words out loud: *"It wasn't paint, Babe."*

Babe blinked, blinked again, then came into his arms as the tears jumped free, and he tried to talk but he couldn't, and Scylla moved inside the room, closed the door, held the weeping kid—no, *professor* if you please, and all he could say was, "There-there, there-there," until Babe had control enough to say, "I knew it, I knew you'd be back," and Scylla said, "I'm here, I'm here," and Babe said, "You're not going to go away again, are you?" And Scylla shook his head. And then he said maybe they could all three take a trip, charter a boat in the Caribbean, banish time, get to know each other, "I know an island I think you'd like," and Babe said, "Deal," then "Damn, I wish Melissa were here," and Scylla asked where she was and Babe explained working on this job for this entertainment company, very big, paid a ton, and that two hundred million people went to amusement parks in America alone last year, maybe half a billion when you added in the world, and Melissa had been recently called in on this project, to help with the accents—

—what accents? Scylla asked—

—with the kids, Babe explained, see, they've got these kids only they're not real and the gimmick was, so Melissa was told, that you paid your money and said where you were from and the kid would talk to you using the accent of your locale, to make it more real, and Scylla tried so hard not to listen anymore, not to hear, but every so often a word or phrase got through, even though he tried to concentrate on the singing of the birds he heard the word "Tring" and the word "Webster" and how they were working Melissa overtime, she had been practically forced to work the whole of last night, getting a last-minute order ready, and even before Babe grabbed their wedding picture, showed the pretty brunette face, Scylla knew why Beverage had gloated so on his last taped message, knew why he had been truly overjoyed when Perkins had suggested bringing him back.

Scylla stared, stared at Babe's face, and then Babe was helpless with tears again, coming toward him whispering, "Give us a hug."

Now both brothers wept . . .

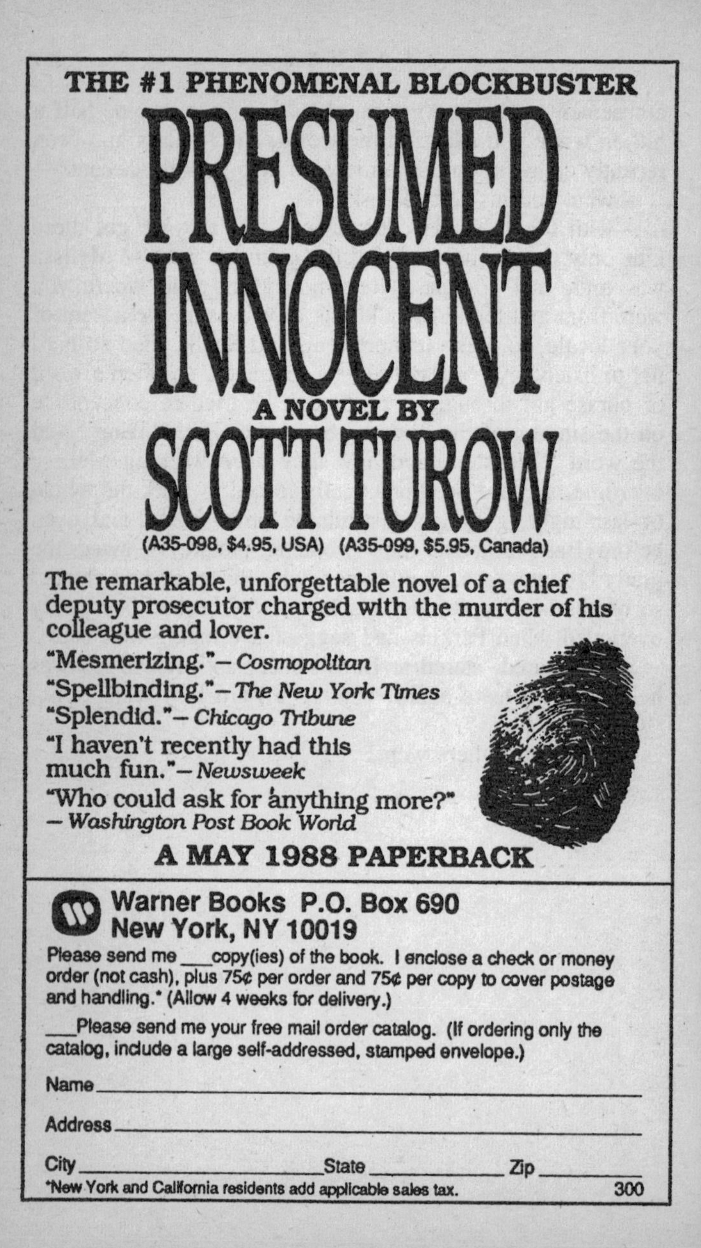

THE #1 PHENOMENAL BLOCKBUSTER
PRESUMED INNOCENT
A NOVEL BY
SCOTT TUROW
(A35-098, $4.95, USA) (A35-099, $5.95, Canada)
The remarkable, unforgettable novel of a chief deputy prosecutor charged with the murder of his colleague and lover.
"Mesmerizing."—Cosmopolitan
"Spellbinding."—The New York Times
"Splendid."—Chicago Tribune
"I haven't recently had this much fun."—Newsweek
"Who could ask for anything more?" – Washington Post Book World
A MAY 1988 PAPERBACK
Warner Books P.O. Box 690
New York, NY 10019
Please send me ___copy(ies) of the book. I enclose a check or money order (not cash), plus 75¢ per order and 75¢ per copy to cover postage and handling.* (Allow 4 weeks for delivery.)
___Please send me your free mail order catalog. (If ordering only the catalog, include a large self-addressed, stamped envelope.)
Name
Address
City State Zip
*New York and California residents add applicable sales tax.
300